DRIVING LESSONS

WILLIAM KRITLOW

Thomas Nelson Publishers
Nashville

Published in Nashville, Tennessee, by Thomas Nelson, Inc., Publishers, and distributed in Canada by Word Communications, Ltd., Richmond, British Columbia, and in the United Kingdom by Word (UK), Ltd., Milton Keynes, England.

Unless otherwise noted, Scripture quotations are from the HOLY BIBLE, NEW INTERNATIONAL VERSION ®. Copyright © 1973, 1978, 1984 by International Bible Society. Used by permission of Zondervan Bible Publishing House. All rights reserved.

The "NIV" and "New International Version" trademarks are registered in the United States Patent and Trademark Office by International Bible Society. Use of either trademark requires the permission of International Bible Society.

Library of Congress Cataloging-in-Publication Data

Kritlow, Bill.
    Driving lessons : a novel / Bill Kritlow.
       p.   cm.
    ISBN 0-7852-8214-9 (pb)
     1. Man-woman relationships—United States—Fiction. 2. Automobile travel—United States—Fiction.   I. Title
PS3561.R567D75   1994
813'.54—dc20   93-27239
                                              CIP

Printed in the United States of America

1 2 3 4 5 6 7 — 00 99 98 97 96 95 94

A Dedication

"Bill. The drapes."

"What about 'em?"

"It's time to do something. The dog pulled the hardware out of the wall a week ago, and they've hung like that for long enough."

"Long enough?"

"Yes, long enough! Now put the computer away and let's do the drapes."

"Just one more paragraph? Mark and Nancy are about to slide down a mountain. I can't leave 'em now."

"Mark and Nancy don't exist."

"Maybe to you they don't."

"We're getting complaints. Andy across the way is trying to sell and he's afraid he'll have to reduce his price. It really looks bad from there."

"But my train of thought."

"Derail it—the drapes or I'm dragging you in front of the elders."

"Andy's one of 'em, isn't he? Hmmm."

Driving Lessons *is dedicated to my wonderfully patient and loving wife, for obvious reasons.*

Chapter One

Nancy Bernard rubbed her locket—a quarter-sized heart that hung around her neck on a thin, gold-plated chain. She rubbed it unconsciously whenever anxious or frightened. This morning she was both. A seed of discontentment had germinated insistently over the week. Now, in church, the sermon just completed, the seed bloomed, leaving Nancy shaken.

A smallish woman of twenty-four, with cinnamon hair and quiet blue eyes, Nancy had not felt pain like this in more than a year. Now the scab she'd nurtured and hardened was being torn away; if it continued, a deep emotional wound would be exposed.

Pastor Bevel's messages were seldom disturbing. Steeped in God's love and sustaining grace, his words and voice were soothing and gently eloquent. When the final "amens" sounded, Nancy usually felt uplifted and recharged for another week. But not this morning.

The congregation was shuffling out, but Nancy remained in her pew. A voice invaded. "Nance."

Ugh! John Dorrie, she thought. *Please, not now.*

A beanpole of a fellow, John had a thin mustache and hollow green eyes that made him look in need of a good meal. And, it seemed, he always wanted to have it with her—sometimes an idea she could live with, but not now.

"I missed you at the singles group last night."

"I didn't go." She didn't like how cold she sounded, and she felt her thumb working her locket again. The frequent rubbing had long since worn the thin coating of gold from its face. She let the locket go—her thumb ached. She must have been rubbing it all through the sermon. "Listen, I can't talk now. I need to talk to Pastor Bevel."

"Can it wait? Some of us are going out for brunch to the little French place—croissants and bagels."

"Not this morning."

His head cocked inquisitively. "You okay?"

"Not really," she confessed, eyes darting between the lines of people—each representing time she could ill afford to waste.

When her eyes returned, she found his face a picture of compassion. "Can I help?" he asked.

Touched, she gathered up a smile. "That's sweet of you. But I have to talk to Pastor Bevel."

"Now? He's usually busy now. Maybe you ought to come to brunch and make an appointment."

"No. You go on and enjoy yourself."

Resigned to defeat and murmuring a few unintelligible words, John slipped away with the rest of the congregation.

The pastor would be a while shaking all those hands, so Nancy swallowed a wad of anxiety and decided to stay put.

Exposed now, Nancy's wound was painfully raw and canyon deep. Unless cleansed and sutured it would only worsen. But there was an even greater reason to deal with it—the Lord, whom she'd only known for a year, wanted her to.

▼ ▼

Through a swampy sleep, Mark Brewster felt a sharp jab in his ribs. Was he dead? He couldn't be alive and feel like this. His mouth tasted like mud, his tongue like moss, his nose ran, and his teeth ached. A lanky guy, his hair now the color and texture of dead grass, he sprawled faceup on a couch, just part of the clutter of beer cans and ashtrays. Neck and back stiff, he inhaled a rancid cloud of stale air—smoke fused with the odor of sweat and spilled drinks. A party—yes, now he remembered—two days of it.

"Get up, Slime Ball." The voice scratched his ears like nails on a blackboard, and Mark felt another rough jab. He remembered. The party had been in his honor—about his screenplay. "Wake up. You're snorin' like a Harley-hog," No Brakes, his buddy for nearly a year now, growled.

Mark moaned, the very center of his skull exploding. He pried his eyes open, and the sun immediately reached through a dirty window and scraped them raw. They slammed shut. "Go away, man."

"You're the one who's goin' away. First out of here and then on to Holly-wood." Nobody said "Hollywood" like No Brakes. Every syllable sliding from his thick lips painted a picture of ultimate glitz.

"Naw, I can't," Mark whimpered, a jackhammer working its way out of his head. "I'm going nowhere," he pronounced weakly, his hands cupping his ears to keep the world out and his brain in. His watery, burning eyes opened and he saw No Brakes. Normally suave, the Puerto Rican had beer and chips staining his black hair and close cropped beard. "Man, you're ugly," Mark mumbled. Gathering together what remained of his strength, Mark pushed himself upright, ran a hand through his tangled hair, and glanced around. "A party or a war?" he muttered, reaching into his back pocket for a handkerchief. None was there. He wiped his nose on his sleeve.

Beer cans and liquor bottles were scattered among cracker boxes and chip bags. Now and then a weary thread of gray cigarette smoke rose from a buried ashtray. Mark saw a pair of legs protruding from behind an overstuffed chair in the corner—red toenail polish. "What times's the bulldozer coming? What time is it now, anyway?"

"Sunday."

Mark rubbed tortured eyes. "The last thing I knew it was Friday night. Where'd Saturday go? Oh, yeah—How'd I do with what's 'er name? Oh, never mind, I never do well enough to want to know. It doesn't matter anyway; I need to stagger to the park and juggle." Mark worked his thick, arid tongue. "Stinks. Is somebody dead under—"

"You're through jugglin'. You're through with everything but getting in that sorry excuse for a car you got, and gettin' on the road. You been delayin' this trip long enough."

"Today? I can't go today. I feel horrible—got a cold coming on or something. Anyway, Sunday's good money. People are just naturally guilty on Sunday. And I haven't delayed anything. I'm downright eager—oh, my head—I need a drink."

"No drink. Just go."

"A little one and then I'll go. I'll go and wrestle Hollywood to its knees. But not today. Please. Sunday's big and I got this terrible headache. What were we drinkin'? There was a brunette in all of this somewhere, wasn't there? Didn't some girl hit me or something?"

"They all hit you at one time or another."

Mark's expression soured as he sighed. "I gotta problem with subtlety. I'don't have any." He worked his thick tongue again. "My mouth tastes like an eagle slept in it. One drink—just one." When No Brakes glared at him, Mark said, "Come on, we both know Hollywood was just a good excuse for a party."

"I don't," No Brakes said firmly as he started grabbing meaty handfuls of stained paper plates, cans, and bags and pushing them into a large, green plastic sack. "You're just scared."

"Me?" A sudden blast in his head nearly brought tears. When Mark dropped his head to his hands he saw the pile of bound pages on the coffee table. "My screenplay," he said with sudden reverence. Brushing potato chips from the grease-smeared cover page, he lifted it as if it were fragile and golden. "Have you ever read this?"

"I don't read."

Mark took a grave breath. He thumbed through the pages, and as they fell open one at a time, he saw the familiar words typed there. "There's a lot of me in here," he mused. Suddenly aware that he lay as open and as vulnerable as the script he fell silent. His friend wouldn't understand.

No Brakes tied off one full bag and whipped open another and continued cramming the spent party into it. "You say something?"

"Nothin'," Mark said, rolling the treasure tightly in his grasp. "You missed a treat not reading this. Hollywood'll buy it. Probably Spielberg himself. But if I wait we can have another goin' away party in a month or two. Maybe at Christmas."

"Nope. We'll have a comin' home party." No Brakes emitted a plume of acrid breath that Mark smelled from yards away. "I'm sick of hearin' about that thing. I need a decent drinkin' buddy again. So get this thing out of your system. Anyway, go now and you miss winter. California got no winter."

"It's three thousand miles, man—Baltimore to Hollywood. That's a whole lotta miles the way I feel this morning. How about another brew before—"

No Brakes set the green trash bag down and took long strides through the rubble to Mark. "I got no brews and I got no patience.

Get home and grab that mutt you got—the one that's probably starvin' to death by now—and get on the road."

"Just like that? Have a heart, No Brakes."

"I ain't got no heart. I ain't never had a heart. But I want you back in a couple months—no more. Then we'll have us another party."

Mark struggled to his feet, clutching the script tightly. As he waded through the debris, his head felt like a nail was being driven into the very top of his skull. Halfway to the door he stuffed the script beneath his shirt and grabbed three empty beer cans. Just to see if he could still do it, he tossed each consecutively into the air and juggled them. All went well until he attempted his famous finale where he'd catch one of the juggled items on the bridge of his nose and balance it there for a moment or two. Actually the finale wasn't all that famous. He'd only been working on it a week or so and had only done it once successfully. Hoping for the second success, he launched each beer can with a spin. Not only did sprays of sour beer drizzle everywhere, but after the can that hit his nose came to rest, the beer remaining in it drooled down the front of him. It balanced there for less than a second and toppled to the floor.

"You're messin' up my house," No Brakes cried.

Mark found a smile somewhere and eyed his friend. "A couple months? I can do anything that long. Why not?" He let the cans fall to the floor and wiped his nose with a sleeve. "Okay, Hollywood, prepare yourself."

▼ ▼

Nancy intercepted Pastor Bevel, his black robe billowing in a chilly October breeze, as he hurried across the grass toward his office.

"Pastor Bevel," she called out, matching his stride.

He immediately stopped. Much taller than Nancy, he looked as he always did, calmly distinguished, with silver wire-rimmed glasses pressed on salty temples. With a father's grace, he extended his hand. "Hello, Nancy. Thank you for coming this morning." He turned to continue on his way.

"I need to talk to you," she said.

"Can it wait? I'm due next door—an elders' meeting."

"Only a few minutes?" she asked, eyes, voice, everything pleading.

His eyes shrank to a perceptive squint. Squeezing her shoulder gently, he said, "Let's talk while we walk."

But his was not a leisurely pace. Trying to keep up while trying to form words from the tangle of thoughts and feelings, Nancy ended with a couple of incoherent grunts. After a frustrated second try, though, she just let the words tumble out. "It's about my father and me."

"The one you left in California."

"The only one I have—you remember?" she said, a bit surprised she was important enough to remember.

"Not many people voluntarily leave California for Washington, D.C. I guess President Reagan was a notable exception." He suddenly shivered and rubbed his arms to ward off the dagger of arctic wind stabbing at them both. "If only a church out there would call me." He laughed. "Now, what about your father? As I recall, your relationship with him wasn't the best. You left him a little upset—miffed."

"Somehow 'miffed' doesn't really capture it," Nancy said, her voice struggling with the pace Bevel set. "I hated him. I know I'm not supposed to hate my father. But I did. Oh, I hope I don't now. He's an alcoholic and it wasn't easy loving him. I don't think I've ever seen him sober. After my mom died, he treated me—well, badly."

Bevel stopped and Nancy stopped and he studied her again for a moment. "The elders' meeting can wait. Let's take a little detour to my office."

Bevel's office was books and paintings and soothing browns and forest greens. When Nancy sat in the soft leather chair opposite his desk she felt a breath of composure return. She hadn't realized how upset she was until her heart stopped thundering in her ear.

"Now," he began, hands folded before him, "what's all this about?"

"You said something in your sermon today."

"Good. Sometimes I wonder."

She forced a smile and continued, "You ended with something like: 'If you love someone who's unsaved show your love by bringing him the gospel.'"

"A common theme."

"Well, I've felt uneasy all week. Like something was wrong—tense, all knotted up."

She noticed Pastor Bevel's gaze drop to her locket—she was rubbing it again.

"A kettle ready to boil?" Pastor Bevel observed.

She self-consciously dropped the metal heart and let her hand fall to her lap. "Right. Sort of." Her face brightened slightly as she realized he was really listening, "I felt like this the first time when I was getting over my mom's death."

"An accident, as I recall."

"Car accident. Very sudden. I was seventeen and I felt lost for more than a year. Then I started feeling like I did last week—like things just had to change. I guess the kettle was boiling. I just couldn't keep moping around. I had to put Mom's death behind me. It took some effort, but I did it."

"That was before you were saved."

Nancy nodded. "Then before I left home three years ago I felt unsettled for several weeks. I'd taken all of my dad I could take. I guess the pot was boiling again. Things had to change before I exploded. After a brief visit to my grandmother's, I applied to a music school out here, got a scholarship, and came here. I play the flute."

"I know. You played that solo a few months ago."

"You remember. Anyway, all this week I've felt that same uneasiness, all knotted up inside. The other times I knew why, but this time I wasn't sure. But something was going to happen." She took a breath. "All this is a little frightening for me. I don't like change. I like things neat and orderly. You ought to see my apartment. Nothing's out of place. I'll be late for work before I leave something out of place. I drive Hamster nuts. He has to put away all his toys before he goes to bed."

"Your hamster puts his toys away?"

Nancy laughed. "No. Hamster's my Great Dane. He's so big and cute."

"Great name for a Great Dane." Bevel appreciated his little poem with a gentle laugh.

Nancy nodded and quickly went on, "I remember talking about how I felt with Hamster—"

"You get everyone's advice, don't you?"

"He's my sounding board." She smiled, but the smile quickly faded. She nervously rubbed her locket again. "And then your sermon made everything clear."

"Your father figures in here someplace. Where?"

Nancy suddenly felt a knot tie around her heart; it constricted her breathing. Her father did figure in this someplace—right in the middle. "I have to go back to see him." Her voice became strained—a trickle of choked sound. She became aware of her right thumb becoming sore as she rubbed her locket. She consciously let her hand drop. "He's my father. I have to love him even though I I—well—don't. I have to share the gospel with him and maybe . . ."

The pastor finished her thought. "And maybe reconcile with him?"

After taking a deliberate moment to force at least a little calm to return, she said, "I'm going to drive."

"Drive? To California? What about the telephone? It's quick, cheap."

"My dad intimidates me. He might hang up on me. He'll probably be drunk if I call, and I could never talk to him if he was drunk. Or he might get mad or I might get mad. I have to do this face-to-face." She suddenly felt the knot in her heart tighten. "Oh, my gosh, that scares me." The constriction leaped from her chest to her throat. "Just the thought scares me."

"Face-to-face is fine, but at least take a plane. I'm sure I can get the church to help."

"No. I've thought all this over waiting for you. I have so much hurt to get over. It needs a lot of prayer. And alone in the car—away from phones and doorbells—I need a week of total peace so I can think and read the Bible and pray."

"But, Nancy, please. So many things can go wrong: flat tires, carburetors, all those thingamajigs under the hood, hoses could explode. I went on a long trip once, and my battery actually melted."

"I used to drive from San Francisco to L.A. now and then, and this trip's only five or so days of doing that. I'll be fine. Anyway, the Lord'll take care of me. Especially while I do what he wants me to. Don't you think so?"

"He also wants us to be prudent, and this time of year there's probably freak storms, snow—maybe blizzards. Oh, my, you remind me of my daughter. She never listens to me, either."

Nancy felt an unexpected surge of excitement. "I have a friend with a tent trailer. She's not a Christian, not yet anyway, but she'll loan it to me. I can save on motel bills. Hamster and I can be campers for a week."

"I wish you'd think this over, Nancy. The church will buy you a plane ticket."

"Thanks, anyway. You've been wonderful to listen to all this and give me such great advice."

"You *are* like my daughter. What advice I have given you've ignored."

"I have?" She didn't understand. "Thanks for listening, though. I'll call you when I get there and let you know how it all went. I have this feeling I'm being a little schizoid. I'm scared to death of seeing him, but I'm excited too. Isn't that strange to feel that way?"

"I guess I feel that way every day of my life," Bevel said, an exasperated sigh escaping from him. "Nancy, the Lord'll take care of you—and while he's doing it, he'll test you, stretch, and grow you." Then Bevel smiled a gentle, loving smile. "And I guess that's what we both want for you, isn't it?"

"It'll be fun. Hamster and me in the Plymouth Champ."

"Isn't that a pretty small car for such a big—"

"Maybe God will stretch the car too." She laughed as she got to her feet.

"I want you to take real good care of yourself." Then Bevel's expression became grave. "I don't believe in premonitions, but I have a bad one about this trip of yours. Take real care."

"Now *you're* scaring me."

"Maybe I'm trying to. Keep Christ in mind every mile you drive."

Nancy moved toward the door, "I'd better get going before you talk me out of it, and I don't want you to do that. Don't worry. The Lord will take care of me. I know he will. And I know he wants me to do this. I'm sure."

"Let's take a moment to pray." They did and when the amen was said Nancy shook Bevel's hand and left.

Chapter Two

Mark's headache had died away to a dull rush, but he didn't think about it now. Instead, he stood outside a grim, weather-carved door, took an anxious breath, and prepared for the gauntlet inside.

Afraid to breathe, he turned the tarnished brass handle as silently as he could, and since the black, weather-battered door normally squealed, he opened it slowly and stopped at the first hint of sound. The door opened into his brownstone apartment building, one in an endless row of brownstones, and it opened onto a dingy entryway. Although smudged with decades of neglect and infected with the odor of acrid spices, sour mash, and stale air, Mark noticed none of it. His attention was riveted to the door just to the right of the entryway.

It was Mrs. Thresher's door, and he had to get by it and up the stairs undetected. Mrs. Thresher was all her name implied—jagged teeth, obsidian eyes, a heart as cold and indifferent as arctic ice. The woman was ideally suited for her job—she collected the rent, and Mark was behind.

Like the door, the stairs were also known to squeal, so Mark stepped as lightly and as close to the wall, where he knew the support was best, as his 165 pounds would allow. And he did pretty well, too, until he got about halfway. Then his nose began to tickle—that deep, canyon tickle that signaled the approach of a sneeze. His nostrils flared as he sucked it back in. The first time the effort worked. But not the second. The sneeze was suppressed and squeaky and it echoed off the dingy walls. Mark froze. Several breaths. No sound from below. As his confidence trickled back, he continued one step at a time. After two steps, from behind and below, came a deafening crash.

After Mark gulped his heart, a voice like a dentist's drill ground into his ear, "Hey, you there—the bum on the stairs. I want your rent."

Mark prepared a gracious face and turned. Thresher still held the garbage can lids, peering up between them with a wicked smile. "Why, Mrs. Thresher! Always a delight."

"Can it, deadbeat," she growled. One of the lids clattered unceremoniously to the floor, and two fingers shot into the air, "Two months' rent. You got two days."

The door above Mark opened, and a guy in an undershirt and sweatpants stood there. A tattooed snake crawled up his arm, and the yellow of his teeth perfectly matched the yellow stains on the walls. "What're ya doin', ya ol' bat?" the guy cried down the stairs. "How's a guy to sleep?"

"Pills." Thresher fired back. "Lots o' pills. Works for me." And she scooped up her lid and disappeared behind a slammed door. For an instant Mark and the snake man eyed one another.

"I'm gonna buy her plastic garbage cans for Christmas," Mark said revealing as many smiling teeth as he could. The guy grunted and stepped back inside, slamming his door, as well.

"Nice to meet you," Mark mumbled, letting the gracious face fade.

Juggling had never been lucrative, but at least before he'd been able to take what he'd found in his hat after the performances and pay rent, buy food, and maintain a car. But recently there'd been a recession. What he made now paid just for food and the car.

Competition.

There were more jugglers lately, and some of them good. Mark wasn't. He knew that. His heart wasn't in juggling anymore and it showed. He was beginning to drop things.

His heart was somewhere else, maybe in his writing, maybe just out there somewhere. One thing for sure, it wasn't in this tenement—maybe it never had been. Maybe the trip would help him find it again.

At his door he rummaged in his pocket for his key.

The few hundred dollars he had stashed would probably finance an escape. Hollywood was as good a place as any to escape to, and selling his screenplay was a good enough reason. But there was more. Brushed off by his buddy, rejected by his audiences, accosted by his landlord, Mark was truly alone. He'd been alone before—most of his life, in fact. So he was used to it, but not comfortable with it. Now, as his key scratched in the lock, his lonely discomfort nested at the core of his heart, making it brick heavy.

He became aware of little Naomi's scratch—her anxious greeting. When he swung the door open, the excited little salt-and-pepper mix squirmed excitedly, then danced on her hind legs, propelled by a blurred tail. Warmed by the greeting, Mark pressed her to his chest and scratched and nuzzled her shaggy body. She lapped at his chin.

"I bet you're starving. I oughta be shot for leaving you for this long, but it was a great party. You'da loved it."

Naomi downed the large can of dog food Mark set before her and then danced before her bowl, cheerfully demanding more. But there was no more. Mark picked her up and nuzzled her, her long hair shedding on him.

"Well, tiger. We're taking a trip. You'll love it. They got palm trees there. You'll love palm trees." He set her down, and she scampered to a pile of dirty shirts by the couch and made a nest there. It was one of many piles in the one-room apartment. Dirty clothes lay where he'd dropped them, dirty dishes were stacked in the sink, magazines and old newspapers lay scattered on the few pieces of furniture and on the kitchen floor for Naomi.

"Yuk! You have been busy." Mark wadded up the offensive paper and stuffed it in a garbage pail.

A sigh pushed from his lungs as he straightened and looked around. All a mess, nothing of value—except maybe the portable typewriter that sat on the spindly legged coffee table. "I'm just not a clean person, eh, Naomi—and why start now?"

Naomi panted up at him as he sat on a canvas-backed director's chair he'd gotten somewhere and said, "We're going to sell the screenplay. You believe that, don't you?" He unrolled it and thumbed the pages affectionately again. " 'Brass Knuckles'—great title. Harrison Ford can star. He's another Bogart." He rolled it again, slapped it nervously into his palm, and eyed the script longingly.

"Maybe it's too cliché." He groaned suddenly, slamming the

rolled pages into his hand with an anger that leaped up from somewhere. Naomi jumped. "Do you know what cliché is?" he asked the little dog. "It's some guy in a dingy, stinking tenement talking to his dog about going to Hollywood. That's cliché." Mark slammed the roll again and felt the anger dribble away. He sniffled back another sneeze and laughed. "It'll be a fun trip. We can clean when we get back. Oh," he whimpered as a stab of pain lanced the back of his skull. "The headache's back. We'll go tomorrow. I need some sleep." He fell onto the couch, pulled a pile of jeans together for a pillow, and lay there until the pain went away.

▼ ▼

"You're nuts! You get lost driving around the block. You'll never get there." A round, red-faced Donna Kingston fired salvo after salvo while standing over Nancy, shaking a pudgy finger. Although she was Nancy's age, Donna was forever assuming the role of mother protector, and this afternoon was no exception. "You're always telling me how miserably he treated you and your mother. And you want to drive all that way to see him? You're nuts!"

Nancy beat back a wave of intimidation. "I have a good map. Anyway, you have to be pretty dumb to miss California. I'll be okay. I need the time, Donna." Knowing how her friend felt about such things, she winced as she said, "I need the time to pray."

"Pray on a plane. Up there you'll be closer—"

"Please, Donna. That's not funny."

"None of this is funny. I'm worried about you. Up 'til now this religion stuff hasn't hurt you—much. But now it's liable to kill you. Winter's coming on. Did you notice that or is your calendar broken?" Then her jaw dropped aghast, and both hands clapped either side of a long, cavernous mouth. "You don't have any credit cards—what'll you do if you run out of money? Oh, my word, you'll be stranded. I told you not to cut them up."

"The Lord will take care of me. He certainly has so far."

Not liking that reply, Donna snapped, "And stop rubbing that locket!"

Nancy glanced down as if to confirm that her thumb was working. She sighed self-consciously and dropped her hand.

"You religious people make me sick sometimes. Did the Lord take care of you when you flunked out of college?"

"I didn't flunk out. I didn't like music as much as I thought I did."

"Or when you nearly got fired a couple months back."

"I didn't, did I? And I am working harder."

"Or when he gave you this father to begin with, or when he took your mother like that."

"Donna, stop it, please." The beating was taking its toll. She felt close to tears. Donna had taken Nancy under her wing soon after she'd arrived in Washington, and although she'd often been wonderfully supportive, she could also be manipulative, sometimes savagely so—like today. But Nancy's father was too important. She couldn't knuckle under. She swallowed hard and said, "I want to borrow your brother's tent trailer."

"You mean the same brother whom you refuse to date?"

"He's married," Nancy protested. She also wanted to point out that he wasn't a Christian, but the fact he was married was reason enough.

"Separated."

"I just want to borrow his tent trailer."

"How can you conceivably ask such a thing? It's not like you're going camping with it. You want to take it on a three thousand-mile trip. And probably never come back. You'll probably drive it into the Grand Canyon or something."

"Come on, Donna, I'll bring it back. And I only have three weeks' vacation. I have to be back by then. Your brother's told me he never uses it."

"I bet you don't even have a trailer hitch."

"I got it all. I bought the car with all that stuff, and I've never had a chance to use it."

"This is the dumbest thing I've ever heard. Winter's coming in those mountains out there, and you'll freeze in that thing."

"I'll be fine. Really I will. Please ask him."

Donna heaved the heaviest sigh Nancy had ever heard and for an instant looked like she was going to give up. But she didn't. "When you get there he'll laugh in your face. You know he will. Like the time he spilled beer all over your high school prom dress. He'll be drunk, and he'll laugh in your face." When pain flushed over Nancy, the pudgy woman leaned against the kitchen counter with a wise, all-knowing look. "And for what? We all hear that nonsense every Christmas and Easter. He's probably heard it more than you. Your tellin' him isn't going to change anything, and it's just going to put you through the same terrible experience you vowed years ago you'd never go through again. Nancy, it's time to wake up and smell the coffee."

That argument began to work. Nancy could feel her insides crumbling and her thumb working the face of the locket, but, as before, she fought back and found a reservoir of resolve. She bolstered herself with a deep breath, placed her locket hand back in her lap, and said, "Please call your brother, and ask him if I can borrow the trailer."

Donna sighed again, looked away as if in great suffering, and nodded.

Nancy's Great Dane, Hamster, waited for Nancy at her apartment. A dog of little emotion, Hamster's posture at these times was always the same: rigidly on his haunches, his long body a few feet from her door—a canine Sphinx. When Nancy opened it, cooing a warm greeting, he'd rise in two fluid motions—first his back, then his massive rectangular head—and she tossled his topknot in greeting.

This morning was no different, and Nancy appreciated his faithfulness more than ever. With so many things swirling erratically around her she was truly thankful for this one important constant.

Nancy's apartment was picture neat. Although sparse, the furniture was meticulously placed to give a homey feel. Beige walls were punctuated with warmly colored posters, framed prints, and wicker things, while yellow and green bouquets of silk flowers added a country charm. Of course, she paid little attention to any of this; instead she bent down and took Hamster's huge head in her hands and cooed, "It is so good to see you." She sat on the sofa and looked her dog straight in the eye. "Remember the trip we talked about last week? Well, it all came to a head this morning, and we're on our way tomorrow—right after I tell them at work. I've got three weeks' vacation saved up—I'm sure they'll let me go. They won't miss me much anyway. You're going to have to be very good. But you always are, aren't you?"

Hamster's big tongue lapped at her hand.

"We pick up the tent trailer later this afternoon, and then we go to the bank tomorrow to pick up some money. There's not much, but we'll be okay. We're going to see my father. You never met him. You probably won't like him. I don't—and I'm supposed to. I need to tell him about Jesus and then try to make up with him." Suddenly a flood of lonely vulnerability washed over her. "I'm going to need you on this trip." Her arms wrapped around the animal's thick neck. "Sometimes I think you're my only friend."

Hamster grunted and pulled away. Sitting down on his huge haunches, he hung his tongue out and waited for his mistress to make the next move. She did. She began to cry.

Within seconds the sniffles grew to buckets of uncontrolled tears. "Oh, Hamster, I'm afraid," she finally said as she knelt before her dog and hugged him, his head on her shoulder. "I don't want to see my dad. He chased one of my dates away with a shotgun once," she choked. "Then he laughed. It'll be just like Donna says. Just like it." She patted the Great Dane on the back of the head and gave him another squeeze. "I've got to stop this. Now." Getting up, she said, "After I blow my nose, I think I'll make some tea, then play my flute and read my Bible a while." When the tea kettle was whistling she found a simple prayer on her lips, "Lord, I sure hope you know what you're doing."

▼ ▼

Ticketed once as abandoned refuse, Mark's car sat waiting for him Monday morning. A 1975 AMC Pacer, it was caramel-colored, shaped like a turtle, and had dirty-white interior. Although a fine car when the first owner bought it, it was a wreck by the time it got to Mark and even more so now. But it ran, and it had good tires. With a backseat that folded down and a wide stance on the road, it was a good traveling car. At least Mark thought so. Of course, it had to be a good traveling car; it was the only car he had.

Mark had only a few clothes, a few toiletries, lots of juggling things, his typewriter, and his manuscript. Everything but the type-writer was placed behind the backseat, and the juggling things, crammed into several cardboard boxes, were stashed everywhere. All was piled atop years of accumulated debris.

Although a garbage dump to most, the car was love at first sight for Naomi. The moment Mark tossed her into the back, she danced and pranced up on everything, sniffing and digging and generally making herself at home.

Mark eased himself behind the wheel, took out his ancient U.S. road map, and spread it out over the steering wheel. He'd gotten it years ago, a first step along a road to adventure—a road he was only now going to take. He quickly found L.A. and worked backward following I-40 through Arizona, New Mexico, Oklahoma, Arkansas, and Tennessee. If he picked up 81 in Tennessee, he could then take 70, which went into Baltimore. "This should be easy," Mark said to Naomi who was already curled in an old blanket that he used at the park to rest on between performances. "And an adventure, Naomi. We ought to make five or six hundred miles a day and be in L.A. by Friday."

Naomi panted as if impressed.

Mark, in turn, took a deep breath, chased away a few aching muscles, and ground the engine into action. The moment the engine fired up, thick doors rattled, the backseat rattled, the juggling things rattled, and everything rattled in unison as Mark pulled from the underground parking area onto the street. "Well, Baltimore, see you later."

Later would be a long, long time.

Chapter Three

Naomi didn't travel well. The little salt-and-pepper fur ball bounced and scrambled from window to backseat, then to the front again, sniffing and pushing her nose into the dashboard vents before posting herself at the window again. After a heartbeat, the frantic ritual was repeated. There was no air conditioning, but the autumn breeze from the vent refreshed them. They had reached the Appalachian Mountains, coal mining country, and the air was filled with rich mountain smells of trees and earth. The forest was brilliantly splashed with reds and oranges of every shade and yellows that could pass for gold. In marked contrast to the fantasy of colors were the few small towns along the road. They presented pockets of dingy reality.

"Real stink holes," Mark muttered to Naomi.

But Naomi paid no attention. She stood, paws against the window, watching the countryside run past in a blur. Whenever her side of the highway lost its charm, she bounded to Mark's. Standing in his lap, between the steering wheel and his chest, she gazed in wonderment for a while. Her vigil always ended the same way. Mark would say, "Hey, pooch, this is dangerous," grab a handful of dog, and toss her gently to the opposite seat. Without hesitation, the dog would stand as before and quickly sniff the window to see if anything had changed like a furry little sentry.

With its wide wheelbase, the Pacer took the mountain curves easily, and the engine's guttural groan, still strong for its age, played like music. The fact that the music was punctuated by a steadily rattling percussion section didn't matter to Mark. For the first time in a long while, he felt in control. Being away from things that troubled him brought a measure of calm. His only responsibility was to drive. He had no rent to pay, no crowd to please, no hat of money to watch, and no concern that it would remain empty. He was a self-contained king in his caramel-colored kingdom.

As the mountains steepened, as the roads buckled back on themselves, he also became a very slow king. In all of Virginia there was only one car slower and he found it as he rounded a sharp curve.

It was a Plymouth Champ struggling valiantly with a tent trailer.

He crept up behind it and camped on its tail. Naomi, too, sensed things had changed, that the world wasn't whizzing by quite so fast. "It's all your fault," Mark complained to her. "It's your weight. If you weren't in the car I'd just buzz around this clown. I ought to chuck you out." The little dog looked up apologetically—but only for a moment. Her eyes were quickly back at the window, her panting fogging it up again.

It didn't take long for Mark to start boiling. The road was an erratic two lanes, bad enough at a reasonable pace, but stuck behind this snail, he found it unbearable. Passing was out. Too much traffic coming the other way. Too much, at least, for his car to pass.

Mark's frustration sometimes buried his good sense. Fortunately, though, just as he was about to push the gas to the floor a passing lane appeared. Relieved, he waited as the other car pulled over, then he jarred the Pacer into gear and floored it. The Pacer began to move ahead dutifully, but suddenly they were on an upgrade and the Pacer slowed. Mark watched sadly as the caramel turtle drew even with but could not overtake the other car. Several times he turned helplessly to the other driver in hopes that his mournful look would cause her to take pity and slow down. But the woman driving never acknowledged him.

Too soon the passing lane ended, and Mark had to ease back and allow the Champ to pull ahead.

"I can't believe this." He slammed a fist against the steering wheel and was about to settle in to another eternity of frustration when the car ahead began to weave and then pulled to a stop by the side of the road. As he passed he saw the woman's face etched with distress, eyes pleading his way.

She'd had a flat and she was reasonably attractive. In his rearview mirror Mark caught a glimpse of her getting from the car. Should he go back and help? Naw. Flat tires were work, and no romance was worth hard work.

Nancy felt the rush of wind as the turtle car growled by. It insulted her with a spray of loose gravel. Although the rocks clattered on her car, the concern for her paint job was dwarfed by the thought of changing that tire.

She sighed and glanced at Hamster. He offered no help.

As part of her plan to grow closer to the Lord on this trip, that morning Nancy had promised herself that if anything bad happened, instead of grabbing for her locket, an act she decided was tantamount to sucking her thumb or Linus grabbing his blanket, she was going to respond like a Christian. Well, this flat tire was bad. Not only did she have a flat, but she was furious at the guy who hadn't stopped to help. Struggling to keep her promise, she plopped down in the driver's seat, grabbed her little Bible from her purse, thumbed quickly to the familiar Psalm 91 and read. When she got to the part she was looking for, she read aloud—there was something more sincere about reading the Bible aloud, and she wanted the Lord to know she was sincere: "If you make the Most High your dwelling—even the LORD, who is my refuge—then no harm will befall you, no disaster will come near your tent."

She closed the Bible and slipped it back into her purse. "I guess flat tires don't fall into the category of 'disaster.' " She pushed her lips frustratedly to the right, then the left. "Maybe the Lord really meant tent, not tent trailer."

She tossed her purse aside and eyed the big dog. "How are you with lug nuts? I've never changed a tire before," she said, suddenly feeling her thumb at work on her locket.

Hamster just sighed disinterestedly.

▼ ▼

Although hunger had been gnawing on him for almost an hour, Mark had avoided stopping. Poverty made him uncomfortable, and these little towns produced a discomfort that easily passed for pain. The hole in his stomach was beginning to set up a vacuum, however, and finally he decided that it was eat or die. "Next town—no matter what it looks like—we're gonna brave it."

The words had hardly been said when he rounded a bend, and the road opened to a small, weed-covered plain. The trees were less brilliant, shrouded in filthy browns and black. They led to and surrounded a small stand of buildings in the distance. Soon he saw the town's name, Harbor View, scrawled unsteadily on a wooden sign, its post leaning against a burned-out truck cab. Both sign and truck were engulfed in tangled vines and weeds.

"Harbor View," Mark repeated cynically. "I can bet the Queen Mary never docked here."

A dog sat listlessly along the side of the road and watched while Mark, concerned about a speed trap, slowed to twenty-five miles per hour as posted on the next sign. A cocker spaniel, whose wheat-brown fur hung knotted in thistles, walked alongside a little girl. No more than five years old, she must have been cold, for she wore only a ragged t-shirt, shorts, and no shoes. Her hair was the color of the cocker's and just as long and ragged. She looked up at Mark with vacant eyes as he passed.

He came to a brick, grease-smudged, two-pump gas station. An auto graveyard was rotting in the weeds beside it, each rusty hulk in a different stage of disassembly. Sitting out front was a young man clad in weariness. He eyed Mark with what could easily pass for contempt.

The only other building was separated from the gas station by a vacant lot of waist-high brush. At one time it must have been the area's hub of activity, boasting several businesses, but now they were all boarded up and only this one remained; it was a cafe, its rusted neon sign eloquently proclaiming EATS. With a porch that stretched its whole length, it seemed transplanted from the frontier, and though it now leaned a bit to the right, it looked substantial enough to withstand a few more winters.

"Well, Naomi, ol' girl," Mark said, regretting his promise but looking forward to the eats, "this is it. There's no telling what you'd catch out there, so I'm locking you in. We'll take a run farther on."

Naomi eyed him, then sat, indicating her consent.

Mark nosed the Pacer into a weed-pocked gravel parking area, made sure the two windows were rolled up, locked both doors, and stepped out. After the heavy door rattled closed, he stretched stiff muscles, then stood for a moment. Looking around, he saw two men, both bundled in heavy plaid coats; a large hound of nameless breed lay motionless at their feet. The older man wore a train engineer's hat propped on the back of his balding head—but what he lacked on top he made up for below. He had a full brush of ramshackle, dirty, gray whiskers, above which grew a bulbous red nose.

The other man was much younger, maybe forty, and wore a sweat-stained Skoal tobacco cap, a wad of the stuff bulged in his cheek. He had a couple days' growth of villainous black beard. Both whittled and both eyed him suspiciously as their gleaming blades eroded big chips from the two-by-four stakes in their hands. Mark had the impression they could have just as easily been whittling on him.

The little girl he'd passed approached him. The cocker bounded to the dog who lay near the whittlers and pushed its nose in its rear. The whittler's dog slowly raised its head in recognition. The movement seemed to take all the energy it had.

"Excuse me." Mark smiled graciously, hoping a friendly conversation would help untie the knot that was forming in his stomach. "Are you two the town whittlers?"

The older one looked up. "Yep. Air you the highway clown?"

"Nice shot." Mark laughed; humor was always the best tact. "Where's the harbor there's a view of?"

The younger man, eyes narrowing, raised his knife and pointed across the road. "There."

Mark turned. A stand of trees rustled in the breeze across the road, knocking the dead, brown leaves off. They fluttered to the ground. "Over there?"

The younger one put his knife down and nodded, daring him not to go look.

Mark couldn't very well refuse the dare. Any act that made them think he was snubbing their town shrine could irritate them. And these guys looked like they could be trouble if irritated.

Leaves crackled beneath his feet as he stepped off the road onto the narrow strip that lay between the two-lane road and the trees. He hesitated but then continued. There had been little sun that morning, and in the trees' shadows a chill suddenly slapped him.

The ground fell away quickly, and before he knew it he was peering down a shale cliff. Below, a river rolled along, washing lazily over the rocks. Mark was surprised by how pretty it was. The remains of a dock jutted a few feet from the bank, its ancient timbers long since eaten away. Now only a few pilings connected by a board or two remained. The battered hull of a boat lay against one of the pilings. "Someone's got a sense of humor," Mark muttered as he returned to the road.

On the other side, he smiled at the men. The little girl and her dog had left. "Nice harbor," Mark commented forcing a cheerfulness.

The old guy grunted. "Nicer 'n your car."

Mark wasn't about to take offense. "She runs good."

"Pacer, eh? I'm surprised there's any left on the road," the younger one commented.

"This one won't be fer long," the older one chided, "it looks pregnant." He laughed, and the younger one joined in.

Mark smiled uneasily. "Clever. Well, I hate to end this sparkling repartee, but I think it's time for lunch."

Eyes followed him as he clomped onto the wooden porch, opened the squealing screen door, and stepped inside. The dim interior smelled of wood smoke from a Franklin stove in the corner and thin shafts of light reached in through dirty windows. The booths along the walls and the counter sitting on barrels were depressingly rustic. The walls, void of hangings, were dark and oppressive. There was only one bright spot in the whole place, and it was one of the brightest spots he'd ever seen—the waitress who regarded him wearily as he entered.

She was gorgeous and he stood for a moment transfixed. Her clothes belonged in this place: faded jeans, a plain gray sweatshirt, worn boots. But the rest of her didn't: auburn hair shimmering with red highlights, large, soft eyes and deep-red haunting lips. She was beyond gorgeous. She was magnificent. Hardly able to breathe, Mark stared for several minutes before he realized that she was staring back, her head cocked arrogantly.

He suddenly felt like *he* was the hick in the room. Recovering, he became suave. "This your table?" he asked, indicating one near the door.

"All of 'em are," she answered, void of charm.

Eyes never leaving her, he sat. The plastic tablecloth was torn and had a greasy feel. He didn't let it bother him.

She grabbed a shabby menu and headed in his direction. Mark's mouth dropped open. He couldn't believe all the jiggling as she walked. When she arrived, his eyes rolled up into hers, and he had to consciously close his mouth. Taking the menu but not wanting to leave her for too long, he glanced at it quickly. Choosing the first thing he saw, he croaked, "Steak and eggs."

"How do you want your steak?"

"Supple."

"What?"

"I'm sorry. My mind must be on something else." He tried to sound roguish.

"Well, get it back where it belongs," she snapped. "We only serve it one way, anyway."

"Which way is that?"

"Burned. Eggs are a little better. Scrambled with a hunk of cheese melted in 'em. Want it?"

"Sure. Both are my favorites."

"You must be easy to please," she said and turned away.

Twenty minutes later she set a plate in front of him. The steak *was* burned, the charcoal edges breaking off and blackening the eggs, which lay cold and in a heap with a naked slab of American cheese on top. The girl was about to leave when Mark found himself asking, "When do you get off?"

"Off what?"

"Work. Off work."

"Why?"

"Why?" Mark was caught a little off guard by the question. "I thought we could get together and have some fun."

"Fun?" She all but spit. "Doing what? Tossing rocks in the river? Kickin' dogs? Or maybe we could get together and whittle like them two fatheads outside?"

"Well, your choice. You are talking *little* dogs, right?"

She sniffed haughtily and was about to turn away when, in desperation, Mark said, "Or we could spend some of this." And he pulled out his money—a wad topped by a couple of impressive twenties and made thicker by a bunch of ones. He held it poised as if ready to count it out. Mark got the effect he wanted. Her eyes grew big as chicken eggs, and she all but licked the drool from her lips.

"What's that for?" she asked, lips a little tighter, eyes hungrily on the bills.

"I just wanted to make sure I had enough for whatever I happened to order here." This was a new act for Mark. No Brakes was the one who used this technique. Mark had always dreamed of trying it, and things were going unexpectedly well!

"It won't be that much. Listen. I got another hour. You just finish your food and have a couple cups of coffee, and that hour'll go faster than any hour you've ever been through."

Mark smiled smoothly. "Not true. It'll pass slower than any I've had."

A satin smile acknowledged the compliment, and she disappeared into the back of the cafe. After a minute or two he heard the faint squeal of a screen door.

Since the cafe was enclosed on either side by dead businesses there were no windows. Had there been, Mark would have seen the waitress run across the weeded field to the gas station, and indicate to the young man sitting there to follow her inside. He would have seen the man rise and follow her wearily. Had Mark seen all this, he would have thought she was telling the local yokel that she'd be late getting off. She might even be using an excuse the yokel had never heard before in an attempt to hide a heart pounding with anticipation. She would soon be with a young, virile, mysterious stranger. Mark would have smiled empathetically as she left the guy and crossed the field, returning to the diner. Of course, he saw none of that and thought none of those things. Had he thought them, he would have been wrong.

The hour crept by. With nothing to keep him company but a tepid cup of coffee and his dreams, Mark frequently checked his watch and the girl. She sat thumbing through a worn magazine behind the counter and never once caught him staring at her. Of course, she hardly looked up at all. In fact, Mark finally thought, she could hardly look less interested in whether he was there or not.

Even though she didn't catch him looking at her, the younger of the two whittlers outside did. Called Tom, he came in a couple of times. The first time the whine of the screen door and the man's heavy footsteps yanked Mark from his reverie. "What 'er ya lookin' at?" the man growled. "She ain't no calendar."

The second time was a bit more dramatic. Mark didn't hear the screen or the footsteps—the guy must have walked on tiptoe. In fact, he didn't know the guy was there until an ugly, bearded face pushed itself into his. Mark also didn't know faces could look like that, like an angry bulldog's who'd gotten caught in a fan—everything was twisted several degrees counterclockwise—lips, brows, cheeks—and the effect was horrific. Even worse was the gleaming knife blade superimposed between both men's eyes. Mark felt his own cross as he studied it.

"What's yer name, boy?" the face growled, much as a bulldog's might.

Mark jerked back, his head rattling with all kinds of grisly possibilities if he upset this person any more. "Uh, Mark—Brewster," he managed, eyes focusing on the blade again.

"Ain't you got somewheres to go, Mark—Brewster?" Mark didn't think it possible, but the face pushed itself closer. The knife dropped out of sight, and the stench of tobacco breath and ammonia body odor nearly made him retch.

"I—uh—been driving a long time. I need rest, some coffee—caffeine—need rest bad," he stammered.

The face hung suspended before him like a map to his doom for several thunderous heartbeats, then it drew back. Never changing its twisted shape, it hissed like a snake to the mouse it had its eye on. "I'm watchin' you, Mark Brewster. I'm watchin'." And after several more seconds of supreme uncertainty, the knife came up again to where Mark couldn't fail to see it. Then the face disappeared outside.

After that, Mark never lost sight of the door. No matter how impressive the girl's posture, no matter how erotic his thought, Mark never failed to realize how vulnerable he was. Of course, he also never lost sight of the fact that it was he, Mark Brewster, the ever famous, ever stammering, ever frightened Mark Brewster who was going to have the last laugh on Mr. Deliverance outside.

Over the course of the hour, there had been two other customers. Both travelers, both alone, both ate quickly, paid, and left. And as the end of the hour crept closer, Mark became painfully aware that no one came to take her place. He was beginning to think she was just leading him on when, with only a minute or two left, her eyes came up to his and she smiled.

Destiny was finally going to smile sympathetically on a simple, wayfaring juggler.

Chapter Four

Having driven at least an hour since the flat, Nancy felt a wash of relief when she saw the Harbor View sign and nearly felt excited when she came to the gas station. She pulled in, came to a stop, stretched, and slid from the Champ, pushing her windswept hair back into place.

Tired, she managed a shallow smile as the grease-stained young man at the gas station stood to wait on her. Hamster cocked an ear but remained aloof. "I had a flat down the road and had to put on the spare," Nancy said as the man approached. "As you can see, it's bald. Can you fix the one I took off and swap it back?"

He glanced at the tire lying in the back. "If I can."

"Thank you. I need gas too. Is this self service?" she asked.

"I'll get it." He stepped to the pump. "Yer tank's locked. Why don't you leave me the keys, and I'll take care o' the tire and gas while you getcher se'f some lunch."

"I had lunch," Nancy smiled, trying not to sound short. But besides being tired, her muscles ached from wrenching the lug nuts free and hefting that big, dirty hunk of rubber around. All she wanted was to get the tire fixed and get on her way. "Thanks, anyway," she said, taking a moment to look around. Having grown up in the crowded San Francisco Bay area, she always found small towns, even scruffy little villages like this, to have a mysterious charm.

Nevertheless, it was hard to find any charm in Harbor View. Beyond the gas station was a field of brush where a small child and a ragged dog wandered aimlessly. Beyond that stood a building where two men sat, and above them was an old sign dripping with rust. Although already waning, her sense of well-being vanished abruptly when she saw the caramel-colored turtle-car. The driver who'd left her to fend for herself amid a stinging gravel shower must be inside that cafe.

She turned back and noticed that the station attendant was glancing at the Pacer, as well. He followed his appraisal with another look at her car. Then he looked back and forth again, as if comparing them.

"He passed me when my tire went flat," Nancy said. "It's a funny-looking car isn't it?"

"Yes'm," he said, as he began pumping gas. "I was jes' think'n how if I was takin' a long trip, I'd take it in yer car radder'n his."

"Oh?"

"Yep. Not only is that car weird, I'd save money with th' trailer. You c'n park off th' road, away from people. It'd be real cozy-like."

"I'm looking forward to just that." Even though Nancy anticipated trouble setting up the tent for the first time, she knew that after she got everything assembled—the lighting, the stove, the area heater—she would be snug and warm. And now, with dirty hands and aching muscles, she *really* looked forward to stopping for the night.

"Check the all?"

"The what? Oh, oil."

"Yes'm."

She nodded and released the hood latch from inside.

The young man was under the hood for only a moment when he stuck his head out. "All's okay."

"How long will it take you to fix the tire?"

"A while," he said, walking back to finish with the gas. "Time'll go faster if ya have some lunch at the cafe."

"I had a sandwich after I changed the flat."

"Then a cupa coffee."

"I can wait." She had no desire to see the driver of that car.

The boy looked cornered, then said, "It's the dog, ma'am. He's too big. You gotta take him somewheres while I work. Dogs and me never get along."

"Sweet little Hamster—I guess he does look a bit intimidating."

"Yes'm."

Leaning back into the car, Nancy snapped a leash on the big animal's collar and pulled. After reluctantly unfolding himself, Hamster eased from the vinyl seat, placing great paws onto the pavement. He and Nancy watched the boy get into the driver's seat and pull the Champ away from the pumps to a place next to the garage.

"Well, Hamster, what say we take a little walk?"

Hamster looked up with huge, sagging jowls. He couldn't fathom why he'd been dragged from a comfortable seat and forced to wander in the cold. No, he didn't want a walk.

"Okay, you win. No walk. But how about a cup of tea? I didn't have my second one this morning and I miss it. They probably don't know what a good cup of tea is around here, but even a bad cup would be good enough. Anyway, I'm starting to get a little curious about the creep who wouldn't stop to help."

About two-thirds of the way past the vacant lot, the small girl who'd been playing there emerged from the weeds. With her dirt-smudged face and arms, her shorts and dirty t-shirt, her tangled hair scattered with thistles, she looked abandoned. She had come over for the sole purpose of petting Hamster, probably the biggest animal she'd ever seen without a saddle, and her hollow, dark eyes became suddenly alive, filled with the wonder of him. Obligingly, Nancy pulled Hamster to a halt.

"Do you want to pet him?" Nancy asked.

The little girl nodded, eying the dog with great reverence.

Hamster remained still as she reached up to touch his sleek back. As she did, Nancy's smile faded. High on the little girl's shoulder, at the base of her neck, was an angry sore. At one time just a cut or insect bite, it had swollen large and red and yellow puss seeped grotesquely from it. Nancy instinctively recoiled, yanking the dog from the child's reach as if afraid Hamster might also get infected. Her dream pulled away, the little girl dropped her hand, and she stood confused, but only for a moment. Suddenly her face became a grim, rock-hard mask.

Nancy instantly felt overwhelmed—the abandoned child, the sore, this whole town—they all needed more than she could possibly give. "He's not used to children," she muttered and hurried off, tugging a reluctant Hamster with one hand while the other grabbed her locket.

Chasing the little girl from her mind was suddenly made easier. The two men she'd spotted sitting on the porch began to argue.

"It shore is yer fault," the one with the short, dark beard said, bouncing a piece of wood off the porch.

"How could that be my fault? It broke 'cause you pressed too hard. You can never take the blame—it's al'ays gotta be somebody else's fault. You pressed too hard."

"But yer the reason—yer such an aggravatin' ol' coot."

Trying to appear disinterested, Nancy stepped up to the Pacer and glanced idly inside. In the shadows, she saw a little dog curled up inside.

"Coot? I'm yer daddy—have respect," the guy with the gray whiskers fired back.

"You ain't my daddy. I couldn't have such a ol' coot fer a daddy."

"Well, this ol' coot's your'n, and if you don't find some respect, and find it quick, I's gonna bang yer head with a club again."

The threat must have been real because the younger man picked up his stick and re-commenced his whittling. He grumbled now and then, but the fight was over.

But not for Nancy. With the windows closed tightly, the little white and black puppy curled up on the driver's seat might suffocate—might die in the accumulated heat. She'd heard of both happening.

Maybe the puppy was dead already.

After rapping on the window, Nancy stepped back, both startled and relieved when the little furball sprang open like a switchblade and bounced against the window with a yipping explosion. Uninterested, Hamster made his way idly to the porch where the whittlers' dog lay. "Well, at least she's not dead," Nancy muttered.

That she wasn't. The barking, though muted, was high-pitched and penetrating, and the men on the porch glared at Nancy with sour disapproval.

"I'm sorry, but the dog shouldn't be in a closed car," she said.

"That may be, but it were quieter," the older one said.

"True." Nancy nodded, an eye on the cafe door. "Is the driver in there?"

"I guess," said the younger one.

"I ain't seen him in a while," said the other. "His eyes pro'bly popped out his head, and he's groping around blind in there."

"He better not be gropin' in there," the son said angrily, as his father laughed. As they spoke, neither missed a stroke with his knife. Nancy figured they must have been whittling for a long while. They were each surrounded by a mound of chips, and the sticks they held had nearly disappeared.

Suddenly Nancy heard a woman's shrill voice coming from the back of the cafe. It anxiously called something. A name.

"Billy! Billy!"

Curiosity and concern for the little girl she'd left in the vacant lot brought Nancy to the edge of the building where she could see. Both whittlers quickly joined her, and together they watched an eighteen-year-old girl sprint toward the gas station calling Billy's name. Only after the girl had run most of the way did Nancy realize what was happening.

She grabbed her throat, then her locket, and as her thumb rubbed, she gasped in disbelief.

"What's Becky up to, Pa?"

But it was obvious to Nancy what she was up to. The fellow at the gas station sat in the driver's seat of Nancy's Champ—its engine running, its passenger door open, poised to accept the running girl.

Nancy was about to scream at them when her attention was drawn to a lanky young man stumbling out of the cafe, his shirt open, his chest bare, his features chiseled and confused. He rubbed the back of his head as if to ward off the effects of being struck.

The younger whittler, when he saw the intruder, said, "Pa, what's he—Mark Brewster, Mark Brewster—" The whittler said the name several times; with each repetition, the sound of it became more agitated, angrier.

"Tom, don't worry about him. Becky's leavin'."

Pa's remark threw Nancy's attention back to the car theft unfolding at the gas station. "Stop!" she screamed, taking several frantic steps toward the grease-stained building. "That's my car. Get out of my car." Nancy spun around to the others. "Don't just stand there—do something! Please, do something."

Mark, still stunned, stood with the others, rubbing the back of his neck in confused silence. At least the others looked interested. In fact, because Nancy stood between them and their escaping kin, they had to crane their necks to see around her.

Too upset to be silent, too confused to know what to do, Nancy spun back around and cried out to the car thieves, "Please, that's everything I have in the world—the trailer's borrowed."

But all her shouting was futile. Becky was already in the car, and the car and trailer were already moving. They spun around, the trailer fishtailing and throwing clouds of gravel. A second later it straightened as the car headed away from them in the direction from which Nancy had just come.

Horror-stricken, Nancy turned back to the men. Mark seemed conscious now, but he clearly wasn't the man of action she needed now. He stood anxiously, bewildered beside the two whittlers who were staring open-mouthed. In a final, masochistic act, Nancy turned again toward her car and borrowed tent trailer and watched them disappear around the first bend in the mountain road.

"Police," Nancy cried, taking a few frenzied steps back. "We need the police. Do you have a car fast enough to catch them? Please, close your mouths and talk to me."

"Huh?" Pa gasped. "Police? They're miles yonder." He threw a hand in the direction opposite from the one the car thieves had taken. "The fastest thing we got is two lame horses out back."

"Anyway, she's my daughter—no police." Tom's face twisted up again, and he shot threatening eyes at Mark. "What was you doin' to my daughter?"

Nancy saw instantly that Mark was in trouble, and the look of terror on his face told her Mark saw it too—especially when the knife came up and the man started twisting it slowly back and forth so the glint would pulse in Mark's brain.

Without hesitation, Mark bolted toward the Pacer, his shirt billowing behind him, his hand reaching into his pocket.

Seeing the opportunity, Nancy ran after him, and as she passed the men, she called to Mark, "Good, we can chase them in your car."

But halfway there, as if he forgot why he had started running in the first place, he stopped, slapped frustrated hands to his thighs, then spun all the way around. "She took it all!" he shouted. "All of it. Keys, money—that miserable—" He swore loudly, his open shirt twisting around him.

"She took your keys?" Nancy squealed, almost to him now. "But they took my car." She became aware of the locket and her thumb pulsing over it. Suddenly the helplessness of her situation flooded over her.

Mark cried to the sky, "I can't believe this. I juggle—I've never killed anybody."

Nancy suddenly heard another bellow behind her. She whipped her head around to see Tom coming unglued. He stomped viciously on the gravel, threw down his knife and wood, and growled something about his precious Becky. Pa, who seemed calmer, grabbed Tom's shoulders and tried to turn him around. "Now, son, behave." Tom neither turned nor behaved.

Nancy turned back to Mark, "We gotta get out of here."

"How? No keys, car's locked—you got a hanger?"

Nancy stared at him. He was serious. "Hanger? HANGER? Are you nuts? Don't you have one of those magnet things with an extra key somewhere?"

Ignoring her, Mark glanced anxiously over her shoulder to the snorting bull who was about to charge, then slapped various parts of his body in a frantic attempt to think of a solution. While he thought, the little dog inside matched his frenzy by yipping and barking and bouncing from seat to seat.

"Hurry, they're getting further and further away."

"I'm about to be killed and you're—are you sure you don't have a hanger?"

Suddenly Mark's face ignited in terror, and he bolted again toward the car. Nancy turned to see Tom moving with measured, furious steps toward Mark. There was Frankenstein's determination in those steps. Sensing that her only hope of saving her things was to save Mark and the car (as slow as they both seemed to be), she did something that upon reflection would have seemed foolhardy.

She stepped forward and placed a restraining hand on each of Tom's shoulders. Suddenly that twisted, revenge-ladened face hovered only inches from her own. "Now, wait a minute," she commanded.

"I ain't waitin' fer nothin'. I got me a city boy to kill."

"Please, don't." She winced, the smells putrefying. "Everything I have went with your daughter—everything. Please let us—"

Nancy never finished; as if he were swatting a fly, the huge man brushed her aside. His powerful arm knocking her off balance, she nearly fell. But she didn't give up. "At least let us phone the police."

"Phone's out," Pa called to her. "We sorta like it that way."

"Like it?" Nancy screamed. She could feel her control slipping away. "How could you like it? Don't you call your friends—have square dances?" She couldn't believe her ears. Square dances? Where did that come from? She was losing her mind. Here, in a rat hole of a town, she was losing her mind.

"You citified creep," she heard Tom growling. Hearing it brought reality back. As terrible as it was, there was no doubt it was reality. "What'd ya do to my daughter that she wanted to leave like that?"

Mark had reached the car and strategically placed himself on the far side of it. "I didn't do anything. Really. Nothing."

"Then why did she run out?" Tom reached the car, too, and began stalking Mark around it. Mark backpedaled, keeping the car in between them.

"She stole all my money," Mark asserted, feeling some safety, but Nancy could tell Mark wasn't convinced that this hulk couldn't just pick the car up and toss it aside.

"Tom Bratton!" Pa hadn't been idle. While all the commotion had been going on, he'd stepped over to the action and now stood near Nancy. "Lighten up here."

"This ain't none o' yer concern. I want t' know what this here manure pile did to my daughter to make her run off like that."

Suddenly, they all heard a growl. It seemed to rumble up from a deep cavern—then a bark, a thunderous, terrible bark. Hamster was aroused.

Tom eyed the Great Dane with immense respect. Hamster now stood at the edge of the porch, his lips drawn high across huge, yellow teeth, his patience coming to an end. "You," Tom fired at Nancy, "get your dog or I'll cut him."

"Cut him?" Nancy gasped, taking a step toward her dog. "Cut Hamster?"

Mark had made it completely around the car and now stood at the driver side window again while Tom was on the passenger side not too far from Nancy and Pa. Everyone was still, waiting to see what the Great Dane would do. Hamster growled again. Nancy had never seen him like this—Hamster was sizing the man up for an attack. It frightened even her.

"Pa, get that stick yonder." Tom pointed anxiously at a twisted tree limb not far away. It would make an excellent club.

Suddenly frightened for Hamster, Nancy clenched her fists and stepped toward Tom, screaming, "You touch my dog and—"

"You'll what?" Tom's bulldog face screwed into an angry challenge that halted her mid-stride.

"Tom," Pa injected, "you gotta stop now."

"She's my daughter, and this pervert here was gonna violate her. He probably raped—"

Mark gasped. "Raped? She stole my money. Raped? You been whittling on your brain too."

"Tom," Pa's voice was on the ragged edge of calm about to cross to hysteria, "she may be your daughter but she's my granddaughter, and him messin' with her would be just one more in a long line."

"I didn't rape . . . She hit me with a baseball bat—it had to be something like that—and she ran. I never touched—well, not really—raped?"

Mark should have kept his mouth shut. When he spoke he only stoked the fire that raged in Tom. The stalking began again. This time it started with the huge man's lunging over the top of the squatty car. Before those meaty hands could reach Mark, though, he darted out of the way.

Pa shook a finger at his son. "Leave that boy alone. You know'd it were just a matter o' time b'fo' she and the Crandall kid took off. She weren't happy here. Look what all this turned her to."

But Tom wasn't listening. He lunged again at Mark; this time the car rocked and squeaked on its shocks while Mark kept screaming at Nancy, "I need a hanger—something to break in. Get me a hanger."

"She stole this boy's money, this girl's car—"

"I need a hanger!" Mark shouted, having danced back to the passenger side on his way toward the front. "Get a hanger!"

"Do you think I just carry hangers around in my purse?" Nancy yelled back.

That's when Pa acted. Nancy didn't see him leave her side, nor did she see him return, but suddenly, when the waltz around the car brought Tom near again, the tree limb—a mighty weapon to say the least—came down. With the sound a melon makes when you thump it, it struck the side of Tom's head. His eyes immediately rolled back in their sockets, his lips pursed, and he collapsed by the side of the car.

"You killed him!" Nancy screamed.

Mark heaved a huge sigh of relief. "We gotta get a hanger."

Pa hovered over his son, leaning on the limb like a crutch. "He ain't daid. Just stunned some. I ain't done that fer years but he ain't thinkin' clear. You two better git."

"We can't 'git.' I need a hanger."

"How about a rock?" Nancy offered eying the big windows.

"All this world needs is one more comedian."

"Well, what kind of fool keeps his extra set of keys inside the car? You need one of those magnet things—" That's when Nancy saw the two-foot length of wire in the gravel. "I can't believe this." Excited, she scooped it up. "Will this do?"

"It might." Mark grabbed it and quickly shaped the end into a small loop. Fortunately, the Pacer's lock plunger was where the adept hanger user could get at it. Unfortunately, Mark was not adept. He got the wire through the window jam and onto the plunger, but easing the plunger up was another matter. Inside, the little dog wasn't sure what was happening and with Hamster near, was beside herself with high-pitched, staccato yipping. The danger gone, a curious Hamster looked in at her. That sent her into an even greater frenzy.

But Mark's time was slipping away. Nancy heard a groan. Mark heard it, too, and his efforts turned frantic.

Pa said, "You better work fast, son. I can't hit him twice't. Ain't no haid can take that punishment. Even one that hard."

One eye on Tom, the other on the wire, Mark manipulated it around the plunger over and over again, but each time he pulled up, the wire slipped off. "Can't you get that horse of yours to rip his arm off or something?" he said to Nancy.

"No," she protested. "That's horrible."

"Better to be horrible than be killed," Mark mumbled, frantically at work.

Tom rolled over, gripping the back of his head. "What happened? My head—you hit me again, Pa?"

"Fer yer own good," Pa said.

"I got it. It's open!" Mark shouted, and Nancy saw him throw the door open and dive inside. Through the dirty passenger side window, she saw him reach over to the glove compartment.

Nancy pounded on the window. "What about me?"

He fumbled with papers and maps. "What about you?" he

shouted back, his voice muffled by the glass. "He doesn't want to kill you."

"No." Tom rose like a mountain beside her. "I want to kill *you*."

"Now, son. You cain't be botherin' these kids."

Growl! Hamster's eyes rolled up at the man, his jowls fluttering over bared, yellow teeth. The huge dog was only a few feet from him now and a real threat.

"I found them," Mark shouted excitedly, jangling the keys at Nancy in triumph. "You hold him off and I'll get away," he called to her. "I'll tell the police about you."

"Open this door." Nancy pounded harder as Tom staggered unsteadily away from Hamster toward Mark's side of the car. "You can't leave me here. You just can't."

Hamster growled—deep and very ominous. Now he was directly in back of Nancy, fiery eyes on his prey.

Tom turned his attention to Hamster. "Gimme that stick, Pa."

"I throw'd it away," the old man said, but it lay on the gravel no more than ten feet away. Tom stumbled after it.

The moment Tom scooped it up, Mark's conscience must have gotten the better of him, for Nancy heard the door being unlocked. She grabbed the handle, threw it open, then grabbed Hamster's leash and pulled him around. The dog leaped into the car and Nancy followed him, slamming and locking the door behind her.

Tom closed the gap, and the moment the door closed, he brought the club down on the roof and then on the window. Though neither caved in, the sound was frighteningly loud. Panicked, Mark fumbled with keys and then the gear shift but finally took a deep breath, calmed long enough to get everything where it was supposed to be and fired up the engine.

The club battered the hood a couple more times before Mark was able to find reverse, but when he did, he backed up quickly, jammed the car into first and jerked forward.

Amid a sudden storm of gravel, their frustrated attacker hurled the club at them.

Nancy's heart still pounding, she watched gratefully as everything but the memory grew smaller in the frame of the rear window. The club landed harmlessly behind them as they sped off.

After a moment to catch her breath, Nancy realized something.

"We're going the wrong way. We have to follow my car. They went the other way."

Mark didn't flinch, jaw set, hands gripping the steering wheel like a lifeline, he stated, "We're finding the police. They're this way—remember?"

"But my car. That trailer's not even mine."

"Sounds like a real problem. But this is my car, and I'm the driver and we're heading this way." Mark's eyes remained fixed ahead, his breathing came in short gasps, and beads of sweat popped on his forehead and rolled down his cheek. Though the terror of the last few minutes obviously still surged through him, Mark's course was set.

With no way of winning Nancy fell back in the seat and crossed her arms defiantly. After a few moments she sighed and let her muscles finally go limp. He might be right. Even if they did give chase, they'd probably never catch them, certainly not in this thing.

Nancy squelched any pretense of hope and slumped back in the seat. Eyes cast sarcastically to heaven, her hand wrapped tightly around the locket, its edges digging into her palm, she muttered, "Lord, the flat wasn't enough?"

Chapter Five

Face chiseled stone and ashen, chest heaving and falling in erratic gasps, eyes glued to the road, Mark was driving as fast as he dared, the mountain roads unwinding beneath them like the back of a snake. After ten minutes, he'd hardly blinked.

Nancy became anxious. He looked as if rigor mortis were setting in. "Are you okay?" Her voice must have made a difference—the muscles in his neck began to loosen. But he didn't reply. "Are you okay?" she asked again.

Hands white-knuckled on the wheel, he mumbled, "They were maniacs. I'm not used to maniacs—I hate maniacs."

Nancy sighed. *Lord, is this really happening?* Filled with anxious energy, she pulled her knees to her chest, draped her locket over them and wrapped her arms around, then planted her chin on top. She sat there for all of three seconds, and after successfully combating the urge to rub the locket again, she let her legs drop and turned to stare out the back window.

The town had long since disappeared behind an eternity of twists and turns as distance rolled beneath their car like an infinite carpet. The only two at peace were the dogs. Hamster's massive body made a canine basket in which Naomi now slept. Nancy enviously watched them, but she didn't know how she was ever going to sleep again. Somewhere out there at the end of that white line that unreeled beneath her, two people were enjoying her Champ and Donna Kingston's brother's trailer. How in the world was she going to tell Donna?

"How much further do you think?" she asked, eyes front again.

"Huh?"

"How much further to the police do you think?"

"Forever."

"What do you mean?"

"Huh?"

"What do you mean, forever?"

"It means forever." Mark's eyes never moved. Nothing moved except his hands as they steered. When the curve was particularly sharp, the squeal of rubber drowned out the constant rattling inside. Otherwise, the rattling was all Nancy could hear.

"What's 'forever' mean? The way you said that scares me a little." Then she heard herself. "A little? It scares me a lot." She groaned, and her legs sprang back to her chest and she wrapped her arms around her knees, rested a forlorn chin on top, and consciously took hold of the locket. She felt like crying, but she held the tears back behind a dam of resolve.

"I can't believe this is happening," she finally said. "I don't know you—you're babbling like an idiot—look like a robot. Here I am—I actually fought to get in this car with you." She sniffled slightly, brushed her nose, then let her legs and the locket drop—all in an effort to regain a little control. "Okay, what's 'forever' mean?"

Mark turned only slightly—most of his attention still on the road—but at least he acknowledged her. "It means that we're never going to get my money back—it's gone *forever.*" He said the word as if it had many, many syllables.

"That's uplifting." Nancy winced sarcastically.

Then Mark's frustrated arms flew around everywhere, one palm finally slapping his forehead. The impact seemed to shatter the shell he'd been hiding in because he suddenly began to talk. "The most beautiful girl I've ever seen, and we were just about to—" He stopped, conscious of Nancy. "She said someone was spying through the window and when I checked, she whacked me. It had to be a two-by-four. Then she took my money and keys—"

"Great." Nancy groaned. "A pervert."

"What?"

"Nothing. What about me? Everything I own is driving the other way. Are you sure we shouldn't be chasing them?" As she spoke she rifled through her purse—it was all she had in the world now. Not finding what she wanted, she fell back against the seat. "They even got my makeup. I hate being without lipstick. My lips get so dry. I usually carry it with me, but this morning I threw it—"

"Lipstick!" Mark exploded. "My world's crumbling, and you're worried about lipstick. What's somebody with chickenlips need lipstick for anyway?"

Nancy fired an angry look at him and was about to retaliate when suddenly everything seemed futile—the anger, getting her stuff back, even the trip itself. She collapsed against the seat and sniffled slightly. "I guess you're right," she finally said. "Maybe I am going nuts. My car and Donna's trailer are gone, and I'm worried about lipstick. But that chickenlips thing—that was cold!"

"We're finding a police station and reporting this—though who knows what good that'll do—then I'm getting my buddy to wire me some money and I'm off again. Me and this twilight zone are parting company."

"You're just going to leave me?"

"You're surprised?"

"But I have no car. My clothes, my flute—everything's gone. Listen to me. Someone's stolen my car." She suddenly felt the urgent need to take inventory of what she did have. She grabbed her purse and rummaged through it: her small Bible, a small pack of tissues, and her wallet. She looked through the little pockets again—then through her wallet. She really had cut up all her credit cards. *Neither a borrower nor a lender be*, ran through her mind. *It'd be nice to, at least, have the choice right now.*

She did have money, but it wasn't much. She'd spent most of it stocking the trailer with food. She'd even bought magazines for the lonely nights. Now she'd have to buy food again and a few bits of clothing. "I'm glad I grabbed my jacket. These are all the clothes I have, and I wore them yesterday. Tomorrow they're going to smell. You can't just leave me," she pleaded, suddenly feeling hard metal rubbing against her lips. The locket—her fingers stroked her lips with it.

Lord, what's happening? Why are you doing this? Satan. It had to be Satan.

It was curious how that thought buoyed her. That was it—the explanation. She was in a battle with Satan. She'd set out to bring the gospel to her father and to use the time for thinking and praying—and just a few magazines—and she was under attack. Satan probably figured that if he took everything she'd turn back, and fear would keep her from trying again. "Well, Satan, I guess you just don't know who you're dealing with."

"Did you say something?"

"No. Nothing," Nancy said, the locket still moving slowly over her lips.

"Yeah, right." He was staring straight ahead again, but he wasn't driving quite as fast as before. "Any time I get mixed up with a woman it's trouble."

The locket fell. "And I suppose all this trouble was a woman's fault?"

"Sure, it's a woman's fault. What do you think she was? An ape? No, she was no ape."

"No. *She* wasn't the ape. It sounds like you were the one wanting to monkey around. And a woman didn't take my car."

" 'Monkey around.' You're pretty quick for someone with chickenlips."

"Listen, King Kong, don't waste your charm on me. It's obvious you're in short supply."

"Oh, blow it out your ear. We only have a few miles to the next town, and then you can catch a bus home."

"Catch a bus?" she scowled but immediately realized that that was the issue, wasn't it? Go home or keep going. Nancy became sullen. The weight of that realization was heavy, and she found herself muttering, "Satan's winning."

"What? Who's winning? You'll get a bus back home. That's what you'll do."

No. She wouldn't. She couldn't. She didn't know what she was going to do, but she wasn't going to do that. She'd press on. But how? Well, that question was just too big to handle just now. She needed a break from thinking and certainly from the bozo behind the wheel—Mark whoever he was. She put her head back against the headrest and slid down in the seat. But after only a few minutes, she restlessly straightened and checked on Hamster. Both dogs were asleep, the little one snuggled into the horseshoe curve of Hamster's body.

"What's your dog's name?" Nancy asked.

"Huh?"

"Your dog—what's her name?"

"Naomi."

"Mine's Hamster."

"Yours or the dog's?"

Nancy had to laugh. "My dog's named Hamster. I'm Nancy —Bernard. You're Mark something?"

"Brewster. But we're not going to know each other very long."

Nancy reached back to Hamster and felt his bristly warmth. "How far are you going?" she asked.

"Huh? Why?" Instantly his face became a mask of apprehension. "Oh, no you don't. Get that notion out of your head right now. I travel alone."

Traveling with him had been the farthest thing from her mind until he said it; then, suddenly, the thought didn't sound that bad. He was obnoxious but—

"Maybe it's something to consider," she said. "The dogs travel well together." But she instantly regretted the suggestion. The mess in his car was bordering on repulsive. The smell was acrid and sickeningly sweet and came from everywhere. But the real reason was him—she didn't know anything about him except that women wanted to beat him over the head. The one back in Harbor View could have been acting in self-defense. Maybe he came at her with an axe. Admittedly, there was something appealing about his face, but that could be why she only slugged him and didn't shoot him or something. No, traveling with Jack the Ripper was not a good idea.

Nancy heard him say, "I don't travel with no chickenlips— never," and she felt relief. But not traveling with him brought back the original problem—the one with no apparent solution. She slumped back into the seat. She found a prayer and said it silently; when the few words were used up, she had an inkling of peace. She knew the Lord would never leave her stranded, wherever Mark might drop her off. He'd keep her on track—somehow.

She closed her eyes and was visited by an image—the little girl with the sore on her arm. Nancy saw her little lost face, her hollow, prisoner's eyes yearning for release. And the sore. She felt a tidal wave of guilt. She'd done nothing to help her. Nothing. Maybe the loss of her car wasn't as devastating as all that. Maybe there were far worse things in life and people were living through them.

They passed a sign, Baker Falls—4 miles.

"Maybe they have a police station," Nancy said.

"That guy back there would have slit my throat—can you imagine what he'd have done to me if he'd hit me with that club? Whew—the look on his face."

Nancy only grunted, pulled her jacket up around her ears for warmth, and nestled against the door. Closing her eyes, she tried to figure out how she was going to tell Donna that her brother's trailer was gone. What if he didn't have insurance? She'd have to pay him for it somehow. She held the locket tightly.

Baker Falls, though small, had a main street lined with hole-in-the-wall businesses, pickup trucks, and old cars—and in the middle of it, a sign that read Sheriff's Office pointing off down a short road.

Mark eased around the corner and parked in front of a red-brick box of a building. American and Virginian flags fluttered lazily out front. Mark stepped from the car and stretched. Nancy did the same.

"It's getting colder," Mark said and pointed off to the sky. It was crowded with mountaintops and piles of darkening clouds. "Rain—maybe snow," he said. He didn't usually mind the cold, but his muscles ached as if a cold were coming on, and the prospect sent a shiver through him.

Nancy studied the clouds with deepening dread. In spite of all the hope she'd injected into herself, a wave of depression crashed over her. He was probably right about the weather; the clouds were coal black and the temperature was dropping. It felt more like snow than rain. Hitchhiking would be terrible.

Hitchhiking! The very thought of it, even in good weather, brought chills. Maybe the bus was the way to go—but it would probably cost more than she had—with food and a magazine or two.

"Well, here goes," Mark said, and they went up the cement walkway to the sheriff's office.

Less than an hour later they emerged. The air had a real chill in it now, and the clouds seemed a deeper, more threatening black.

"Juggler." Nancy pushed the door open and stepped into the cold. "At least you're not wanted by the police anywhere—but a juggler? Somehow it figures."

"At least I'm not a loon. All that business about the devil in there. I bet you're gonna have a ball this Halloween."

Nancy became serious. "Do you think they'll find our stuff?"

Mark just grunted. "I gotta find a phone and you'd better find a bus schedule."

"I guess you would be calm about all this. You only lost a couple of bucks."

"A couple *big* bucks. But I'll get those replaced, then you'll get a good look at my exhaust."

"I've already gotten a good look at your exhaust. That's your most prominent feature."

"There you go being quick again." Mark took a sweeping look around him. "Phone. I gotta find a phone." He caught sight of one hanging in front of a coffee shop across the street. "See you later, Chickenlips."

"You're not really going to leave me here."

"I'm obnoxious, remember? An ape-type. I'm sure they've got buses."

"But I'm going all the way to California," she said as if that made a difference.

"Yeah, sure. I'm going to make a call. See you later." Mark walked across the street.

By the time he reached the phone, Nancy had already fought off the urge to return to the sheriff's office and ask about a bus to Washington, D.C.—going back wasn't an option.

Since she had to call Donna anyway, she followed Mark. When she got closer, she heard Mark's voice rise in volume. "Come on, man, I'll pay you back. Just a couple hundred. I'll get me a regular job and pay you back. Sure, I'm good for it. Man, we're friends—" When she heard his agitation, she hung back a discreet distance— just far enough so he'd think she couldn't hear. Seeing her, Mark turned his back, but it didn't matter, she still heard everything—she just took a few extra steps forward.

After a long silence, she heard, "Come on, I didn't mean anything by that. I was just kidding, man. I like your sister. She's beautiful, gorgeous. Even if she does have lips like Buick bumpers... Aw, come on, these are the jokes, man. You're m'buddy. We've been through too much together. We're buds. . . . How can you say that?" he said, his voice a symphony of hurt.

Nancy glanced toward the coffee shop window, where a couple of older guys in baseball caps sat in a booth. They seemed to be able to hear through the window because they began to take notice of

Mark—first with concern and then with a burst of audible laughter as one of them cracked a joke.

But Nancy's attention was quickly yanked back to Mark, whose voice was noticeably more agitated. "Don't say that. . . . Where'd you learn a word like *impetuous?*" Then he fumed. "I know where you learned it—laying in the gutter with your other friends. Well, listen, I'll get where I'm going without you—" Then more silence, and finally Mark's voice became painfully desperate. "No Brakes, I need help. You're my pal—you're the only one I can call. I need some money. . . ."

More silence, then he exploded. He slammed the receiver onto its cradle and stood staring at the phone, collecting himself. Finally he turned, and without taking notice of Nancy fell against the wall next to the phone, his eyes cast toward the pavement.

"I need to use the phone," Nancy said gently. Mark responded by moving further away, turning his back on her again, and planting himself against the wall.

"You okay?" Nancy asked, but he didn't respond. After a small, helpless shrug, she grabbed the receiver and looked at it for a moment while she thought about running and hiding behind some tree someplace. But she just put it to her ear and made a collect call.

After a slight hesitation, Donna accepted the charges.

Nancy took a tense moment to gather her courage and then started talking, and she didn't stop until the dreadful story was finished. Although she expected an explosion, none came—nothing came—only a thunderous silence. Through it Nancy thought she heard a fuse crackling on Donna's end. "Are you still there?"

"Sure, I'm here. Where else would I be? How could you have allowed it to happen? Pete's going to kill me."

"I feel terrible. But it really wasn't my fault."

"I promised him you'd take care of it. Are you sure the police won't find it? What kind of police are they? And what kind of a friend are you? He's going to kill me."

"He has insurance, doesn't he?"

"It's a tent trailer. Who insures tent trailers? You better get back here and pay for it. That's the only thing that'll keep me alive."

"But I can't come back now."

"You can and will. It's your fault and you have to make good."

"But don't you see?" Nancy was about to explain that Satan was trying to keep her from seeing her father and that she couldn't let him win that battle, but she knew Donna wouldn't understand. Instead she said, "I can't come back. I'll pay for it; I promise, but I have to keep going." She spoke over the locket, now pressed to her lips.

"You have to get home and take your medicine—now."

Nancy shook her head, but there was nothing more to say, except, "Donna, I'll pay for it, but it'll have to be in a few weeks. I'm going to keep going."

The phone went dead, and a dial tone hummed in her ear. Friends were supposed to understand but this one sure didn't. Shoulders down, eyes glazed, Nancy stood for several seconds looking at the dead receiver, but finally she dropped the locket she'd been rubbing. It was only then that she realized that Mark, still leaning against the wall, was watching her, a broad, viperous smile stretching across his face.

"You okay?" he asked.

Nancy's brows dipped suspiciously. "Fine. I just thought friends were supposed to be more understanding."

"You'd think so, wouldn't you?" He pushed himself erect. "Well, we need to make some plans."

"We?"

"Yeah. I mean we both got this problem."

"Both?"

"Yeah—both. English is your first language, isn't it?"

"I thought I was to get a bus schedule and fixate on your exhaust. Swallowed some of your own exhaust, have you?"

"Okay, I was a little insensitive. I admit that."

Nancy laughed ironically. The afternoon was wearing away and a frosty chill had settled on it, causing her to pull her jacket collar up. It helped a little, but she still shivered slightly. Winter was coming to these mountains, and if they didn't keep moving they'd be caught in it. A covey of dead leaves danced and twirled by. "Let's get in the car. It'll be warmer," she suggested. "You can try to talk me out of my fortune in there."

"Now who's being insensitive?"

"Not insensitive—careful."

The interior of the Pacer wasn't much warmer, but at least they were out of the wind. When the doors slammed shut, they each pressed into their respective corners, half facing each other, half not.

Mark looked thoughtful, as if measuring and arranging every word. From somewhere out in the ether came some words Nancy's father had said once: "Talk first and lose." She couldn't remember when she'd heard them, but right now they sounded like good advice. She waited patiently, amused that she was now in control.

But what did she really want? It was *her* money, not *theirs*. Did she want to share it for a ride with someone she didn't know in a car that either wouldn't make it or would make her sick if it did? Anyway, she didn't even know how far he was going.

The answer came quickly. "You don't know this yet, but I'm going all the way to California too. Southern California—Hollywood. Destiny, huh?"

Nancy began to wonder. "Maybe."

"The way I figure it, if I go on alone, I starve—"

"No gas. You walk."

"Right—walk. And no matter how much you have, it'll be cheaper driving with me."

"Probably. But I don't think this turtle thing—"

"Pacer. AMC Pacer. Great car."

"Pacer-thing'll make it."

"It'll make it. It's made a hundred and twenty-seven thousand miles already. It'll make three thousand more."

"Somehow that logic isn't comforting." Nancy leaned back and thought for a moment. In the backseat the dogs were curled up together; Hamster snored while Naomi breathed softly. Again she envied them. A thought stirred, and she found it as calming as the dogs' gentle breathing. *The Lord's in control.* She remembered Pastor Bevel saying he relied on that every time things seemed to be ricocheting in directions he didn't understand—times like this one.

"Perhaps traveling together sounds sane to you," Nancy said. "It did to me, too, a little while ago. But I'm not sure now. All I know about you is that you're disagreeable and you juggle. And the reason we're in this mess is because you did something lewd, maybe violent. My traveling companions usually have different qualifications."

Mark groaned. "Listen, I know it sounds bad. But that's not me—not the real me. I'm usually a pretty shy guy. I'd never done anything like that before. Never. I guess I'm asking you to take a chance."

Nancy took a long moment and looked into his eyes. He looked so sincere, so trustworthy—maybe they *could* make it.

"I want to take a walk. Just me and Hamster. We need to talk. The fact remains, I have to get to California, and right now you're the only real option I've got." Looking Mark up and down, sighing, and slowly shaking her head from side to side, she muttered, "Some option."

She turned and slapped Hamster unceremoniously on the top of the head. The sleeping dog, eyes still half-closed, raised up as if to say, "Huh?"

"Come on, boy. Let's take a walk." She opened the heavy door, made sure she had her purse, and clipped the leash on the dog. That done, she eyed Mark with an "I must be crazy for even considering this" look, and she and the dog stepped from the car into the growing cold.

Chapter Six

Around the corner and not far from the sheriff's office, Nancy found a fallen log stretched across a vacant lot. There she sat and Hamster lay, his tongue lapping at the cold air.

She took out her wallet. $515 and some change. "Gas will be $150 each way, at least—$215 for food, something to wear, lipstick. . ." She groaned. She'd started out with nearly $800 and, thinking back, had spent lavishly on food (she'd even bought a couple of steaks), extra camping gear, and things to make her nights comfortable—$50 on a comforter alone. She hoped Becky and Bill, the thieves who had put her in this fix, choked on those steaks—not much of a Christian thought, but she had a hard time repenting of it.

"What are we going to do, ol' boy?" she asked Hamster rhetorically. "I guess we'd better check the roundtrip bus prices. I don't want to get stuck out there. And if I take the bus, how am I going to get around when I get there? I'll have to think about that one."

A stiff wind blew, and she brought the jacket up around her neck. Night was coming.

"The Lord has allowed all this to happen. You know that, don't you, Hamster? I'm finally coming to grips with that. 'All things work together for good.'"

But then the image of the little girl came to her again. "Will it all turn out all right for her? I should have done something. Just a little soap and water would have made a big difference. You don't suppose I'm being disciplined for not helping her? No, I don't think so. But I sure am thinking about her a lot. Why, do you suppose? Probably because I acted like a jerk—that's why."

She sighed and pressed the locket to her lips. "Well, anyway, that's over now. We have to figure out what we should do." Nancy patted Hamster's large head, and he looked up at her with pleading eyes. "You don't care as long as you get back in that warm car, do you? Well, what say we phone Greyhound and see what a ticket would cost."

"Well," the man said on the other end of the pay phone, "you'd have to get it at Lynchburg or Roanoke, seein's how yer comin' that way and to San Francisco—"

"And back to Washington, D.C."

"And back to D.C. . . . $243. It's cheaper if you was back in D.C. now—$228. But you ain't."

"Really? That's not bad. Actually sounds cheaper than buying my own gas. Is there an extra charge for my dog?"

"Dog? What kind of dog?"

"Great Dane."

There was hesitation on the other end of the line. "If it was a small dog we could put it in a carrier—but a Great Dane? There's no way."

"He's gentle."

"He'd scare the other passengers to death. Sorry. Anyway we're pro'bly going on strike in the next couple days—I don't think we're gonna be much help to y'all."

Suddenly the bus option had crashed and burned. "Well, thanks." She hung up and glanced toward the coffee shop. A cup of tea suddenly sounded very good and very, very warm.

She looked down at Hamster who'd remained dutifully at her feet. "The bus is out." She eyed the coffee shop again. "I want a cup of tea. You'll stay out front, right?"

Hamster looked up at her with soulful eyes. It was cold and his light coat wasn't much protection. Having been an apartment dog, his coat had thickened only slightly.

Maybe she should go back to Washington—no! She'd already been through that, and she just couldn't go back. Forward was the only direction now.

That reaffirmed, it was time for tea. "Okay, sit right here. I'll only be a minute."

She watched Hamster with one eye as she went inside, then kept one eye on him while she ordered.

A woman in her mid-thirties stood behind the counter. "What'll it be?"

"Tea."

"Lipton's okay?"

"Sure—just so it's warm."

"It'll be that." The woman said as she sauntered to the coffee pot and poured hot water into a Styrofoam cup. When she returned she said, "That your dog?"

"I wish he had a sweater. He's cold."

"You on the road?"

Nancy dipped her tea bag, a ribbon of steam rising from the hot water. "Going to California. But I've had some car problems, and the buses may go on strike—I'm not sure what to do."

"Train—boring as all get-out but they get there."

"Train?" The idea suddenly sounded good. Just the other night she'd seen a rerun of the movie *Silver Streak* on TV. Even though Gene Wilder had been attacked by murderers, she doubted that the same thing would happen to her. "Train. Where do I find out about schedules and prices?"

Before the woman could reply, a man in a flannel jacket entered and threw a stack of newspapers on the counter next to them. "These musta just come outside, Wilma," he said. "Quite a wreck."

"Wreck?" Wilma asked.

"On the front page. Worst rail disaster in history—track gave out." His thick, calloused finger jabbed at the front page.

Nancy looked down. The headline read "Worst Wreck Ever: 'Tracks old, unsafe . . . ' consumer groups charge."

"Probably wouldn't take dogs, either," Nancy mused.

Mark stood outside leaning against the car, his arms folded for warmth.

"Lock yourself out again?" Nancy jabbed, as she and Hamster approached. Her tea had disappeared, consumed slowly while she weighed all the issues and alternatives.

"Do we have a deal?"

"Get in the car. Let's talk," Nancy ordered, completely in command.

Hamster leaped into the back and immediately curled up. Naomi quickly buried herself into the warmth of the big dog's belly.

Nancy climbed in the passenger side and pushed herself into the corner between the seat and the door and looked across to an expectant Mark who sat the same way.

"Now," Mark began, obviously taking the offensive, "before you set a lot of conditions, you remember that I'm supplying the car and without the car, you don't go anyway."

"Just lighten up. I'm not going to take advantage of your attack of generosity here. I just want to make sure of a few things." Nancy could never remember being so firm.

"Okay—what?"

"First—and foremost, no—uh—advances toward me. Not only will Hamster rip your throat out—I think you know he's capable of getting upset—but I don't want you to think that I want anything from you but a ride."

"Don't worry about that. Chickenlips don't turn me on."

"Good negotiating ploy," Nancy said. "Being obnoxious really helps your cause." She went on, "The next thing is this car."

"What about it?" He'd taken offense.

"It's a mess and it stinks. We're going to clean it out. There's no way I can take this for four or five days."

"What mess? What're you talkin' about?"

"What mess!"

"Okay, I'll admit things could be tidied up a bit. But you don't want to do this right now."

"Soon, very soon." She swallowed hard; this next one was a little selfish. "We're going to northern California first and dropping me off. I'm sure I can figure out transportation once I get to familiar surroundings."

"Northern—?" He pulled forward as if to fight but just fell back. "Okay, a few more miles won't make any difference."

"And finally—"

"Only finally?"

"I'm a Christian, and I don't want you ridiculing my beliefs."

"You mean in order to share a car I have to start believing in fairy tales?"

Nancy snorted angrily and grabbed the door handle. "That does it. I'll brave bad tracks before—"

"Wait, wait. I'm sorry. You're right. What you believe is your business. But you have to understand that what I believe is my business. And frankly, I do as I please. But I'll—uh—be careful what I say."

She turned back to him and exhaled triumphantly. "Okay. Then it's a deal. We both get what we want. I do have some money. Not much but probably enough for gas and food. I'm a little worried still, but I'm sure we'll work things out as we go along." Nancy paused. She'd thought about not saying this but had decided she had to. "There's something else we have to come to grips with."

"More?"

"You won't like hearing this, but I find you to be—well—a real jerk. You're rude, self-centered, a bit dumb, morally corrupt, and as far as I can tell, you've got all the charm of a speedbump."

Mark's hand went up for her to stop. "All that aside, you're still going to share your money with me if I share the ride with you?"

"Let me finish. I'm not supposed to feel so negatively about you. I'm supposed to love you and do nice things for you. But I dislike you. You're a real scum ball. Anyway, to get to the point—"

"You mean this assassination has a point?"

"Please try to be nice to me. I'll try very hard to be nice to you. But when you're not nice to me—when you call me Chickenlips—"

"You just called me a speedbump."

"No, I said you have all the charm of a speedbump. There's a difference—a slight one, but a difference. No—I have to stop this. I'm sorry. You're not a speedbump. You're more like a little road debris. No, no—see what you do? You have to be nice to me because when you're not I want to murder you, and I'm not supposed to want to do that."

"Sounds reasonable, Chickenlips. I'll be nice as I can be . . ."

"Which probably isn't saying much, Speedbump."

"Maybe we ought to continue all this fun we're having later. The weather looks like it's turning bad. For the record, I don't like you either. You're not my type—a little short, a little sweet, a *big* mouth. But I can be nice. I'm nice to whole audiences when I'm juggling—and they pay me. So trust me, I'll be nice. I'll be so nice you'll probably fall in love with me."

"There's not that much nice in the whole world. All I ask is that you be civil. Enough said. You're right about the weather. We'd better get going, Speedbump."

Chapter Seven

"We've been driving for almost an hour and we haven't said two words to one another," Nancy finally observed. Even though there'd been a gentle bantering when they'd first gotten in the car, the moment the engine roared and the rattling started, when Mark turned his head to back up, he went silent. More than silent—he went sullen. At first Nancy found the silence welcome. Not liking to drive, she appreciated Mark's giving her time to unwind and think. But now each passing minute made the silence between them seem increasingly forced.

But what actually bothered her, what framed every minute in a growing discomfort was the lack of silence—the incessant squeaks and rattles—swarms of them—from everywhere, buzzing and ricocheting about her head. These sounds were maddening enough, but one squeak in particular, which occurred without apparent provocation or discernible rhythm, set at a pitch that pierced the back of her skull like a nail, was driving her nuts. Talking seemed the only possible relief.

"It's only been about forty-five minutes," Mark replied, eyes still on the road as they drove into the dying afternoon.

"What year's this car?"

"Seventy-three. Their first year. I got it a couple years ago for a real steal. They never were as popular as they should have been."

"It rattles," she said flatly.

"You'll probably rattle in your twilight years too."

"No, I'll just sag." She thought that would get a smile but it didn't. "Are we going to drive all night?"

"Not unless you want to take the wheel and let me sleep."

"No," Nancy said without hesitation. Driving at night frightened her a little, particularly on unfamiliar mountain roads. "I'm used to a smaller car."

Mark nodded and lapsed back to silence. *He must be getting tired,* she thought. *He seems so tense—hunched forward, eyes glued ahead. Oh, well . . .*

The rattling and that one squeak in particular buzzed around her again, and she brushed it aside as well as she could. Her first shot at conversation wasn't a total success, she thought, but it wasn't a complete failure, either. She'd try again later—after the moment that she knew was coming—when that squeak began to drill a hole right at the base of her skull again. In the meantime, she grabbed her little pocket Bible and forced herself to read the Twenty-third Psalm.

Words and page melded together at times as the light continued to fade. *Somewhere above those iron-gray clouds there must be a beautiful sunset,* Nancy mused when she lost her place. But she quickly finished reading, and when she did she realized that even though she'd read the psalm a hundred times before, this was the first time it had real meaning. And as she thought about it a moment longer, she found it giving her comfort as never before. With her Bible clutched tightly in her hand, she scrunched into the corner and closed her eyes.

She must have slept for a few minutes because when she opened her eyes it was darker than before. The day was dying—not in a spectacular splash of crimson and fire but in a whimper of gray.

The squeak hadn't died. It seemed more real, more alive, more incessant—more disturbing than ever. Nancy cocked her head in an attempt to locate its source. It could be anywhere in the scattered debris. She was about to start rummaging around to find it when they came to a town large enough for a grocery store and hamburger stand. After getting a bag of dog food and feeding Hamster and Naomi, Nancy and Mark headed for a hamburger. They ate and spoke sparingly and got back on the road quickly. Even though he wasn't going to drive all night, Mark seemed determined to grind out a few more miles.

After they achieved highway speed the squeak began to drill again. This time it found the spot—right at the top of her spine—where every nerve in her body came together. After only a few annoyed moments, she'd reach her limit. She had to either find its source and stop it or die trying. It came from the backseat—she knew that much—so without waiting another second, she turned her head back.

"What are you doing?" Mark asked.

"That squeak is driving me nuts. It's coming from the backseat somewhere."

"Only one squeak?" He shook his head incredulously. "Find something on the radio," he ordered.

She found nothing but static. After covering the whole dial she flipped it off. "It's back there."

"Ignore it. That's what I do."

"I can't—it's like a nail being driven into my brain."

"Well, no loss there. Don't you think you're being a little dramatic?"

"No," she said flatly and turned completely toward the back. Planting her knees in the crack and hanging over the back, she listened. "It seems to be coming from way in the back. With all that junk."

"Will you sit down?"

"No. I'm going to find it."

"Please—sit! It's hard enough to drive without your playing mountain goat."

"I'm okay."

"But I'm not!"

His words still rang in the air as he rounded a curve and came face-to-face with two beady red eyes on the back of a slow-moving truck. He jammed on the brakes and slowed in time, but Nancy shot, bottom first, toward the dash. Instinctively trying to break her fall, she grabbed for something. The "something" she grabbed was the steering wheel.

"Let go," Mark roared but she didn't.

It was too late, anyway. Her head had already slapped against the dash and the car was cannonballing to the right. Nancy screamed. Mark gasped. And the car plowed off the road into a field—and kept on going.

As her head repeatedly slapped the glove compartment, Nancy had little time to think of anything but pain. But when she saw Mark reach frantically down to the floor, she knew the gas pedal was stuck. The world jiggled wildly as she saw Mark straighten and jab at the brake, but because of the car's violent bouncing, he kept missing.

Of course there were two others in the car. Panicked, the dogs launched themselves into the front to get a better view. Naomi leaped frantically about the unoccupied passenger side while Hamster settled on the driver's side—in Mark's lap.

Hamster's weight instantly drove Mark's foot and the gas pedal beneath it to the floor. The Pacer reacted and bounced and fishtailed even more violently.

Nancy watched Mark struggling to regain control. That included throwing the bewildered Great Dane into the passenger seat on top of Naomi who yelped then squirmed free. Nancy caught jarred glimpses of Mark as he jammed his foot at the brake. He must have finally made contact, for she was suddenly thrown toward her seat, her nose flattened against Hamster's dejected black snout.

The Pacer slid to a stop and the engine, meeting resistance from the transmission, died. Mark gasped for breath and pushed himself back into the seat. He sat there rigidly while Nancy heaved an immense sigh of relief and rubbed the back of her aching head.

The dogs were less traumatized. Naomi stood at the window looking out into the darkness, wagging her tail and fogging the window while Hamster sat where Nancy should have been sitting, his head down, a little hurt that he'd been thrown there so angrily.

Looking up into Mark's glazed eyes, Nancy said, "I'm so sorry. I'm such a klutz sometimes. Are you all right?"

But Mark remained silent—his eyes bulging and his lips clenched. One hand still clutched the steering wheel, while the other pushed against his forehead as if holding his head up.

Nancy became concerned. "Are you all right?" she said, struggling to regain her seat. "Oh, my goodness," she groaned, every muscle screaming at her. She pushed Naomi and Hamster into the backseat. After she'd allowed herself a moment to rest, she asked again, "Are you hurt?"

He sighed heavily then winced as he moved his arms and shoulders. "You sure are something to get used to," he muttered, working his stiff hand. Then he looked her way with eyes that were obviously glad to be seeing anything at all. "Nearly more than this body can bear."

Nancy thought she heard his heart thundering as the hand on his forehead dropped to his chest and he worked his neck. After several deep breaths, he announced with a groan, "Muscle strain—and we probably don't have a car anymore."

"Do you really think so?" she shook her head remorsefully. "I think it was just dirt outside—my dad always said I was a klutz—always. I could trip on a carpet. I'm so sorry. Really I am."

Mark moaned and waved a weary hand at her.

Nancy fell deeply into her seat, rubbed her locket, and let her guilt simmer for a minute. Outside, the headlights cut a shallow tunnel in the black and lighted nothing but more rugged earth and clumps of bumper-high weeds. In the distance, a stand of trees was illuminated like tall ghosts against deep shadows. "At least we missed those trees," she said. "The car did take a little beating though."

"A little?" Mark said disbelievingly. "I suppose you call Niagara Falls a little damp." Then he rubbed his eyes with the palms of his hands as if trying to erase the torment behind them. It must have worked, for when his hands fell, the person behind them was reasonably calm. He switched the headlights off. "Command decision time—we stay here tonight."

Meekly, Nancy asked, "But do we know where here is?"

"No matter what's out there, it'll be less of a problem in the morning. There has to be something about that in your Bible somewhere. It makes too much sense for me to have thought it up myself."

"Shouldn't we look around though?" Nancy suggested, still meekly, her locket clasped deep in her palm. "We might be sitting on something that could sink or something."

"If you don't look for trouble you won't find it," Mark stated flatly, but he still took a quick glance to the front and sides.

Nancy nodded uneasily. Mark might be right. There were some good reasons for staying: it would be difficult to navigate through the field in the dark, there might be holes to fall in, even big rocks that could rip the bottom out of the car. But it still might be more dangerous staying than leaving. "Do you have a flashlight?" she asked.

"Why?"

"I want to scout around a little."

"No flashlight."

"You came on a cross-country trip without a flashlight?"

"You're surprised? You came without your brains."

Nancy suddenly felt weighed down by her own stupidity. "I am sorry. I really am. I can't blame you for being cross."

"Cross!" Mark growled. "I left cross in the road back there. I'm heading toward homicidal." But he caught himself and forced calm again. "I'm tired—very tired. This has been an incredible day—incredible." He looked at Nancy with a moment of understanding. "I'll turn on the lights inside and out, and with the doors open you ought to be able to see if we're teetering on the edge of a cliff or anything."

"Thank you," Nancy said, feeling a bit relieved—he seemed to be working up to forgiving her.

She could see about fifteen yards to the front and sides and a little less in the back. Stepping from the car into ankle-deep weeds, Nancy found a field of frosty dirt clods and hidden furrows. Although she found walking treacherous, there seemed to be no hidden obstacles. A semi thundered by, then a few cars telling her that the highway was about fifty yards away. Perhaps spending the night in this quiet meadow was a good idea. It seemed peaceful enough; crickets chirped, somewhere an owl hooted, and one frog croaked, then another. There must be a pond in the meadow.

"Lord," she whispered, "I make you work overtime, don't I? We'd still be on the road if it wasn't for me, and now I have to ask you to keep me safe in the middle of a field—in the dark."

It *was* dark—no stars—the clouds were still piled high up—perhaps ready to rain. Rain could turn their little bit of earth to mush—mush that could quickly swallow the car's wheels to the axles.

"Lord, keep us dry. And begin to prepare my dad's heart for me. Oh, Lord, I feel like such a klutz—Dad was right." The locket felt cool against her lips but it dropped away as she heard Mark.

"How long you going to stand out there?" he called to her. "It's getting cold."

Only after he'd mentioned it did she feel the night's icy fingers poke at her. "I'm sorry. I didn't think about it."

"How could you not think about it? You numb or something?" Mark commented as she slid into her seat and pulled the door closed. Mark pulled his closed, too, and with a shiver asked her gently, "You okay?"

"Yes, I guess. Listen, I'm really sorry—I'm always doing dumb stuff like this. Always."

"Now you tell me." Mark managed a smile.

She fumbled with her locket as she thought back. "I can remember when I was about twelve. I made a birthday cake for my dad. After working all afternoon, I topped it off with powdered sugar for the icing. When he bent down to blow out the candles I beat him to it—he ended up with powdered sugar all over him. I ruined that birthday for him."

"How could a little powdered sugar—?" Before Mark could finish, he heard something and cocked an ear.

"What?" Nancy asked.

"Footsteps!" He slapped the headlight switch and the world went black.

Nancy heard them too. Unmistakable, they crunched toward them. Her thumb dug into the locket's face as she opened the window a crack.

"What are you doing?" Mark whispered.

She called out through the crack, "Is anybody there?"

"What are you doing?" Mark's whisper was like forced steam.

"Is anybody there? Are we in your field?"

"Quiet!" Mark threw a hand her way. "Farmers carry guns."

"Oops. I hadn't thought of that," she whispered back.

The footsteps stopped. The night was again only croaking frogs and chirping crickets. Then they heard more steps—this time two distinct sets. Terrified, Nancy's brain ran scenes from horror movies—axes splitting heads open, spikes puncturing necks, and a hundred other scenes—all with pools of blood in them.

Steps crunched from behind. She spun but saw nothing through the dirty back window. Turning back, she slid down in the seat, the locket digging into a gripping palm. "This is not my favorite thing."

Mark cranked his window down an inch and strained an ear. "When you pick a field, you sure pick a good one. I think they've lost sight of us and aren't exactly sure where we are."

The two sets of footsteps must have seen them for they were relentless now.

"Maybe we ought to get out of the car and run," whispered Nancy.

"Maybe we ought to just get out of here." Mark fired up the engine and slammed it into gear, but before he could release the clutch, a hideous face appeared at Nancy's window.

She screamed. Hamster erupted in barking and Naomi yipped.

Mark grabbed his heart and sank back against his door. The engine died.

The intruder mooed.

"A cow." Mark gasped.

Bossie's head extended and she mooed again mournfully.

Hamster, satisfied that he'd done his best, lay back down. Naomi, however, had more to say, but after a few seconds, even she found her protests more pomp than circumstance and she quietly settled down with Hamster.

Nancy, still recovering, started laughing. She had to. It was her only release, and when she stopped, she leaned back and laughed some more.

The cow plodded around to the other side of the car, eying it casually. Another cow came up with a calf. Satisfied that the turtle-shaped intruder wasn't a real menace, they moved away.

Mark sat silently as the cows were swallowed by the darkness. After several more minutes to allow the world a chance to normalize, Mark took a deep breath, rubbed his chin then his neck, and chuckled—it was the kind of chuckle that said he was finally giving up. "I'm exhausted," he said expelling a body full of air. He reached in back of his seat and pulled out a blanket. "I need some sleep."

"That sounds good—is there another blanket?"

"No, I don't think so," Mark said, covering himself.

"Really?"

"Only one of me started this trip."

"Come on. You must have something back there—a coat or something. We've been through a lot tonight."

"And whose fault is that?"

"Mine, I guess. But we have to stay together for a little while, and no matter what I did it's not punishable by freezing to death. Anyway, you promised to be nice."

"On the road I'm nice. Not among cows."

"Well, that wouldn't be for lack of practice," she fired back and then softened. "I'm sorry." She looked at him with big, pleading eyes. "Just a coat? Anything? It's really getting cold."

He sighed wearily, "I must be getting soft. There is something you can probably use."

"I'll be forever in your debt."

"Lot of good that'll do me." Mark pushed his door open and stepped out and around to the back. Opening the heavy hatch, he rummaged behind the backseat. A few minutes later he got back in the car, slammed the door, and handed Nancy an old, moth-eaten brown cloth coat. Perhaps beautiful once, it was now torn, stained, and permeated with a deep, oily, musky smell. "Here. Use this."

"This?" She held it at arm's length. "You roll a bag lady or something?"

"It'll keep you warm."

"I nearly had a nice thought about you. I don't feel quite so obliged anymore." She eyed the coat, disgusted. "Mark, you can't really want me to use this. It's dirty and it stinks."

"It's probably warmer than this blanket."

"Then you use it."

"No. It's dirty and it stinks." He wrapped the blanket more tightly around him and did his best to get comfortable.

Nancy sighed heavily. With no alternative, she decided to do the mature thing and concentrate on the good side of all this. The coat *was* heavy, and it would keep her warm as long as none of her stuck out through the holes. She wrapped it about her, placed her locket in the palm of one hand, and nestled into the corner. After a few moments of being closed, her eyes sprung open again. "I'm not really tired," she finally said. "Don't you want to talk a while?"

"Not really." Mark groaned, muffled by the blanket.

Nancy hated the feel of the coat. Slimy with age, it smelled like it had been buried for years in an auto wrecking yard. "Are you sure you don't have a flashlight? I'd like to read."

"Come on, Chickenlips, give me a break. Aren't you religious people supposed to like other people?"

"Well, yes. I guess." Doing her best to disregard the odor, she pulled the coat collar up under her chin while she tried to force her mind to peace. She *was* tired. The day had been exhausting. Suddenly all those things that only moments before had kept her awake—anxiety about the theft, being thrown into the same car with a very strange person, the accident, and their nocturnal visitors—were now the same things that weighed her eyelids down. Her senses melted away.

Mark, on the other hand, stirred uncomfortably. The blanket still over him, he sat beneath the steering wheel unable to stretch. He turned on his side but was quickly on his back again, trying to coax himself into sleep. But sleep wouldn't come, and the longer he sat there, the more awake he became. All the snoring was irritating. Not only did both dogs snore—Hamster's sounded like a groan, Naomi's like a tragic little whimper—but that woman snored too.

Not an offensive snore, so he could hate her easily, but a gentle, peaceful rattle that he envied.

"I need some air," he whispered to the darkness.

Nancy groaned when the inside light came on but she didn't wake. Mark eased himself out of the car and closed the door as gently as he could.

Outside, the cold stung his face and arms. To work up some circulation, he found three dirt clods and juggled them until they broke to pebbles in his hands. He hated juggling. It was a worthless skill. The world was no better because he juggled. There were no fewer poor people. In fact, if he counted himself, there was one more. He relieved no hunger, avoided no war, sent no one through college. He just threw things in the air, caught them, and threw them up again.

But he also loved juggling. When he juggled he thought of nothing else. When the dirt clods were in the air he forgot, if only for a single, wonderful moment, how worthless he really was.

After he scattered the dirt in the weeds, instead of juggling more clods, he remembered an old Beatles song that he used to put his own words to. He hummed it then quickly found courage and sang it. Softly at first, then loudly, then louder still:

Not here, dude—you're nothin'.
Not here, dude—life's wantin',
What you never had.

He stopped. He heard a dog barking. Turning, Mark came face-to-face with the Great Dane—his paws plastered like suction cups against the inside window, his jowls flapping violently. Nancy's door opened and her head rose above the roof. "What are you doing?"

"Nothing. I couldn't sleep."

"I thought I heard something terrible. Big cats fighting or something."

"I was singing."

"Singing? Really? I thought it was big cats."

"Go back to sleep."

The head nodded vaguely, then disappeared into the car again. The dog quieted, and after a moment punctuated by two quick sneezes, Mark stood alone again with his thoughts.

Chapter Eight

She must have slept, but she didn't feel like it. Her neck ached, and she moved trying to relieve the pain, but no position helped. She eased herself to a sitting position and allowed her eyes to drift open. She had pulled the old coat over her chin to protect her from the cold. To Nancy nothing was more unbearable than an uncomfortable night, and she was smack in the middle of one. Rolling her head toward Mark, she was surprised to find his eyes wide open. A few scattered rays of light reflected from them as he stared vacantly at the windshield.

"You okay?" she said just above a whisper.

"Tired," Mark said softly, eyes still.

"Have you slept at all?"

"A little, I guess." A small, furry head peaked from beneath Mark's blanket, her coal black eyes wide, her pink tongue lapping frigid air.

"She keeping you warm?"

"We're keeping each other warm."

"I wish I could do that with Hamster but he'd crush me."

"She's my little teddy." Mark jostled the little animal beneath the blanket. He turned his head and sneezed.

"You okay?" she asked.

"Fine—I might have a little cold."

"You warm enough?"

"Sure—fine."

Nancy nodded and after a moment said, "Those hamburgers didn't have much staying power." The center of her stomach was caving in. "You don't have anything to eat do you—a Lifesaver, anything?"

"Nothing," Mark replied, scratching Naomi below the chin. "I went through every pocket in this car. Nothing."

"Every pocket?"

"There's some interesting stuff in that coat you're covered with," he pointed out.

"I don't even want to think about it."

"I could use a Snickers right now."

"Good choice," she said, smacking her lips at the vision of a huge Snickers on a conveyor belt being assembled, layer by gooey layer, peanut by crunchy peanut. "Oh, do I love Snickers. But I think a cup of tea would taste better right now. A good hot one. I make good tea."

Silence replied. The crickets and leaves were suddenly still, and the night seemed bleak and void.

"We haven't really talked, have we?" Nancy whispered.

"Things have been a little hectic."

She laughed gently. "I'm sorry."

Mark tilted his head toward her. The gathering of light lit the edges of his face. His features looked soft and understanding. "It's been about fifty-fifty."

Nancy became aware of a renewed wash of crickets. Muted by the car, they sang softly and she allowed them to lull her into a peaceful place. "Have our bovine friends come back?"

"I hear only one moving around now and again," he said, eyes moving slightly. Then he turned his face forward again, and she heard him murmur, "And I used to like doing this."

"You mean camping?" she asked.

He chuckled under his breath, then muttered, "I guess you could call it camping."

"What would you call it?"

He didn't answer in words, but his head moved slightly from side to side and he gave a hint of a shrug. A little lost for what to ask next, Nancy laid her head against the seat back and studied his profile again. She found strength there, his features were definite—pronounced brows and nose, defined lips and chin, all slightly angular and together, curiously handsome. "You told the police back there you lived in Baltimore—what's living in Baltimore like?

"Like any city. I'm luckier than some—nice apartment, friends. I like the city."

"I'm not sure I do. Washington's too congested—too much traffic. The parks are nice though—I've only one friend. Of course, now that I've lost her brother's trailer—well—" She listened to her voice fade, and she found the silence that followed uncomfortable. "You also told the police you were on your way to Hollywood—to juggle?"

"I wrote a screenplay."

"Really?" Nancy exclaimed, sensing an opening. "Can I read it?"

"It's back there."

"Doing something like that's really creative. I tried to write once, but it didn't turn out very well. I guess I'm best at doing what other people have already done." She paused, consciously hoping he'd say something. He didn't. "I play the flute—other people's notes. I don't play very well but I enjoy it. Was it hard to write a screenplay?"

"Not very," he said, his eyes drooping closed.

"I'm going to northern California," she said. "But you know that."

"Why?" he asked, his eyes still closed, his head back, not moving.

Nancy's excitement at finally being asked something was dampened slightly by her search for the right way to phrase the answer. Her eyes scanned the blackness beyond the windshield. "I'm going to see my father." She smiled uneasily and faced Mark again. "I'm on a mission," she said.

"Aren't we all?" Mark said and faced her, eyes open, as if interested. "What's yours?"

"My dad's been an alcoholic all my life." She suddenly felt uncomfortable proceeding, but she forced herself. "I'm going to present Christ to him."

Mark gave a shallow nod. "I don't know what that means."

"Would you like to?" Excitement and dread were surging together. She'd never been any good at witnessing.

"Not really." Mark tickled Naomi's chin, a bit more awake. "I've never been religious—never thought much about it, really."

"Maybe it's time to," Nancy said, a little surprised at herself.

"I've been on my own since I was sixteen—juggling for nickels in the park. Religion seemed very far away, like—well, like hunting lions in Africa or something. I never thought about it. And I guess I don't see much use in starting now." The glow lit his profile again. "Did you have much to do with your father?"

"No. I don't think I like him much—I'm trying to change, but I'm not having much success," Nancy admitted softly, her hand feeling the outline of the locket as it lay between her breasts. "That's why I'm driving instead of flying. I need time to think about things."

"What things?"

She shrugged self-consciously. "Just things."

"Any time to think so far?"

"A little." In the cold, her weariness began to melt her defenses, and she found warmth from Mark. "This morning when I was driving—which reminds me—thanks for all the help with my tire."

"What tire?"

"I got a flat and you didn't stop this morning."

Mark thought for a moment. "This morning seems like a century ago. Oh, yeah, I remember. If I'da known we'd be cooped up together in a cow pasture all night I would have."

"I broke every one of my fingernails fixing that flat."

"Broken fingernails or not, I'm impressed."

"Really?" The compliment suddenly meant a lot to her. She pressed the locket to her lips. "After that I stopped thinking and just tried to make it through the day." Then she added, "The Lord knows what he's doing." To herself, careful that Mark didn't hear, she muttered, "I hope." When Mark said nothing, she asked, "Are you thinking about anything?"

"No," he muttered. "I work to avoid deep thoughts. It's an art."

A bit overdramatically, Nancy asked, "Are there dark secrets rattling around deep inside you—skeletons you don't want to look at?"

"Very deep and very dark," Mark said, just as dramatically. "What's with that locket?"

Nancy became aware of it again.

"You're always rubbing it, eating it—"

Nancy shrugged. "It's just a locket—an old locket."

"It means something special to you?"

Nancy shrugged again. But before she could figure out how to answer, something slapped against the back window, a shocking pop that jarred them both. Thinking it gunfire, Nancy instinctively ducked, but when she saw Mark only flinch, she turned cautiously. Through the fogged glass she saw someone with a huge brass belt buckle walking from the rear of the car to the driver's side. When he stopped, he lifted a shotgun and pointed both barrels at Mark.

Chapter Nine

"I can't believe you," Mark began as the Pacer bounced and squeaked onto the highway. "He's got a shotgun—he calls us hippies out to destroy his garden, and instead of groveling, you tell him God led us there. I'm just glad this thing still runs."

"I meant that he led us through the gate. We didn't hurt the fence or the cattle guard or anything."

"Good thing. He kills people who touch his fence. He said that—'kills people.'" Mark pushed the gas to the floor. "I've never had a shotgun pushed in my face before. I could never get used to that—never."

Thunder! A jagged tear of lightning exploded behind them, and rain immediately began. As the road became a dark blur, Mark turned on the windshield wipers. Ragged rubber smeared dirt in great arcs for a moment until the rain washed the glass clean.

Mark groaned. "Watch, in a second it'll hail."

"Come on, everything's turned out okay," Nancy said, feeling strangely cheerful. "And, if you slow down a little, everything's likely to stay okay." She placed a hand on his shoulder. "For a little while we were friends. Why don't we try to keep it going?" Above the drumming rain, she noticed something: "The squeak's gone. That squeak I hated is gone. The bouncing around must have fixed it."

"Well, my day's made," Mark said flatly and flipped the radio on. He quickly found a rock station; although static frequently interrupted the music, it just gave him more to grumble about.

After a few minutes of throbbing, grinding sounds, he began to tap the steering wheel and move his shoulders rhythmically. Nancy watched as he quickly lost himself in music that she found aggravating at best.

Her hope for a quiet moment vanished.

The rain stopped about twenty minutes later, and Mark picked up speed. Nancy slipped into an irritated coma.

"Are you hungry?" Mark finally asked her after an eternity of screeching singers, drums, and DJs' patter.

"I could use some tea," she said. "I wonder if they know how to make tea out here. What time is it?"

"Your watch broken?"

"It's in the trailer."

"Good place for it."

The jabs were back, and she sighed defeatedly. "What time is it?"

"About six. My eyes hurt, and the sun's coming up back there. I can't sleep during the day." Then he groaned. "I need coffee."

"Wanna get a thermos? They're cheap and you can take coffee along."

For the briefest instant Mark tossed a thankful look her way, but the look quickly faded. "You like pancakes?"

"Waffles. Lots of syrup and butter in every little hole. My mom used to come unglued when I used up all the butter filling all the little holes."

"You going to see your mother?"

"No. She died years ago."

"Mine too," Mark said, and Nancy detected a hint of softening, of regret.

Deciding to leave it at that, she glanced back to see how the dogs were faring and saw a pile of bound pages behind his seat. "Is this your play?"

"Be careful with it."

"Can I read it?"

"Just remember, my ego's a tender thing."

"I know," Nancy said and found she meant it. "Brass Knuckles," she read. "Charming."

"Let the other guys write charming. Mine is powerful."

"The title probably captures the mood," she said, falling back into the seat and starting the first page.

She hadn't finished it when she heard Mark ask, "How's this place look?" He pointed to a small diner not far ahead. "Looks a little better than yesterday's."

It did. Like a gingerbread Swiss chalet, the little building sat atop a small knoll and, a quaint staircase, bordered by flowerbeds, wandered up to it. Perhaps in summer bright colors framed the walk and warmly invited the traveler. Perhaps the cafe was busy and from the parking lot below you could hear voices and clattering china. But on this cold October morning, as fall was dying with a last gasp of red and gold, there were no flowers—and only silence. Mark and Nancy were the only customers.

"Is it open?"

"I see lights," Mark said.

They got out of the Pacer and stretched. "We need to feed the dogs." Nancy reminded him.

"The bag's in the back."

She watched Mark step to the rear of the car. "We're going to clean this car of yours. Maybe even today."

"After breakfast," Mark insisted. "I need coffee first."

After climbing the wooden steps, they went inside, the whining screen door slapping behind them. The interior was clean, sparked with yellow and blue plastic flowers on all the tables, and as wooden inside as out. A polished wooden counter ran down the center of the room, while perfectly appointed wooden tables sat next to the windows. The only compromise to the "olde worlde" motif was a small wire stand near the cash register and two boxes of candy—Baby Ruth and Snickers. Both sounded good to Nancy, but she didn't dare spend money on empty calories like that, no matter how wonderful they would have tasted. A woman in her mid-forties greeted them from behind the wood-grain cash register. "Sit anywhere," she told them.

"Over there, by the window," Nancy suggested, and they walked on hollow wood floors to a table not far from the door. The woman followed them with menus.

"You kids are up early," she said, setting the menus in front of them. Nancy asked her, "Does it snow here this early?"

"Which way you heading?" the woman asked.

"West," Nancy answered, then pointed. "That way."

"Then further along you'll hit snow—in the Ozarks. They had an early storm a day or so ago," the woman answered, her smile shaped with warmth.

Mark grimaced. "I don't like driving in snow," he mused, eying the menu for a moment. He set it down and asked the waitress, "Where's the restroom?"

"Back there." The woman pointed toward the cash register. "Order me coffee," Mark said and left.

Nancy set her menu down and looked up. "Hot tea for me, and I'm sure you heard his order—lots of coffee."

"Lemon for your tea?"

"No, just a little cream."

"How's he like his coffee?" she asked, pencil poised over a small order pad.

Nancy stopped to think. Mark hadn't said—he'd never said. "I don't know."

"You must be newlyweds."

"No, we're just together."

The woman's gracious look vanished. "I'll bring cream and sugar," she said curtly then hesitated for an instant. Nancy found a lot average about her—average height, brown hair, neither fat nor slim— but her eyes were distinctive, expressive, and now a hint of anxiety charged them. Those eyes searched over Nancy for a moment. But the woman turned and headed back to the counter, her sneakers whispering over the boards. Nancy considered calling her back to explain how innocent everything was when Mark reappeared.

"Did you order?"

"Just your coffee," Nancy said, throwing a wary glance at the woman. She stood behind the counter pouring Mark's coffee. "I didn't know how you take it."

"Cream and sugar—candy coffee," Mark said, idly looking out the window. "What do you think's going to happen to us today?" His eyes followed a semi thundering east. "You ever see the movie *Duel?* Spielberg. Makes you wonder about the truckers we'll meet out there."

"Pleasant thought."

Still concentrating on the highway, Mark paid little attention to the waitress as she approached. The two cups jiggled noisily on her tray. He also didn't notice that she deliberately avoided looking at him. Nancy saw both. She saw the woman's hands tremble slightly as she placed the cups and small stainless teapot on the table. After a moment's hesitation, she made a quick half-turn to leave. But she never completed it.

She turned back, and Nancy immediately saw she was greatly upset. She glared at them both with tortured eyes and quivering, bloodless lips.

"Are you all right?" Nancy asked, brows knit with concern.

"Do you two know what you're doing?" the woman blurted out.

Mark turned from the window, bewildered.

"Do you know how this hurts the people closest to you?" she continued, her voice strained and backed by anxious breathing. "All those people who don't want to see you destroying yourselves."

"What?" Mark's face twisted inquisitively. "Are you talking to us?"

She hovered almost vulture-like—but not quite. Vultures possessed a harshness this woman didn't. Behind the irrational intensity of her eyes lurked an anxious vulnerability—a silent pain, a pain now soaring in judgment. "Do you know what God thinks of what you're doing?" she said, eyes darting back and forth between them.

Mark fell back. "Is this the floor show?"

Nancy pleaded, "You don't understand—"

"Living together—you're sinning against God," she continued emotionally, her brows perched like dark cliffs. "Do your parents—?"

Mark now leaned toward Nancy. "Get rid of her before I—"

Nancy turned confused eyes toward the woman, "Please," Nancy began, feeling the unwelcome pressure from Mark, "we're not—"

Stung by a sudden surge, as if the pain behind her eyes had broken loose, the waitress said shrilly, "People are touched by this. People are hurt." To Nancy's consternation, she suddenly dropped to her knees, grabbed Nancy's hand and, holding it firmly with tears flooding her eyes, pleaded, "Stop this. Go back to your home—they love you there and—"

"Barbara!" A voice molten with rage exploded from the kitchen, and a thickly built man stood in the kitchen doorway. He wore cook's whites. "What in heaven's name—?"

The woman fell self-consciously silent. Still trembling, she rose unsteadily, brushed off her dress and, with eyes cast down nervously pushed tears away.

"Let's get out of here," Mark said indignantly, scraping his chair harshly against the floor as he rose.

"I think you're right," Nancy said still confused and suddenly a bit frightened. Mark let her go first, and as she passed the woman, mascara-smeared eyes peered up at her. Nancy had never seen such anguish. Her eyes were reservoirs of confused and jumbled emotions, indistinguishable from one another, except for one that haunted Nancy the instant she recognized it—a mother's fear.

After a quick, regret-filled glance her way, then a fleeting one at the angry, embarrassed cook, Nancy hurried out. Mark was a few steps behind her, and as the screen door slapped behind them, Nancy heard the cook's voice erupt in indistinguishable sound. She could only imagine the heated words that boiled over the woman.

After clomping hurriedly down the stairs, she opened the car door, threw herself inside, and slammed it. She sat numbly as Mark climbed in behind the steering wheel.

"You're all nuts. 'Jesus this' and 'God that.' What'd she think we were doing—eating babies? This trip isn't real. I get robbed, bounce into a pasture, spend the night with cows, and get threatened with a shotgun. Then, when all I want is my morning coffee, I get the Bible thrown at me. You religious types are giving me an ulcer."

Surprisingly, Nancy felt the same frustration. Like Mark, she felt like she was starring in a nonsense play. Irrational, explosive events seemed to be detonating randomly all around them—unpredictable events populated by unpredictable people. It was like being around her father when he was drinking.

He'd be soothing one moment, a volcano the next. He'd praise her, then in the next breath, damn her. He'd be helpful, then destructive. His moods would shift abruptly, sometimes for no discernible reason. When he was like that she'd try even harder to please him. She wanted to please him, to hear kind, encouraging words—even just a thank you—but she seldom did. Even on those rare occasions when she succeeded, his pleasure was short-lived. It could fade as quickly and as randomly as the sun on a cloudy day. And when that happened it brought the same chill and shadows.

She slid into the corner of the car, fumbled with her locket, and numbed her mind. She'd think about it all some other time.

"There's got to be peace out there somewhere," she heard Mark say, Naomi cradled on his lap. "All most people need to cross the country is gas. I need bodyguards—to protect me from robbers, farmers, waitresses—and chickenlips."

Chapter Ten

Rock music, a different station, but more of the same: DJs talking in funny voices, names Nancy associated with drug busts, the incessant throbs and screams over and over again.

"Could you turn it down a little?" she finally asked.

"It keeps me awake. If you'd bought that thermos I'd be buzzin' on caffeine now instead of groovin' on tunes."

"I just forgot," she said. After leaving the Swiss chalet they'd found another small town and an equally small and inexpensive breakfast. A general store snoozed next-door to the cafe, and Mark reminded her about the thermos while they sat at the cafe's gaudy red Formica table. When they left, however, they both forgot it. But because he'd reminded her, forgetting became her fault. "Please, turn the radio down," she pleaded.

He did, reluctantly. For a moment, until even that volume level became more than she could bear, the pain in Nancy's head subsided.

The Ozarks seemed more rugged than the Appalachians and as predicted, when they'd climbed high enough they saw snow. At first just a few scattered crystalline patches huddled in the shadows, but soon the patches grew and before long they came to a glistening field of white, the aftermath of a substantial snowfall. The ground billowed and puffed over what lay beneath and reflected the gray sky radiantly. "Feel the window," Nancy said. "It's freezing out there."

"I don't have to. I really hate snow."

"But it's so beautiful. Especially the way it piles on the black tree limbs."

"And falls down your back. Then there's shoveling it—as much fun as a root canal."

"In the city? That's somebody else's job."

"I didn't grow up in the city."

"Where did you grow up?" she asked, sensing another opening.

"Outside the city," he responded flatly. "Can't we just be quiet for a while? Being friends makes my jaw ache."

She pointed at the radio. "Quiet? With that?"

But he didn't answer, and as time ticked away his silence hardened.

She missed the Mark that had dropped his guard just a bit last night, he'd still shut her out, but there hadn't been the hostility or the high walls. Even afterward, on the road—he'd jabbed at her a little, but she sensed a bit of humor behind it. But all of that had vanished. Ever since they'd left the diner she'd been aware of the fortress Mark hid behind and the walls that stood—no, the moat—that stretched between them. For a brief instant she became aware of her own walls—and how vulnerable she felt wandering outside them as she had briefly last night. Maybe she and Mark weren't that different, after all.

No, they were different, she protested to herself. When she looked at him, his stern eyes staring at the wet blacktop disappearing beneath them, his equally stern hands gripping the wheel, she knew beyond doubt that she and Mark were very different. And yet...

Nancy sighed and made a conscious decision not to let him bother her. Decision or not, though, it did.

She turned back to the endless stand of forest that passed on the right. Like a riverbank seen from the river, the forest erupted tall and majestic from the clearing that ran along the highway. She had always been amazed at the Midwestern forests. They began abruptly and never seemed to end; when she entered them, the world became all trees. In California, although there were patches of forest, most of the Golden State was desert and farmland. A real tree was an event, clumps of them a miracle. And only the most remote were ever beautifully piled with cottony puffs of snow like these.

"It's all so peaceful," Nancy said.

"I only hope the road stays clear," Mark said, eyes never leaving it.

"Once I hit a patch of ice and turned all the way around—three hundred sixty degrees. I don't drive well in snow, either."

"Nobody's going to ask you," Mark said flatly.

If his unpleasantness was aimed at irritating her, it was working. Who was this guy, anyway? He was using her gas...

Oh well, she knew of no way to snap him out of it, and she certainly wasn't in the mood to find one now. Instead, she just grunted and turned a defiant back toward him. Palming her locket, she tried to sleep. But no matter how heavy her eyes, enough comfort to sleep eluded her. She rolled onto her back, then to her side facing him, then away from him again. After repeating the cycle the third time and ending up facing the window, she tried to gain support by propping her arm on the floorboard between the door and seat. And that's when she felt something—alive! She gasped at sudden visions of snakes and darting lizards, but when whatever-it-was didn't move, a tenuous calm returned. She felt the object cautiously and determined that it was just something slimy. "What's down here?"

"Who knows?" Mark said, dismissing her.

With thumb and forefinger, Nancy grasped it and pulled it out— an old, rotting brown banana peel. "That does it—pull over."

"What?"

"Look, have apes lived in here?" Nancy asked, the sarcasm feeling good. "I told you when we started that this car's got to be cleaned. The time has come."

"You're kidding," Mark bleated disbelievingly. "It's cold. Snow means cold. It's one crummy banana peel, for cryin' out loud!"

"There's no telling what else is living in here. In another minute we all might get typhoid." She threw the peel dramatically into her trash sack and as firmly as she could, barked, "Now, Speedbump."

Mark swore, then growled, "I don't need this. Bug off, lady."

"Pull this car over. Look, there's a rest stop. Pull in there."

Mark eyed her with daggers, but after a moment he softened and a sigh steeped in defeat hissed from between clenched lips. Using dramatic movements to emphasize his displeasure, he pulled into the parking area.

Although the rest stop had been used often since the snowfall and the frozen slush crackled as they drove over it, the sprawling meadow beyond the cinder block restrooms was still pristine white. They pulled up in front of a couple of picnic tables, also still piled high with unfettered snow. Mark and Nancy sat still for a moment. In summer the place probably looked ordinary, even desolate. But the festoons of snow piled on the rest room roof, the billows of white blanketing everything beyond created a peaceful winter postcard.

But the postcard lost its charm the instant the chill hit them. The sudden blast as Nancy threw open the car door was like opening a deep freeze. As she stood ankle deep in the snow, her ski jacket of little help, she began slapping her arms and rubbing her hands to keep her circulation flowing. Mark warmed his nose by breathing into cupped hands. Festoons of white breath rose up in front of his face while Hamster, still in the car, took a healthy sniff and reburied his head in the coil of his body. Naomi, on the other hand, became instantly animated. She leaped from the car into the chest-high snow. Without missing a stride, she bounded and spun, yipping joyfully.

"Stupid dog doesn't know when she's well off," Mark said, watching the black-and-white pup grow quickly tired of plowing through the snow and sit, her pink tongue lapping at the frigid air. "I don't think you do, either. You're leaving a warm car to work out here?"

Nancy felt her stubborn streak solidify. She had to admit to herself that there was just a touch of revenge in what she was doing. "I'm leaving a pigsty, and I'd do that in any weather."

"Well, when your hands grow numb they'll make a matched set with your brain."

"Like this conversation. Now, take that wonderful coat you had me sleep under and curl up on one of those benches. This won't take long."

"It never takes long for you women to take over, does it?" Mark charged.

"What's that supposed to mean?"

"It means what it means," he said belligerently. "It's not the mess—you just want control."

"That's not true!" Nancy protested.

"Sure, it's true. That's all women ever want—to run our lives. Well, it won't work. That's my car and my stuff. You own the gas but that's all."

"Sure it's your car. Who else would want it? Maybe Evil Knievel would drive it off a cliff or something, but you're in no danger of losing claim to this car."

His expression became a pout, as if his best friend were taking the marbles home. "This car is just the way I like it. Now you're going to change it all. But don't let my feelings bother you."

"What year did that rotten banana bring you such fulfillment?"

"A better year than this one's turning out to be," Mark muttered angrily as he and Naomi slogged over to one of the tables. When he got there he brushed the snow from the end of it and sat down.

Eying him suspiciously, not sure how seriously to take his ranting, Nancy finally said, "You look like a spectator at your own execution."

"That's about right," he said, eyes deep set like one of his own footprints. "Listen, I can't watch this. Do what you must, but I'm going for a walk."

"All this drama isn't going to work. I'm cleaning the car."

"All what drama? You're the one who's being dramatic. I can see you standing at the door to a ward for the terminally ill clapping your hands and saying, 'Perk up in there. Your death's for your own good.' Well, I can't watch this particular assassination." He stood, but before his first step, he shook a threatening finger. "Clean all you want, but don't throw anything away. Nothing—until I've said you can. It's my stuff, and if you're anything like my mother—and believe me, you're looking more like her every minute—you're not to be trusted."

"Does that go for rotten bananas too?" Nancy fired back.

"It goes for everything—everything!" Mark exploded. Turning with a great show of anger, he and Naomi plowed toward the forest.

However, Mark was never one to be angry long. As he walked, his little companion panting happily beside him, he found his anger quickly dribbling away. After all, there were other things to think about. The chill for one.

There was something exciting, something exhilarating about it, something manly in enduring it—something cleansing. Nancy was right—not about the car—but about the generous mounds of snow that stretched in every direction. They were beautiful and the laden trees were lovely.

He chuckled to himself.

He'd lied. Winter was his favorite time of year. Summer boiled hot and humid, and spring and fall were wimpy—winter was a man's time of year, when you chopped wood, survived blizzards, and warmed yourself by the fire.

But Mark knew there was more to it than that. It was a time to forget, a time to coast, a time when all earth's corruption lay stashed away out of mind. The filth of his neighborhood lay hidden in the purest white, even the twisted and torn chain-link fence around the basketball court looked picturesque under a cover of new fallen snow. For a few months at least, he could pretend all that squalor didn't exist and that the purity that covered it would remain forever. Such were his thoughts as he wiped a cold, red nose on his coat sleeve and he and his pooch walked alone in the cold.

Mark suddenly felt removed from the activity going on behind him. He could hear Nancy clattering about—even humming—and in his mind he could see her circling darkly over his car and his life, a ravenous creature bent on recalibrating all those things he wished left untouched.

Overwhelmed by his impotence, depression came; by cleaning and rearranging, Nancy was taking control of what was rightfully his, and he'd done nothing to stop her.

But he could be depressed later. Right now he had snow to enjoy and trees to admire. He suddenly thought of something he used to do as a boy, and he longed to do it again—stand beneath a low, snow-covered branch and jiggle it. The shower of snow would cascade all over him, on his head, down his collar—wonderfully cold everywhere.

But even that thought evaporated after a few more steps. The white earth suddenly dropped away from him toward the woods, gradually at first, but it became moderately steep after twenty yards or so. A thought took hold of him and he turned excitedly and scooped up Naomi. As she yipped just as excitedly, Mark thrashed through the snow back toward the car.

Nancy saw him coming and for a moment thought he was going to attack her, but when she saw his playful smile, she called out, "What did you find?"

"Fun!" he called back. "Forget the stupid car. There's fun over there."

"Fun? What kind of fun?" she asked, a touch of suspicion in her question.

"How many kinds of fun are there? Several kinds, huh?" He smiled with all his teeth as he rushed by her to the car's opened back hatch. Dropping Naomi, he fumbled around noisily.

"Hey, I got some of that stuff in order."

"Who cares?" he tossed back, finding what he sought. He held up a cafeteria tray triumphantly. "It's back here for emergencies."

"An emergency would be my last guess. What are you doing?"

"There's a hill back there."

Nancy perked. "Really?"

"Come on, Mizz Clean, let's go sledding."

"How big a hill?"

"A hill's a hill. They're all fun."

Nancy hesitated, eying the car and the footprints that led off through the meadow. "No, you go ahead. I want to get this done."

Losing none of his enthusiasm, Mark shrugged, scooped up Naomi again, and high stepped through the snow, the tray swinging at his side.

Nancy leaned against the cold car and watched him. When he finally reached what she figured was the top of the slope, she had to laugh. He unceremoniously dropped Naomi and the tray. Then she saw him poise his bottom over the tray and plop down. The moment his seat hit, his arms went into the air, and with a whoop muffled by distance disappeared beneath the white horizon.

"He's no fool," Nancy said to Hamster who still lay curled up in the backseat. "I'm cleaning his car and he's sledding." Her head shook in disbelief. "Do you think he planned all this? Maybe he wants it cleaned. What'd' ya think?" Hamster didn't even flick an ear. "No," she said with assurance. "He's a slob. And he's not a bit clever. No. With Mark what you see is what you get."

She returned to work.

At first she'd hoped she could just move things around a bit and clean between them, but before long she realized that the trash and dirt were too well entrenched and that she'd have to remove everything. She filled box after box with an incredible array of junk. There were tools, various sizes of balls, something like bowling pins—probably all his juggling gear. She found cassette tapes of groups she'd never heard of and paper—lots of paper.

She found every conceivable size of it—note size, lined school size, legal size. It was all scribbled on, some doodled on—he'd drawn elaborate mazes—some colored on, some intriguing, some intricately beautiful. But most was just trash.

Then there was the debris, the refuse—the real garbage: piles of

Twinkie and Ding Dong wrappers (he must be an addict), an empty oil can, soiled rags, wrappers from McDonald's hamburgers and Taco Bell tacos, Styrofoam cups, and a hundred other kinds of trash. Among the rags were a couple of torn shirts and a single gnawed shoe. His suitcase was a small paper bag.

At times Nancy's stomach twisted around itself as she dealt with the rotten, moldy food—half-eaten bags of cookies, a box of fish-shaped crackers with two mossy, green remains inside, an apple core, a couple of peach pits, and a half-eaten banana with its peel carefully replaced. She even found several half-eaten bags of French fries.

Everywhere was dirt—oily, black, in all the cracks and crevices. Nancy was determined to get it all out. If this was going to be her car for the next few days it was going to be clean. As she cleaned, as she used the rags dipped in melted snow to scrub and scour, she kept saying over and over again, "How can he live like this? Why hasn't he died from tuberculosis by now? Coal miners are cleaner."

But as elbow grease was expended, floor mats were shaken out, the dirt was dislodged from its home of years—maybe eons—the Pacer began to look actually habitable. Even the dash glistened as a thick coating of grime fell away to reveal a whitish background.

True to her word, Nancy kept everything. The things that looked like keepers, she repacked in the boxes. The stuff that looked like trash—an amazing pile of it—she stacked in the boxes that were left over after she repacked. She placed all the boxes of "keepers" back in the car and left the other two boxes sitting in the snow.

Finished—if only she had a vacuum cleaner—she stepped back and admired her "new" car. There was more room. There was order. It was clean-ish. And never again would she stretch out to grab hold of a slimy banana peel. She smiled.

As she did, she listened to the whoops and yells from the distant hill. They'd always been in the background as she worked—an annoyance, a reminder of Mark's indifference to her efforts. But now that she was finished and she saw Mark shout excitedly and slide from view, the noise became inviting.

"Come on, Hamster," she said as she nudged the huge dog. "Work's done. Let's go find out what that guy's up to. Maybe there *is* some fun over there."

Chapter Eleven

Nancy concluded that Mark might be a lot of disgusting things, but he knew how to have fun—at least in the snow. Now that the car was clean, she was ready to put him to the test. No cars had driven by in quite a while, so she figured leaving the Pacer open would be all right. She took the money from her purse and slipped it into her pants pocket, then tossed the purse on the passenger seat.

Hamster didn't enjoy snow. Hamster didn't enjoy anything, except Nancy's coming home at night. While other dogs panted excitedly through life, Hamster sauntered through it halfheartedly. Now he sauntered beside Nancy, meaty paws breaking through the crusty surface with tortured steps. When they came near, Mark was just rising above the horizon. Covered in white, cheeks cherry red, Mark's face was wrapped in a wide grin. When he saw her, he darkened. "The execution is over."

"I even saved the apple cores," she said to him with a certain air of self-righteousness. "You look pleased with yourself."

Mark brightened again. "Take a turn. It's a kick."

Nancy shrank back. "I don't know. I'm not good at these things. I usually fall off and get hurt."

"That's the whole idea."

"Getting hurt?"

"Well, falling off, anyway." Mark tossed the tray toward her. It just missed Naomi who pranced on top of the hill waiting anxiously for Hamster, who approached with grave caution.

"But I don't like snow down my back," Nancy said, eying the tray apprehensively.

"That was my line," Mark laughed scooping up a handful of snow. "You just need to get used to it," he said. Smoothing the snow quickly into a ball, he fired it at her. Before she could duck, another one was on its way, then another and another. She spun and dodged, squealing with a mixture of fear and delight. The snowballs came so fast she couldn't retaliate, but her dodging worked. All missed but the last one. It nailed her squarely between the shoulder blades. "Ouch! That hurt," she exclaimed, turning toward him with what began as anger and ended as uncontrolled laughter.

"It couldn't have," Mark called back. "Come on. Take a turn on the tray. You'll love it."

Nancy eyed the plastic rectangle but only for an instant. After a breath of ice, she straddled it and awkwardly plopped down. She stuffed her locket inside her blouse where it would be safe, then braced herself and waited for Mark. He didn't disappoint her. Placing strong hands on her shoulders, he pushed. The bumpy ride began.

The hill was about forty yards long and fell gradually at first but after the first ten yards dropped earnestly to a flat area below. Mark had worn a path with deep sides and a packed, irregular base—a base that now jolted her, slamming her teeth together and making her shout an endless series of warbles. The warbles grew louder and more excited the further and the faster she went. As the bottom of the hill flew up at her so did the trees beyond. Elated, she hit the flat, bounced, and spun off the tray into the wave-like avalanche of cold—blistering, wonderful cold.

She lay there for a moment, only long enough for the cold to bite her hands and the snow down her back to yank her to her feet. She slapped her hands together and stood for a moment looking back up the hill. Mark stood at the top, hands on his hips.

"That was great!" she called up to him.

"Am I smart or what?" Mark called back.

She found the tray half-buried, grabbed it, and started back up the hill, her heart far lighter than her trudging steps. Halfway up she tossed the tray to Mark. "Your turn."

With a maniacal whoop, Mark climbed on and seconds later slid wildly past her, his cries just as wild. By the time he reached the bottom, Nancy was at the top. He flung the tray up to her like a frisbee, and without hesitation, she started down. But this time when she was just a bit ahead of him, the tray leaped the bank and she careened into him.

In a riot of arms, legs, and splashing snow, the two tumbled in cascading white all the way down. Laughing and squealing, Nancy pulled away from Mark. She grabbed a handful of white powder, pulled his collar back, and drilled it down his back. He yelped and grabbed a scoop of his own. "No," she laughed, leaping to her feet and backpedaling. "No you don't." She grabbed more snow and flung it and then pitched handful after handful until he shrank back beneath the barrage.

Beat back only for a moment and bent on revenge, Mark scooped up an armful. Cradling it like a baby, he charged her. With a glass-shattering yelp, she spun and ran, but when she reached the hill, Mark, on lanky legs, caught her. Dodging him, she slipped and fell. Now helpless, hands high to ward off the inevitable, Nancy giggled and squirmed like a puppy. Standing over her, laughing diabolically, he opened his arms and dumped the frosty white all over her. Dropping to his knees, he rubbed the snow all over her face and hair and into her screaming mouth.

"There," he said, laughing. "Take that, Chickenlips."

"Don't you call me that, Speedbump." She sprang at him. She was smaller than he, but with the strength reserved for the drowning, she wrestled him over onto his side, then rolled away. Scrambling to her feet, she avoided his counter-lunge and kicked great splashes of snow at him. One wave caught him full in the face. The only thing visible was his dark eyes and open mouth. She kicked at another pile of snow and instantly regretted it. It was a snow-covered rock. Pain rifled up her leg and she fell back. She hopped and grabbed at her injured foot. "Oh, that hurts," she screamed. It did hurt, but having fun was too exciting to take the pain seriously. She laughed in the midst of it and finally lost her balance and fell again. "You put that rock there, didn't you?"

Mark was up now. He hovered over his injured foe and prepared to attack again. But his attention was suddenly drawn away. Nancy saw his eyes turn toward the hill, his head cock in disbelief, a smile form, then a grin. When she finally broke away from watching him, she, too, folded with laughter, her sides aching.

Atop the hill, his bony chest in the snow, legs out like the points of a compass, Hamster slid down the hill. Straddling his back like a fuzzy, salt-and-pepper jockey was Naomi. Although they didn't go far, they went far enough. "I can't believe it," Nancy squealed, trying her best to straighten.

"Now that's a hot dog," Mark cried, collapsing.

"Hamster, the ski dog!"

"Come on." Mark charged up the hill. "Let's put 'em on the tray. Come on."

The two dogs watched with apprehension as the two people ran toward them. Naomi, naturally excited, jumped and yipped as Mark approached while Hamster, his fear of the cold gone, lay in the snow piles waiting, unsure of what was coming.

Mark quickly picked up Naomi while Nancy grabbed Hamster by the collar. Pulling him to the top of the hill became a struggle. Hamster was tired. He had had his fun and had no desire for more. He just wanted to rest, and no amount of coaxing was going to dissuade him. He was going to lie down. Some of the exhilaration gone, Nancy finally said, "I give up."

"Naomi's had it too," Mark said, panting like the dogs, sweat breaking on his brow.

Tired, but not wanting to let go of the moment, Nancy grabbed the tray. "I'm going down just once more before I freeze to death."

"Okay," Mark announced, "Nanook's last ride."

With her muscles lagging, Nancy sat on the tray. Mark, now struggling to breathe the icy air, gave her a shove. Overcompensating for weary muscles, he shoved a little harder than before, and Nancy felt herself sliding faster than she wanted. At first it was exhilarating, the jolts exciting, the instances when she bumped off the tray heart-stopping. Suddenly, as before, the tray left the path, but this time it headed in a different direction, one that carried her where neither she nor Mark had been.

Suddenly the whole earth dropped from beneath her. One moment she was on firm snow, the next she had lunged over a steep embankment into a funnel of snow at the base of which stood a thick, black, formidable oak!

Mark saw her disappear over the edge, and immediately his heart lodged in his throat. Not because she'd disappeared but because of the scream—a strangled, terrified corkscrew of a scream that rifled right up his backbone. The instant he heard it he bolted down the hill to where Nancy had dropped from sight. Within seconds, the dogs at his heels, he stood on the rim of the snow funnel looking down. What he saw was more terrifying than the scream.

The snow had made a deep cone around the oak. Nancy lay at the base of it, her back slammed against the trunk, bent unnaturally. The sight of her was horrifying. She lay gasping for air, small, tortured puffs of white coming from thin, drawn lips. Her arms uselessly flogged the air while her tight chest wrenched with each attempt to breathe, and her legs lay twisted under her.

Fearing the worst, Mark scrambled down. While both dogs remained at the rim watching, snow flew everywhere as Mark bounded quickly down the embankment. Careful not to fall on Nancy, he slid to a halt and knelt. Though he felt totally inadequate, he knew he had to do something; afraid to touch her, he also knew he had to get her help. "You okay?" he sputtered, his hand going cautiously to her shoulder.

Nancy's eyes darted toward him, and he realized instantly how stupid the question had been. She struggled to say something. "I need to sit here for a minute," she said, lungs straining for air.

"Do you think your back's broken?" Mark wasn't sure what he'd do if the answer was yes.

She struggled to shake her head. "Knocked wind out of me." She groaned.

Now what? He fell back against the snow and found himself loosening his coat collar. He suddenly felt very warm. "I couldn't believe it when you—"

"I'm sorry," she said, the words coming a bit more easily now. "I don't think I am hurt."

"You're sorry?! I probably pushed you too hard," he said, still worried. "I knew this was here. I'd been avoiding it all the time—I pushed you too hard."

"No, I'll be okay."

A wave of relief began to build on the horizon as he saw her chest begin to rise and fall more normally. When it did, a sense of tension fell away from Nancy's face and shoulders. As a kid Mark had fallen out of a tree near the house—a place where he used to stash things—and landed on his back on a dirt mound. He knew just what she was feeling now as the muscles slowly decided the trauma was over and relaxed—strand by knotted strand.

"You look like you're doing better."

"A little," she said. She cautiously brought an arm around and rubbed her opposite shoulder. "Seems okay." She winced then brought the other one around to check out that shoulder.

"Can I do something?" Mark felt helpless; he needed to do something to make amends, yet there was nothing to do.

"No. Not just now." Suddenly her face twisted and a pained groan slipped from her. Her back arched slightly, and one arm shot back, the hand at the end of it grotesque in its shape. "A spasm," she said breathlessly. But the spasm ended quickly, and she relaxed, even more than before. "If God ever wanted to discipline me all he'd have to do is give me a backache," she said.

"I was so worried—you don't think you're hurt, do you?"

"We're about to find out. I think it's time to get me on my feet."

Mark stumbled uncertainly in the snow, but then he established his footing. "What do you want me to do?"

Although Nancy still felt pain, her back seemed strong enough to move. She looked up at Mark, who peered down at her with huge, concerned eyes.

"Maybe if you could put your hands under my arms and pull?" she asked apologetically.

He nodded then moved closer and placed his hands under her arms.

"Tell me when to pull," he said.

Nancy tucked her legs beneath her. "Okay, now," she signaled.

Mark pulled, and he could sense her legs pushing. Although she winced at first, the pain seemed to rush out of her as she straightened, breathing heavily.

Standing directly in front of Mark, the top of her head meeting his nose, Nancy looked up. A very different Mark stood there, still holding her. A Mark that seemed reluctant to let go. This Mark looked concerned and caring, a little frightened and vulnerable. This Mark had forgotten and let his defenses down—had stepped outside his fortress to care and help. This Mark ignited a warm ember of feeling deep inside of her—at her very center. "I'll be okay now," she said gently, and she felt his strong hands loosen and stroke her sides warmly as they fell away.

"Is your back bruised at all?"

"It's still tender," she said, stretching a bit to check things out. "But maybe we should call it a day."

"Well, this has certainly been a day." He smiled.

"Looks like one to me too."

"You able to make it to the top?" he asked.

She looked up the steep wall of white, the two dogs at the top of it, panting and looking down. "Maybe if you held my hand?" she asked meekly.

"Hand holding's what I do best."

She reached out with just a heartbeat of hesitation, and he took it. Seconds later they were trudging up the embankment, Mark in the lead, Nancy struggling behind. Her struggle wasn't so much from her back—that seemed strong enough—but she was tired out from all the fun they'd had. When they were halfway and she was panting pretty strongly, Mark slowed.

"Let's take a sec to rest," he suggested.

"Good idea," she said breathlessly. She'd never been one for aerobics and jogging. Although she wasn't fat, she had to admit she was a little fleshy. Maybe she'd think about an exercise program when she got back to Washington. After a minute, she looked up at the warm face that continued to look down at her and said, "Okay, Nanook's ready."

The dogs crowded around them when they reached the top. Hamster, who was usually as demonstrative as a doormat, leaped on his hind legs, planted reassuring paws on Nancy's shoulders, then panted a warm "Welcome back to the living" directly in her face. "We're getting your teeth brushed—I never realized," Nancy said, patting him firmly on the ribs. "Okay, Hamster, down."

He pulled back obediently as Nancy bent again to check her bruises. Finding them minor, she said, "I think I'll make it from here." She took a step or two. "I always do this—this klutz in me is always fighting to get out."

"You okay now?" Mark asked, walking beside her.

Nancy nodded, the pain in her back now just a dull ache. "That was fun," she said, looking his way and filling her eyes with him. "Thanks for inviting me." Feeling a tremor of self-consciousness she reached for her locket.

"This is equal opportunity snow. Everybody's welcome."

She couldn't find it. She felt her neck again, but the thin gold chain was gone. "My locket—the chain must have broken." Her heart caught, and she ignored the ache in her back as she spun around. Scanning the snow for just a glint of gold, she saw nothing but a confusion of light glistening off the now ragged surface.

"It could be anywhere; it's lost," Mark stated.

"It can't be lost," Nancy said, stalking back through the snow.

"It's lost—you'll never find it," Mark said, trying to sound as understanding as he could.

"I'll look up here. You go back down by the tree."

"Come on, Nancy. Give it up. It's only an old piece of tin anyway. You said yourself it wasn't anything."

Nancy glared at him, then returned to her search. She kicked at the snow and walked every inch of the path starting at the edge of the drop-off and working up to the summit of the small hill. When she reached it she turned to see Mark still standing there, hands on his hips, looking a little befuddled. He probably wanted to tell her again that her search was futile, but he didn't dare. "Mark, please, this is important to me."

He finally shrugged and a moment later disappeared below the drop-off. A few seconds later the tray came flying over the rim. "I forgot this," he called.

In the meantime, Nancy walked the path again, back aching severely now as she bent low trying to see everything she could. At one point her heart leaped with excitement, but the golden fleck turned out to be an old candy wrapper they'd unearthed.

Suddenly she heard Mark's muffled cry, "I found it."

Hugely relieved, she ran toward the embankment. Seconds later his cherry cheeks appeared, and he all but fell over the edge, the locket hanging from his hand. She took it from him and cradled the heart in her hand as he said, "The necklace is broken. When you hit the tree, maybe. It was just sitting there on top of the snow."

"Praise the Lord," she whispered and threw her arms around Mark's neck. Only when his eyes were less than an inch from hers did she realize what she'd done. She hesitated, then pulled him to her and gave him a hug. A bit sheepishly, she pulled away. "Thank you," she said, very softly.

"It *is* important to you, isn't it?"

She didn't answer but held the locket tightly for an instant as if welcoming home the dearest of friends. "Memories," Nancy said, as if it were all that needed to be said. "I know you think I'm a little crazy—"

"Just a little."

"—but it was sweet of you to go looking for it." Afraid she might do something dumb again, she quickly changed the subject. "It was good that I sent you down there. We probably would've gotten all the way to the car before missing your tray," she said, carefully pushing the locket and broken chain into her pants pocket. She'd never known such relief.

"I've had that tray a long time—stole it from a high school."

Catching only a couple words, Nancy smiled at him fondly, the smile fed by that warm ember nestled just below her heart. The fact that she was smiling that way prompted her brain to admonish her heart, *This is Mark you're smiling at—non-Christian, obnoxious Mark.*

Her heart didn't pay a whole lot of attention.

"I never thought I'd use it on this trip. That was fun," he said softly, as if trying to say a little more.

"It was," she affirmed. "Really fun. I haven't just played in years."

"Adults need practice."

Then she said sheepishly, eyes cast just a little away from him, "It was fun playing with you, Mark." When she'd said it, her eyes came up and searched his face. She became aware of a handsome innocence there—a certain Jimmy Stewart naiveté in his longish features and richly dark eyes. There was a slight crook in his nose that heightened his vulnerability while the three-day growth of beard brought a mature ruggedness. Yes, she did find him handsome—very handsome. The ember caught fire.

"It was fun playing with you too." Mark smiled with a hint of roguishness.

She ignored it and said, "It doesn't have to end." She bent and as a hint of back pain returned, she scooped up a handful of snow. "Make a snowball."

"No. No snowball fights."

"No fight. I want to see you juggle. You keep talking about it. I want to see." She quickly had two snowballs made and tossed him both. As he deftly caught one in each hand, she made the third.

"I've never juggled snowballs."

"Good. We'll expand your act. Of course, now you'll only be able to juggle in fields in the dead of winter. But that's show biz."

She laughed, tossing him the last one. The moment it left Nancy's hand, the juggling began.

Effortlessly he caught it while one of the others was in the air, then the three balls shuffled from hand to hand to air to hand and around. Becoming more confident, Mark tossed one over his shoulder. Catching it, he became even more courageous. While Nancy laughed and clapped and the dogs howled their approval, Mark began to flip them under one raised leg, then the other, and finally between his legs, over his back and head, catching one while continuing to keep the other two snowballs shuffling. Thrilled, Nancy yelled and clapped more excitedly. Finally, when he straightened and as the snowballs moved from hand to air to hand, he announced, "It's time for the great finale. I haven't done this too often, but it's neat. Watch."

She did.

The snowballs shuffled for a couple more revolutions, then one went particularly high. When it came down, it landed on the bridge of Mark's nose. It was obvious that he wanted to balance it there, and he caught it as gently as he could. But instead of balancing, it smashed against his nose, leaving a frozen white splotch of ice.

"You did that well," Nancy laughed. "Here, let me do that too." She grabbed a handful of snow and hurled it at him, laughing. But instead of responding with snow of his own, Mark raised a weary hand for her to stop. "No, I'm bushed."

"That was great. You are good." Nancy beamed. "That last move was particularly good."

"It's not perfected yet. I'll have it soon. But what about the rest of it? Do you really think it was good?"

"Yes, I really think so," she said, becoming serious. "You're a natural entertainer."

"Really?" Now he beamed. "Thanks," he said, smiling with great warmth.

A sense of oneness caused Nancy to reach up and rub his back and pat him encouragingly. "Well, I guess we need to get back on the road."

She turned toward the distant car. Only then, seeing the boxes stacked on the roof, did she remember that things were left undone. "I guess we need to get this car cleaning thing over with," she said, fumbling with her feelings. Had she known she was going to feel this good, she would have never worried about the car—or at least she would have put off cleaning it. But she hadn't and now she regretted it.

The moment Mark saw the car and his stuff stacked on top of it, he became sullen again. He was heading for the fortress.

"I'm sure you'll like what I did," Nancy babbled, a curious panic assaulting her. "I saved everything—you can even put everything back the way it was, if you want."

But Mark remained silent except for a muffled cough, and after a few steps, Nancy, too, fell silent. She heard only the crunch of the snow and the sound of a wind growing in the trees behind them. It blew in an iron-gray sky.

When they reached the picnic benches, Mark said, defeat in his voice, "I have to sit for a while. I guess I'm out of shape." He planted himself in the seat he'd cleared off.

"Don't be this way," Nancy found herself pleading. "It's not that bad really. It's clean—just clean, that's all. The dirt's gone. You can even, heaven forbid, put the apple cores back." She stood before him, waiting for some sign that the Mark she'd just played with in the snow was returning. When no sign came, she anxiously turned toward the car. "I'll start putting things back. Just look through the trash boxes, and save what you want." Her back still stinging, Nancy grabbed the two trash boxes from the roof and set them gingerly at his feet. She hesitated, hoping he'd get in the spirit of the thing. He didn't.

An immense wave of sadness washed over her. She didn't understand it all, but she knew she was drowning in it, and at the crest of the wave foamed an edge of anger.

Feeling herself harden, she ignored the ache in her back and began taking boxes from the roof and placing them inside, as neatly and efficiently as she could. With each box, her anger grew—an anger she found a little mysterious, but an anger that was definitely at work. When she fit the third box—a particularly heavy one that drove hot painful spikes into her back muscles—into the back, she turned to see a surprising sight. Mark was peeling the brown wrapper off a Snickers candy bar. Before Nancy said anything, he'd taken a huge, gnawing bite and was chewing with what appeared to be anger of his own.

"Where'd you get that?" Nancy asked, brows knit.

"I had it all along. It fell out of my pocket when I was sledding," Mark explained coolly and took another huge bite.

Nancy's shoulders drooped as the angry wave broke over her and pulled her down for the third time. Raging foam swirled about her senses. "You've rested long enough," she said, iron hard. "Pick out the junk you want to save."

Suddenly, as if just making it back to the surface for needed air, she cried, "You stole it, didn't you? Back there, at the cafe. You stole it." Just as suddenly, the energy was used up. Anger gave way to confused frustration, and she fell against the freezing car. "My goodness," she said, pushing her palm to her forehead, "you're a thief as well as a jerk."

"Thief? I'm no thief," Mark protested.

"And I nearly fell—" Though she didn't say it, she thought it: she'd nearly fallen in love with him. The thought came down like an axe severing her from those wonderful feelings she'd just experienced and from the warmth she'd felt. Although it didn't extinguish the ember burning inside her, it shattered it. She muttered, "I guess God's just showing me—I guess."

"I told you what happened," Mark said.

"I saw them there. I love Snickers. I'd kill for a Snickers, but I didn't buy one because I knew we didn't have enough money, and you stole one. Probably when you came back from the rest room. You stole it!" Her heart deflated, all she could do was turn away from him.

"I didn't steal this. I'm no thief."

Nancy looked back at him. It had been so long since someone showed concern for her—so long. But after a moment, she gathered herself up and looked at him again. "You went through all your pockets at the meadow last night. Remember? We even talked about Snickers, and I wanted one so bad. Why do you have to be a thief too?"

"I'm not a thief." Mark was on his feet now, pacing the snow. He turned and with a grand flourish, said, "Okay, so what if I did take it?" He took an angry bite for emphasis. "I'm still not a thief."

"Sure, you're a thief," Nancy stated with dismal matter-of-factness.

Mark was furious. "Taking one lousy candy bar from a crazy old lady who yelled at us is not being a thief. She owed us this candy bar."

"She hadn't yelled at us yet when you took it, and even if she had—" another wave of immense sadness broke over her. "I can't believe the feelings I had." Nancy turned her eyes toward the forest, bewildered.

"You're nuttier than this candy bar, Chickenlips. That's what you are. Yes, sir. You're an accessory to the great chocolate caper. You rode in the getaway car!"

Suddenly all the sadness and frustration was gone. Now there was only anger, and a steel rod of it went up her backbone. "You have to take it back."

"I what?"

"You have to take it back and make all this right again," Nancy announced with great rigidity.

"A half-eaten candy bar!" Mark was beside himself. He sputtered and wheezed and spun completely around in a rage of his own. "Throw a half-eaten Snickers on the counter? Or maybe I ought to rewrap it so the next person who buys it gets a surprise—like Cracker Jacks. Maybe they could get even more money for it as a collector's item. It'd be the half-eaten remains of the great chocolate caper turned in by the infamous Snickers Bandito."

"Or you could just pay for it. You stole it; you take it back," she said definitely.

"Listen, Chickenlips, you're not my warden. You're not anything. Stop being anything; better yet, stop breathing, but above all, stop being my mother!" His whole face puffed red, eyes bugging, lips quivering. Nancy was thankful he had no weapons.

"No," Nancy bawled back at him, "I have one more motherly duty to perform. Thieves don't get to choose."

"What's that mean?" He didn't have to wait long to find out.

She quickly grabbed the two boxes of trash—the wrappers, cups, apple cores, oil can, all of it—and took them to the garbage cans on the far end of the rest stop. "What are you doing?" Mark's rage was overshadowed by a growing gravity.

"It's all trash," Nancy said as coldly as the snow. "It all goes."

"It's not all trash. None of it's trash."

"Old apple cores aren't trash?"

"Are old flowers pressed in books trash?"

"The only way these would get pressed is if you stepped on them. Which, by the way, you've done frequently."

"You put those things back. They're mine." A bony finger came up and pointed at her like a gun. "Now who's the thief?"

She thought for a moment, then said, "You take the candy bar back, and I won't throw this trash in the bottom of this very wet can." The snow in the bottom of the cans had melted, making a pool of ugly black.

"You're going too far." Mark's mood was grave; had there been even a hint of humor before, it was gone now.

Nancy suddenly hated him. "Which is it going to be?"

Mark was beyond rage and stood a few yards away from her with eyes like steel beads and a jaw set like concrete. "Throw it all away. All of it. And when someone stops to rest here, see if they're going to California and if they need your money."

"Which I'm going to have to check. You might have stolen that too."

Without another word, Mark turned and scooped up Naomi. He walked purposefully past Hamster who started to follow him to the car. As Nancy watched Mark climb behind the wheel, a seed of fear began to germinate. Without so much as a glance in her direction, he fired up the engine.

Now he looked at her.

For an instant she thought she saw him soften. Then she propped an "I told you so" expression upon her face as he stepped from the idling car. The expression broadened as he stepped ceremoniously to the other side and opened the passenger door. She expected him to stand by it while she got in.

But he didn't.

With a hint of flourish, he turned toward the inside, bent, and grabbed something. He held the moth-eaten coat she'd slept in tightly in one fist, her purse in the other. The fist extended, he let the coat drop to the wet snow, then dropped her purse on top of it. He smiled a toothy "I told you so" smile of his own.

A moment later the door slammed, and the Pacer ground through the snow toward the highway. Without so much as a backward glance, Mark drove off toward California.

Chapter Twelve

Now the locket really got a workout. But not before Nancy grabbed her purse and slapped it under her arm. She eyed the coat with a mixture of disdain and longing. She was cold; there was no way to convince herself she wasn't. In her playful excitement she'd been able to ignore her stinging fingers and ice-gnawed ears. But now, standing outside in the mountain deep freeze, Nancy could not ignore the cold stalking her senses like an angry grizzly.

But picking up that coat was more than she was willing to do. "I'll turn to ice before I give him the satisfaction," she proclaimed to Hamster.

Hamster, on the other hand, wasn't quite so locked into pride. The moment the Pacer and his friend, Naomi, disappeared beyond a distant fold in the mountain, the dog stepped cautiously over to the coat. After sniffing it for a moment, he turned his huge, angular head in Nancy's direction. Sorrowful eyes begged her to throw it over him. "No," she said, feeling her lower lip shiver. "He'll be back and when he comes, I want that coat lying exactly where he dropped it."

Hamster cocked his head inquisitively, as if asking her to reconsider, then eyed the brown mound of cloth as if hoping it would leap over him by itself. When it didn't, he sat next to it and gave a calculated little shiver accompanied by a helpless whine.

"No," said Nancy, but with a bit less resolve. She'd taken the locket from her pants pocket, and now her thumb worked it feverishly.

Only then did she realize the boxes of trash were still balanced on the edge of the garbage cans. A single glance toward them reminded her that she truly hated Mark. *What a scumball!* she thought and, while calculating the pain it would bring him, she tossed the boxes and their contents unceremoniously into the can.

That done, she clasped her hands together, rubbed them until circulation returned, cupped them over her ears until both hands and ears were freezing, breathed on her palms and cupped them over her ears again until the initial warmth vanished again, then she cupped her hands and breathed into them to warm her nose and cheeks. After going through the whole cycle three or four times she realized how hopeless it was.

That realization plunged her heart somewhere dark and oppressive, and she gripped her locket firmly.

"You know, if he really does leave, we have a problem," she said to Hamster.

Hamster seemed to sense that and gave a strong shiver to emphasize the problem part of what she'd said.

Immensely concerned, Nancy dropped her knees into the snow and wrapped warming arms around him. The muscles just below his thin coat quivered uncontrollably, but after she pulled him against her, the warmth of their two bodies mingled. Soon the dog's trembling ceased. In appreciation, Hamster lapped the side of her face with his huge, wet tongue. Nancy smiled and hugged him even tighter.

"Come on. Maybe we should walk. It'll keep the blood pumping, and soon someone will come along and give us a ride."

Hamster reluctantly left the coat lying on the ground and followed Nancy. The length of the rest stop was seventy-three paces, and after they had paced it twice, there were two nearly straight paths from end to end—one thick, one with small, paw-sized holes in the snow. On the third trek a large station wagon, with a covered load tied on top, swooshed by.

"I'm sure someone will stop, soon," Nancy repeated. *They'd better*, she thought. *I'm getting really cold.*

So cold, in fact, that she thought of the scene in the second *Star Wars* movie when Han Solo was looking for Luke Skywalker, who was lost on the cold, ice world of Hoth. Han was riding on that big, furry white thing—what was it called? Oh, yes, a Ton-Ton—and he'd kept himself from freezing to death by splitting the creature open and crawling inside. She even remembered the line he'd said:

"And I thought they smelled bad on the outside." She could see the scene as clearly as if it were on a screen in front of her.

She glanced down at Hamster... *No!* She bit her lip. *What a horrible thought.* She winced, then fumbled with the locket.

"Lord, what's going on?" she asked as she cast her eyes to an iron-gray sky, a sky that seemed to hold acres of more snow. "I guess I've asked that question a lot this trip—of course, you haven't answered me, either."

Another car hissed by.

"Please stop," she whined to the car as her heart sank even further.

"But if someone does stop and we leave, what happens when Mark comes back looking for us?" She couldn't believe she'd actually asked herself that. "If he comes back and we're gone, it's his hard luck—of course, there's no such thing as luck—it'd be his hard providence—the creep."

Nancy and Hamster kept walking, white breath puffing before each of them. When they passed the coat again, she mused, "Up until now my life's been pretty much like everyone else's: warm apartments, warm cars, cold runs from one to the other, my flute, tea. But something's changed here." They'd reached the end of the parking lot and turned back. She eyed the clouds, then the coat, then dropped to her knees, and hugged Hamster. "It's as if I stepped into a different life. Someone else's life—someone with real problems."

After feeling his warmth for a while, she stood and planted her hands on her hips and threw her eyes to the clouds above. "God, you really are going to save us, aren't you? You're not going to have us found lying here in the spring when the snow thaws—are you, Lord?"

She shook her head and patted Hamster's. "Of course, he'll save us."

She continued walking, but now Hamster leaned against the warmth of her leg. The responsibility for the animal suddenly weighed heavily on her.

"Maybe we ought to go into the rest room. It's got to be warmer in there." But then another dismal thought: "If we do, he won't see us when he drives by, and he'll think we got a ride. He might keep on going." She shoved brittle hands in her jacket pockets. They warmed slightly, but the movement pulled her coat collar down and her neck began to sting. It was then that she remembered that her coat collar had a hood folded up inside it. She quickly unzipped it and brought the hood up. It offered a little protection—protection that quickly waned as the chill penetrated the nylon. She pulled the string around the hood, and it puckered about her face, leaving only her nose and eyes exposed.

That's when it started to snow.

Hamster was the first to notice it. Only two things caused Hamster to move quickly: cats and falling snowflakes. He lived to chase them both and, although he looked ferocious chasing cats, he looked foolish chasing snowflakes, as he did now. As a big, lumbering projectile, he stalked, then dove at a gently falling fleck of white. Catching it with powerful jaws, he spun to devour the flakes that tried to slip by his unprotected rear. Hamster was a true warrior when it came to snowflakes. But this combat lasted only while the flakes fell individually; it ended when they attacked in armies. And there were armies now—great swirling armies. With the armies came defeat. Shaking the growing avalanche off, he finally sat, his sagging jowls sagging further while snow piled on his head and snout. Looking dejected, he watched Nancy watching him.

"I'd probably be warmer if I did that too," Nancy admitted. "But I don't think I'd have quite the flare."

At that moment a small car pulled into the area. It parked right behind the coat, and the moment the engine died, a round husband and equally round wife got out amid the sound of squeaking, over-burdened seat springs. Three round children in the back squealed with delight at the prospect of playing in the snow. But the father ended that idea with a snap, and after a few groans the kids contented themselves with fighting where they sat.

Satisfied, the man straightened, eyed Nancy coldly, and joined his wife on the way to their respective rest rooms. The man was the first to reappear. As he returned to the car he noticed the coat lying there. He walked over to it and hovered there.

His wife joined him. "What's that?" she asked.

"Looks like an old coat," the man replied.

"It looks pretty grubby."

"It looks like a good old coat."

"A grubby good old coat," the wife pointed out.

The man leaned over to pick the coat up.

"That's mine," sprang from Nancy. The man stopped and still bent over, turned his round face to her.

"Yours?"

"Mine," Nancy said again, this time hesitantly. She had the gnawing feeling she was lying.

"Why is it here in the snow?"

Good question, Nancy thought. She sputtered for a moment, then said, "Personal reasons."

"Don't touch it, Ralph," the wife cautioned, with a suspicious eye on Nancy and a restraining hand on her husband's arm. "There might be something dead underneath."

"Oooh." The man winced, his hand darting back as if it had touched something hot. He straightened and peered at Nancy as if looking at something dangerous. One eye went to his wife. "See if the kids need to go."

He remained on watch while she bawled at the kids to be quiet, then asked each by name if he or she needed to go "potty." None did.

"They say no," she reported.

"If they have to later I'm just pulling over to the side of the road," the man warned, his eye still on Nancy.

The wife asked each child again. When they all nodded in turn, the man, still casting a watchful eye Nancy's way, quickly got behind the wheel. When the sound of the squeaking springs died away, he fired up the engine and spun his rear wheels in the slush as he launched the car onto the highway. Seconds later they disappeared down the road.

Nancy stepped to the coat and stood over it. Maybe it was time to put pride aside. As slimy and as grungy as it had been, it had been warm. And warm was important right now.

The instant she shook the wet snow from it and slipped it on, she knew she'd made the right decision. The mid-afternoon chill was suddenly broken and although she wasn't warm, she didn't feel as threatened. She transferred the locket to the deeper pocket, then stuffed her purse and hands in and felt her fingers begin to thaw.

A moment later she heard the whine of an approaching semi. The air brakes squealed as a large Kenworth pulled in, blocking all the parking spaces. A young man got out and without hesitating said, "Nice coat—you okay?"

"Okay? Sure, I'm okay," Nancy said coolly and immediately felt vulnerable. She thumbed her locket nervously. The trucker didn't look particularly savage standing there; in fact he was rather nice looking with blond hair and a chestnut complexion, but he was a guy and she was a girl—alone. "My friend went to get help. My dog here nearly ripped his arm off when he got near me, and he needed to get bandaged up," she said, sounding as tough as she could.

The guy nodded gravely. "Why didn't you go with him?"

"Too much blood," she answered quickly. "Lots of blood. I didn't want to get blood on the dog. He goes crazy when blood spatters."

"Happens often, does it?" The guy cast an eye toward Hamster.

"All the time—when guys hit on me—he gets crazy."

The trucker nodded.

Nancy thought she saw something bubble in back of his tight lips, something he was holding back. He said, "Well, I'll just have to keep m'hands to m'self."

"Good thinkin'," she said, matching his drawl as he disappeared behind the men's room door. That's when she found out what he was holding back. Through the vents she heard a cackle of laughter, and although she felt instantly foolish, she also felt relieved—rather him laughing than plotting her rape.

A few minutes later he reappeared. "I got a warm cab if you need to get somewhere down the road. I'm going all the way to the coast. I can drop you just about anywhere."

"Really?" she said, but she wasn't as excited as she thought she'd be. In fact, there seemed to be a cork locking in her excitement. "I can't—no. Can't," she babbled.

"Listen, I ain't gonna hurt ya, and that dog 'ud protect you. Ripped the other fella's arm off, remember?" He smirked, but even for the smirk, his sincerity shone through.

"No—wouldn't be right traveling with you—no." More babbling and this time she stepped back.

"Ma'am, it'd be less right me leavin' you like this—you'll freeze out here. This here is snow fallin', miss."

"I'll be all right—really. I'll be all right," she said, nodding her head like a spring-neck doll.

"Well, okay," the trucker said reluctantly. He turned toward his truck, glanced back in her direction as if thinking he might try again but gave up and just said, "Well, wrap up warm." When he'd taken his place behind the large wheel, he powered down the passenger window and tossed something red and white out of it. A woolen ski cap. "That ought to help a little," he called to her as she grabbed the woolen Frisbee going by.

The truck growled to life, the air brakes squealed their release, and after a throbbing start he pulled onto the interstate.

"Thanks," she whispered, glancing down at Hamster who sat beside her looking up. He was shivering terribly now. She wrapped the coat around him and let her warmth radiate through him. His distress lessened. Then she took the red and white cap and being cautious with his ears, placed it on his head. "Maybe this'll help. I did it, didn't I? I let him go. I could have put you between us, and we'd be warm right now. You got a real smart companion here, you do." She hugged Hamster close and realized again that she had let the nice trucker go, and the reason that was starting to emerge was frightening.

While she held Hamster beneath the tent of the oily, smelly coat, she thought not of Mark's cold, arrogant expression as he dropped it in the snow but of how, just a few minutes before that, he'd burst over the snowy cliff to save her, concern for her engraved on every line of his face.

After dwelling in the warmth of that concern for a while, she was suddenly buoyed again by the freedom they'd experienced rough-housing in the snow—the delicious cold, the laughter, the trust and acceptance they'd shared. They'd thrown things *and* each other around a bit but neither would have hurt the other. As if surveying a list of her favorite things, she slowly inventoried every other good feeling those moments in the snow had brought. When she reached the last one, she surveyed them again.

On the third pass she admitted that she didn't want to leave the rest stop because she hoped Mark would return.

Of course, the fact that most of the trip she'd been mad at him, even hated him, made her immediately question her sanity. But during those moments in the snow and those minutes that had just passed, she had seen the real Mark—she thought.

"But he's not a Christian, is he, Lord? Not even close," she found herself saying to Hamster and the snow falling and drifting around her. "And he's a jerk most of the time. This is unreal. I feel like I'm rationalizing a date with Dracula: 'Well, he'll only take a pint or two,'" she said, using her best Transylvanian accent. "No, I can't do this," she said as if slapping herself into consciousness. "Next offer of a ride I take."

She patted her furry friend on the ribs and got to her feet. In spite of the heavy coat and the cap, the cold was beginning to seep in, and soon another chill shivered through her. But her new resolve gave her an injection of strength and she began to pace again, Hamster alongside of her, the ball of his cap bobbing as he walked.

"He is a jerk, isn't he?" she said again. "And what we're going through is his handiwork." She walked even faster, her hands plunged further into the coat pockets—the anger storming back.

"He's not coming back and I'm freezing!" she finally cried out. "That miserable jerk isn't coming back. Well," she corrected herself, "he's not the jerk, Lord. I'm the jerk."

She spun around. White was everywhere. Although it had only been snowing for a little while, it had been long enough to cover the path she and Mark had made to and from the forest. It seemed only right that those tracks be deeply covered—buried. Who'd want to be reminded of a walk with a jerk? And a juggler. "Would you believe a juggler? Did you see those things he juggled? Junk. I bet he drops 'em too. What a jerk."

That's when she saw it. Humming by in the opposite direction, a caramel-colored Pacer. She leaned forward to get a better look at the driver, but it disappeared too fast. Mark? She wasn't sure. The driver looked like a man. "There can't be two of those cars in the world still running."

Sure there could. And why did he go past her?

When the car hadn't returned after a while Nancy sank back into her hurt. Was it someone else? "Jerk!" she screamed.

The snow stopped falling for a few minutes but started again. This time Hamster was too tired and cold to care about the snowflakes. He just watched them float down and pile upon his nose. "We're going to die out here," was Nancy's immediate assessment.

After a few minutes while depression and snow piled up together, she made a command decision. "Come on, Hamster, let's go into the rest room. It'll be a little warmer in there."

Hamster didn't argue. He immediately followed his mistress into the shelter.

Inside wasn't much warmer, but at least the slight wind chill was gone. "This afternoon stinks." She groaned as she sat on a bench that ran along the far wall and planted elbows on knees and chin in hands. Hamster lay at her feet and they waited.

She didn't know how long she'd been sitting when a diesel thundered outside, and a truck door squealed open and slammed shut. To Nancy's surprise the footsteps led to the ladies' room. When the door whined open an attractive woman in jeans, a western jacket, short auburn hair, and a brightly colored blouse walked in. She didn't look at all like a trucker.

At first the woman ignored Nancy, but after straightening her hair and applying lipstick, she glanced her way.

"Hi," she said, peering at Nancy's reflection in the mirror.

"Hi," Nancy replied, sounding a bit flat.

"You okay?"

"Cold."

"Dog's got a nice hat there."

"Thanks. He's into compliments."

"You hitching?" The woman asked, her face road-weary but concerned.

"Waiting for someone."

"Waitin' long?" The woman faced Nancy now and slipped her lipstick into her jeans.

"I don't have a watch—a couple hours now, I think." It had probably been only a half hour but it felt like three days. Nancy decided to split the difference.

"Can you use some hot coffee?"

Nancy brightened. "Hot anything would be great," she said and bounded to her feet. Sensing something good was about to happen, Hamster jacked himself up as well. Nancy continued, "I've never been so cold in all my life."

"Come out to the truck. Do you want me to take you somewhere?"

Nancy hesitated. "I just want something warm right now."

The woman smiled as if she understood—didn't necessarily agree but understood.

Outside the swarms of falling flakes were large and wet and they clung tenaciously to Nancy's clothes and eyelashes.

"Why don't you come up and warm yourself inside?" the woman suggested when they reached the Mack truck.

The roomy cab was comfortable and as warm as promised. After pouring the steaming, black liquid from a stand-up thermos into a mug and Styrofoam cup, the woman introduced herself. "Rheta Johnson. I run this route two or three times a week. This rest stop always turns up just in time for coffee."

"Nancy Bernard," Nancy extended a hand in greeting. "I'm going to California." She took a sip and although she preferred tea, the coffee brought such warmth to her hands and insides that she found it impossible to think badly of its bitterness.

"Looks like you're going nowhere," Rheta said. "I could be tactful, but why you sittin' in a john in the middle of a snowstorm?"

Nancy hesitated and took another sip. How much did she want to say? Finally, "I was left. But he'll be back."

"Ah. There's always some guy wrapped up in these things somewhere. You know for a fact he'll be back?" Rheta cocked her head as she challenged.

"Yes—no—I don't know for a fact. No," Nancy admitted. "I guess hope springs eternal."

"This ain't spring. If I had a boyfriend that treated me like this I'd break his nose."

Nancy knew this trucker sitting before her would. The thought of it made her smile. "He's not my boyfriend, but the thought of breaking his nose has occurred to me more than once."

"I been around this block a few times," Rheta said, taking a long, slurping sip of coffee. "When they leave you in a john in the middle of a snowstorm, it's time to stop waitin'."

"He'll be back. I know him."

"No you don't," Rheta insisted. "Did you ever think he'd leave you here?"

Nancy knew truth when she heard it. She really didn't know Mark at all. "No, I didn't," she replied, realizing that a change of subject was in order—this one was getting uncomfortable. "I don't usually like coffee, but this is great."

"I could take you to the next town—Laurel?"

"I know you could. I can't leave though." She was doing it again. It was as if these weren't her words. Her mind was standing on the sidelines and letting some other part of her take over—her heart, for instance.

"You sure? I don't have time to argue. But if he don't come back, what then?"

"He'll come back," Nancy said, sounding much less convincing than the situation demanded. But the part of her that demanded convincing had abdicated.

Nancy drank the second cup of coffee standing in the falling snow, Rheta's truck disappearing around the same fold in the mountain that had claimed everyone else.

The cup warmed her hands then unfroze her face as well as she pressed it against one cheek and then the other until the Styrofoam cooled. Setting it on the picnic table and watching the snow melt around it, she kicked herself again. She'd declined the ride. Her brain was back in the driver's seat—but too late. She and her brain were back in the snowfall, back in the cold, back telling herself she'd take the next ride offered.

Even though each passing heartbeat made him more of a jerk, each also made the vision of the real Mark more vivid—and her desire to see that Mark again more arresting.

Her mind conjured up those concerned eyes, eyes that said he understood her and what she'd been through, eyes that proclaimed he needed her—non-Christian eyes, blind eyes. That's where it all broke down. But Christian or not, the longer she waited, the stronger her commitment to seeing him again. Her brain was abdicating again.

She ran a hand over Hamster's cold back. "Come on, let's find a seat inside and warm up a little." She started toward the rest room.

From behind came the honk of a car horn and the crunch of tires on ice. She turned to see the caramel-colored Pacer roll up. When it stopped, the passenger door swung open, coolly inviting her to enter.

Nancy was immediately deluged by conflicting currents of joy and rage. Hamster, on the other hand, had no time for such silliness. He was too cold and the car too warm. He leaped in and, as his hat fell to the floor, he curled up as if returning home while Naomi yipped excitedly and dove into her old familiar place. Nancy spent as much time as she could watching the dogs, but before long she had to look at Mark. Bathed in sullenness, he looked angrily resigned to picking her up.

"Get out of the cold," he ordered.

Nancy instinctively obeyed and slid onto the icy vinyl seat and closed the door. He didn't even glance her way but kept his eyes glued on the windshield. She gazed where he gazed. Outside snow swirled indifferently about them, and the wipers warred with it, keeping up as well as they could.

Now, with the cold locked outside, the heater blowing a wonderfully warm stream of air on her, she suddenly didn't care about Mark or how he felt or how she felt about him. All that mattered was the rejuvenating warmth permeating through her. She felt the cool metal of the locket pressed against her lips, and she let it stay there a moment as all of her body became warm again.

After a few seconds, Mark pushed the gear shift into first and felt the rear tires spinning before they finally gained traction and pushed the car forward.

That's when Nancy looked at him. He was the picture of a pout—the child cleaning his room because he'd been ordered to, doing his homework when he'd rather be playing ball outside. Mark was everything she remembered—a jerk.

As he pulled to the highway entrance and waited for a semi to hiss by, she said, "I'm not sure I want to go on with you. I've had two ride offers already, and I'd probably get a few more before nightfall." Although she knew she sounded as childish as he seemed to be acting, saying it felt good.

"You should have taken them," he said flatly. The road was mined with patches of ice, and his tires lost traction once after taking off, but Mark deftly slowed, allowed the tires to regain their grip, and soon they hummed at full speed.

After she'd sacrificed for so long in the cold, turned down the two rides just to be there when he returned—after all that—she'd expected more—a brass band or something. "Why'd you come back then?" she asked.

"I saw you. If I hadn't, I wouldn't have stopped."

"Maybe I would have been in the building keeping warm."

"Then you'd still be there keeping warm." He glowered at her.

Surprisingly, though, his glowering didn't matter. She knew he was just hiding behind that wall again, and his anger was only the mortar that held the bricks together. The Mark that cared if she was hurt, the Mark that found her locket for her again and juggled just for her would come back again one day. Until then she'd just have to be patient—and keep praying that the Lord would bring him in.

She allowed his remark to hang between them and leaned back in the seat. Although there was still a nagging uneasiness, it was overshadowed by a larger, more powerful feeling of rightness, a rightness that brought with it a satisfying dose of peace. She slipped her purse from her coat pocket and lay it on the floor and snuggled into the coat collar. Placing her hands into warm pockets, her right hand gripped her locket and felt the metal warm.

Maybe she slept. She wasn't sure. But she suddenly found herself thinking about her father—and her father's father, Walter Bernard.

Walter Bernard died young, an indirect casualty of World War II. He'd taken a bullet in the lung and, although he'd survived, after he got back and built a family of three daughters and a son, he finally died. Nancy's father was seventeen when he suddenly became the man and "father" in the house.

Upon high school graduation, when others were looking forward to the future, he became responsible for a family he hadn't created. Nancy pictured his shoulders aching from the weight, his youth rushing away with the indifference of a passing train. She figured that he had found that booze lightened the load and kept his mind from focusing on the train's dying whistle. Perhaps he'd been unable to face it; perhaps he was proclaiming his manhood in the only way he knew how. But when all was said and done, it didn't matter to Nancy why he drank, only *that* he drank. And that he drank continually.

Nancy could never remember him not being surrounded by the musky smell of liquor. After years of emotional brutality, Nancy's mother left and then died in that horrible accident.

Nancy lived with her father for a couple more years, but like her mother, her loyalty was chipped to dust by a thousand hurtful blows. One angry night—a surge of guilt rushed through her as she remembered that it had been on his birthday, when all he'd done was mess up his cake—she fled.

First she took refuge at her grandmother's. Nancy knew immediately that she was only an interruption there, and after a couple months she cast eyes toward Washington, D.C. Although at first the music school was just a dream, she now remembered how remarkably courageous she felt that morning she applied. Music school hadn't worked out. She quickly found that musicians truly love music. They had to practice and remember all that theory. She didn't love music that much. She quit and found a job—then found Christ—or rather, he found her.

From the moment she'd left her father she'd felt a nagging guilt. He needed her, needed someone to love him. She knew that his cruelty, his drinking, and his outrageous behavior were just feeble cries for love. But she'd ignored them and taken the easy way out. Now there was Christ to bring to him—now the love she'd offer would be the truest, most wonderful kind.

What would her father look like now? When she left, his hair was thinning, his teeth were brown from the rancid cigars he smoked and falling out from lack of proper food. His knees were giving out from an injury he'd sustained in an auto accident twenty years before—now and then he used a cane. Picturing him made loving him that much more difficult—which, she thought, made loving him that much more important.

Nancy heaved a great sigh and felt a sea of tension drain away. As it did, she regained a tenuous level of contentment. She didn't completely understand her situation, and she still felt a sense of uneasiness about her feeling for Mark. Yet if the Lord was really in control, she was right where the Lord wanted her to be. Everything would work out all right.

Suddenly she had a thought. "Let's have a picnic," she suggested.

"What!?"

"Let's get some hamburgers and Cokes, find a little back road somewhere, and have a picnic."

"Get real—no picnic," Mark couldn't have sounded more definite. But her concerted pouting must have done some good, for he softened. "Haven't you had enough cold for one day? It's a zillion below zero out there. Give me a break."

"We can eat in the car. Come on, let's have some more fun."

"No. No more fun. You complain that I leave you to freeze your toosh off and the moment you're out of it you want to run right back. Your bag o' marbles got a hole in it, lady."

"We're not quite so high in the mountains now. The snow's gone. It won't be cold now. Besides, I'm still the one with the money."

"No picnic!" Mark had firmly retaken the rudder and barked his command. This time he remained granite until they'd gotten to the next town with a McDonald's.

"You havin' this here or t' go?" the young girl with large eyes asked.

"To go," he replied, and Nancy felt her heart balloon.

"I saw a little jewelry store further down the block. I need a chain for my locket," Nancy told him as they stepped from the restaurant.

"That's money we really don't need to spend," Mark admonished.

"Yes, it is. Come on."

They found an inexpensive gold brushed chain and seconds after being handed the bag, Nancy had hung the locket handily around her neck.

"Someday you're going to tell me the story around that thing," Mark predicted, sliding behind the steering wheel and firing up the Pacer.

"Someday—maybe," Nancy said seriously.

Mark just shrugged. "Okay, where do you want to have this picnic? There's nothing here in town."

"Keep going. I'm sure we'll find something."

After the town died away to a few scattered shacks, the road stretched and lay inexhaustibly before them again. But soon Nancy pointed out a side road, one that wound up a wooded hill. The asphalt road narrowed and wound arduously as it clung to the hillside. After a while the asphalt ended, and a dirt road continued even more steeply up the hill. Where the asphalt ended there was also a turnout ideal for what Nancy planned. Flat, dirt and gravel, the small shelf on the mountainside provided a visual feast—the highway below, the eternal woods now brown and expectant, and finally a broad valley that faded to distant smoky mist. Evening shadows lengthened as the sun crawled toward the horizon and the sky, gilt-edged and streaked with flags of orange, cast the trees in a glow of gold. Across the highway, on the left side of the valley, veiled in a silver mist, was a vertical brushstroke of white—a waterfall cascaded from a rocky bluff and fed a river that meandered idly through the valley. Without any prodding, Mark pulled over and stopped.

For a moment they said nothing. Finally Nancy spoke. "I'll get out the dog food. We can tie them to the bumper or something."

"That's okay, I'll do it," Mark offered, the angry edge to his voice worn down.

"You sure? How's your cold?"

"I'm okay—just a little muscle ache."

After the dogs were fed and lying on a nest of deep grass, Mark returned to the car.

"It's a little warmer here," Nancy said, as he slid into the seat.

Mark nodded from his reverie. "It's pretty. Peaceful," he said, and Nancy sensed his tension beginning to dribble away and the wall around him eroding. "The breeze is warm. The trees even have color. I can't believe we nearly froze an hour ago." After a second when he seemed to savor it all, he turned to her, "Hungry?" And he held out the bag of burgers. "That valley's beautiful."

"Beautiful," Nancy repeated reverently and reached in and grabbed a burger and a bag of fries. "I'd like to say grace."

Mark sighed but he didn't protest.

She bowed her head and she noticed that he did too. "Heavenly Father," she began, "thank you for this food you've provided and the day you've given us. Thank you for Mark and for bringing him back, and please reveal yourself to him. Keep us safe through this night and for the rest of our trip. In Jesus' name, amen." After a warm look at Mark, she took a large bite. The hamburger tasted wonderful as she scanned the distant valley again.

So peaceful, she thought, *it seems so wrong to have those black clouds forming over it.*

Chapter Thirteen

Chewing her burger ravenously, Nancy looked over to see that Mark wasn't doing the same. The sullenness had settled over him again, and his chiseled features stared at the burger in his hand. She saw him shiver.

"You okay?" she asked.

"I guess," he replied. Then what he wanted to say started to break the surface. "You thanked the right guy, anyway."

"I know." Nancy nodded, waiting for the rest of it.

It came. "It had to be God that caused me to pick you up."

"I know that too," Nancy said, feeling rather noble. But her nobility quickly melted as she saw Mark struggling. His breathing was more erratic, and his eyes never looked at her but kept gazing at the untouched hamburger; his voice sounded strained.

"After I left I was king again," he began. Nancy had the distinct impression that what he was saying was important to him. "I found a rock'n'roll station and turned up the volume. I didn't have to worry about being driven off into cow pastures or having someone rifle through my stuff. I even crumpled up some paper and threw it on the floor."

"Why'd you come back?" Nancy asked, sensing he was taking a direction that brought her a flicker of hope.

He finally took a nibble from his hamburger. "I wasn't going to," he said. "I pictured you freezing, standing in the snow—shivering, regretting how you treated me, wanting me to rescue you. A wonderful picture. I wanted to gaze at it all the way to California." He'd picked up steam now and he turned to her. "I had one more thing to do, and then I would be off to sunshine. But then it started snowing—and I weakened."

"I'm glad you did," she mused. "What was the one more thing you had to do?"

"Nothing, really." Mark took another halfhearted bite. Nancy hated the way he ate—she'd devoured almost two hamburgers and her fries, and he was still nursing his first burger. Skinny people always ate that way and she resented it.

"What did you have to do?" she persisted.

Mark's eyes dropped, and he put on a reluctant, wounded child's expression. "I took back the loot from the great chocolate caper."

"You did?" Her eyes lighted.

"Yes, I did," he admitted, screwing his lips up. "I'm no thief," he insisted again. "But you were right. Just because I wanted to strangle you and bury you in the snow didn't change the fact that I shouldn't have taken it."

"You wanted to strangle me?" She winced, feeling the ghost of his hands around her neck.

"Sure."

"Oh," she said, swallowing hard. "Was the woman as weird as before? What did she say when you showed up?"

"Nothing. I set it on the counter and split. I guess they'll just throw it away."

"You didn't even leave money?"

"Money? I took the stupid thing back. What else do you want from me?"

"Nothing," Nancy said quickly. "Nothing more." Even if he hadn't done all the right things, he'd done enough to tell her something very important. He cared what she thought—he cared about her. As she squeezed her locket like the hand of a close friend, her heart inflated with the helium of what she now knew and floated happily inside her. Smiling warmly, she felt a drop of moisture form at the corner of her eye.

"Now, wait a minute," Mark warned, pushing away from her. "You're reading more into this than there is. I haven't found religion or anything. I've stolen some things—" Nancy noticed that he suddenly glanced at a far away memory, then, just as quickly returned. He hardly missed a beat. "—to survive, but that doesn't make it right."

His memory trip troubled Nancy for an instant. What had he stolen to survive? But her concern was fleeting. She found a smile and brushed a joyful tear from the corner of her eye. "Good," was all she managed to say, her insides turning to a pleasant sort of mush. But she could easily tell that her reaction to the good news was frightening Mark and chasing him back behind his wall.

So when he said, "Listen, Chickenlips—" she forced a casual chuckle and pocketed her feelings—feelings she wasn't completely comfortable with anyway.

"Relax, Speedbump, I promise not to think more of you than I absolutely have to. I'll never use words like—" she counted them off on her fingers, "—like honest or lovable or honorable. Certainly will never describe you as nice or handsome."

"Now you're going overboard."

"No. The watchword is honesty. No matter how generous I might want to be, to me you'll always be a scumball pervert."

Mark heaved a satisfied sigh. "Thanks. I appreciate that."

"Your reputation was hard won, and I know that one simple, thoughtless compliment could destroy it all."

Mark nodded. "You understand."

"More than you'll ever know." Nancy groaned. And as she did she caught sight of the sunset—one so lovely it arrested her mid-thought. The car was pointing west, and through the sprawling windshield they saw the crimson sun kiss the far gray horizon. Sparse banners of clouds waved orange and candy apple-red. Above the clouds was a faded blue wash of vacant sky that swept toward them and bumped into that bank of black clouds Nancy had noticed boiling there before. "That's the most beautiful sunset—"

"Why didn't you take those rides you were offered?" Mark asked as if he'd been storing the question up for a while.

"Why?" Nancy stalled for time. She swallowed. The question was suddenly difficult to answer. The tension inside was intensifying. With every passing moment her feelings for Mark congealed further, and the more they congealed, the warmer their center and the stronger their force of gravity—a force intent on pulling the rest of her in. And yet, the greater the pull, the more the part of her that refused to be drawn in fought to escape. It kept crying in her inner ear, *Listen, bozo. Speedbump is not a Christian—and he really is a bozo, right?*

But the stronger her feelings for him, the more they demanded a voice of their own. She said again, "Why?"

"Yes, why?" Mark replied. "Now it's your turn for the third degree."

"My turn?" She winced, but she was horrible at stalling. "I thought you'd worry if you came back and I wasn't there."

"Like I'd think maybe wolves had dragged you off or something?"

"Yeah, the two-legged kind—or something."

Mark grunted a cruel little laugh. "Dream on, Chickenlips."

"Yeah," she responded, an uncomfortable bout of honesty coming on. "I probably was."

"You said one of the truck drivers was a woman, a nice one."

"She gave me coffee—yes. Very warm, very welcome." Nancy shivered again just thinking about it. Then she came alive reliving it. "My fingers were ice; my ears felt like squirrels were gnawing on them; even my eyes ached." Remembering, she suddenly slammed a fist into his shoulder. "I nearly froze out there, you jerk."

"Why didn't you leave with her? Why'd you wait?" There was an expectant glint in Mark's eye, and his mouth twisted as if prepared for an inevitable victory.

The tension within her grew, and it was a kind she'd never experienced before. On one side of the tug-of-war was an immense longing—a battered heart reaching out for someone she could care about and someone to care about her. The ache to fill that void was every bit as immense as the longing itself. The other side was piled high with all her fears and had its heels firmly dug in. Holding all those fears loosely together were God's admonitions and warnings. For the first time in Nancy's Christian life God's side was losing.

"Okay, you win," she finally said. "Listen. I'm going to admit something."

"This ought to be good." He grinned victoriously. The grin that was nearly more than Nancy could bear.

"In your own charmless little way you've wormed your way into a small corner of my heart."

"I knew it," Mark bubbled.

"Not a big corner," Nancy pointed out. "And it's filled with frightening cobwebs and icky spiders—a place where charmless speedbumps like yourself flourish."

"No," Mark argued, "not into a little corner of it—right in the center. And not where all the spiders are but right in the middle of all that warm, mushy stuff."

Nancy cocked a disbelieving ear. "Are you suggesting I've fallen in—it's almost impossible to say the word in connection with you—fallen in love with you?"

"You said it, I didn't."

"What!" Nancy exploded, shaking her head in fits of incredulity.

"See!" A triumphant finger pointed right at her.

Nancy recoiled. "There's obviously no point in trying to talk intelligently to you about things that matter." Then she fired, "Love you! I could just as easily fall in love with a snake. I just wanted to tell you that I don't find you quite as nauseating as I used to, and you—well, never mind. I'm through." She took a large bite of her cold hamburger and tried to make noises like she was enjoying it.

Mark said nothing but drove home his point with a know-it-all snicker of vindication.

There was a long silence between them. Mark finally started eating and now and then he'd rummage noisily in the bag for ketchup, but Nancy ignored him. Yet ignoring him didn't get a particular nagging question of her own answered, so after what she thought was an appropriate time, she said, "Now it's your turn," Nancy pushed a finger of her own at him. "You came back for me. Didn't you? And if I hadn't been out front you would have searched for me, wouldn't you?"

Mark shrugged, then tilted his head. "When I drove up to the rest stop I took one look—not even a look, a glance. If I hadn't seen you standing in the falling snow, knee deep in the cold, shivering in desperation, I would have gunned this car and not let up until I got to California."

"This car is ungunnable. And you would have gotten only as far as the next gas station."

"Aha," he exclaimed with even greater triumph. "Money—I can earn money."

"Doing what—crawling on your belly and flicking your tongue?"

He just tossed a smile back at her.

Suddenly Nancy felt a small, frightened knot in her stomach. At first she wasn't sure who tied it, but then—he could earn money pumping gas, cleaning out a store room, mowing lawns. He could get across country without her. He didn't really need her after all.

"I'm tired," she said finally. The cold, the anxious waiting, the hope, the fight—together they'd taken their toll and she was exhausted. "I guess we'd better get the dogs in." She opened the door and listlessly went to the back of the car. Hamster lifted a weary head in acknowledgment and when untied, quickly resumed his place in the backseat. Naomi curled up within his coil, and the two were soon sleeping as if they'd never been awakened.

When they'd gotten out of the car to get the hamburgers, she'd thrown the thick, oily coat in the back; now she retrieved it, wrapped herself in it, and scrunched into the corner. "I guess you deserve a 'good night' so 'good night.'"

Mark turned to her, his expression no longer triumphant. "I guess I do tend to ruin things," he said.

"I guess." She groaned with little heart for anything else, then turned her back to him and tried to let the drowsiness settle in.

Mark couldn't sleep. He tried, but every time he felt sleepy, the very act of closing his eyes woke him. Maybe he'd had too much caffeine. He felt as if he had, yet he couldn't remember having much at all. He suppressed a sneeze and glanced over at Nancy. She snored gently, half on her back and half turned away from him, her locket held lightly in her hand.

He wondered about that locket. She used it for security like a child's blanket, and yet she wasn't a child—there had to be some significance to it. Maybe her father had given it to her—his only gift; maybe her mother, before she died. He mused about it for a second or two and then Nancy's hand dropped away and the locket lay on her coat, reflecting what light there was invitingly.

Mark took only a second to decide—was he a snoop or not? Of course he was. As silently and as breathlessly as he could, he reached over toward Nancy. The locket lay on her chest, near her arm, but the thick coat would cushion any mishaps, so he moved quickly. He plucked it off the cloth and ran his fingers over the warm metal, searching for the clasp. When he found it he pressed it and it popped open. There was a picture in there, all right.

Leaning as close as he could while being careful not to pull on the chain, he moved the picture around, trying to see if it would catch enough light. A face—but whose? Was it male or female? Mark finally turned on the interior light for an instant and although Nancy stirred, she didn't wake. He instantly recognized the face. It was a young Maureen O'Hara. The light out again, Mark gently closed the locket, laid it on the coat and leaned back in his seat.

He stared out the window into the black. *Why in heaven's name would she be so attached to a locket with ... ?* He finally just sighed. It was too much to think about this late.

He decided to stretch his legs and got out of the car. He closed the door quickly to extinguish the interior light, then took a few steps and looked up. No stars above usually meant clouds still hovered. At sunset he didn't like how black the clouds had been, and now that he couldn't see them he liked them even less.

But the clouds were just a minor annoyance.

His reaction to Nancy was a major one. She'd tried to say something nice to him, and he did what he always did when women got close—he'd pushed her away. With the others it hadn't mattered so much. But with Nancy ...

There had been a time when he smoked, and for an instant, there in the dark, his cold making him sensitive to the brisk night and the coming winter, Mark thought a cigarette would taste good. Well, it wouldn't taste good—they never really tasted good—but drawing the smoke into his lungs had always had an element of relaxation to it, of being in control, of being a man. Right now he felt neither relaxed, nor in control, and less like a man than he had in a long time. John Wayne wouldn't play these games. *But John Wayne probably wasn't haunted by the same ghosts I am,* Mark thought. *Of course, now he's probably doing his own haunting.*

He took a brief walk, first down the hill where the road, carved from the hillside, dropped steeply toward the highway below, then up where it rose just as steeply to a place he couldn't see. From the highway this hill had looked like a small knoll, but now the hill had expanded to a good-sized mountain.

It began to rain, a few drops at first, then a gentle downpour. Although his first inclination was to leap back into the car, after only a second or two he began to hum "Singin' in the Rain." When Mark was a kid his mother had insisted that he find something he could do on the stage. She was sure that all great men could handle themselves on the stage, and she certainly wasn't going to be the reason her son wasn't great.

She didn't think he was smart enough to be funny or handsome enough to act, but he was lanky enough to dance. From the time he was five she'd sent him to dancing school—mostly tap. By ten he'd refused to go anymore, but for five years he'd stolen the best from Gene Kelly and Fred Astaire—well, actually he ended up dancing more like an inebriated Buddy Ebsen. Right now, though, he just wanted to have some fun, and the growing puddles gave him the opportunity. He started singing, then splashing around from puddle to puddle. But soon he ran out of words he knew, and then the fun had gone out of it.

The rain fell steadily now and Mark was wet to the bone. But he didn't care. He felt remarkably free again—as he had those first few minutes while playing in the snow.

My goodness, he thought, *that was only this afternoon.*

He heard the splattering of falling water and looked around until he found it. Above the road and a little down the hill, an old, gutted log acted like a rain gutter. It stuck out a foot from the road cut, and a steady stream of water fell from it to the road below—it was a natural shower.

Seeing it Mark suddenly realized how grungy he felt. He hadn't shaved in days, his hair and skin itched and seemed coated with oil. A shower was just the thing he needed. After glancing into the car to make sure everyone was still asleep, he quickly opened the hatch, found where she'd put the bag with the toiletries in it, and grabbed them. He gathered up his soap, shaving gear, and shampoo, gently closed the hatch, and ran down the hill to the "waterfall."

There were some root ends sticking from the road cut, and Mark quickly got out of his jacket and hung it on a root, then unbuttoned his shirt and hung it on another root—both hung limply in the rain. With a certain sense of adventure, he spurted a mound of shaving cream into the center of his palm and although the rain eroded it, enough remained to slap onto his face. He worked it onto his face and was about to take a firm swath with his Bic disposable.

Above his head came a frightening flash, an explosion that sent shock waves through the ground and up to his knees, and an ear-splitting rip. Sensing real danger, Mark plastered himself against the road cut just as a charred and smoldering tree fell from the cliff above him. Jagged limbs crashed only inches away from Mark, as it slammed into and across the road. After its limbs splintered and wrenched, the thick trunk finally came to rest—the end closest to Mark glowing red and steaming until the rain snuffed it out.

Heart pounding, he quickly realized how close he'd come to becoming a cinder. Terrified, he threw on his jacket, grabbed the toiletries, wrapped them in his shirt, and sprinted through the mud toward the car.

When he'd run only a few yards there was another growl of thunder—this one more distant, the flash less brilliant. The storm was moving away. Another roar of thunder, even farther away, the flash little more than an afterthought. When Mark reached the car, the rain had already lightened perceptibly. But in spite of that, he was still only a heartbeat removed from his own incineration and, as his mind cleared, he began to realize that the tree that had nearly crushed him now blocked their way off the mountain.

He threw open the door and fell into the seat. Slamming the door behind him, he came face-to-face with Nancy who now sat stiffly upright, clasping Maureen O'Hara as if clinging to a lifeline.

"What happened?" she asked, her voice a sleepy choke.

"Lightning hit a tree just above me," he whispered.

"You okay?"

"I was nearly burnt to a crisp—the tree's across the road. We'll have to try going up the hill."

"What goes up comes down. We should be all right. What's all over your face?"

"Shaving stuff. I was taking a shower," he said.

"Out there?" She pointed into the blackness.

"Sure. It felt good," he said, then sneezed and sneezed again.

"Good thinking," she said dryly and settled back in the seat still clutching the locket. "I was dreaming about something and suddenly—*Bang!* I've never been so scared."

"The storm's lightening up, but I think we should leave. If a tree can fall on me it can fall on the car." Without waiting for Nancy's reply, Mark fired the engine and backed up toward the road quickly. But after only a few feet they both felt a sharp bump and then a strong wrench of the steering wheel.

"What was that?" Nancy asked, her heart gaining speed.

Mark didn't answer. He slammed the brakes, then slapped the steering wheel angrily. When the car stopped sliding in the mud, he stepped outside. The car door must not have closed tightly, for the interior light remained on. It immediately revealed that all he feared was true.

The driver's side tire had a huge gash in it, and the metal rim sat deep in mud and water. The cause was just ahead of the tire: a very sharp rock. Two inches protruded from the ground, the soil around it washed away. It looked like the tip of a shark's tooth.

Fighting off a wave of defeat, Mark looked around. Could they stay there and ride the storm out? The chances that a tree would fall on them were remote, the lightning storm having moved on. He was about to decide that they could remain in the car and change the tire in the morning when he noticed something else.

Water broiled around his shoes and washed beneath the car. Mark looked over to the road rising up the mountain. Illuminated by the car's headlights, a shallow river ran down the mountain, washing away the dirt and exposing the ragged underlying rock. He spun around to where the tree had fallen. Although the car's interior light provided only dim highlights, Mark saw enough to be further alarmed. Where the hollow log had once provided a nice shower, now water thundered over the cliff, only some now channeled through the log. As he watched, the intensity of the waterfall increased. It must have been raining hard farther up the mountain, and they were stranded in the middle of the growing runoff—a river.

In his mind's eye Mark could see small lakes forming above them, reaching a maximum depth and sweeping away the land containing them—he could imagine his car suddenly swept away with it as a wall of water fell on them. He didn't know how much time he had, so there was definitely none to lose.

Their only way out was up the dirt road—which had now become a shallow rapids. There was no way to make it with a flat front tire. Even if they were able to negotiate it, the rocks would further batter and bend the rim. The choice was simple.

Mark heaved a deep sigh, pushed wet hair from his eyes, and was about to open the car door when he heard Nancy.

"Can I help?" she asked. She'd gotten from the car and now

stood on the other side of it, her cinnamon hair flat and draining into her eyes.

"It's build a dam or change the tire. There's no time to build a dam, and I hate changing tires."

At that instant, the rain began falling more earnestly.

The rain splashing off his face, Mark said, "That God of yours has quite a sense of humor."

"The turnout's washing away on this side," Nancy cried to him.

He splashed over to her and saw what she'd seen. The turnout had looked like an earthen plate, as if formed by a single, circular swath of an earthmover's blade. Now bathed in the dim light from the car's interior, it looked like someone had taken a large, triangular chip out of the plate's edge. Making matters worse, the runoff had quickly found the chip and was now devouring even more. The chip was now a notch and it was moving toward them.

"I've gotta change that tire and get us out of here."

"I'm sure I can do something," Nancy stated. "I can get you things."

"I'll do it—there's just no time." Breathing rapidly, Mark ran a frustrated hand through sleek, wet hair and stared back helplessly at the avalanche of wet. He tried to remember any time he'd succeeded in a pressure situation like this—he couldn't. He hoped this would be a first. "Listen, I need to get to work."

"At least put a shirt on. I'm sure there's a dry one . . ."

"It wouldn't stay dry very long."

"Well, okay," Nancy said defeatedly.

"Get back inside. I'll work as fast as I can."

Nancy could only nod. She heard something behind her and turned toward the edge of the turnout. Another chip had broken off the plate, and it quickly eroded into another notch as the water continued to devour the turnout. Soon there'd be a third and fourth. How many would it take before the Pacer was washed off the mountain? She eyed the dogs curled in the backseat and knew that if Mark had any prolonged trouble she'd have to evacuate them. Climbing out of the wet for a minute, she grabbed her locket and began to pray.

Chapter Fourteen

After Nancy's short prayer her head came up to see Mark stumbling around looking for something in the light thrown by the headlamps. When he finally straightened and spun in awkward desperation and frustration she decided her place was beside him. Knowing she'd need the coat's warmth later, she twisted out of it, tossed it in the back and then, after another quick prayer, opened the door. The rain was only rain—wet and cold, and it caused the world and everything in it to become a grayish blur. But the runoff had increased. The water was thundering off the cliff behind them with greater force, the water around her shoes broiled more ravenously, and the notches in the turnoff were appreciably larger, their apexes steadily reaching for the car. In the muddy syrup, she steadied her first steps by clinging to the car.

Mark's back to her, he bent, searching through the brush at the edge of the clearing.

"What are you looking for?" she called.

He straightened and looked around. With no time to question why she'd left the dry car, he called back, "Rocks to wedge the back wheels."

"What about the emergency brake?"

"Doesn't work."

"Somehow I knew that." Nancy groaned. "How about that one?" She pointed to a rock suddenly exposed by rising water.

"I must have missed it."

"I'll get it," she called. But though her brittle fingers pawed at it, abrasive grit now packed under her fingernails, it wouldn't budge. "It's too heavy or something!" she bawled to Mark, wiping her muddy hands on her pants.

"I'll get it. You find another one." Mark attacked the rock, which was squarish and flat, eight inches on a side. He dug around its perimeter and finally dislodged it. But it immediately displayed a mind of its own and slipped out of his hands. When Mark tried to catch it before it hit the mud, he lost his balance. Nancy caught his arm and steadied him. With a glance of appreciation, he retrieved the rock and splashed toward the back of the car.

Nancy figured she had a gift for rock finding because she immediately spied another candidate. Not waiting for Mark, she scraped the mud from around the rock, washing the persistent grit from her hands in the swirling muddy water, then pried it loose. Although it was as heavy as the other one, she lifted it and followed Mark back to the car.

Even though she loved the California beaches, she hated the sand—it got into everything: clothes, shoes, sandals, hair, bathing suit, between the fingers. She hated this mud the same way. She hated the grit, the feel of it; it was as if she could feel every grain, and as she carried the rock, the grit ground into her hands. When she got to the back of the car Mark had already pushed his rock in place and was reaching for hers. She gave it to him and felt immense relief as she held up her hands and let the pure rain wash them. In the meantime Mark unceremoniously dropped the rock in back of the passenger side wheel. A wave of mud splashed all over her, but her hands were clean now and that's all that mattered.

"What now?" she shouted over the rain.

"I need a flat rock to set the jack on."

She winced—more grit. "I saw one back there," she said, heading to where they'd found the other two. She glanced toward the edge of the turnout. Another larger piece of the plate had broken off between the other two, the muddy runoff pouring over it. Fortunately, the erosion had met an obstinate slab of rock that looked like it might stall its advance for a while.

Resuming her search, she quickly found a flat tablet of shale. The shale was heavier, and her back, still not completely recovered from her accident in the snow, pinched as she lifted the rock. Mark saw her struggle, and he grabbed it just before her muddy fingers gave up.

"I'll take it. You get back in the car."

Letting the rain wash her hands again, she protested, "No. I can help. I changed the flat I had—the one you wouldn't help me with. Maybe if you had, God wouldn't be putting you through this right now." She laughed.

Mark didn't hear her. He took the shale from Nancy, splashed to the flat tire, dropped the rock, then positioned it behind the flat and under the frame.

"What should I do?" Nancy called to him.

"Get in the car. I just have to get these nuts off and the spare on."

"Are you sure I can't—"

"Get back in the car. It's cold out here. You'll catch pneumonia."

"You could too," she bayed at him. "With your cold. And you look like you're getting tired." He did too. She had noticed it a few minutes ago. His movements were slower, more exaggerated, his steps more plodding. Of course, he could be just fatigued, but it seemed more than that.

"Get out of the rain!" he ordered back to her.

She hesitated, but when she saw him busily positioning the jack and realized there was nothing more she could do except get even wetter—if that were possible—she made it back to her side of the car. The first two notches in the earth had also seemed to stop growing; maybe there was an underlying rock strata. Maybe there wasn't as much danger as they thought.

Nancy's hair hung down her face in grotesquely twisted strings, her clothes clung like a clammy second skin, and her water-resistant jacket resisted no more. She hadn't realized how battered and bedraggled she was until the rain was locked outside. She also hadn't realize how cold the rain had become until she'd climbed into the warm.

A few seconds later, after she'd pulled the thick, oily coat around her and the chill began to break up, she felt the car jerk and groan as Mark jacked it up. When the jerking stopped, Nancy sat on an angle watching the top of Mark's head as he worked feverishly, hidden from her by the hood.

That's when something very spooky happened.

Nancy saw it first, and then Mark sensed something was amiss, turned and saw it too.

The waterfall that thundered over the cliff at the base of the hollow log suddenly lightened, then died to a trickle.

Mark stood for several seconds staring at it. Then he turned to her and shrugged. "Maybe the rain stopped up there," he called, his words muffled by the glass.

Nancy nodded. But then she noticed that the steady stream cascading down the dirt road was stronger than ever. That seemed to contradict Mark's thought. She glanced back to where the waterfall had once raged. Now there was little more than a trickle. What was going on? An eerie chill danced up her spine.

When nothing else happened for a moment or two, she turned her attention back to Mark who'd bent down and resumed his work. By his position she knew he was working the lug nuts. Nancy remembered how hard hers had been to loosen. She remembered her broken nails and how it felt to strain every muscle in her body and have nothing happen. Now Mark must be doing the same. She could see his facial muscles become granite as he pushed, pushed harder, then threw his whole weight against them. One must have given way for he caved in and disappeared beneath the hood. Then he reappeared a moment later smiling, the nut in his hand, showing it to Nancy.

She laughed her support.

He reapplied the lug wrench to the next bolt.

Suddenly the cliff beneath the hollow log, near the level of the road exploded. Dirt, mud, stones, and broken limbs blew out, propelled by a powerful fist of water. Like a huge pipe bursting, the water punched through, sending debris flying and picking up more debris as the earth above it collapsed into the torrent. When the hollow log finally toppled in, the river tossed it into the road, then carried it over the cliff as if it were kindling. After its original frenzy, the torrent subsided slightly, the pressure released, but then it kept up a steady, though at times erratic, flow from its new channel. When it thundered onto the blacktop, it fanned out, mostly running under the fallen tree and, some, still propelled with great force, escaped over the cliff. For an instant Nancy thought the tree that blocked their exit might be pushed aside, freeing them, but it wasn't. Its branches formed an amenable passage for the mud-laden flow.

"Did you see that?" Mark cried.

"What happened?"

"I don't know. It must have developed a sinkhole or something, traveling along a layer of rock and punched through."

"What happens if something punches through below us?" Nancy asked.

But she didn't need an answer. Mark knew immediately what would happen and so did she.

Now they really were in trouble.

"Maybe we should just leave," Nancy called out to him.

But he didn't hear her. He quickly threw himself at getting the nuts off and to his surprise he did, one at a time, but quickly. Throwing off the wheel, he stood, stretched, wiped his eyes, and dipped down below the hood again. Nancy heard the grind of metal against metal as the spare was put in place.

As Mark tightened the nuts, Nancy heard a tearing sound. She turned to the now ragged edge of the turnout. The rock that held the eroding flow at bay had given way. Its edges compromised, it lost its grip and toppled into the valley. There were less than four feet between the car and the cliff now. Nancy knew they'd be following that rock soon—unless some underground river blew them off first.

She was about to abandon the Pacer when she saw Mark overcome whatever weakness he had been feeling and run to the back of the car. Tossing up the hatch, he hefted the old wheel in, made no effort to restack anything, closed the hatch violently, and quickly threw open the driver's side door.

"Here goes nothing," he said, grinding the ignition. The car didn't start. "It always starts. What's happening?"

"Wet?"

With no time to reply, Mark ground it again and this time it fired up. He mashed it into gear and slowly backed up enough to get a run at the inclining road.

Looking like a drowned puppy, Mark sneezed, took a huge breath and eased through the mud and water to where the road began its ascent. The rapids had long ago washed all the dirt away revealing an irregular rock foundation. Both Nancy and Mark felt the tires take their first grab, and they began to move forward.

"The tires should be okay on the rocks," Nancy said trying to sound hopeful, for the road was steep and it had to be slippery.

"The oil pan. The Pacer's low to the ground—it wouldn't take much to rip it open."

At that moment the tire ruts in the road deepened, and the mound between them raised and became more threatening.

Nancy grabbed her locket and said another quick prayer, although she didn't dare close her eyes.

After several heartbeats she noticed Mark's lips—they were thin, purple bruises and they were trembling uncontrollably. She grabbed the blanket and tucked it awkwardly over his shoulders. Then, while he kept his eyes riveted to the road, she pressed her palm to his forehead. Warm. "We have to get you dry clothes."

"Let's get off the mountain first," he said, but his voice trembled with his lips.

Suddenly from behind they heard the muffled sound of earth rending, trees grinding and tearing at one another, and the roar of rushing water.

Nancy turned and peered through the back window.

Mark didn't dare. "What happened?" he asked, the strain in his voice acute.

"The turnout's gone," she said simply but in awe.

"Gone?" Mark gasped. He glanced over his shoulder for the split second it took to verify what she'd said.

As if the earth had been blown out from under it, the turnout had collapsed into the valley, taking with it the surrounding earth and trees. Nothing more than the memory remained, and even that was being quickly washed away by an ever growing mudflow.

"Maybe a dam broke on the mountain," Nancy said, numb from their close call.

"Somewhere up there is a herd of angry beavers," Mark said, eyes frozen ahead. "I hope they give us a wide berth."

Their biggest fear, of course, was that their road might be next. Mark eased the pedal down, but the Pacer was going as fast as it could and although the engine whined a little louder, nothing else changed.

The road suddenly steepened and the car slowed. But then, after twenty or thirty yards the road dipped again. When the Pacer reached the bottom, it plowed and bumped through a newly-formed river that reached up to the doors. Ascending again, they slid around a hairpin turn, and Nancy felt deep ruts take control of the steering, forcing them over jagged rocks that gnawed at the Pacer's vulnerable underbelly. Nancy soon wondered if she were better off not praying. When she did, things seemed to get worse. But she bit her tongue as punishment for that thought and prayed again.

"I can't believe the headache I have." Mark groaned, massaging his forehead.

Nancy pushed his hand away and placed hers on his forehead. "You're burning up," she stated flatly. "Do you want me to drive?"

"No," but his response was gentle and understanding, even thankful. "I know this car, and that's important right now."

Suddenly the car shuddered as its belly ground against gravel and dirt.

Mark tightened, then sighed. "I didn't hear anything tear. I think we're okay." Then he rubbed his eyes and continued to stare at the blurred arcs made by the worn wiper blades. In front of the car torrents of water bubbled and flowed like rapids down the road they were struggling up. "I feel like a salmon. Worse. All the work, none of the fun." Mark moaned. "I hate this."

"You're going to hate what's ahead even more," Nancy said as the headlights struck a fallen oak. Its limbs brutishly tangled, it blocked the road completely.

"Things were just going too good." Mark sighed. Fortunately the road had leveled off a bit, and he brought the car to a stop in what seemed to be a safe place.

"Maybe we can move it," Nancy offered feebly.

"Maybe the car can push it out of the way," Mark said, his voice flattened by a punishing weariness.

Nancy studied him. He was sweating now; rivers of it ran from his forehead down his cheeks, and his eyes were red and exhausted. She pressed a palm to his forehead again. He was on fire, and for an instant she thought about having him stand in the cooling rain again, but she figured he'd just die out there and she didn't want that. Anyway, the rain was little more than a mist now.

Mark eased the car closer to the oak. It, too, had been hit by lightning. Although the base no longer burned or steamed, it was charred black and burned through. The limbs lay broken and twisted, and there was no way the car could get close enough to push it.

"It's hopeless." Mark sighed, lying back defeated.

"No it isn't," Nancy suddenly said brightly. She'd seen something.

"Huh?"

"Look—tire tracks leading off into the forest." She pointed into the brush on the right. The rain had beaten down the grass and brush, exposing two parallel tire ruts that ran a short distance into sparse trees and quickly disappeared.

"Maybe there is a God," Mark said, backing up slightly to position the car.

"No maybe about it," Nancy affirmed, increasingly worried about Mark.

Without responding, Mark laboriously turned the wheel, and they plowed into the wet underbrush. Surprisingly, after driving about the length of a football field, they broke into another dirt road. Although battered by the rain, it seemed in far better repair than the one they'd just left. It climbed more gradually through the woods.

"This easier for you?" Nancy asked, concerned.

"You drive for a while." Mark groaned as he stopped the car in the middle of the road. "I'm tired."

Not rain but a wet chill hit Nancy as she slid from her seat and met Mark halfway around the Pacer. He steadied himself by holding on to the car. She helped him into the passenger seat, and he groaned. "The fever came so fast."

"You stay as warm as you can," Nancy told him and tucked the blanket around him again. As he sat back, eyes all but closed, his breathing labored, his fever raging, she kissed him lightly on the forehead, then lingered there a moment. She felt so helpless. At least she could help by driving.

Even though she hadn't driven the car before, she confidently threw it into first and started rolling. After only a few hundred feet, things started to look up. She found herself at the crest of a hill, and the drive down the other side looked much easier than the way up.

Relieved, she was about to start down when a man stepped from the brush into her headlights. She only saw him for a split second before slamming on the brakes, but she saw enough—he had longish hair peeking from beneath a stylish Stetson, a thick mustache, and a shotgun cradled across the front of his hunting jacket.

She grabbed Mark's arm. "Mark, wake up!"

Mark stirred. "Huh?"

"A man with a gun is stopping us."

"That figures." He tried to straighten. After giving it all he had, he finally just fell back without seeing the hunter.

Although the white light made it hard to tell what the man wore, Nancy thought he appeared to be more gentleman than woodsman and closer to both than to a criminal. He was tall, broad shouldered, probably in his fifties, and his Stetson, long hair, and thick, waterfall mustache gave him the look of a Bill Hickock or Custer without the flair. He wore the stern, brooding expression of a man who meant business—the fact that Nancy didn't know *what* business gave her real concern.

His next move gave her more cause to fear. He leveled the shotgun in her direction, then motioned her to get out of the car. Nancy reached back and slapped Hamster on the head. He groaned but offered no assistance. Since Mark and the dog were going to be of no help, she had no alternative but to comply. She opened the door and stepped out.

"Why are you here?" he asked, his voice resonant, his coal-black eyes tunneling through the drizzle.

"We're going to California and have spent most of the night in a small clearing down the road but couldn't get back to the highway because a tree was hit by lightning and blocked our way. Then the storm came and nearly washed us off the mountain. We finally made it here. Is this your road? I guess it's yours, isn't it?" She stopped herself. "I'm babbling . . ."

"What's wrong with your husband?"

"He needs a doctor. He's had a cold for a couple days now, but it really got bad in the storm. He had to change a tire in the rain. He's got a bad fever—very bad. Maybe it's gone into the flu or something. But he's not my husband; he's just a friend."

The man dropped the point of his gun. "You folks can get warm at my place," he offered. "The nearest doctor is a long way. Anyway, I know as much about these things as he does." The man moved around the car so that he could get a closer look at Mark. The moment he opened the door and peeled the blanket away he registered deep concern. "No shirt? Did you try to break the fever by packing him in mud?"

"It was horrible down there. Like we were in the middle of a river."

The man nodded and placed a hand on Mark's forehead. He left it there only a second.

"He's definitely warm. You had breakfast?" the man asked, looking at her over the car's roof. "It'll be dawn soon. You can clean up at my home."

Nancy put a cap on her appreciation for a moment. "Why are you out in the rain this early?"

He gave her a long, evaluative look, then said, "Visitors need investigating." Then he spotted the dogs in the back. "Please keep them quiet."

"No problem. Really. They're very quiet dogs." Naomi immediately proved her wrong by lapsing into a yipping fit, but Nancy grabbed her and, after being cuddled for a moment Naomi quieted and lapped at Nancy's chin affectionately.

The woodsman smiled warmly at them, then became stern again. "Drive a little farther. You'll see a driveway on the left. The house is behind the trees. Park on the gravel. I'll be right behind you."

A few minutes later Nancy parked next to a forest-green jeep, and the man stood beside Mark's open door. The shotgun slung over his shoulder, he helped Mark to his feet. "Come on, kid. You can make it." Mark draped a listless arm over the man's shoulder and a few seconds later was being helped into the house.

The house was a large cedar A-frame set far back from the road and hidden in a grove of oak. The man led them along a walkway that skirted the house and led to a large porch. This was not a mountain shack, nor even a seasonal cabin. This was a luxurious home—and it was a man's home. The porch teemed with hunting trophies, countless hides, elk and deer horns, a couple of boar heads with large, coiled tusks, all hanging from walls of glistening knotty pine. A large door with an imposing stained-glass forest scene opened into the house. The man took Mark to the kitchen table and sat him there. "I'll get him a pill and then you can clean him up." He tossed his Stetson onto the kitchen table, and his glistening white hair showed the impression of his hatband. Nancy nodded and stood beside Mark.

She couldn't help but survey the rest of the first floor. Reminders of the city were nowhere to be seen in the sprawling room. There were only warm browns, oranges, and accent yellows, and the overstuffed furniture oozed comfort. The walls were cedar and each held its own personality. One was draped from hardwood floor to ceiling with books—shelves and shelves of them. Another was alive with more hunting trophies—a couple of deer heads and some stuffed fish. Another was covered with all sizes of paintings—original forest scenes—and the fourth was ribbed with shelves that held every conceivable kind of memorabilia: pictures, collectibles, one-of-a-kinds, each next to another, some several deep. The floors were accented by expensive, warmly-colored rugs.

The memorabilia and artwork spilled over into the rest of the room. On various end tables were silver-framed pictures and porcelain statuettes, small antiques, and music boxes—some simple, some exquisitely elaborate. On a table near the back were several bronze castings—cowboys, a stagecoach with frothing horses, and a couple of American Indians. Whoever this hunter was, he had money.

The man took down a large bottle of aspirin and shook two tablets into his palm. After he filled a glass with tap water, he stepped toward Mark. "You're admiring my trinkets. I'm a hopeless collector," he said.

"I love stuff like this. It's so homey," Nancy told him. She remembered that her home had been void of art, not even knick-knacks. Her mother was allergic to dust, and anything that collected dust ended up in the trash.

"Here, take this, guy." He pushed the tablets between Mark's lips and spilled the water down his throat. When Mark swallowed and lifted a finger in appreciation, the man turned toward the kitchen. "How about a hot breakfast—oatmeal or something? I'll have coffee made in a minute. The guest room's in the back—you two can use that."

"Mark can. I'll be fine out here." Nancy eyed the comfortable floral sofa that stretched in front of a deep, richly mantled fireplace.

"Your choice. I'm Fletcher Harris, by the way. And you folks are?"

"Nancy Bernard, and this wreck is Mark Brewster." When she said Mark's name she looked affectionately down at him. He looked worse than ever. "I'd better get him cleaned up and into bed. You wouldn't have any tea, would you?"

"Only the loose kind."

Nancy couldn't believe her ears. "Could you make me some? Not real strong, but I love loose tea."

Fletcher nodded and smiled obligingly. "Well, I'll get busy in here while you two get your showers. The shower is off the guest room through that door over there. Make yourselves at home. After breakfast we'll get busy making you well, Mark."

Nancy hesitated. "I want to thank you, Mr. Harris. When I saw you with that gun out there I wasn't sure what was going to happen. But—well, anyway, thank you."

"That's all right. I'm not a man who likes company, but you two need a hand and I'll not turn you away."

Nancy smiled awkwardly and slipped an arm around Mark, "You ready?" she whispered to him.

When they'd walked about halfway to the door Mark whispered to her, "I don't trust him." Without waiting for Nancy to react, he turned toward the man. "Are you really going to help us?"

Fletcher was in the middle of rattling some pans around and stopped when the question reached him. "As much as I can. I'm alone up here for a reason. But I'll help. Just remember that I like my privacy, and I like people to stay where I put them. Do that and everything will be fine."

"We'll respect your privacy, and we'll stay where we're put," Nancy assured him, a little annoyed at Mark's question.

Satisfied, Mark let Nancy guide him to the guest room door. "You gonna wash my back?" Mark asked as Nancy reached for the expensive brass knob. She looked into beleaguered but impish eyes.

"I'll drown you first."

"But I'm too weak to wash myself." She felt his weight double as he slumped in her arms.

"Get in there and get your shower. You're not that far gone." Nancy pushed the door open and pointed him toward the bed. "I'll see you in a few minutes to get your clothes. I'll wash them."

Mark leaned beside her for a moment, eying the comfortable bed before him and the wash of dawn's light that lay across it. "This is too good, Nancy. I still don't trust him. No accent. This is the South and he's got no accent. Watch yourself."

Hearing the concern in his voice, she looked deeply into his eyes, eyes that told her how really serious he was.

Chapter Fifteen

Fletcher made the tea first, and Nancy was sipping it gratefully when she heard the shower go on in the guest room.

"I need to wash our clothes. Is that okay?"

"Through there." He pointed to a door on the other side of the kitchen.

"I'll get his clothes."

"I'll get you a robe. You can change in my room," Fletcher offered and walked to a second bedroom not far from the guest room door, which Nancy cautiously opened. Finding Mark's clothes piled on the floor at the foot of the bed, she scooped them up, deposited them in a large sink by the washing machine, then stepped toward Fletcher's room and passed him on the way out of it. She closed the door and found a rich, red terry cloth robe lying on his bed.

A few minutes later she emerged from Fletcher's room wearing the robe and carrying her clothes. She heard the shower turn off as she crossed to the washing room. She threw her muddied clothes on top of Mark's in the deep sink, then washed as much of the mud out of them as she could before loading them, jackets and all, into the large, heavy-duty machine. With the washing machine humming, she returned to the kitchen, took another sip of tea and looked toward the guest room. "I'm worried about him."

"If death had a body, it would look like he does," Fletcher said, stirring a pot of oatmeal.

"I'll go see if he's okay."

"There's a thermometer in the bathroom. It's time we found out what we're up against."

"You've treated these things before?" Nancy asked hopefully.

"A fever's a fever," Fletcher said.

Somehow that didn't reassure Nancy. She listened at the guest room door for a moment, then knocked timidly.

"Come in," Mark said from inside.

When she opened the door, she saw him lying on the bed—naked. After an instinctive gasp, she whirled around and stepped from the room and slammed the door. "Would you please get under the covers!"

"I'm too weak—you have to tuck me in."

"Get under those covers or I'll send Fletcher in here with his gun," she called back through the thick door, and after a few seconds she heard the bed squeaking and thought she heard sheets flapping.

"Okay, Miss Prude. I'm ready."

"You'd better be," she fired back and cautiously opened the door again. Mark lay beneath the covers, his head planted deeply in a pillow.

"Nice robe," he croaked.

"I'm washing the clothes," she said, looking toward the bathroom. "He said there was a thermometer in there—"

The door opened behind her, and Nancy turned to see Fletcher walk in with a tray. On it was a bowl of the oatmeal he'd been stirring, a glass of orange juice, and a small shot glass with several pills rattling around in it. "I took the liberty," he said, a broad smile stretching across his face. "Feed him the oatmeal after he downs the pills—they're antibiotics and some other things. If it's a virus nothing can help. We'll see." He handed Nancy the tray.

She took it and he smiled again down at Mark and left them alone, closing the door behind him.

"I still don't trust him," Mark said, eyes still on the door.

"Well, so far he's been nice. Now take these and we'll give you the oatmeal."

"I hate oatmeal."

"Well, haven't we gotten bitter."

Mark eyed her and then broke down and smiled. "I still have that headache—and I feel like I'm burning up."

"Let's get your temperature, then the pills, then the oatmeal you hate."

Nancy sat on the edge of the bed and studied the thermometer for several seconds before setting it down. "One hundred and two.

That's high—at least my mom used to say it's high. Come on, take the pills. Maybe they'll help."

"I heard that the brain starts falling apart when it hits one-oh-four," Mark said, concerned.

"Well, at least that won't hurt you too much. Take the pills."

He took them two at a time with the orange juice. When they were all down Nancy scooped up a spoonful of oatmeal and pushed it to his lips. He groaned but opened his mouth.

"I'm probably capable of doing that myself," Mark said, after some of the second spoonful dribbled from his lips and Nancy retrieved it from his chin. "I'm not a baby."

"Maybe," she said, shoving in another spoonful.

"I hate this stuff." He groaned again as she dabbed his lips with a napkin. "Can we take a break?"

She nodded and set the spoon down. "How do you feel?" she asked, knitting her brows and feeling very maternal.

"Horrible—hot—weak," he said, eyes sinking back in his head. "I feel like I could sleep forever."

"I'm almost afraid to let you."

"Afraid?"

She nodded. "Come on, let's finish this stuff. It's getting cold."

"No. Please no more." He turned his head to the dawning light. "I think he's trying to poison me. He can't be all he seems."

"You need to eat," she urged, another spoonful hovering over his chest.

"I don't. I never need to eat. I think he's going to kill us later—when we're asleep."

"Nonsense." She set the spoon down. "He's just trying to be nice. He's probably running from the world and ended up here. Earned a bunch of money doing something and escaped—maybe like you and I have done once or twice in our lives." She looked toward the door and in her mind saw the man beyond it—he was probably still working in the kitchen—his kitchen—away from all the other kitchens in the world and all the other people working in them.

Suddenly she heard Mark laughing, a choked, distant laugh and she turned back to him. "What?"

"That robe makes you look like a fire engine with hair." He laughed so hard his shoulders bounced, but stopped and grabbed at his throat. "It's sore."

"Serves you right," she said, but she felt the pain he felt and longed to hold him and make him better.

"I'm tired," he finally said.

"I'll be back in a little while to check your temperature again."

A listless hand came out from beneath the covers and waved her good-bye.

She stood over him for a moment, then bent and kissed him lightly on the forehead. His eyes were closed and when her lips touched his burning brow, he groaned with a certain pleasure.

She closed the door behind her and took the tray back to the kitchen.

Fletcher Harris sat on a high stool at the kitchen counter, sipping a cup of coffee and leafing through a gun magazine. "How's he doing?"

"His temperature's high. He's sleeping now."

"We'll know if the pills worked in an hour or so."

"I can't thank you enough for your help. Really. We're not used to people being so kind—at least not on this trip," she said, feeling a wave of weariness break over her. "As soon as he's feeling better we'll get out of your hair."

"When you're ready. More tea?"

She shook her head, a head that suddenly weighed a ton. "Thanks anyway. I'm suddenly very tired. Is there a place I can take a shower?"

"The room where you got the robe. Bathroom's in the same place." He took another sip of coffee and idly flipped a few more pages.

"This is such a beautiful home. I wouldn't expect it up here."

"That's why it's here," he said without looking up.

As she moved beneath the shower, the water rushed across her in pleasantly warm waves, and when the last of the mud disappeared from her hair she felt renewed. Her skin seemed alive again—clean, fresh, reborn. She found herself standing there for a while and letting the world wash away too. She prayed, thanking the Lord for everything. And when she finally toweled off and donned the thick, red cocoon again, she was ready for a nap. But she didn't take one. She used Fletcher's hair dryer and did the best she could without a curling iron.

The washing had finished, and Nancy put the things in the dryer.

When she found Fletcher gone, she poured herself another cup of tea, took a couple of sips and decided to check on Mark. She listened at his door, and hearing nothing, she quietly opened it.

A shaft of morning light fell across Mark as he lay curled beneath the blanket. A patch of wheat-blond hair was all that was visible. His forehead burned and his lips were desert dry. What had her mother done with fevers? Should he stay warm, protected from another chill, or should he be cool so he didn't incinerate right there between the sheets?

The only thing Nancy felt comfortable doing was checking his temperature again. His lips never opened as she shoved the thermometer under his tongue. While it still protruded, Fletcher appeared at the door.

"How's he doing?"

"Are we supposed to keep him warm or cool with a temperature—I can't remember."

"How high is it now?"

Making sure the time was up, she took the thermometer out and checked it. It had risen. "It's a hundred and three." She groaned helplessly. "He needs all the brain cells he has, and soon they're going to start boiling away."

"We'd better wash him down. Get a cool, wet cloth from the bathroom."

When Nancy returned with a cold, dripping rag, she found that Fletcher had pulled the covers away and there Mark lay, naked again. Her face flushed, and she turned away, pushing out the hand with the cloth. "I'm sorry," she heard Fletcher say. "I just assumed—" She heard the sheets move, and she cautiously turned. There was still more of Mark exposed than she wanted, but she decided to ignore it.

To the outstretched cloth Fletcher protested. "He's your patient. I'll count pills and give advice, but—" He indicated the body.

"He and I don't have that kind of relationship."

"You think he and I do?"

"Well," Nancy said, feeling a frightened resolve settling over her, "no."

"Every little girl wants to be a nurse at some time or another. Pretend you made it." He moved to the door. "Keep the cloth cool. Get his arms, legs, chest, back, face—all of him a couple times. Then wait a few minutes and take his temp again."

Mark didn't remain listless long. The moment the cold cloth touched his chest, his eyes bolted open and he cried loudly in protest. "Argh! What's happening?"

"We're fighting your fever—shut up and take it like a man," she barked, for Nancy felt excruciatingly uncomfortable with her task. It was far too intimate, rubbing his chest, taking his hand and rubbing his arms, then his legs. She did it all mechanically, void of warmth, callous to the cries of, "No! N-n-no—sadist!"

Callous because she was afraid of feeling anything else.

After she'd refreshed the cloth at least five times and finished Mark's back for the second time, Nancy pulled the sheet up to his chin and smiled into his large, staring eyes. "Get that temperature down or we do this again," she ordered. Then feeling a wave of caring, she kissed him again on the forehead. "I'll see you in a while." After squeezing his hand, she left.

Fletcher was gone when she emerged from the room. But his touch was still present—a fire crackled in the fireplace, and the two dogs lay warming themselves on the woven-rag rug before it. "A dog's life isn't all that bad sometimes," she mused. The dryer was still working its magic in the back and her tea had gotten cold. Nancy gave way to her weariness and curled up on the couch in front of the fire, Fletcher's robe large enough to cover her with some to spare.

She heard Mark coughing—deep, rasping coughs, his body struggling to break up the phlegm in his chest. First the coughs mingled with her dreams, but when she woke, they were so violent that she became immediately frightened.

But she calmed a little when she heard heavy footsteps and saw Fletcher walking quickly from his room to Mark's, several prescription pill containers in his hands.

When she made it to Mark's side, Fletcher was already pushing the pills down.

"Antibiotics," he said simply, but the word was edged in a sense of urgency.

"The coughing's bad," Nancy said, her eyes searching Mark's tortured face.

The last pill given, Fletcher planted a large, meaty hand on

Mark's brow. "Still hot. We'll check his temp again in an hour or so."

Nancy suddenly felt helpless. "He'll be all right, won't he?"

"I promise. Now get some rest."

Mark's vaporous voice rose up, "Why don't you guys just fill a coffin with ice and throw me in—then you'd only have to move me once."

She woke to two sounds, both mingling in her mind. One was the pop and crackle of the fireplace. There were a couple of new logs on it and the flame gnawed hungrily at them. She felt almost too warm. The other was a muted, low-pitched buzz—the sound of a small plane landing.

She patted Hamster's head then looked around. Fletcher was gone and the plane was out back. Curious, Nancy walked to the wall of windows that formed the back wall and pushed aside the veil of expensive lace that covered them.

The house was built on a steep, wooded hill that fell quickly to a large, glistening lake in back. Picturesque anytime, now it seemed mystically so. Far below a small sea-plane had just landed. Churning up a fresh wake, the plane's single engine growled as it motored toward a long pier. Fletcher stood at the end of the pier waiting, his Stetson crisp and white in the high sun.

When it was only a few yards away, the plane fell silent and floated to within a few feet of the pier. The door beneath the wing opened, and the pilot leaned out and handed Fletcher a heavy, foot-square box. Fletcher set it on the pier, then accepted an envelope. He opened it and looked inside. The transaction done, the pilot disappeared into the cockpit, and the engine sputtered, then ignited. Pulling away from the pier, the plane turned toward the middle of the lake, revved, then taxied. When it had gained speed, its wake cutting an ever-widening path, it lifted from the water and soared above the distant hills. A few minutes later it was just a memory.

"Now that's what I call special delivery," Nancy muttered, as she watched Fletcher push the envelope into his back pocket and carry the box off the pier and out of view.

She looked out over the lake for a minute or two longer. Even with the trees stripped for winter, the scene was remarkably beautiful. But then she remembered Fletcher's speech about being a private person and decided to move away from the window.

She checked on Mark and found him in a labored sleep and still on fire—no worse but no better. She stood over him in the shadows. In times like these she cared for him so—he was so childlike, so in need . . .

"How is he?" Fletcher's voice came from behind.

"Still feverish," she said.

"The antibiotics take time. They'll heal him."

"The Lord will heal him," she said, a little surprised that she had.

"All sorts of things will. His desire, the medicine, his body, millions of years of survival. All of it."

Nancy sighed. "He believes that too."

They both stood silently for a heartbeat or two, then Fletcher asked, "Want some lunch?"

"Thank you," she answered, eyes still on Mark. "I need to get dressed."

"I folded your clothes. Yours are laid out in my room. Why don't you change while I get lunch."

She didn't like the fact that he'd handled her underthings, but she did find her clothes neatly folded and waiting for her. She hadn't realized how crusty they had become until she felt so good going back on. Clean and still warm, her blouse and jeans made her feel almost like she was home.

The afternoon passed slowly. After a submarine sandwich stacked with at least four different meats, one of them filet mignon, Fletcher excused himself and left Nancy with several gun magazines to read. She went through them in about a minute. Then she attacked his bookshelves. She found a Hemingway and found that she didn't like Hemingway. Then she found *Tom Sawyer*. After checking Mark every fifteen minutes, at about three o'clock she just decided to station herself in his room. Just when *Tom Sawyer* was getting a little boring, Mark began to cough.

As first it was listless sputtering that lasted for a few seconds. But after a minute or two of silence, he suddenly exploded with deep, scraping coughs that dug deeply into his chest.

A little frightened by the violence, Nancy sat helplessly on the edge of her seat; when the coughing persisted, she slid over to his bed. Mark would lie on his pillow and cough, then he'd rise up as if he were sleepwalking and cough some more. Finally, as if in pain, he rolled on his side, folded in two, and coughed into his pillow. Yellow mucus drooled out. Either too weak to move or still asleep, he made no move to help himself.

Nancy instinctively turned away but realized that it was time to be the nurse again. She ran into the bathroom, grabbed some damp cloths, and ran back. Scooping up the mucus with one, she washed Mark's face with the other, then gently raised his head to her breast, turned the pillow over, and lay his head back down. Through it all he never woke.

He became peaceful again. But then, suddenly, he was too peaceful. Before her eyes the color drained from his face and his complexion turned to wax.

"My throat's so sore," he whimpered through the death mask as if saying his final words.

She had never felt such overwhelming fear. She refreshed a pile of washcloths with cold water and rubbed his arms, then worked his face and neck—he moaned when the cold touched him, and he moaned louder after she washed his chest and even louder when she rolled him on his side and did his back. Then she went through the cycle a second time and laid him back and covered him with the sheet.

"Mark, can you hear me?"

"You really do want to kill me, don't you?" He groaned, mouth open and pressed against his pillow, breathing in huge, rasping gasps.

There was little change in Mark through the evening. He woke only once near eight o'clock and moaned like a tortured ghost. Nancy brought him some chicken noodle soup and spooned about half of it down. Only once did he even appear to be awake—when he choked on one of the noodles and sprayed her with it. The rest of the time his eyes remained closed, and if it weren't for the action of his Adam's apple, she would have thought him in a coma.

About ten o'clock Fletcher retired. He put down the book he was reading—the latest Tom Clancy, announced he was off to bed, then got up to build a small fire in the fireplace. He'd seemed preoccupied and had hardly spoken all evening. So his sudden voice gave

Nancy a start. She thanked him for all he'd done and said good night.

After dinner she'd switched to reading *Wuthering Heights* and finally, at about eleven, she put that down, mussed Hamster and Naomi's heads, brushed her teeth with the toothbrush Fletcher had provided, kissed Mark's still fevered forehead, and curled up on the couch before the fire and slept.

She heard his coughing first in her dream—the thunderous, rasping sound that seemed to be the residue from an explosion deep in his chest. When Nancy realized what it was, she sprang to her feet, nearly tripped twice over furniture that she didn't expect, and finally all but fell into his room.

Mark sat straight up in his bed, his whole body heaving with the coughs, his chest tight with something that the coughs were desperately trying to break up. She pressed a hand to his head. He'd never been so hot—her hand almost sizzled as if on a burner. She felt helpless. The antibiotics were doing no good—his fever raged higher than ever. She had to get him to a doctor.

Suddenly Fletcher was at the door. He didn't even look at Nancy as he crossed quickly to Mark and pressed a hand to his forehead. It was quickly slapped away as Mark lurched forward to cough again.

"We have to get the fever down. Run a cold shower."

"Cold?"

"Run it," Fletcher ordered.

She didn't hesitate. She quickly flipped the cold knob all the way on and returned to the room. Fletcher already had a wilted, naked Mark cradled in his large arms and was heading for the shower. Nancy left the room just as she heard Mark scream. It sounded like her scream that moment she went over the edge of the snow and headed for that tree. She remembered how every part of her was screaming, how her lungs tried to scream louder but couldn't. Mark's scream was just like that. Then he moaned and swore and called out for mercy. But the big man would have none of it. Mark's cries went unheeded. Finally, the shower went off and a minute later Nancy heard the bed creak under Mark's weight. She entered to see Fletcher toweling him off.

"I'm so afraid for him. Shouldn't we get him to a doctor?"

"No. No doctors." Fletcher was ordering again and at the same time working quickly to dry Mark off. When finished, he covered him with a sheet, then stood looking down, appraising him. "Wash him down every hour, and I'll leave the window open in here—it's getting cool out there."

"Every hour?" Nancy winced. "I'll never stay awake."

"I'll get a timer from the kitchen. All you have to do is remember to set it each time."

It went off an hour later and then an hour after that, and then an hour after that. It had been about two in the morning when Mark had awakened the first time. By four she was staggering. But staggering was the best of it; having been up most of the previous night and now this one, her eyes burned, her mind operated in an unthinking fog. When she worked on Mark, her muscles sometimes just stopped, not sure what to do next and her brain not sure either.

It all became worth it at six o'clock, the fourth time she stumbled into his room. Through painful, blurred eyes Nancy noticed something that perked her right up. Mark's breathing was less labored and his forehead less fiery. As she finished his arms for the second time, she saw that his waxy, "he'll be dead any minute" pallor had given way to real, flesh-alive color. And, as she collapsed on the chair and looked at him in the shadows of a dawning world, he took on an aura of peace. All the night's work, the lack of sleep, the immense relief came together, and she cried. Not many tears, but enough, and when she finally left the room and reset the timer, she knew that Mark was going to be all right.

By eight o'clock, when the morning was agonizingly bright, Nancy's relief had given way to a deep fatigue, her excitement had faded to inevitability, and her sense of purpose had become a desire to fold up and die. So, when she went in to give Mark a rubdown and found him sitting up in bed, eyes weary but no longer peering out from behind death's door, she gave him a small smile and said, "Good, I can stop."

"I can remember someone trying to drown me in ice—was that a dream?" he asked, still a bit of a groan in his voice, but obviously on the mend.

Nancy fell into the chair. It was her turn to groan. "We had to get your fever down. Want some breakfast?"

"I remember a waterfall—I was drowning under a cold waterfall."

"The shower—a cold shower." She almost sounded irritated. She didn't like sounding irritated. She wasn't. She'd never been happier seeing him alive and getting well, yet she sounded irritated.

"You gave me a cold shower?" he managed a taunting smile.

"No, Miss Prude didn't. Fletcher did," she answered, managing a little taunt in return. "I am glad you're feeling better. You are, aren't you?"

"Some—you mentioned breakfast."

"What do you want?" she asked, sensing distance from him.

"No oatmeal—I had a dream I was drowning in that too. Eggs, bacon, cereal, something like that."

"Coffee? He's got some brewing."

"I smell it. Cream and sugar."

"Anything else?"

"This isn't going to be too much trouble for you, is it?"

"What's that supposed to mean?"

"Nothing," he said, turning away as if talking to her at all was the supreme act of futility.

"No, what's that mean? I just got through losing my second night's sleep—last night saving your miserable life. I've . . ."

"Your favorite word, *I*."

"What's that supposed to mean? I've been—" She stopped self-consciously, trying to figure out how to get the self-centered little wretch to understand the work she'd done for him without her using *I*. It was hard with a brain swimming through a stormy fog bank.

"It means you're just like every other woman—selfish. You didn't care anything for me."

"I've been up all night . . ."

"You didn't care—you've never cared for me. If you cared you wouldn't have thrown out my stuff."

Exasperation brought a groan, a whine, and a stifled cry together. "But it was junk."

"It was junk just because you thought it was junk—"

"A natural conclusion—old Twinkie wrappers, old banana skins, an old can. Were those your treasures? Anyway, I didn't throw them away until after you left."

"You threatened and that's all that mattered. It was my car and you threatened me."

"It was junk—junk."

Suddenly the fight went out of him. His chest deflated, his eyes glazed, his hand rubbed a very weary forehead. "Okay, have it your own way—you will eventually anyway. It was junk."

"I don't understand this—it *wasn't* junk?"

"I don't want to talk . . ."

"You can't leave it like this. I can't take it. If I'd just gotten up from a good night's sleep, then I could take it. Now, I can't. I care too much about you to have you leave it like this."

"Like what?"

She gave him her whine-groan-stifled cry again. "Like what?" She leaned back, face twisted in frustration. "You act like I've driven a knife right through your liver. I'm up all night trying to keep you from dying, and I get the knife-through-the-liver routine."

"This is no routine. You hurt me—ruined my life—you did drive a knife through my liver."

"Don't you think you're being just a teensy little bit dramatic? What did I do?" The whine and the groan were gone, but the cry remained.

"Nothing."

"All this because I threw away an old oil can—why would anybody keep an old oil can?"

"Because, Miss Chickenlips, it was the last thing my uncle touched before he died!"

"What?" It took a moment to sink in but when it did, her heart became tight as a fist. "You're kidding, right?"

"No," he said, his voice centuries distant, "I'm not kidding. He was changing the oil in his car, and I was helping him when his heart gave out—died right there in front of me, the can in his hand. I've kept it for over twenty years."

"Why didn't you tell me? I would have never . . ." Nancy's intestines were suddenly a snake of knots.

"Now let's talk Twinkie wrappers. I waited all night for this girl once—Joanie Barnes—beautiful girl. To keep myself busy I ate Twinkies. I loved Joanie Barnes. She had eyes that cut right through me—right to my heart. Her parents hated me and one day they just sent her away—to an aunt's or something. I showed up for a date and waited all night for her eating Twinkies. I didn't save all the wrappers—just some."

"Why did they hate you?"

"I was eighteen and she was fourteen."

"Fourteen? Aren't there laws about that sort of thing?"

"We're talking memories here, not jurisprudence—I could talk to her. There are so few people in this world who will listen." That last statement was a lance aimed at Nancy.

"But you didn't tell me."

"You wouldn't have listened. That was my stuff. I don't have to tell you anything. I collect things. Some people take pictures, I collect things that remind me of other things. That was my life you threw away—my photo album."

"And the banana?"

"That was trash. But not the other things—well, most of the other things." His voice became more animated. "That box of crackers . . ."

"They were mildewed."

"I met this girl in the park. Never knew her name. I was juggling, and she came up and started talking to me. She was nice looking—not really beautiful but really nice. She had the crackers and ate them while I juggled. Afterward she stayed and we talked some more. I felt good around her. She left the box, and I never saw her again. I went back to that place at least fifteen straight times, but she never came back."

"But you didn't tell me," she muttered again. She moved to the edge of the chair and looked deeply at Mark. He looked so overwhelmingly sad. She finally said, "Mark, I had no idea. I'm so sorry—" Then something happened, a thought that started at the center of her heart, a disturbing earthquake of a thought, guilt, regret, and the reason why. "Oh, Lord, it's happened again," she whispered.

"What's happened again?" Mark asked.

"I'm so sorry, Mark," she felt her thumb working her locket, her heart about to explode, tears waiting in the wings of her eyes. "I have to go—please forgive me, Mark. It happened again . . ."

"What happened again—Nancy?" As she ran from the room, she heard a voice of frustration call out, "Give Maureen O'Hara a rub for me, too, while you're at it."

Chapter Sixteen

I t hung there before her eyes with clarity yet by such a thin thread
that she thought if she breathed, the thread would break and she
would be left with only the immense feeling of guilt.

But clarity belonged not so much to what hung there but to who
placed it—the Lord, the Spirit, her Christ, the one who had loved
her enough to shed his blood for her, who had sweat blood in the
Garden for her, who had agonized as nails plunged through his
flesh, one hammer blow at a time, who, before the dawn of time,
had determined to make her his own. She knew God was there
because in a single beat of her heart he'd revealed himself by showing her the immense gap that existed between her love for others
and his love for her.

She clawed through her purse and found her New Testament.
Matthew—Matthew, yes, 25—ah, there it was—Matthew 25:35.
She read hungrily. Before she knew it she was on the back porch
overlooking the lake, the brittle morning chill still in the air, frost
lacing the fallen leaves. But she saw none of that. She sank into a
chair, set the Bible down, a huge weight bending her shoulders.

In these verses the Lord identifies those who love him as those
who minister to others: visit the sick, feed the hungry, minister to
those in prison—treat the infected sores of dirty, lost little girls in
small mountain communities . . .

The memory of the nameless child haunted Nancy again. Those
large searching eyes, those dirty cheeks, that lifeless expression
—they all gazed up at her. And the sore—the festering sore. Just a
little soap and water, just a little caring, just a little of herself left
behind in the little town—Harbor View, was it?—yes. What was the
little girl's name? She'd never know now. In a single thoughtless

moment Nancy became part of the world that had victimized that child.

The child's face faded and the face of the waitress in the coffee shop appeared. Nancy felt the discomfort all over again. There was little doubt that the woman had overstepped propriety—she had assumed the untrue and had assaulted them. But lurking restlessly behind that was a very troubled person. Something had driven her to behave as she did. Something Nancy could have taken on herself, lovingly, empathetically. After all, Nancy was no stranger to trauma—no stranger to doing things she later regretted. She could have asked what was wrong. She could have probed, helped. Instead the woman was left with a half-eaten Snickers, not a listening ear. Nancy had done this to a fellow believer!

Then there was Mark. She'd stayed up all night with him, worried over him and done all the things that showed she cared. But those were the simple things—just time and sweat, and she couldn't have left him to smolder and die. When it came to putting herself out, putting his needs before the comfort of her own, trying to understand who he was and what drove him, she'd failed. And he'd suffered for it.

She hadn't cared for any of them.

Yet wasn't it love that had kept her from strangling Mark several times, that took her out into the rain to help him change the tire?

It was, she replied defensively to the voice that whispered within her.

Wasn't it love that kept her on the road to her father? Wasn't it love that made her want to overcome her hate for him, her desire to see him rotting alone somewhere, paying penny by penny for the countless wrongs he'd done her? Wasn't it love that wanted to forgive him and present him with the greatest of gifts? *Sure, it was*, she chided the voice.

But, the voice countered,—*that's easy. Will you be there when he really needs you? Will you be there for him if he offends you again? Will you put his needs above your desire for justice? Will you be there for him like I was there for you? While you were yet a sinner, I died for you.*

Nancy looked out toward the lake. A wedge of geese clipped the distant horizon. "Yes, I will," Nancy replied.

Her head dipped, and a wordless prayer took wing—a prayer of feelings, and longings, of unfathomable thanksgiving, and unintelligible sound. Her heart prayed, longing for forgiveness. She had not loved. She had turned away from those whom the Lord had brought to her, who needed her, and in doing so she'd offended the Lord. So often he had loved her, revealed himself gently, supporting, correcting, providing, nurturing, carrying her along—so often. And she'd let him down.

I'll never leave you nor forsake you, said the voice. The words were a gentle mist easing over and enveloping her consciousness—cleansing words, words of undying love and support, words that would never fail, words that gained strength and flowed through her like a surging tide lapping at every hidden bay. For the first time in her life Nancy truly knew what they meant. She was forgiven—a forgiveness that was truly miraculous, for she knew it spanned the infinite gulf that separated her unworthiness from Christ's goodness.

Now, in the middle of this forest, overlooking a nameless lake, this strong, faithful God cradled her in her Father's arms; now Nancy knew she must be faithful to him as he'd been faithful to her.

She was to walk beside him. Like blind Bartimaeus, she was to follow Jesus along the way. She could do nothing to undo the past, but there was a future lying directly before her. A large part of that future lay back there in the guest room.

She paused in the guest room's open doorway as if to enter would be violating Mark once too often. "I did a terrible thing to you," she said to him. "Please forgive me."

Mark let out a whispering sigh as if to say she was making too much of it. "You thought it was trash—who wouldn't have thought it was trash? I guess my memories were partly trash anyway."

"No," she protested, taking a seat on the edge of his bed. "I didn't consider you. I didn't even try to understand. I didn't care. I didn't love you like I should."

"You didn't love me?"

"Mark, I'm really sorry."

"Love?"

"Please, forgive me."

"Love?"

"Will you stop that? Forgive me, please."

"Love?"

"Mark!" Irritation snuck in. "You just can't take sincerity, can you? I really don't know why I care about you."

"Love?"

"Yes, love," she whispered, frightened that God might hear. "I don't know why. But I sort of care for you." She stepped away from Mark and glanced toward the door. "One thing I do know is that I'm not supposed to—not this way, anyway."

His head cocked like a puppy's hearing a strange sound. "What are you saying?"

"I don't know," she said, a frustrated hand going to her forehead, then waving a palm at him. "Listen, I'm just tired. When I'm tired I do and say strange things—very strange things."

"Are you saying loving me is strange?"

"At this particular moment I can't think of anything stranger. It's actually too bizarre for The Far Side." She took a step toward the door. "I'm very sorry I did what I did to you. Please believe that. But right now I need sleep."

"Nancy," Mark called to her, his voice gentle, "I'm sorry too."

"You? Why?"

"For driving you away just now. I guess I don't handle sincerity very well."

"Maybe we're both—" But she didn't finish. She wasn't sure why; maybe it was because she noticed her thumb working her locket nervously. Maybe she suddenly hated her dependence on it and wanted to throw it away—yet maybe the thought of doing so was too frightening to consider seriously. Or maybe it was because she remembered something. "What did you say before about Maureen O'Hara?"

Mark straightened. "Well . . ."

"What did you mean by that?"

"Nothing—really nothing."

"When did you—while I was asleep? You—while I was asleep?" Now it was Nancy who felt violated—but only a little. Why didn't she mind?

"I just wanted to know why you cared so much about it. Why Maureen O'Hara?"

For a moment Nancy saw Mark's wall crumble, saw his hand reach out to learn something about her. People learn about what they care about, and she truly liked the idea of his caring. But another wave of weariness broke over her, and she knew his question would take too much emotional energy to answer. "Not now," she said and stepped toward the door. "I'm beat. I'm very glad you're feeling better—now it's my turn to sleep."

She'd told Fletcher earlier about the night and how Mark was mending and how she really needed sleep. So when she emerged from the room, drooping and exhausted, he suggested that she lie down. She didn't need the suggestion repeated. Still in her clothes, she patted Hamster and Naomi's heads, pulled the blanket over her, and planted her head deeply in the pillow. And instantly started to worry.

She couldn't believe how wishy-washy she'd been. Here she'd promised the Lord she was going to follow in his footsteps, walk alongside him, be everything she was supposed to be, and then only a few seconds later she was in Mark's room professing love for him—a non-Christian bozo. She started to fixate on how they didn't have anything in common and what Sunday mornings would be like—Mark with his hangover and her with her Bible and how disciplining the kids would be difficult because he'd be too lax or too strict and she'd be just right . . .

She remembered dreaming—a waterfall rushing—no, a plane swooping over her as she relaxed in a fishing boat—the growl of a motorcycle. The motorcycle was real. She woke to the noise out front. She could hear the grind of gravel beneath its wheels. When the engine died, she heard voices—agitated voices—and soon Fletcher came through the front door from the porch and moved with quick, agitated steps to stairs that led to a lower level. A few minutes later the motorcycle engine roared to life again and after fading away it returned. It growled loudly outside, was gunned once, then roared away.

She thought about her kids and how they'd be so confused by Mark's lack of discipline and her firm, godly hand that they might run away and join a motorcycle gang and get snake tattoos.

When she woke at around noon, the memory of the motorcycle was little more than a fading impression—even when she saw Fletcher sitting at the kitchen table, two pistols dismantled in front of him, a cleaning kit between them. "Sleep well?" he asked, pushing a cleaning rod with a cloth patch through one of the barrels.

Nancy nodded. "Going hunting?"

"Maybe later," he said, smiling. But the smile didn't seem real. "Lunch?"

"I'll check on Mark. Maybe he'll want some too."

"How much better is he?"

"I'll take his temperature—we'll find out." Nancy sensed there was more to his question than curiosity.

When she opened the door Mark stirred, and by the time she stood over him with the thermometer he was awake, and narrow, sleepy eyes looked up at her. "How you feeling?" she asked.

"You woke me to ask?"

"Temperature," she said, pushing the glass tube between his lips. "Nod if you want lunch."

He grabbed the thermometer and took it out. "I smelled sandwiches yesterday."

"He makes good ones," she said. "Now put that thermometer back."

A few minutes later she saw that his temperature was nearly normal. "I think we'll be heading out of here soon," she told him.

"Maybe not. I'm safer here."

"That may be true. You're still weak. Maybe we'll stay here 'til the morning."

"That'll give you time to read my screenplay."

Nancy groaned. "Three pages wasn't enough, eh?"

"Now that you've professed your true feelings for me . . ."

"Watch it, Speedbump, I wasn't responsible. But I'll bring ol' Skinned Knuckles in."

"*Brass* Knuckles," he corrected.

"Whatever." She set the thermometer on the end table. "He's got just about every conceivable lunch meat. What kind of sandwich do you want?"

"Any tomatoes?"

"This is November on a mountain—ketchup will have to do."

"Then surprise me."

She chortled evilly. "Now there's a challenge."

"I didn't mean to upset you by looking in the locket," Mark injected when she was about halfway to the door.

"Do you say these things for maximum effect or what?"

"No."

"I think you do." Then she smiled, an ember of warmth behind it. "We'll talk about it someday. But all you had to do was ask to see it."

"Bologna."

"What?"

"I want bologna—mayo and ketchup."

"Oh, okay."

Mark slept after lunch, and Nancy settled in to reading the play. By page 8 she wished the play were already on television so she could turn it off. But it wasn't and the more she read, the closer she came to that terrible moment when she'd have to tell the anxious author the truth. The play stank—worse than stank—it was horrible, even pornographic. Every other word was filthy; there was sexual innuendo throughout and two very torrid scenes that were so explicit that she couldn't finish them. Ten pages from the end, and faced with another scene of reckless debauchery, she set it down.

She needed air.

The afternoon sky was lifelessly gray and it turned the lake the same. The forest that surrounded it was void of leaves and seemed an army of gnarled, black forks. They appeared to be anxiously waiting to skewer winter when it fell.

Suddenly a sound she didn't expect—would never have expected. It was the muffled spitting of what had to be a machine gun down below, near the lake—out of view. She leaned over the wooden railing and craned her neck to see, but the trees obscured everything.

There it was again. Three quick bursts of ten, maybe twenty rounds each—then silence. Nancy leaned out further and nearly lost her balance. Pulling back, she waited for the next burst. It didn't come.

Maybe we shouldn't wait to leave, she thought. But maybe she hadn't heard what she'd thought she'd heard. Maybe the echoes were playing tricks. Maybe it was just an outboard motor or something—sound was only sound, and it could change with distance and be distorted by things in-between.

A machine gun seemed so out of place up here.

No. It couldn't have been a machine gun.

But it sounded like one.

Nancy waited a little longer and felt the smooth tin locket in her hand. A hawk circled above the lake, then came to rest on the tallest tree on a narrow finger of land that jutted into the gray water.

There was no more sound, save the clattering of tree limbs all around.

She resumed her place in the chair inside, read another page of Mark's script, then gave up on it. It had gotten every bit as bad as she expected. But that wasn't the only reason she'd set it down. What she heard *had* been a machine gun—she was sure of it.

With renewed determination she went back to the back porch. She walked the length of it, peering down through the trees with each step, looking for something—anything to confirm or deny what she'd heard.

When she saw and heard nothing but the wind rattling through the trees, she straightened. Five Canadian geese, their beautiful dark bodies and white spotted heads, winged in. Gliding to rest on the water near the end of the dock, they honked to one another and began leaving gentle V-shaped wakes behind them.

Suddenly one honked loudly, the sound a frenzied screech. Immediately two others reached out with anxious wings, their legs churning beneath, their necks stretched like javelins. The moment they were airborne, the machine gun spit again, and both birds, caught in the same sweep of bullets, one then the other, lurched, their bodies torn and twisted, feathers blown into a grotesque halo about them as they were thrown from flight into the lake. As their battered bodies floated lifelessly, the other geese honked and flapped frantically. Disoriented, they scattered.

Nancy stood transfixed. Hope and horror taking voice, "Come on—come on," she encouraged the geese and kept up the rhythm of words as if they could affect the life struggle below.

One goose that had been paddling and flapping back toward the dock suddenly decided to fly for it. Wings flapped, legs churned, and he lifted into the air. The instant he was airborne, the bullets spit, but they missed, and the bird flapped off.

Nancy was just appreciating the sense of relief, when the one that had headed straight out toward the center of the lake decided the time was right. Like the others, it began its takeoff, webbed feet splashing wildly, its voice a cry. The machine gun fired, and the wake behind the bird erupted in several spouts as the bullets struck.

The goose rose, and there was another burst. The bird escaped unscathed.

The last goose remained on the surface, paddling madly, afraid, honking, its neck outstretched.

The machine gun fired and spouts erupted near her. The goose cried frantically and paddled harder. The gun fired again, and the spouts sprang up closer. Suddenly the goose could take no more. It began its ascent, feet paddling, wings beating against chilled air. Another blast of bullets, the water spouted, the goose flew as hard as it could. The machine gun fired—missed—fired again, and the goose exploded—hit. Feathers and parts blew out from the twisted, lifeless rag of a body, the neck limp and whipping about as it was blown off path and fell into the water. It bobbed there for a minute or two, then was swallowed by the water—as the other two had been.

"Target practice," Nancy heard behind her. Mark stood there, his blanket wrapped around him, his eyes riveted on the lake.

"He was cleaning two pistols this morning."

"Did you hear the argument out front?" Mark moved to the railing and looked over the side.

"With the biker?"

"I was in the bathroom. It's hazy, but they were going at it pretty hard—threats going back and forth."

"Threats? Maybe we ought to leave."

"I'll gather up my stuff. I'm still feeling weak, but I think he's practicing for a reason."

Nancy searched Mark's face for a moment, then said, "I'm truly sorry, Mark—that I did that to you."

"We'll talk about that later too."

Nancy looked off toward the lake. "He has been good to us. I hate to just leave."

"Write him a note. I'm getting dressed. Get your stuff."

Nancy nodded and went quickly inside; Mark followed her and went to the bedroom. She donned her jacket, made sure her dwindling money supply was still in her purse, then checked around the room for anything that might be hers. She didn't know why—she didn't have anything. She found notepaper near the phone and wrote:

Dear Mr. Harris:

Mark's feeling better, and with all that machine gun fire we think we probably ought to be moving on. We can't thank you enough for your hospitality.

God bless you.

Nancy and Mark

It felt strangely right signing it that way, and Nancy looked at the two names for a moment before setting the note on the kitchen table.

Mark emerged from the bedroom. He'd been moving quickly to get dressed and gather up his things, and he looked a little winded when he joined her.

"You set?" he asked.

"Come on, Hamster, Naomi," she called to the dogs. Hamster rose up and Naomi bounced over to Mark.

"Okay, let's get out of here."

The Pacer was where they had left it, and they were quickly behind the wheel and pulling onto the road that had brought them to Fletcher Harris.

"Did you hear any of the argument?" Nancy asked.

Mark shook his head, concentrating on the road that wound down the other side of the mountain.

"What if we're jumping to the wrong conclusion and he's just a nice guy somebody's mad at?"

"You mean like those somebodys?" Mark said, pointing off in the distance. Somewhere down the mountain, now only a snake of trembling black, was a long line of black motorcycles heading up the road toward them.

Chapter Seventeen

"How many are there?" Nancy leaned forward, her chin nearly on the dashboard.

"A lot," Mark said, easing up on the gas pedal.

Nancy's eyes never left the string of motorcycles that wound up the hill toward them. Maybe a mile or two away, they snaked from fold to fold in the mountainside, sometimes half disappearing at a time, but they always reappeared in their relentless climb.

"I count thirty," Nancy finally said.

"That's quite a gang."

"Maybe it's just a club or something."

"Think so?" Mark asked rhetorically. Then he pointed to the right. "How about over there—we'll be hidden." He pulled the car off the road, they bounced a bit over some rough terrain and came to a stop behind a thick stand of brush. Through the tangle of limbs they could see the road only slightly but well enough to see the cycles pass.

The engine silent, they waited. Nancy felt a prayer sneaking into her head and, after she said it she remained forward on the edge of the seat, her elbows resting on the dashboard, her chin on her hands. But it didn't rest there, it seemed to hover anxiously above her fists. "I'm not sure I've ever been in a situation like this—I mean, this is dangerous," she said.

"Me too. But, then, that's par for this trip," Mark said, eyes on the road and beads of sweat breaking out on his forehead. "I think we'll be all right here," he said, head bobbing around, making sure they were covered from every angle.

Nancy opened the window a crack and immediately heard the rumble growing. Soon the rumble became thunder. Nancy ducked down in her seat and peered through the tangle of branches. A few minutes later the thunder changed; it became the roar of engines—individual engines—and they began to pulse past them one by one. These motorcycles were all low-slung choppers, and the shadows astride them were large and threatening. Clad in jeans and denim jacket, head wrapped in a red bandana, a large horseshoe insignia on his back, each man planted his eyes on the chopper ahead of him.

Nancy's dry throat rasped as she swallowed with each passing bike. Nancy counted twenty-seven swallows. Each biker looked more threatening than the one before. "Harris must have done something pretty bad," Nancy said, when the thirteenth one hammered by.

"I hope he's made enough coffee."

When the last one had disappeared around a mountain fold, Mark glanced at Nancy, then started the car and eased onto the road again.

While Mark drove as quickly as he could down the mountain, Nancy kept her eyes in back of them. But she found with the frequent turns, she was beginning to feel sick so she turned back, eyes front. "Can you see them in your rearview mirror? I'm feeling a little woozy."

Mark glanced up. "A little—sometimes better than—oops."

"What?"

"I think we have a problem. They spotted us."

Nancy forgot her dizziness and turned completely around. Two of the cycles blasted down the mountain roaring after them. Fortunately they had a long distance to cover before they would reach the Pacer; unfortunately they were covering it quickly.

Mark accelerated, but he'd already been going faster than the muddy road allowed. After nearly careening into a ditch, he slowed. The choppers gained rapidly, but the Pacer had a knack for going downhill, and Mark pushed it to the limit. That only meant that the choppers gained a little less rapidly.

"They'll catch us soon," Nancy cried.

"The highway's ahead," Mark shouted back, as he strained to follow the serpentine road.

Sure enough, a state highway loomed ahead. Because they were approaching it, the road they were on suddenly turned to blacktop.

The moment it did, Mark slammed the accelerator to the floor and, before the choppers could reach them, he climbed the on ramp.

The choppers followed. The men were so close that Nancy could see their faces—sun darkened, bearded, thick, meaty brows, teeth clenched, long hair tied by the red bandanas—everything about them meant business.

Mark roared down the highway now, but the choppers no longer had curves to slow them down. Mark pushed the car as fast as it would go, but that wasn't as fast as the Harleys. With the growl becoming a deafening thunder, Nancy saw the meanest looking of the two motion the other to pull around to the side of the car. When they split to come up along both sides, Nancy saw the same one reach under his denim jacket and pull out a pistol.

"They've got guns!" Nancy warned anxiously.

"I'm not good at this," Mark said, glancing at the rearview, his eyes afraid to stay there too long.

There was little traffic—few witnesses.

Suddenly Mark saw a red light far back, blazing and pulsing between the choppers. It belonged to a state trooper's car. Mark's chest collapsed as he heaved a huge sigh of relief as the bikers saw it too.

Nancy yelled excitedly when the guns were pushed back in their belts. As the state trooper gained, the cyclists gunned their Harleys and shot by them as if the Pacer had been standing still. Nancy noticed that one of them had a round Indian war shield, the outline of an Indian brave on it, strapped to the back of his roll bar. The moment they were in front of him, Mark released the gas pedal, and the Pacer slowed. He pulled off to the side of the road and waited. He expected the trooper to roar past him and chase the choppers. But he didn't. The green car pulled up in back of the Pacer, and the green-clad trooper with a flat, wide-brimmed hat got out.

"He's going to give me a ticket?" Mark exclaimed, shocked.

"No, that can't be—open the window—tell him—"

But the trooper was already there. He took off dark glasses from a hawk nose and peered down at Mark who rolled down the window and peered back up at him. "You're not going to chase those guys? They were going to kill me."

"License, please."

Mark was dumbfounded. "They were going to kill us—there's this gang . . ."

"License. Looked to me like you were going to kill yourselves, racing them like that."

"Officer." Nancy tried respect, seeing that Mark was about to lose it.

"Just give me your license."

"But they were chasing us," Nancy said as Mark gave up and reached into his back pocket. But before the officer could take the license, he straightened and Nancy saw him step back as if trying to get a better look at something.

"What's happened?" Mark asked.

But the officer said nothing. He stepped back further, stood still for an instant, then ran to his car. Nancy turned around as did Mark, and they saw him throw open his passenger door and reach inside for his radio mike.

"Something's going on," Mark said, puzzled.

At that moment they both heard a muffled blast.

Scrambling from the Pacer, they stood beside it transfixed. At the crest of a hill that stood among a whole rumple of hills, right where Fletcher Harris lived, there was a sudden eruption of flames and a high-arcing shower of flaming debris—all of it blown skyward by a tremendous explosion. As they watched, the top of the mountain turned into a flaming jaw, opening to devour the sky, a crimson tongue of flame lapping hungrily at it.

Mark and Nancy forgotten, the officer spoke frantically into the mike. After a flurry of words, he threw himself behind the wheel and made a wide U-turn across four lanes of traffic and a weeded median and headed in Harris's direction.

Nancy watched the trooper peel off the highway and head up the same mountain road they'd just been chased down. Then she followed the mountain to its top where half of it seemed engulfed in flames—the jaws had widened, and now huge, crimson flames lapped at the clouds, black billows staining the blue. A fire truck passed, sirens blaring, on its mad dash down the other side of the highway.

"Can you believe that?" Mark shook his head, befuddled. He glanced at his watch. "It was about three-thirty when we left—it's four-oh-five now. We missed all that by a half hour."

"That sure looks like Fletcher's place."

"Time to go," Mark announced with mixed anxious purpose.

They climbed back in and Mark sprayed gravel getting back on the highway. But after only a few hundred yards, Mark pulled off the highway and stopped in the back of a Shell gas station.

"What now?" Nancy asked.

"We've seen them—the motorcycle gang. They're not just going to let us go. They may be waiting for us up ahead. We'll stay off the main highway for a while."

"Works for me," Nancy agreed, glancing worriedly over her shoulder.

The map they bought at the Shell station showed an alternate route that essentially paralleled the highway. They found it after only a couple of wrong turns, then discovered a local radio station. As they drove along the country roads, sometimes crisscrossing the highway, the drama they'd nearly been part of on the mountain unfolded on the news. As it did, Nancy listened with increasing disbelief.

"A gunsmith for organized crime?" Mark winced, after one news report went into the findings of the state's organized crime bureau.

"Why'd he take us in? He seemed so nice." Nancy leaned back and shook her head. The reports continued to pile up on one another and before long a clearer story emerged. The owner of the cabin was called Fletcher Harris. ("At least he didn't lie about that," Nancy said, still feeling a sense of betrayal.)

Harris had angered a chapter of Satan's Army, a powerful motorcycle gang, because he wouldn't work with them. They came to call. Harris either accidentally or purposefully ignited a large stash of explosives in the basement of his home, causing real damage to the gang—at least three deaths and a score of injuries. Harris remained missing.

"We'd be part of the dead right now," Mark finally said.

"I bet he got away."

"We could have been killed. Ten minutes more in that place— seconds if you think about the chase. That was close—and you took us there," Mark's eyes were right on Nancy. "Do all the people you love die of fever, or explosion, or getting trampled by cows?"

"Only the truly obnoxious ones," she shot back. Then she said, "The Lord's watching out for us—he's in control." But even though she said it, she was beginning to wonder. *Lord*, she thought, *you cut it very close that time.*

"Makes you wonder how long our 'luck' will hold," Mark said, anxious thumbs tapping on the steering wheel. Then he added, his eyes very tired, "I'm really not up to this." Sweat beaded down his chin. "I'm feeling weak again. You know, we were sitting on enough explosives to blow us—or at least pieces of us—all the way to California." He held his hand in the air, flat, palm down—it trembled noticeably. "I need a break. You drive for a while."

"He seemed so nice—until those geese—if he hadn't killed those geese that way . . . mafia gunsmith," Nancy mused. She whispered, "Thanks, Lord," and then tagged on, "You, too, geese." She repeated another whisper that the Lord was in control. Just saying it again was reassuring. He really was in control—she knew that. And yet, when she glanced in the rearview mirror and saw the black smoke boiling on the distant horizon, she suddenly felt the way Dorothy might have the moment she lost the yellow brick road.

Driving definitely had its advantages. While Mark tried to sleep, frequently groaning and tossing, Nancy chose the speed (the limit), the lane (the slow which was often the only), and the radio station (the quiet). It felt good to be in control again, even if it wasn't for real and although she always had one eye on the rearview mirror in case the bikers should suddenly appear, she drove feeling reasonably relaxed. The Pacer was an old, funny-shaped car, but it drove easily and even all the squeaks and rattles didn't bother her all that much anymore.

By avoiding the main highway, she was also treated to beautiful countryside. Ready for winter, there seemed to be an unusual peace about it—an expectant silence in the farms and small towns and roadside shops. People drove more slowly than she even wanted to at times, and now and again she'd find herself in back of a tractor or something even bulkier snailing along. During those times, when the smells had a chance to catch up to her, the area lost a bit of its charm. Deep, rich clouds of manure smells were everywhere. Mark had been sleeping soundly for the first time in a long while and suddenly, from nowhere—seemingly from a world of rolling hills and stands of naked trees—came a rancid, billowing odor that engulfed them and caused him to wake—nose tight, eyes narrowed, mouth clamped shut. He glared at her as if the odor were her fault.

Not long after that she saw the billboard—for a Christian radio station.

She fumbled with the radio dial and found it. A hymn rose up and filled the car, and it brought a therapeutic renewal.

"Oh, come on," Mark suddenly said, rolling onto his back. "That other stuff was bad enough."

"The driver chooses," Nancy affirmed.

"Then pull over."

"No, you're still tired. You need your rest."

"I don't need it that much."

"Go to sleep and you'll never hear it."

He groaned and stayed that way for a minute or two, but when a sermon started he rolled back.

"You believe that stuff, eh?"

"Yes—believing wouldn't hurt you, either."

"It'd change my whole personality."

"That would be bad?"

"I wouldn't be this fun-lovin' guy anymore," he said, eyes still closed. "I'd have to go around serious all the time—'tsk'ing at everyone who's having the fun I want to have—hey, I have an idea. You can pay me to use my radio."

"What?"

"Sure. I need some money so I don't go around stealing candy bars from strange and possessed waitresses, and you want to listen to your superstitious nonsense."

"When we started this trip you said you wouldn't make fun of my—"

"Okay, your—whatever."

"How much would this radio rental be?"

Mark thought. "Two bucks a half hour."

"Two dollars—a half? That's more than a movie costs!"

"Seems like a reasonable figure to me—after all I have to listen to that drivel too."

"What about three dollars for two hours?"

"Two hours? That's more than I can take."

"Two dollars for an hour."

"Money in advance?"

"A dollar now, a dollar at the end of the hour."

"Done."

She grabbed a dollar from her purse and handed it to him.

"I figure you have twenty minutes left on this time slot."

"Oh, no!" Nancy protested. "The hour starts right now."

"Pull over, Chickenlips—deal's off. Here's your buck back."

"I'll go for forty minutes, but no less."

Mark sighed but nodded, then glanced at his watch. "Forty minutes. It'll be dark before long. How's the gas?"

"About empty."

"Me too."

"In about forty minutes we'll stop for dinner," Nancy said, feeling she'd won the negotiation. When she stopped a few minutes later for gas, she even kept the radio on while he pumped it. It was so comforting to hear a hymn and to hear Jesus' name mentioned— it told her she wasn't alone, that there were other believers out there.

Back on the road, Mark remained silent, curled up as comfortably as he could, and seemed to be listening to the praise music and hymns and the occasional brief message. The messages were gentle, too, like Pastor Bevel's back home, filled with the love of the Lord—something Nancy needed to hear. Only once, after a particularly long message, did Mark say anything, and that was under his breath with his head turned, "Hogwash."

"Not to me," Nancy defended, feeling strong.

But soon afterward, the station began to evaporate to static. They were out of range.

"Too bad. All gone." Mark smiled and flipped the dial.

"How much time was that?"

"What's the difference? It's gone."

"How much?"

Mark glanced at his watch, "Twenty-two minutes."

"Then I've paid for eighteen more minutes."

"That's not my fault."

"Give me my money back."

"No way, Chickenlips," Mark said. "I sold you time on the radio. Not a particular station. Just the time."

"Then I've got eighteen minutes left. Turn it off."

"Off?" Mark looked at her like the word didn't exist.

"Off."

Mark hesitated but must have come to the conclusion that fair was fair and the radio went off.

Now, except for the whine of the tires, the incessant rattling inside, and the dogs snoring, there was silence. Mark rolled over toward the window, and the countryside faded to gray.

Nancy thought about her father—that last night when, like Mark's guard sometimes, his guard had come down and she'd missed an opportunity to love him. She'd made his birthday cake as a peace offering—peace she really didn't feel like offering. They had had a minor skirmish that morning, but there'd been so many of them lately that the scars were beginning to add up to the wounds one might expect from a major battle. But it was his birthday and an opportunity for a truce.

German chocolate cake. Her mother's recipe and her father's favorite—with burnt coconut frosting and served with French vanilla ice cream. A wonderful cake—more than he deserved. He'd come home drunk. Not roaring drunk, but the day had ended early for him, and he'd gone to his favorite bar for the remainder of the afternoon. Normally he would have been late getting home—early enough to say good night but late enough so he wouldn't have to spend time with her. But that night he floated in at about seven. Nancy remembered trying to hug him. Although he had a belly on him, when she wrapped her arms around him, his chest and back were bony and unmoving—it was like hugging a stop sign. After a reheated dinner of something or other, Nancy went into the kitchen to bring out the cake. He followed her in to get a beer and when she had turned her back to get out the ice cream, he nudged the small utility table the cake was on. All she heard was the splat and the cake dish shatter and her father swearing.

She turned to see something she did not remember ever seeing before: the look of deep remorse on her father's face. Maybe it was that touch of weakness in him that gave her the courage to explode. Whatever feelings he might have allowed to surface were lost in the outpouring of her rage. She looked at the cake, not at him, and screamed and stomped her feet. She remembered what a sense of release she felt while she screamed, yet how nothing was relieved—

the ache was still there when she finally stormed from the room, then from the house.

The next morning she returned for her clothes. She'd tiptoed around his snoring form lying comatose on the couch with a near-empty bottle of Jim Beam on the coffee table, retrieved some of her things, then fled to her grandmother's.

If she'd only been more patient—if she'd only seen the open door instead of giving way to the fire within her. She suddenly wanted to hug her father again, even if there was no response.

"When do we cross the Mississippi?" Mark asked, taking a long stretch standing beside the car.

Nancy had found a small diner and, testing her wings as Pacer-pilot, turned in without waking him. Now they both stood outside the car eyeing one another over the roof. "The Mississippi? You're kidding, right? We crossed that long ago—before the Ozarks."

"Oh, no. We missed Graceland too."

"Graceland?"

"He's still alive, you know—in a witness program someplace."

"Maybe you could join him. With all you know about geography you could both get lost."

"Be nice and there's no charge for the radio."

"I wouldn't pay you anyway. How you feeling?" she asked, surveying the small, ramshackle diner.

"Better—I feel pretty good, actually," Mark said. The rhythmic whine of honky-tonk suddenly reached them as the door opened and a farmer in a denim coat and sheepskin collar stepped into the cool night. His wife followed, putting on her gloves. The music ended when the door slammed behind them. "I'm not sure if I like that stuff or not."

"We came here for the food."

"That might be a little iffy too."

"Well, let's find out."

The inside was everything a small country diner should be—the music was too loud, the tables clean but just a bit wobbly, burnt-red Formica everywhere wood wasn't, and an old Wurlitzer jukebox blared at them from the far wall. Pictures of picnics and men holding huge fish hung intermixed with a collection of old license plates in back of the counter.

Mark chuckled. "Makes you wonder if they're not out front right now stealing ours."

"The gas is eating into our reserves so go easy. We were getting better mileage on the highway."

Mark nodded. "Tomorrow we'll go back to it again. I doubt if they followed us. We couldn't tell the police any more than they already know."

"He was such a nice guy—but those geese . . ."

There were only a couple of people in the place, which made finding an empty table easy. They both thought that one far from the jukebox was best.

The food was okay, the waitress pleasant, and when Mark finished his second cup of decaf he leaned back, looking quite content. "So what'd you think of my screenplay?" he asked, a toothpick making its way around his teeth.

Off guard, Nancy thought quickly. "I haven't finished it yet," she said, hoping that would get her off the hook. She didn't want to have this conversation, especially not here, in front of strangers.

"You finished most of it."

"Most." She shrugged. "But not all."

"What do you think so far?"

She fumbled uncomfortably with her napkin. "I want to wait until I get the full impact."

"You're avoiding—you didn't like it."

"Do we have to talk about this now?"

"Was it too hard-boiled for you—too real?"

"There are people here."

"Too much like real life—that's it. You religious fanatics turn your back on real life—you live in the clouds. It's too . . ."

"It's too horrible," she said, getting some revenge.

Mark leaned back, probably deciding whether to be hurt or pull one of the big fish from the pictures and slap her with it. "It's just too much for someone like you."

"Way too much," Nancy played with her finger, the cork on her rage starting to loosen.

"It's too hard-hitting—it'd be rated R."

"For Revolting."

Mark was getting heated, and Nancy immediately knew she'd gone too far. She softened. "Listen, Mark. You're right. It's not what I enjoy—but let's take it objectively. The characters are one dimensional, the plot is old and—" She glanced around to see if anyone was listening. No one was. "There's nothing beautiful about the way your characters make love—you shouldn't show it anyway—but it's just sex—dirty, sleazy."

"So that's where the hang-up is," he said loudly, not as concerned about people hearing him. "It's sex."

"Will you keep your voice down?"

"See—you're ashamed of sex."

"I am not ashamed of sex," she said uncomfortably. "I think it's wonderful. I look forward to it—I guess—when I'm married."

"How old are you now?"

"What's that got to do with anything?"

"You're what, twenty-four?"

"Yeah, twenty-four."

"And still . . ."

"If you say that I'll strangle you right here."

Mark immediately softened. "What did you think of the mother?"

Nancy found it a strange question. "The mother? She didn't figure in it much. I didn't even think about her."

"Really? I struggled with her. I wanted to put more of her in the story, then when I did, I'd cut it. Maybe I cut too much."

"With everyone jumping in and out of the bushes—"

"You take it all so lightly. But that's me in those pages. I worked for almost a year on that thing. When you reject—"

"No," Nancy said, leaning forward. "That's not you—you're not like that at all."

Mark wasn't listening. He'd drifted away as if she'd driven him out and he'd found a distant, safe haven. He drifted back. "Come on, let's get back on the road."

"Mark, I'm sorry I didn't like your screenplay."

"Well, you can't please everyone," he said, trying a smile and failing miserably.

"You want to drive?"

"I guess." He walked out while she paid, and when she joined him he was already behind the wheel, the engine running, a rock station growling from the dashboard.

It was going to be a long night.

Chapter Eighteen

Night clapped over them like a cup and their world shrank to black. The sky was black, the country on either side and in back was black, and the road ahead was lighted only by an occasional streetlight. Sometimes a farmhouse with exterior lights would open things up a bit, but most of the time the only light came from the front of the car. Although it lighted the road ahead and cast the winter-stripped trees in a ghostly gray, it did little to break up the black they drove through.

The road twisted irregularly, wandering here and there, sometimes crossing beneath the highway, sometimes heading far afield. Never more than two lanes, it was often pocked by huge potholes that they either swerved suddenly to miss or slapped over, jarring bones and teeth alike. It was difficult driving, and usually when faced with such an effort, Mark hunched over the steering wheel, his chin inches from it. But not this time.

He lay back in the seat, one hand on the wheel, his eyes half open. He was either tired or depressed or both and seemed to be growing more so by the minute. Had Nancy known he was going to crawl into a hole when she told him what she felt about the screenplay— "Mark's Mess," she named it to herself—she might have been more diplomatic. But he'd been acting with such assurance— getting them away from the mountain cabin, escaping the motorcyclists, keeping them safely on the road—that it never occurred to her that he'd climb back within himself quite so quickly. But now she could see his stifled energy dribbling away as the dark miles rolled beneath them.

What scared her was she cared. Normally she had little patience with people who hid themselves in fogs of depression. They never said what they meant, they found something negative in everything, and they slumped and grunted from place to place. Donna Kingston, back home, was like that sometimes. In general, such people were difficult to deal with and certainly no fun to be around. At times Nancy, too, dove into grand funks; and maybe that's why she had so little patience with them because she had less with herself. But Mark's depression brought out the mother in her, and her heart reached out to him. She wanted to work him out of it somehow.

She tried conversation, but no matter what she said, he responded with a single incoherent word or a nod or a grunt. She tried asking questions, but he answerd in the briefest, coldest way possible. She tried being happy—whistling even—but she suddenly missed her flute and found herself drifting away to whistle familiar flute tunes and forgetting about the depressing lump beside her. Finally she found herself just staring at Mark with long, evaluative looks.

After a few minutes of doing that, she realized it wasn't the depression that was getting to her. It was Mark himself, coupled with the now familiar question that played in her mind over and over again—how did she really feel about him? What part of her heart had he wormed his way into? It couldn't really be the center, could it? The more she examined her feelings, the more she realized that it didn't matter how she felt; the admonition was clear— "Do not become unequally yoked!"

In Washington, D.C., with the shortage of men around her there were few opportunities to get yoked—equally or otherwise. But now there was just good old, heathen Mark, and to care about him would only lead to hurt.

Did she love him?

No. Strong feelings, yes—but love? No. Love is when you can't get along without someone, and Nancy knew, beyond any doubt, that she could get along without Mark. Not only could she get along without him, but she probably would cherish every moment without him. And the thought of spending a lifetime with him? An hour was more than she could stand.

And yet . . .

When she thought about all those things was she evaluating the *real* Mark—the one who stepped out in the open occasionally? She wondered what it would be like to be cradled in the *real* Mark's arms, to drink in the *real* Mark's eyes, to have the *real* Mark be the one she always prayed for, the person she talked to and shared everything with. With that Mark those things might be possible. But he emerged so infrequently. If only he would stay put long enough to grab and hold on to.

She knew that Mark had a great capacity to love, to understand, to empathize—at least she thought he did—she was *sure* he had. Those were just the qualities she wanted and needed, had prayed continually for. And they all lived just in back of his emotional wall.

She slugged him in the shoulder.

"Ow! What's that for?"

"Are you there?"

"Where else?"

"Come on—come clean. What are you hiding from?"

"I suppose that means something."

"Whenever life's a little rough you jump behind your wall of self-pity and hide. What are you hiding from?"

"You nearly get us blown up and you have to ask that?"

"You blame me for that?"

"You chose the road—you stopped there in the first place. If I hadn't suggested we bail out you wouldn't be able to tell us right now from charred motorcycle parts."

"I was afraid you were dying."

"Better by fever than by fiery dismemberment."

"See what you do? When I try to be nice—"

"Slugging me and accusing me of sitting around pitying myself is being nice?"

"There you go. You're changing the subject."

"You nearly have pieces of us flying all over the state, and I'm on trial for changing the subject?"

"Nobody's on trial." Nancy groaned with immense frustration. "I just want to know you. Instead all I get are smart comments and—"

"You read my play. You know me. That was me—right there in those pages. You didn't like my play—you don't like me."

"That wasn't you."

"It was—that's me."

"All I want to do is understand—get close."

"I don't want you close. When you're close I end up in cow pastures being threatened by shotguns, with crazy women screaming at me in diners, escaping floods, getting away from mountain cabins just before they're blown sky-high, and, let us not forget, being chased—maybe still being chased—by some very bad guys. Close! I want you on one end of California and me on the other. And I want that soon."

Nancy felt a stab of hurt pierce her heart. It sounded like the *real* Mark saying it. "Do you really mean that?"

"Do chickens cluck? Do bears scratch?"

"Yeah. And do idiots drive Pacers?" She sighed. "We're going to end up fighting again."

"Only if you keep talking."

"All right, you win," she said, grabbing a dollar from her purse, wadding and throwing it at him. "I'm buying a half hour's worth." Then she reached over and angrily clicked off the radio.

But after a moment, when rattling and tire noise were the only sounds, Nancy saw Mark find the dollar between his legs, unwad it, and hand it back to her. "My treat," he said in a conciliatory tone.

"Thank you," Nancy responded, feeling an uneasy warmth return.

He gave her a shallow smile, and after a few more miles and sounding like some of the spark had returned, he said, "What say we make a little time before we shut down for the night?" He pointed to a small sign indicating Interstate 40.

It was getting on toward 9:30 P.M., so there were few cars on the road and Mark showed little regard for the speed limit. Nancy settled into the seat and massaged her locket for a time out of habit and was about to nod off when Mark came upon a couple of semis in the slow lane. Although they were moving at a pretty good clip, Mark's clip was faster. As he nosed ahead of the first one, his brows suddenly slammed together, and he took his foot off the gas and immediately dropped back.

"What?"

"They're between the trucks."

"The bikers?"

"Two—I only saw the front wheels but I don't want to take a chance." He let the trucks ramble ahead. Mark suddenly pointed to the glove compartment. "In there's a pair of binoculars—I use 'em at the Redskins' games."

Nancy grabbed them and pushed them to her eyes.

"What do you see?" Mark asked.

"It's them—they're rounding that curve up there—there's the Indian head on the back." She brought the binoculars down and returned them to the glove compartment.

"I'm not sure I like this," Mark said.

"Why would they still be after us? We couldn't tell the police any more than they already know."

"They don't know that—anyway, maybe they just want revenge." Mark looked up ahead. "There's an exit coming up. We'll take that and stop for the night. We'll let them get far ahead."

Nancy nodded and rubbed her locket and said an earnest prayer.

Mark pulled the car slowly onto the exit, one that proclaimed in small letters, Fort Baxter Army Base.

"That's handy—if they bother us tonight we'll call out the army."

Mark didn't stop right away. Now he bent over the steering wheel, his chin almost resting on it, his fingers fidgeting nervously, as he struggled with the black country road ahead.

Nancy felt the strings around her heart tighten, and she half-expected the motorcycles to be hiding behind trees and barns, expected them to leap out with shotguns blasting. Now that she'd seen what a machine gun can do, she pictured it doing it to her. She found that her prayers didn't quiet her, and she rubbed the locket and lay back in the seat, hoping to force rest.

That's when she saw her. "Isn't that girl a little young to be hitch-hiking?"

"If she were fifty she'd be too young to be hitching. I wish her luck."

The headlights splashed her ghost white. Walking backward, her thumb poised, she moved with an assurance of someone far more experienced than her twelve or so years permitted. Ragged, her long hair flared and hung in disarray and framed a child's face that now winced in the sudden light. Her crop top hung over just a hint of breasts. Somebody's ancient bell-bottoms were frayed and, like the little girl with the sore on her arm, she wore no jacket. She had to be freezing on a night like this.

"We'd better pick her up. I wouldn't want those Satan guys—"

"We're not going to pick up any hitchhiker," Mark pronounced, shaking his head in disbelief.

Not willing to pass up another opportunity to help, Nancy insisted, "She could end up raped or murdered."

"This is Arkansas not Baltimore. Anyway, we pick her up, and it could be us who end up murdered."

"She's no more than twelve. And she must be freezing out there."

"A midget terrorist."

"Stop."

"You have to be kidding. Everything that's happened to us has started just like this. And now you want me to pick up a hitchhiker?" Mark's head still wagged incredulously, but he fixed a gaze on Nancy. After shaking his head again, his fingers drumming, he pulled over onto the soft shoulder, near a wire fence and a little ahead of the girl. Then they both watched in the rearview mirror as she ran toward them.

Chapter Nineteen

Nancy saw it as God's opportunity to redeem herself, and her heart immediately reached out to the hard, little hitchhiker. The girl's eyes were dull and etched indelicately with dark mascara. The harshness of it made her face seem gaunt and dirty. Her clothes were as dirty as her eyes seemed to be and as ill-fitting as the mascara. Her tennis shoes were torn, worn, and the laces were loose and knotted where they'd broken. She wore no socks. But for all her obvious poverty, she pushed the boxes in the back aside, dislodged the dogs, and climbed into the backseat with the cockiness of wealth.

"I'm late gettin' home," she drawled after she'd glanced around the car appreciating the variety of stuff.

"How far?" Nancy asked.

"Couple miles," she replied. "Up ahead."

"I'm Nancy Bernard, and this is Mark Brewster," Nancy said, trying to sound as friendly as she could. "What's your name?"

"I'm in a hurry," the girl snapped. "Can't we get goin'?"

"Your command is our wish." Mark tossed a net of sarcasm over Nancy and his I-told-you-so eyes pulled it in. He slipped the gear shift into first and pulled onto the road.

"What brings you this far from home?" Nancy asked.

"Boyfriend. We got to messin' around and it got late. You know how it is," she said casually, eyes on the window and the darkness beyond.

"Messing around?" Nancy's brows knit high.

"Sher. Like you and him."

"But we don't . . . I mean, we're not married and I'm a Christian," Nancy felt the pressure to emphasize her beliefs.

"Fine, you're just missin' out aintcha? No sermons, please."

At a loss to know what to say next, Nancy turned toward the front. For the next few minutes she stewed—certain that she should say something profound but not sure what it might be.

When they came to a gravel turnoff, their guest said, "Let me off right here," her voice rock hard.

"No, we'll take you home," Nancy offered.

"Suit yourself. Turn here."

Mark did, and the road became instantly like the one they had taken off the highway that took them to Fletcher Harris's cabin—so much like it that Mark fired another I-told-you-so glare at Nancy. The only hill for miles, it wasn't as high as the last one, but it was wooded and the road wound and climbed and finally came to an end at what looked somewhat like a single-story home, but more like a shack. Nancy took in as much as the headlights washing across the front of it would allow. When they parked parallel to it in a mud yard, she had the opportunity to see more.

The sides were a ragged mix of tar and wooden shingles, and a battered porch sagged the length of it. Anemic yellow candlelight flickered through the two front windows and the tattered remains of lace curtains. On the porch, leaning against the house, stood a rusted bicycle frame, and stacked beneath one of the windows, next to a door, was a cord of chopped wood. Other piles of debris completed the picture—the country's version of a slum.

"Thanks," said the girl, squeezing between the seat and the door to escape. "See you around."

"I'd like to see your mother, please," Nancy said.

"Why do you want to see her mother?" asked Mark.

"You gonna convert us?" the girl chuckled.

"No. I'd like to see her." Something boiled inside Nancy. She knew she'd been brought here to make a difference, and since there was no difference she could make with the girl, maybe there was with the mother. She stood outside, the mud closing in around her sneakers. "Mark, I'd really like you to come with me." She felt the sudden need for moral support, and even though he'd probably do no good, he was the only one handy.

"Listen, Chickenlips . . ."

The girl laughed. "Chickenlips—boy, does that fit."

"Nancy, I don't want to go in there. I want to turn this car around right now and get back on the road. Every time I do what you tell me I end up regretting it—and believe me—I'm already regretting this."

"If you want to see my ma, come right on in, but it won't do you no good."

"Mark, I have to do this. Please stand by me."

Mark looked angry but relented and stepped from the car.

The air smelled of smoke and an underlying sourness of decay. Nancy stepped onto the porch and felt the timbers sag and heard them creak beneath her. The little girl led the way, her smile fixed with anticipation of some kind of victory. When Nancy reached the door, she heard Mark's footsteps behind her. The girl opened the door and let it swing slowly open.

"Come on, she's in here," she said, her eyes suddenly alive and sparkling. "I'll lay you odds you've never seen what you're about to."

The inside was like the outside, except with walls. Smoke and decay filled the air while candles, stuck in several hurricane lamps, threw dim, trembling shadows everywhere. A fire was locked inside a potbelly stove in the center of the room and glared at them through crimson slits around the square door. On the floor lay things from cars and bikes—things Nancy didn't recognize, black iron things and small, carburetor-like things. The one item she did recognize was an exhaust pipe that snaked across the far wall; a bike with no wheel frame leaned over it. The black walls hung with tar paper, some peeling to reveal ancient gray studs, while an oil-stained remnant of a red rug covered a warped, plywood floor.

But the things were only things—the kids in the place were heartrending. All girls, the oldest seemed about seven, the middle one about five, and the youngest probably three. They all sat alone at a card table in what was probably the kitchen. Although they glanced up when Nancy and Mark entered, they showed little interest in them. Their vague eyes peered from vague faces, their attention on dinner which spattered plates in front of them. The only thing Nancy recognized was an open bag of Oreo cookies. The three-year-old slid from the folding chair. She was naked except for a ragged gray t-shirt. After standing there for a moment, she reached up to her plate, grabbed a handful of mashed potatoes and squished them into her thin, blonde hair.

Nancy felt overwhelmed as if shocked by a sudden wave at the beach—only she liked the beach. She hated it here. Deflated, near tears, whatever coping mechanisms she might have had broken down, she grabbed for Mark's hand. Finding it, she squeezed it and with the other hand she grabbed her locket.

"My mom," the twelve-year-old said, bowing broadly and indicating a sofa across the back wall.

A woman lay on her back, her head propped up on a dark pillow. She didn't move, as if unconscious. "Is she all right?" Nancy asked.

"Who knows? She'll pop any time now. A soldier done that."

"What?"

"Can't you see the lump?"

Only then did Nancy notice the woman was pregnant. Her dark clothing against the dark sofa had masked it, but now the woman's condition was obvious. Her stomach was huge and she lay on her back, her hands around and beneath the bulge. She breathed laboredly.

"We all got soldiers for dads. Different soldiers. My mom's a waitress—meets 'em there. We ain't seen that one for about a month now." There was a huge, knowing grin on the girl's face. "Mom just likes messin' around."

"Mark, we have to help."

" 'Liz'beth, that you?" The voice rose from the sofa like a vapor—thin and fragile and ailing. "I hear voices. Is Mike here?"

Elizabeth's eyes never left Nancy, "No, Mamma. Go back to sleep." Then she grinned again as the naked three-year-old ran over and wiped mashed potatoes on Nancy's jeans.

"I'm outta here," Mark announced with grim finality. "Stay if you want, but I'm history." He dropped Nancy's hand and had cleared the doorway by the time Nancy turned.

"You can't. We have to help."

He was to the steps when he said, "Stay, then—hitchhike to California. She'll teach you how, but I'm gone. I have to."

Nancy followed, pleading. "Mark, please, we can't leave them like this. That woman needs our help."

"Yours maybe, not mine." He opened the car door and turned back to her, a finger of emphasis pointing her way. "Nancy—no." This wasn't Mark being obstinate, this was Mark being troubled. His features were chiseled, eyes strained and definite—this was a Mark ready to break.

But these were people God had given her, and Nancy couldn't just leave. "We have to help—somehow," she pleaded.

Mark slid behind the wheel, closed the door, and rolled the window partially down. "I'm not kidding, Nance. Get in or get left."

Nancy suddenly felt a hand in hers. She looked down to see Elizabeth looking up. "Go ahead," she said, all traces of arrogance gone. "There's nothing you can do. We're okay. Honest. We'll be all right."

Nancy eyed the suddenly very adult face. There was appreciation there but also immense defeat—they would be all right because nothing would ever make it better. Nancy turned back to the car. "Mark, please."

"In or out."

She hesitated for another moment, but when he shrugged and fired up the engine, she knew she had no choice. She faced Elizabeth and suddenly wanted to say so many things—magic and wonderful things to bring her into the kingdom, the only thing that would truly end her struggle. Yet there was no magic but the Lord's, and he was drawing her away. Helplessly, Nancy finally said, "Please, Elizabeth—there's a God. He put you here so you'll search for him—search him out—please." She squeezed Elizabeth's hand and stepped through the mud to the car and got in. Her eyes fixed on the waif surrounded by a smoky, decaying world, Nancy saw her fade into the black as Mark drove back down the hill.

About halfway down, Nancy finally turned to him. His eyes were nailed to the windshield, his hands gripping the wheel like a lifeline.

"Don't say it," he said, to beat her to the punch. "Browbeat me later. Now I need you quiet—for just a little while."

Nancy heard a note of desperation she'd never heard in Mark before. "I wasn't going to browbeat you."

"Good—now quiet."

Nancy nodded slowly and kept her eyes on him. The edges of him reflected the light from the dash, and he looked like stone—his eyes never wavered, his chest remained flat as he breathed, his chin jutted as rigidly as his eyes. Only two things moved—a throbbing vein on his temple she'd never noticed before and the index finger of his right hand beat tensely against the wheel. Mark was agitated and frightened.

They met the road that paralleled the highway and turned toward

California. Mark never spoke. He moved only enough to make the turn; otherwise, he remained a zombie.

At least twenty minutes passed, then ten more. Finally, "What's wrong, Mark?"

Locked in some other time and place, he didn't answer, didn't move—only the vein throbbed and the finger beat.

In the distance grew a cluster of lights, a McDonald's sign among them. Mutely, Mark pulled into the parking lot and drove to the furthest corner and turned off the engine. Still stone, he sat there for what seemed forever. But then, as if time had finally returned to earth, the rigidity dribbled away and he turned to her, his eyes weary and red-rimmed. "Would you get me a vanilla shake?"

"A vanilla shake?" she repeated. "After all that?"

"Please," he pleaded as if the shake were the most important thing in his life.

"Okay—vanilla shake."

When she returned, he took the shake and sucked hard on the straw for several minutes.

"How long are you going to keep this up?"

He pulled the straw from his lips but kept his eyes away from her. "I'm in the twilight zone—or some kind of morbid *Candid Camera*." His voice was hoarse, and he whispered as if speaking from eons ago.

"What happened?"

He didn't answer right away. His chest heaved and fell as he breathed heavily. "That was me back there."

"Where?"

"That was like my mother before she had me. The shack, the stove, the junk everywhere—the soldiers. That was me in the womb back there. I had four older sisters—I never knew my dad . . ."

"Your uncle was your dad . . ." Nancy heard herself say, the thought a tragic discovery.

"Until I was ten or so."

"That's why he was so special."

His eyes fell away and he gulped more shake. "We lived in a place like that—around Fort Meade." He paused for a moment as if to gather the strength and courage to continue. "I couldn't believe what I was seeing up there—it was like a play—a horrible, personal play. No electricity—on a hill—junk everywhere—soldiers would come and fix their cars up there and leave stuff—a one-story shack with a broken chimney—Frankenstein's lab for a kitchen." He worked the shake some more, eyes staring nowhere, his breathing erratic, nearly panting.

"She was a waitress like that one. She actually liked living there—I heard her say it one night when one of her bozos asked her to live with him. But she kept all of us in that shack. In that pigsty. Five kids . . .

"I was a soldier's son too. Sometimes I marvel at how stupid I was growing up. It never occurred to me that my dad was army—I thought he was something special. Even thought he left because he had to—I used to imagine all the reasons why he had to leave. Secret missions or that he died and my mom loved me too much to tell me the truth. We kids never talked about it—we didn't talk about much of anything—still don't. I have no idea where my sisters are now— not one of them stayed there past sixteen. In fact, it was when Mom was mad from finding that the last one left with one of her soldier friends that she got mad at me and told me everything."

His breathing became deep, more aggravated, a tear formed from the pool under his eye and broke free. "I always had the feeling she was just a whore." Mark stared off toward the dumpster, and while he sipped his shake Nancy rubbed her locket, not sure what to feel or what to say.

"What did she expect?" Mark continued. "My dad cared so much for me that when his hitch was up and I hadn't been born yet, he just got out of the army and went home. She never saw him again." He took another long sip.

Helplessly overwhelmed for the second time that night, Nancy reached a hand to his shoulder and rubbed him gently.

"You can't believe anyone cares," Mark went on. "You get to believing that you don't deserve to be out of the pigsty. That's you there because it's right you should be."

"I'm sorry, Mark—I'm so sorry." Nancy felt tears pooling beneath her own eyes, and she let go of her locket to push them away.

"It isn't your fault—none of it's your fault," he said as if trying to protect her.

"You asked me about the locket."

"What's that got to do with—?"

"My mom gave me this for my seventeenth birthday."

"Your mom's Maureen O'Hara?"

"No. My mom was Celia Bernard—real estate tycoon. And she was late to my seventeenth birthday. I wasn't having a party because she was going to take me out—a special dinner—but she got hung up with a client and missed it."

"Are you trying to one-up me?"

Nancy's tears gushed, and anger rode out with them. "No—but now it's your turn to listen."

His hands went up submissively, and his eyes narrowed.

"I'm sorry, but this is hard for me," she said.

"Okay, I understand. Go ahead."

Nancy swallowed hard and fortified herself with a deep breath. "On the way home she stopped at Kmart—Kmart for crying out loud—and bought me this locket. She told me it was gold, but by the time she died the gold was already rubbed off. She said she'd get me a picture of her to put inside, but a month later she was dead." She worked the locket with her thumb. "This is all I have from her—my mother," she said, lifting the locket to look at. It looked worn; the metal beneath the gold was tarnished, and the constant rubbing had caused a dent in the center of the heart.

"Mothers can be thoughtless," he whispered. "I can't even remember mine hugging me."

"Now who's trying to one-up who?" A laugh convulsed through her tears.

"She'd tuck me in, and I'd smell some new perfume or other. They were always bringing her perfume—she probably stunk of the place we lived in. When I was supposed to be asleep, I'd hear things—but she never hugged me."

Accompanying Nancy's helplessness, so many other things reared up and converged—immense sadness, relief that she'd actually verbalized her pain, longing to be even closer to Mark, disbelief at the absurdity of their lives and the equal absurdity of their coming together, fear of her feelings for him. Emotions and impressions collided and joined—at her heart—at the center.

She heard Mark's voice breaking through. "When you touched me just now, I started to think about it—I can never remember being comforted."

In the light from the parking lot she saw a tear form at the edge of his eye. It sat there suspended for a moment. Before it fell, Nancy gently touched it—the moisture was warm and rolled down her finger.

Mark turned to her—she'd never seen such longing. "I need a hug, Nance."

Without hesitation, Nancy leaned toward him, her arms moving up his arms, around his shoulders, then around his neck. When they united in back of him she pulled him to her. He responded and nuzzled his face in her neck—his warm breath soothed her skin, and she felt his lips kiss her lightly. Eyes closed, she kissed his hair and spread her fingers and let her hands roam his back lovingly, as she thought his mother should have done—as she wished her mother would have done so long ago. After too short a time, she felt him pull away, and she released him.

"Thank you," he whispered, his eyes soft and moist and searching all over her. Moving to her lips, her ears and up to her hair, they stopped at her eyes. "You're beautiful."

"You just like good hugs and will say anything to get another."

"No—well, yes—but you are beautiful." As if to prove his sincerity, another tear emerged and rolled toward his cheek, but Nancy caught it on her finger and watched it roll to her palm where it beaded, then disappeared, mingling with the moisture in her hand.

She looked up and saw intense eyes searching over her again. She thought she should feel self-conscious but didn't. He moved toward her again, but this time she instinctively moved away. But when she saw the hurt that came to his eyes, she moved to him. Their lips touched shyly, and only for a moment. Then, after another, they came together again. This time her arms went around his neck and his around hers, and they pulled each other tightly together. When the kiss had ended, when Nancy's lips rested against Mark's ear, she whispered, "I wish I could make it all better."

"You have," he whispered hoarsely, and they kissed again and hugged again, and as they did her heart was filled to bursting.

All the feelings that had been pushing at her melded into one. "I've wanted to do that for a long time," she slipped the words gently into his ear.

"It wasn't such a new idea to me either. Want to do it again?"

Nancy answered him with lips searching for his, and she felt his hands rubbing her back and felt safe and warm as he pulled her close. All the hurts of a lifetime seemed to fall away—they became tattered rags peeling away, hitting the floor around her.

"Can we get a room somewhere?" he asked.

"No, we can't." The words leaped from inside her and she stiffened. To her horror the idea didn't sound as repugnant as it should have. "I can't," she finally said, as if driving the last nail. But she kissed him again and took his hand and kissed his palm, then the back of his hand and his lips again. Now there were tears, gentle tears rolling down her cheek. Mark stopped one with his finger and let it roll down into his hand. She watched it until it came to rest in his palm, then she kissed it there.

"I know you can't," he said, understanding in his voice. "But you can't blame a guy for trying."

She pulled back. "I can't—really."

"We're going to spend the night together, of course. We've done that before."

Nancy sat up straight. The thought was disturbing now. "I know, but it's different now. Anyway, we can't spend the night here. Ronald McDonald wouldn't like it. We'd better get going. That is, if you're feeling up to it."

Mark leaned back against the seat and took a long satisfied breath. "I'm fine—now. We'll find someplace and we'll figure all this out."

Not far up the road they came upon a dark baseball field, its bleachers and fences vague outlines. Adjacent to it was a parking lot. Mark pulled in, and the tires crunched to the far corner where he parked beneath a sprawling oak. The engine and rattles silent, a muted chorus of crickets outside, he leaned toward Nancy and kissed her lightly. "I know we said we'd talk. But I'm tired, and talking might mess all this up."

His features glowed soft as they gathered what light flitted about. Then he offered her his shoulder, and she accepted. Although Mark was thin and should have been bony, she found a most comfortable little spot that seemed just made for her. Within seconds of placing her head there, his arm encircled her, and she fell asleep.

"I'll get it, I promise." The voice rose around her through the black. A mist of sound enveloped her. "It was beautiful and I saw it hanging there—I'll get it, I promise." Through the dim she saw a person, transparent, the sun dying behind and through him. She shrank. The sunset grew gray—obscure. "I'll get it, I promise. I always keep my promises." She shrank again. "You know I love you. My love is like gold—it will last forever." The figure became smaller, transparent, fading, eyes cast up to her, a huge smile with nothing behind it. The sunset a memory and the figure fading to only an impression—but the voice remained strong, maybe stronger—and the words never changed, "I'll get it, I promise, and I always keep my promises."

Sometime in the night Nancy woke. The dogs snored, and Mark breathed gently as she nestled on his chest. The night was so peaceful that she didn't understand the sea of uneasiness that surged around her. But then she knew.

She was sleeping with him. Although it could be said that she was merely comfortable, that nothing had happened, that they were only caring for one another, she knew that she was sleeping with him and that in her heart she'd made love to him. And when she realized that his hand cradled her breast, she knew it was all wrong.

After several moments of turmoil, she gently moved his hand, then his whole arm and eased to her place in the corner by her door. She put the blanket over Mark and grabbed the old coat she'd always used and curled up. Feeling unusually troubled, she grabbed her locket and tried to sleep, but everything was different now. They loved each other. They weren't just car mates. Their lives were entwined. Maybe not inseparably but enough to make a huge difference.

She couldn't sleep. Nestled at the very core of their love were the seeds of its destruction. Nancy prayed for guidance and the answer she received was more troubling, more definite than she expected. She brought the coat up around her chin and waited for the cold to turn to warm. She slept the executioner's sleep. She would tell Mark the bad news in the morning. The morning would be soon enough.

Chapter Twenty

Nancy wasn't sure exactly what she thought when the knocking on the window woke her. It was either something about rams butting heads over a young, innocent ewe or a washing machine spinning out of balance, which she learned about only after her mother had died and her father fired the woman who came in to clean up a couple days a week.

Whatever it was, it was only a dream, and the moment her eyes opened the dream vanished, and she looked into the ketchup-smeared face of a young boy. He was laughing and rapping his knuckles against the window.

She saw immediately that they weren't in the baseball field parking lot—the tree was gone, the dirt had given way to asphalt and white lines. Eyes wide, still a little groggy, she straightened. Morning had come like cymbals—bright with rich blue skies and an invigorating chill. The car was parked with its rear to a building, and she looked at a narrow road and a field beyond.

She pushed the coat down, stretched, and looked around for Mark.

The kid at the window knocked again and smiled broadly, his middle teeth gone and giving him a goofy look.

Nancy rolled down the window. "Hi," she greeted.

"The man told me to watch you. He's inside," the boy said.

"Why'd you wake me?"

"I wanted to." He smiled.

That's when she heard laughing from more kids to the rear of the car. She turned to see Mark entertaining them by juggling Egg McMuffins. He had at least four of them wrapped in paper, and five kids were standing around him enthralled.

Nancy couldn't help but laugh. He was so much at home with the attention, the juggling, the funny faces—the kids were in the palm of his hand. Anything he did they enjoyed, and when they enjoyed it he enjoyed doing it all the more. After a few minutes, a mother and father stepped out, bags cradled in their arms. They, too, became interested, and then another adult appeared. This one stood behind a couple of young boys, a hand on each of their shoulders. Before long the crowd had grown to a good-sized audience, and the McMuffins had spun out of their coverings and had fallen to the ground. The moment they hit, Hamster leaped from the open window, made it to the McMuffins in a flash, and devoured all four in as many bites. Just as quickly he returned to the car, leaped back through the window and resumed his position in the backseat. "You must have incredible hearing." Nancy laughed, looking back at him. It was impossible to tell that he'd ever moved.

Great "ahs" of sympathy bubbled up for Mark, and one of the men stuffed money into his pocket. Nancy heard Mark tell the crowd to wait a second, and he ran to the car. "I can't believe it—the guy gave me a twenty!" Mark exclaimed to Nancy after throwing up the back hatch. He grabbed a few props, and the juggling began again.

Nancy was outside the car now, leaning against it and watching. She got such satisfaction from watching him; it was like he was hers and she was sharing him—probably like a proud wife might feel.

Mark was happy. His face glistened with smiles and mock worry and all the expressions jugglers make to keep the audience interested. And he did it well.

Of course, he dropped things now and then. But the crowd cheered him all the more when he did. And when Mark attempted his great finale—this time with one of his prop rubber balls—and it worked, the ball balancing on the bridge of his nose for as long as he wanted it to, the kids went wild. Beaming, Mark waved his hands graciously in the air, accepting their applause, then retired to the car out of breath and completely fulfilled.

Nancy felt fulfillment with him.

"You were wonderful," she said as he fell against the car next to her.

"I did it. Did you see that? I did it. It was so easy. I love it and I can get better at it—I know I can."

"They gave you money?"

They had. As they went to their cars and some said personal good-byes, several people, mostly men, stuffed money into his pocket. Now he dragged it out. "Forty-three bucks."

"Gas money," Nancy exclaimed.

But Mark shook his head. "No, I want to do something else with this."

"What?"

"You'll see. But first it's time we replaced that breakfast I juggled away—then we'll find a place to do a little shopping."

"You looked good with those kids. You like kids?" Nancy asked, her raised brows indicating there was more to the question than was asked.

"Sometimes—other people's."

Nancy laughed, and she wrapped an arm around his waist. "I feel scuzzy—having showers regularly at Fletcher's spoiled me."

"I used the rest room inside."

Breakfast over and teeth brushed, hair combed and face splashed, Nancy rejoined Mark in the car. He lay back in the seat, sipping coffee, eyes closed, his arm resting on the gear shift. "All set?" he asked.

"I feel a lot better."

"Thanks for listening last night," he said, eyes still hidden behind his lids.

"That must have been a real shock to see all that."

"It was. Thanks for telling me about the locket too. That must have been hard for you."

"Not as hard as other things have been," she said, suddenly remembering the vow she'd made before falling asleep. She was going to end it all this morning. She'd repeated the words she was going to use over and over again—they'd changed slightly over the course of the rehearsal, but the content remained the same. *Mark, I don't know why I feel about you the way I do. But as a Christian I can only become involved romantically with other Christians, and since you've yet to take Jesus Christ as your personal Lord and Savior, I have to put an end to this brief relationship.* It was a fine speech, and when she woke in the middle of the night and moved over to her side of the car, she'd rehearsed it a couple more times before finally falling asleep.

But now, with the morning so bright and the vow so distant— with Mark doing so wonderfully with those kids, she slipped the speech into the back pocket of her mind and vowed to revisit it later. "You have a real gift," she said to him.

Mark's eyes opened and he smiled. "Come on, time to hit the road." And he leaned over and kissed her as naturally as if they'd always been doing such things. She kissed him back with equal calm, and a few moments later they were on the highway again.

"Don't you think we ought to keep to the side roads?" Nancy asked.

"Hopefully they're far ahead. But I do want to find a little town."

"It was weird seeing them last night. I've never been chased like this before." But then she realized she was wrong. *Satan's pursuit is like that: relentless, deceptive, remorseless,* she mused.

Mark didn't turn the radio on, and when he finally said he would like some music, he suggested that Nancy find a station she'd like. She found a golden oldies station and played it softly. This Mark wasn't half bad. In fact, she found herself just staring at him sometimes—studying the small crook in his nose, the height of his cheek bones, and how a day's growth of beard didn't look as ragged on him as it had on her father. He had never shaved Saturdays or Sundays, and by Sunday night, after he'd been drinking, the beard was haphazard and looked more like uneven smudges than respectable growth. Mark's looked very respectable.

"I sort of like your beard," she finally said.

"Really?" he brought the rearview mirror over and glanced at himself, running a hand over his chin. He grunted with satisfaction as he straightened the mirror.

It took them a good hour before they found a town—a small cluster of shops and gas stations, with its single street branching off at a right angle to the highway. Mark didn't hesitate. He turned off and began scanning the storefronts.

"What are you looking for?" Nancy was intrigued but actually more flattered than curious. She knew this was going to be a gift— and she liked gifts.

"There's one," he pointed excitedly.

He pulled into a parking spot and jumped from the car. "Stay here—I'll be right out." Then he ran into a jewelry store.

Nancy's heart sank—he wasn't going to get her a ring? Suddenly this game she had been playing at became very serious. Not a ring! The speech came back and screamed in her mind's ear. If it was hard to say a couple hours ago just because he looked cute, what was it going to be like when he was handing her a ring and proposing—and could she trust his proposal? He might just be trying to get those hands of his all over her again—and why didn't that sound as bad as it should?

"Oh, Lord, when am I going to learn? When you say jump . . ."

She remained glued to her seat, her eyes glued to the door, her heart pounding, her lips moving as she said, "No, we've only known each other for—and you're not a Christian." She must have been on her two hundredth pass over those words when Mark emerged, a small silver box between his fingers.

It was a ring. She knew it. She said a prayer, but the prayer seemed jumbled because she knew she didn't deserve to be saved from what was about to happen. She deserved to go through the hell she'd built for herself.

Mark slid behind the wheel and turned to her, his face the picture of childish anticipation. He must have seen her anxiety because he instantly registered hurt. "What's the matter?"

"Nothing—I guess I was just worried about the motorcycles," she lied and immediately felt a jab from her conscience.

"I got you something."

"What?" She bit her lip at the sound of the reluctance.

"Here," he said, eyes wide and excited as he handed her the box.

Afraid and yet a little excited as well, Nancy pulled the silver elastic string away and took the small square lid off. Inside sat a blue ring box. To her surprise there was a strong part of her that suddenly wanted the ring. She beat that part back and opened it. There on a crushed velvet base was a golden locket—a little smaller but much more beautiful than the one she now wore. Her eyes immediately filled with tears, and she looked up at the man she loved with a heart as golden as the one she held in her hand.

"Open it," he whispered.

"Open it?" she said, taking it from the box and working the clasp. Inside was a small piece of paper cut to fit, on which was written *Mark*. She sniffled and wiped her eyes and nose on her palm and then could hold back no longer. She fell forward into his arms and kissed him on the cheek and lips and finally on his neck as his arms wrapped around her and he hugged her mightily.

"I wish I had a picture."

"It's beautiful—oh, Mark, it's beautiful." She cried some more and kissed him some more and then pulled back and took the locket she wore off carefully and put it in the box, then slipped the necklace around her neck and clasped it. The heart fell nicely on her chest and she patted it. "How's it look?"

"It's not expensive. You know how much money I had. But it's as much as I could get."

"How does it look?" she insisted.

"You're the only thing more beautiful," he said, wrapping his arms around her again.

This time she stayed there for a while, feeling his large hands stroke her back and the safety of his embrace chase at least some of her fears away. After a while, though, the speech mumbled at her from a distance. She pushed it away, but the fact that it had come dulled the moment and she pulled away.

"Maybe we ought to get going," she said.

"Are you sure you like it?"

"I love it—it's a wonderful gift."

He kept smiling her way as he started the car and only stopped looking at her when he backed up. Suddenly his smile faded to grave concern. He threw the car into first and eased back into the parking space.

"What?" Nancy asked, then turned to see what he'd seen.

Coming from a feeder road and turning away from them toward the highway were their friends on the choppers. When they'd made the turn, their backs to them, Nancy could easily make out the Indian head.

"They know the car but not us," Mark whispered.

"It looks like they're heading for the highway," Nancy said, her eyes never leaving them, the throb of their engines like sandpaper on her nerves.

But they didn't go to the highway. When they reached the end of town near the highway, they turned to make another sweep.

"We'd better get out of the car," Nancy said, as they grew nearer with each heartbeat.

"They'll just stake it out—well, get everything you need."

Nancy grabbed her purse, toiletries, and Hamster and opened the door just enough to squeeze out, Hamster right behind her. Mark grabbed Naomi and a few other things and joined Nancy on the sidewalk. They moved quickly down the block and waited in a doorway as the motorcycles growled slowly toward them. The bikers' heads moved from side to side, the bandanas bright crimson, their hair fluttering about their shoulders, their beards black as their eyes. They looked powerful, almost reptilian in their determination.

A mother, holding the hands of two children began to cross the street near the choppers. The kids were probably boys and looked somewhere between seven and nine—both wore overalls. When she'd gotten a couple yards from the curb, the one with the Indian head peeled off from his friend and eased his bike over to the woman. He said something to her, Nancy could barely hear a faint voice over the engine. The woman ignored him, a remarkable feat since the biker had already circled her completely. He said something again, and she ignored him again and kept walking.

"She's got more guts than I'll ever have," Mark said, his voice raw.

Nancy just watched. Now the biker shouted an obscenity at the woman and rode around her again.

The boys clung tightly to her side, their heads following the biker as he circled them. His eyes never left them either—a circling vulture focused on his prey. The woman kept walking. Another shouted obscenity. She continued to ignore him, but he was not to be ignored. When she'd made it about halfway across the road, the biker eased off and moved up the street away from Mark and Nancy. After about fifty yards he turned around and brought his bike to a stop, the extended wheel pointing directly at the mother and her children. He revved the engine and it cried like a banshee; he revved it again, and the engine whined louder still. The rear tire screamed and smoked against the pavement as he launched himself in the woman's direction.

The woman was brave but not stupid.

The moment she saw him coming she ran, dragging the boys behind her. But they soon developed speed of their own and passed her, screaming wildly. The moment they reached the relative safety of the curb, the woman, still in the street, stumbled. She fell head-long onto the pavement and knowing the danger, spun quickly onto her back so she could see the chopper speeding toward her.

She screamed and pulled her legs up to her chest to make as small a target as possible.

The chopper roared by, the distance between the wheels and her feet undiscernable. As the bike pulled around for a second shot, the woman scrambled toward the curb where her sons stood, one crying, the other shouting through his tears. Nancy heard him, muted by distance, yell, "Come on, Mom, please! Mom, faster."

The chopper spun around and was gunned toward her again. This time she'd made it to her feet and was flailing headlong toward the curb when the chopper passed. The guy aboard reached out an arm and scooped the woman up by the waist. She screamed and he laughed. As she kicked and beat on his arm with her fist, he headed toward the highway.

"He's kidnaping her!" Nancy gasped, her heart in a knot.

But just as suddenly as he'd grabbed the woman, he threw her down in the middle of the street. Though a good distance away, Nancy could tell that she'd struck her head, and after she rolled a few feet lay motionless. A man from the side of the road stepped out to her and received a blow to the side of the head from the cyclist's friend who'd come alive and was following his buddy toward the highway.

When they'd gone a few blocks, a siren suddenly erupted not far from where Mark and Nancy stood. They turned to see a light-green and white police car emerge from a side street. The outlaws straightened in their saddles, saw what danger they were in, and gunned their choppers. In seconds they reached the highway ramp and thundered off toward California.

Still shocked by the violence but undeniably relieved, Nancy stood for a moment watching a knot of people begin to congregate around the injured woman. Someone called to get an ambulance while others took charge of the kids who'd run up, crying loudly.

"Why didn't anyone help her?" Nancy asked Mark.

"Better her than them," Mark said, eyes still glued to the drama.

Nancy couldn't help but look at him. The remark was so cynical, yet she couldn't deny its truth.

Someone had brought a pillow, and several people helped the woman rest her head on it.

The police car had originally given chase to the choppers but now returned. When the officer got out, he mumbled something about the ambulance to the crowd.

"Come on," Mark urged. "Those guys will be running for a while. We'll find a parallel road as soon as we can."

The heavy doors to the Pacer slammed shut, and when they were safely inside, Nancy allowed herself a sigh. She instinctively grabbed her locket—and felt the shape of the new one. It was slightly smaller, and there was no dent for her thumb to work. She immediately remembered how wonderful the surprise had been.

"I really like my locket. Thank you, again."

Mark smiled broadly with a strong glint of pride. "I wish we had time to enjoy it, but we'd better make tracks."

An hour passed. Since the car hummed along and the motorcycles had disappeared, they decided to stick to the highway and make better time. There was little talking. Both seemed to settle into the trip as one settles into a slipper—comfortably—like being with an old friend, as if the trip had become an accepted way of life.

In fact, Nancy began to dread getting to California. The trip would be over, and she'd have to make a decision—a decision she would rather postpone.

When she thought about that, that part of her she'd stuck in the back of her mind woke. *So he's given you a gift—so what?* it said. *So it was thoughtful—so what? So you feel more strongly about him than you've felt about any man before—so what?* And then it ended by screaming in her inner ear, *Don't become unequally yoked.*

"You okay?" she heard Mark ask.

"Sure. Why?"

"You suddenly looked sour—that cute little nose of yours wrinkled."

Nancy shook her head and escaped by looking out the window. She felt very alone and depressed, but she couldn't risk his asking her why. She might have to tell him, and she just couldn't do that—not yet anyway.

Lunch was at a Wendy's. Nancy had never gotten used to square hamburgers, but she and Mark were hungry and it was the only place that presented itself.

The burger lay in her stomach most of the afternoon and she was glad of it. It gave her a reason to look a little down in the dumps when Mark asked.

For she was down there. The war inside was huge as two sides of her battled ferociously. The one who wanted Mark and longed to see his sparkling eyes over coffee in the morning stood her ground against the one who kept quoting Bible verses and saying that no matter how his eyes sparkled she was going to have to give him up. They locked horns all afternoon. Once the Bible verse side was so strong that she felt her hand reach for the door handle, and for an instant she almost considered leaping from the moving car. But a moment later the sparkling eyes advocate wrestled the other into submission and she found her hand resting on Mark's as his rested on the gear shift. The smile he gave her woke the Bible verses again, and she pulled her hand away.

Even though the war raged inside, outwardly Nancy leaned life-lessly against the door, as if moving took more energy than she had.

By late afternoon they'd reached New Mexico and the sun blazed persimmon red across the western horizon. She suddenly realized that she hadn't even thought about the bikers all afternoon, and when she felt Mark's hand stroking hers, the warmth gave strength to the part of her who loved him.

"You about ready for dinner?"

"Let's have something kind of nice—not incredibly nice—sort of Denny's nice."

"Denny's nice—hmmm."

Mark pursed his lips as if pondering the problem, and a few minutes later the solution presented itself.

Brandon was like most of the other towns they'd come across: small, surrounded by rough terrain, a few cacti, piles and piles of boulders—evidence of an approaching desert. Like a bead on a string, the town clung to the road that left the main highway. In the dying day, lights came alive, one in particular was green and blue neon that announced something that had to be cute: Bramble Bumpkins—too cute to pass up. Having seen its sign, Mark parked in front.

After feeding the dogs and making sure they were comfortable, Mark and Nancy made their way into Bramble Bumpkins. Obviously designed by a person who loved fairy tales, the walls were playfully colored and covered with wooden cutouts of Mother Goose, Humpty Dumpty, and all their neighbors while the tables and chairs were modeled after a children's nursery. It was a curious oasis from the harsher reality outside.

There were only a few people inside. A family cocooned in overalls sat in the corner booth, and a lone cowboy sat at the counter, his hat sitting beside him, his denims worn and gray. The waitress stood behind the counter, her back to them, and the cook's white hat bobbed back and forth behind the tall counter in the back.

The waitress, a pretty girl of seventeen or so, turned and motioned for them to sit anywhere. They picked a booth in the corner furthest from her. "I'm going to the rest room," Nancy announced.

"Want tea?"

"Just one cup or I'll be awake all night. See you in a minute." Leaving him on his own, she hurried off.

When she returned, things began to happen. Although what she saw was probably very innocent, it fed a part of her that neither wanted Mark nor quoted scripture. It had been lurking uneasily in the back of her mind ever since she began to have feelings for him. It was the part that knew he was only toying with her and that had been waiting patiently for the right moment to point it out to the rest of her. That moment had arrived.

The young waitress stood at the table, an order pad in hand, her large, fetching eyes all over Mark. As Nancy approached, the girl giggled coyly at something Mark must have said. She was enjoying herself far more than Nancy thought she should. Mark, too, was enjoying himself far, *far* more than Nancy thought he should. His large, brown eyes gazed up at the little morsel as Nancy imagined he'd stared up at the girl who'd stolen her car and tent trailer.

Why, Mark Brewster, you're flirting your little—and I mean very little—brains out, Nancy said to herself.

Although she thought she should feel jealousy or anger or hurt, or a thousand other emotions, she didn't. Something far more puzzling bubbled up around her—relief. The battle was over. And relief brought a sense of rightness—all the cobwebs of doubt suddenly fluttered away and the smoke of battle lifted. Nancy saw things clearly.

The sudden onrush of clarity caused her to act with uncharacteristic firmness. When she finally stood at the table beside the waitress, she said, "Would you excuse us, please?" The young girl immediately soured. After a brief, appraising glance at Nancy, she shrugged smugly and strode toward the counter.

"You mad about something?" Mark asked with just a hint of defensiveness.

Nancy thought of a number of things to say, but suddenly none of them mattered. "I'm going."

"Going? We just got here."

"No. *I'm* going."

"Alone? That's ridiculous. Now? Why? You don't think there was anything going on between—shouldn't you just get jealous or something? Leaving seems a little hasty."

"Jealousy isn't it," Nancy said, afraid to sit because then she might decide to stay. "Well, maybe it is. Partially, anyway."

"You're not making sense."

"I don't have to make sense." She reached into her purse and took out her wallet. After counting out four twenties, about half what was left, she handed them to him. "This will buy most of your gas, and what it doesn't you can juggle for."

"You're serious. All I did was flirt a little bit. You're leaving because of that?"

"There's more," she said, her eyes beginning to burn. She desperately didn't want to cry. "We're different."

"Everybody's different."

"Your heart and my heart are different. Too different. Seeing you do that just made me realize how different. How could you? Would you cheat on our honeymoon?"

"Honeymoon?"

"Good-bye, Mark." She stood for a moment waiting for the tears, but they didn't come. Here she was leaving someone she thought she loved, yet she felt physically and emotionally strong. That wasn't like her at all. Maybe she felt this way because she wasn't leaving someone she loved but, rather, she was returning to someone she loved more.

Outside the restaurant, however, the physical reality of what she'd done came up to meet her. Night was falling, and as darkness hung over everything, it brushed away what remained of the warmth. The cold that replaced it seemed lethal. Although her ski jacket kept her top warm, her face began to sting immediately as white breath plumed from cold lips, and her jeans did little to help her legs. She'd scampered back to the Lord, but his arms were far colder than she'd hoped.

Back at the car, she opened the door, grabbed her small bag of toiletries and clipped a leash on the sleeping Hamster's collar. After a strong tug followed by a moment of spasmodic shaking, she eased the huge dog from the car and Hamster stood wearily beside her. Nancy closed the door, and Naomi immediately stood, her little paws pressed against the window, yipping a sad protest.

Nancy had to think. Making this decision was one thing; carrying it out was something altogether different. What was she going to do now? No car, a town she knew nothing about, a thousand miles or more from her destination—talk about a step of faith. "Well, ol' fella," she said to Hamster, "we're on our own now."

Hamster yawned away a vestige of sleep and looked up at Nancy with large, liquid eyes. There was little doubt those two dark pools in this large angular head were taking this opportunity to question her sanity.

Chapter Twenty-One

It took Nancy about a minute to grab her locket—her new one—and begin rubbing it. She didn't realize she was doing it until her thumb began to chafe. But as the lights flickered on in the little town and when the only people she saw were cow-folk with sweat-stained hats and sheepskin jackets and when all they did was angle off the highway down the single road in their pickup trucks and when the people got out of their trucks to go where they were going as quickly as they could because it was getting horribly cold, she realized her decision was going to be costly.

The enormity of it came home when a pickup truck stopped with a squeal of brakes in front of a darkened store she was walking by. The man who stepped from the cab had a beat-up, felt cowboy hat with the rolls tight and the protruding brim bent over his eyes. His neck was surrounded in white wool, and his hands were planted deeply in his coat pockets. He bumped into Nancy as he went by and said nothing, even though she'd nearly been knocked down.

That moment of complete indifference told her as clearly as any words that, except for Hamster, she was alone—just like at the rest stop in the snow. A listless laugh bubbled up from inside as she compared that time with this. Mark had left her then but she'd left him now. She'd only begun to care for him then, she loved him—or at least thought she did—now. She'd been waiting for him to come back then; now she was waiting for someone to take her away from him.

There was one thing, however, that was exactly the same: the cold. Even though there was no snow on the ground, as night fell, the cold was every bit as penetrating—maybe more so. It felt like millions of needles jabbing icy points through her jacket and jeans into her skin. Her bones were next.

She needed a ride soon yet as she scanned the town that looked unlikely. Not only were people scarce but those she saw were coming to town, not leaving and even if they had been leaving, they weren't the kind she wanted to ride with.

"Okay, Lord," she whispered, "I'm doing what you want me to do. It's time for one of those rescue miracles you're so famous for."

A church. Every town—even those built of tumbleweeds—had a church. A church would be warm, and maybe there'd be someone to help her. The Lord would surely have a church nearby. While she craned her neck in all directions looking for its steeple, a man and woman, bundled against the cold, got out of a late model car and hurried toward Bramble Bumpkins. Nancy summoned courage. "Excuse me," she said. "Is there a church around here anywhere?"

"A what?" the man replied, his ears covered by a high woolen collar. "What'd you say?"

"Is there a church around here?"

The woman answered, "Not around here. There's one a couple miles down Raspberry Road. But I think it went out of business."

"That's a real estate office now," the man corrected. "This ain't church country. Will's Mesa got one. Catholic, I think."

"Thank you," Nancy nodded politely and watched the two go inside.

Focusing again on the street and trying to decide which way she should walk, she heard a familiar voice. "Are you ready to come back yet?" Mark stood behind her, his hand planted firmly on his hips—she turned to find him the picture of arrogance.

"No. I'm not coming back."

"Don't you think this is just a little silly?"

"Silly?"

"Sure, silly." He glanced self-consciously around to make sure they weren't being overheard, then he said, "I mean we said we loved—" Another sheepskin jacket wrapped around a leather neck stepped from Bramble Bumpkins and caught Mark off guard. He quickly stopped, shuffled, and waited for the intruder to pass. "Loved each other, for crying out loud. You just can't suddenly leave."

Nancy cringed. He was right—but so was she. A familiar feeling swept over her—the same feeling she'd had when she'd decided to leave her father. She knew what she was doing would be seen as an overreaction—leaving just because he ruined a cake—but she'd made a decision, one that was long in coming. It was the right decision, and no one was going to talk her out of it—not her father, not her grandmother. And not Mark now. She said simply, "Silly or not, that's the way it has to be."

"Listen, Chickenlips . . ." His tone was a bit defensive.

"Yes, Speedbump?" And hers was childish, but it felt good.

He puffed up slightly. "You're gonna have to go a long way to catch a guy like me."

"Just to the nearest mud hole."

"Watch it—I'm about to get offended."

She stepped back, feeling increasingly vulnerable. Any second he might come up with the words that would make her change her mind, and she didn't want to hear them. "I gotta go. From this moment on you're free to roam this earth seeking whichever girls you may wish to devour." Then she added sadly and a little confused, "I'm history." She turned away.

"This is unfair!" Mark protested. "Any healthy red-blooded American guy would have done the same thing."

"Well, that doesn't explain why you did it." A surge of anger accompanied the statement and with it came a tremendous burst of freedom.

Mark shivered slightly and vigorously rubbed his forearms. "Is that God of yours the God of ice or something? Does he like his people to freeze to death?"

"No." At the mention of God, Nancy drew her claws back. "He'll keep me safe. I know he will. I have to go now."

"Go where?" Mark made a dramatic sweep of his hand. "Look around. There's no place *to* go."

"I'm going to see my father. I don't know how I'll get there but I will. I'm doing what I should have done in the first place—go alone."

Mark suddenly softened. His eyes became repentant, and he shuffled his feet uncomfortably. "Be reasonable, Nance. We've had our first fight. And, you—like every other woman in the world—are being a little emotional. Why don't we work this out? What if I promised to leave you completely alone for a while—not even talk to you until you feel like it? We have a good thing here—I really care for you."

Those were the words she feared, and the way he said them was certainly sincere enough. It was written in his drooping eyes, his bowed head, his hands working together nervously. But her will suddenly possessed a spine of iron, and she immediately reaffirmed to herself that his sincerity wasn't the problem.

"I can't, Mark," Nancy said, softening as much as he had. "I really can't. Being with you the way I feel is wrong. What happened in there just showed me how wrong it was—and what kind of a man the Lord wants for me. I have to leave. I just have to." She turned slowly, a strong part of her suddenly wanting to run back to him and throw her arms around him and kiss him and tell him that she'd never do something stupid like this again. But that wasn't possible. So, with her bag of toiletries tucked under her arm, Hamster's leash firmly in hand, her locket in her other hand and only a moment's hesitation to look at Mark one last time, she took her first step away, then another, and before long she'd made it past the edge of Bramble Bumpkins and had left Mark standing alone in the cold.

"That direction's a good choice," he called to her. "Tell the desert hello."

He was right; she was walking away from the highway toward the harsh terrain beyond the town.

"In ten minutes you'll cry out to me with frozen vocal cords, but I won't hear you."

She didn't turn but just placed one foot ahead of the other and pulled Hamster along. Hamster wasn't sure this was a good idea, and a couple of times he turned back to see if Mark was still there. After a few minutes Nancy heard the door to Bramble's slam. A quick glance over her shoulder confirmed that Mark had gone inside.

The sidewalk and the town ended at the same point. The road became narrow, and the pavement dissolved to sand and rocks and an occasional bush. Nancy felt the cold sting her ears and looked back to where she'd come from. Most of the buildings stood dark, but across the street from the diner was a bar, and in front of it, bathed in the country and western music from inside, were several cars and pickups. Leaning on a couple of them were two men and a woman who laughed occasionally between draws on their bottles of beer.

Everything was so foreign—so different from what her world ought to be. She was totally unprepared for all this: this place, this sudden independence, this cold. "Okay, Lord, anytime you're ready."

She and Hamster walked back toward the highway, past Bramble's and a yipping Naomi, past a gas station to the highway on ramp. There she stopped. A sign at the on ramp entrance proclaimed No Pedestrians.

"I guess that means us. Can't go back, can't go forward. We're trapped, Hamster, ol' boy. Maybe I'd better swallow a little pride and compromise with Mark."

Glancing over his shoulder toward the diner, Hamster indicated that he thought that idea had merit.

A snowflake fell and landed wetly on Nancy's nose, then another danced by and another. The rugged countryside would be white in the morning, her body frozen beneath the snowy mantle, the only blemish on its otherwise pristine beauty. How long had it been since she'd been stranded at the rest stop? Days ago. Three, four—she couldn't remember, and she didn't care enough to figure it out. It just seemed long ago—another time, another world.

It was love that made it so, she suddenly thought. Love changes everything—or at least those feelings of love do. She remembered one of Pastor Bevel's sermons and smiled, remembering the gossip sparked around the singles group in connection with it. Pastor Bevel's daughter had supposedly told him that she was in love with a not-so-great guy—a guy probably like Mark, Nancy had to admit. The next Sunday there was a sermon on what love was—1 Corinthians 13.

"Love is total commitment to the other person's well-being. Love isn't feelings. Feelings often fade; feelings often need rekindling. Love doesn't exist without Christ in the middle of it," he had said.

And yet after the feelings come, Nancy thought, *everything's different. What came before no longer has relevance; it doesn't exist. Old relationships dissolve, old places no longer mean what they did. Life takes a sharp turn into something incomprehensively new—never to turn back.*

She allowed herself a moment to feel them again—to feel the

awakening of wondrous things inside her, feel the glorious surprise like an unexpected sunrise, feel the freedom. Yet, as the moment matured, she couldn't forget that the object of her love was in the wrong army—was a flag bearer for the wrong commander, the usurper of the throne, the evil renegade.

She sighed and let the memories fade and reality reemerge. Truckers—where were those truckers now that she needed them? Now she'd accept the rides. Had she taken them up on their offers back there at the rest stop, she would have avoided all this—if only she'd gone with the woman with the hot coffee—what was her name? She would have avoided standing out here in the cold again. Avoided the hurt of dumping Mark. Avoided falling in love.

No. Even if the person she felt it for was the wrong guy, she never wanted to avoid feeling. The feelings were wonderful—toweringly warm, magnificently fragile, feelings of belonging, of being understood and desired. No. Even though the path led her to a place out here in the cold she was glad for having walked it.

"You okay, miss?" The voice was soothing and shy, and it came from behind her. She turned. A young man stood about fifteen feet away. He was about twenty, lean, wore tired jeans and a thick sheepskin jacket, and his cowboy hat sat squarely on his head. He looked strikingly trustworthy.

"No. Not really."

"Does that dog eat people?" he asked, offering a cautious smile.

"Just the bad ones," she said, but she had the distinct impression that this fellow didn't fall into that category. "I need help," she said. "Do you have any to give?"

"What sort of help?" His cautious smile faded to just plain caution.

"A ride."

Now his expression became concern. "Where?"

"California or any place in between."

The young man thought, one eye on Hamster, probably weighing his chances for survival. Finally he came to a conclusion. "I'm goin' about ten miles that direction. If that dog don't eat me, I'll take you at least that far. Maybe you can get another ride after that."

"Really? Thank you. What's your name?"

"Harry Woods. That don't matter though. I saw you walkin' around, and I just wondered if you was in trouble."

"No trouble. I just need to keep moving on to California."

"I can certainly help you do that. I'll get my truck." He spun on boot heels and ran down the slight incline to his truck. It was in front of the bar and although that concerned her for a moment, Harry seemed steady enough. She hadn't realized how welcome the sound would be, but relief washed over her when she heard his engine roar and saw him back onto the road. Seconds later he pulled up alongside her, leaned over, and opened the cab door. "It'll take a minute to warm up in here," he said as Nancy and Hamster got in.

Hamster took his position between them. Nancy was glad it was one of those full-sized trucks and there was room for Hamster to curl up. Harry was right, the cab did warm quickly, and before long, Nancy loosened her coat.

"What's your name?" Harry asked a bit sheepishly.

"Nancy Bernard," she answered, eyes ahead, peering into the night. "It's very dark out here," she mused.

"Dark, but friendly. I've lived here all my life. Work a ranch not far down the road."

"Really? Are we going there?" Nancy didn't want to go to a ranch; she wanted another town where she could negotiate another ride.

"No. A turnoff. But you can get a ride easy from there."

"I can?" She didn't like the sound of that. "What kind of turnoff?"

"A road, sort of. A trucker'll give you a ride."

"Is it like one of those trucker gas stations or something?"

"Naw—out here? It's a streetlight and a turnoff."

"Just out on the highway?"

"Sure. No problem."

Nancy was instantly nervous. Standing out by the highway was not what she had in mind. "Maybe you could take me back to town. I really don't want to stand out on the highway."

"Can't. Gotta get home. The boss called—cow problems."

"Cow problems?"

"Don't know more than that, but when he calls—he calls."

"But you can't just let me stand out by the road . . ."

Suddenly she heard a growing growl in back of them. She quickly turned and peered into the black. Two headlights moved up from a distance and now sat on their bumper. A moment later they gunned their engines and sped around them. Choppers. One of them had the Indian head war shield on the back. Nancy's heart deflated for an instant, and then they disappeared into the night ahead, their taillights fading to black.

Slightly shocked, she pushed herself back into the seat and laid a hand on Hamster—she worked her new locket with her thumb. *They only know the Pacer,* she said to herself, *and the Pacer was back there—did they see it?* Had they killed Mark? No. There was no time for all that. Mark was still all right. It was she who had the problem.

A problem that suddenly became very real. The turnoff came, and it was everything she hoped it wouldn't be. A dirt road met the highway at a right angle, the turn illuminated by a single street-lamp. The light bathed a small area in a white cone, but everywhere else was ominously black. Harry pulled over and then, with his smile still just as fresh and innocent as it had always been, he leaned against his door. "This is it. Just stand over there by the light, and someone'll be along to pick you up. Us folks out here are pretty decent."

She thought of the two choppers who'd been stalking her. They were out here someplace, and they were not decent folk.

"You're kidding. You are kidding, aren't you? I can't stand out there on the side of a road in the middle of the night in this cold."

"Ain't nothin' gonna hurt you." The smile was as large and as friendly as ever. Harry eyed Hamster. "Anyway, he'll take care of you."

The huge dog looked up at the cowboy as if to ask who was going to take care of Hamster.

"Now, go on. I gotta get going."

"What if I went with you to the ranch? I'd at least be safe."

"No. This ain't my truck. I ain't supposed to take no hitchhikers in it. No. Time's come to get out." His smile was gone, and the young cowboy, used to having his way with critters of all description, glared at this female one firmly.

With extreme reluctance, eyes darting first to the tall cone of light then back to the stern face, Nancy opened the door and slid out. A few moments later, with Hamster sitting beside her, Nancy watched the truck's taillights disappear down the dirt road. The moment they did a huge semi exploded by, throwing rocks and dust everywhere. Hamster shielded himself behind Nancy while she turned her back to the barrage. With the dust still swirling and the semi roaring away, Nancy turned back to the highway.

If she thought she was alone before, she was really alone now. She began to fume at herself. Why hadn't she just refused to get out of the truck? Why hadn't she clung to the door and not let him throw her out? Why hadn't she kicked and screamed? Of course, it didn't matter why. She hadn't and now, as the semi's thunder died to a distant whine, she peered after it in immense defeat. She'd done some dumb things in the past but nothing like this. Not only was she in an incredibly vulnerable position, but she'd let it happen.

But that was spilled milk, she thought. Now she had to deal with it.

She took a quick scan of the area. The dirt road quickly disappeared in the darkness, and there were no lights to indicate that it went anywhere. Sure, there was a ranch down there somewhere, but it could be miles and there could be many things between here and there far more dangerous than staying put. Not far away, bathed in the scant periphery of the light, was a large pile of boulders. They offered a little shelter but that was all. Snakes were probably in hibernation but, of course, other things might also seek the shelter of those rocks—coyotes, maybe wolves, scorpions—who knew? She was familiar with the dangers common to the backyard, not the desert.

Brandon lay on a plain below her, as she now stood on what appeared to be foothills that lay rumpled around a larger mountain. The road left Brandon and climbed. Even now as she turned to look up the mountain, Nancy could see the semi's beady red taillights appear and disappear in the mountains' folds.

Below, there were occasional headlights. Like the fireflies back in Washington, they'd come alive for a time, then travel the highway, only to turn off and die in the darkness. Some would turn the other way, white lights turned red then to fading crimson particles in the distance. Nancy stood there detached from all that, and as she stood, time passed and as time passed no one came by—nothing to avoid and no "friendly folk" to pick her up.

The longer she stood there the greater her quandary. Chance seemed to be pushing her loving God from his throne—was there a celestial roulette wheel spinning up there somewhere, the little bead coming to rest on something good for her, then on something bad? After all, her loving God had the opportunity to make things work out for her in town. Instead, he'd turned her over to this darkness and this cone of light, neither of which offered any protection.

Just like he turned me over to an abusive father and an indifferent mother. She heard the anger voiced in the thought.

Nancy shook the idea away. No. God was loving. God had placed her in situations so that she would seek him. Acts 17:26-27—she'd studied it more than once at those times when she wondered why the Lord had brought her down the path he had. Yet, for all of that, the darkness still held its terror, and she still felt vulnerable in that very small cone of light. Everything out here was quite foreboding.

She decided to step out of the light. Leash firmly in hand, her toiletries stashed beneath her arm, she gave Hamster a tug and they stepped over to the boulders. Using one as a high stool, Nancy sat there. Now within the black, she felt comforted by it.

She looked up to the sky. A splash of stars sparkled here and there around a sliver of moon. The clouds that had brought the brief snowfall must be breaking up. "Praise the Lord," she whispered. "At least I don't have that to deal with."

A distant set of headlights appeared to be coming from Brandon. When they kept coming, she felt hope and stepped back into the light. As they approached, she did something she thought she'd never do. She put out her thumb and waited. As the car grew closer, she made out the shape—a squat turtle. She immediately retracted her thumb and stared at the driver as the Pacer roared by. Mark smiled viciously.

How could he have done that? Just left her standing out there? Even though she had put her arm down, how could he have left her as prey for any deranged cowboy who might happen by? Or worse yet, those bikers who seemed to be scouring the countryside for them? She suddenly hated him.

By ignoring her—since he was the only person within a thousand miles who knew and supposedly cared about her—he reaffirmed her predicament; she was definitely alone. As she watched the taillights climb and disappear, she resettled on the boulder and thumbed the locket desperately.

His locket, she suddenly thought.

Without hesitation she took the small box out of her jacket pocket, and a few moments later she was wearing her mother's locket again. The dent fit her thumb so much better than the other's perfection.

Hamster growled—a cavernous barrel growl from deep within him. He hadn't moved; he still sat next to her by the boulders, but now something, somewhere, threatened him.

"What is it?" she whispered, not wanting whatever or whomever it was to hear.

Hamster ignored her question. His ears perked, and his huge head pulled around in the direction of the darkness behind them.

Something Hamster didn't like was out in the desert.

Hamster stood, rigidly facing away from the road. "Easy, guy. You have to stay here." Nancy gripped his leash tighter.

More growls, this time louder, more urgent and far more menacing. Was it a wolf? A coyote? Bobcat? Oh, why didn't she watch those Disney true life adventure things more closely?

Hamster took a step away from the highway toward the dark world beyond and growled with teeth bared, eyes wide and ears cocked.

In an effort to reestablish her authority, Nancy tugged on the leash and tried to get him to sit. But it was a lost cause. The huge animal, committed to something out in the blackness, brushed her efforts aside with a cool glance in her direction. Having effectively told her to "bug off," he returned his attention to the cause of his fear.

Suddenly, his body stiffened, what hair he had on his shoulders turned to sand paper, and his head pointed rigidly—but he made no sound.

He held his pose for about ten seconds, then, with black lips curling above yellowed fangs, Hamster exploded in a cannonade of growling and barking. And just as suddenly, he leaped forward. Although he pulled Nancy for a few steps, the leash quickly became too much to handle and she let go. Her heart wrapped around itself as she saw the gray animal lose the light's reflection and disappear.

"Hamster, you come back here this minute!" she shouted. But her shouts were no competition for Hamster's own barking. Then the barking, now a good distance away, fell silent. She cried out again. But all she heard in return was her own forlorn echo. Far off,

the sound muffled by distance, she heard Hamster explode ferociously again—and the sound had all the earmarks of battle.

Then she heard something else, a softer sound—sniffling? No,
sniffing—insistent like a hunting dog. The sound was very near.
Afraid to move too quickly, Nancy pivoted on her heels. No more
than six feet away, a raggedy skinny gray dog-like animal, its nose
dancing on the end of a narrow snout as it sniffed the air around her,
slinked from behind the pile of boulders. A coyote! There was no
mistaking it, and each step brought it that much closer to her.

"Oh, Lord," she whispered, eyes full of the mangy creature. His
eyes never once glanced up; rather they stared where his nose
pointed. Suddenly he stopped, froze, and, his sniffing over, he
glared up at Nancy with hollow, yellow eyes. For a moment both
the coyote and Nancy stood motionless, each appraising the
other—Nancy in terror, the coyote as if he'd not expected to find a
person at the top of those legs.

Stifling her desire to bolt, Nancy called upon instinct. Having
been around dogs most of her life, she abruptly stamped her foot.
"Shoo, go on, shoo!" she commanded, waving her arms emphati-
cally.

But the coyote didn't shoo. He stood his ground and, with lips
curling over fangs ripe with decay, he growled. It was a whiny
sound but effective enough; he was not to be intimidated.

Such courage triggered another thought. He might be rabid!

Fear like she'd never known grabbed all three chambers of her
heart and held it so tightly she thought it would stop. She took a step
in retreat, but the coyote merely stepped forward, his growls
becoming fiercely confident. He took another few steps and was
now only a yard away. Nancy took another two steps back and
stumbled against the boulders. Quickly regaining her balance, rubbing her locket furiously, she felt a strangled prayer work its way to
the surface, "Lord, please."

A semi thundered by. Hitting the highway shoulder, it sent dust
swirling in a hundred tornadoes and rocks flying everywhere.
Taken by surprise, the coyote took an instant to assess the sudden
danger, then bolted into the darkness, his ragged tail a flag of sur-
render. Alone again, Nancy fell against the boulders gasping for
breath. Her hand worked her chest to keep her heart from leaping
out through her ribs, and her eyes remained focused on that hole in

the blackness that the coyote had leapt through. She knew he'd soon realize the truck was gone and return. But after she stood there for what seemed like forever, the coyote hadn't returned. Although that fact brought a bit of calm, she knew he was still out there somewhere, perhaps just beyond the light's perimeter.

Another gray animal suddenly appeared—Hamster. He returned from the blackness, a dog with a purpose. Back in Washington, on hot, summer Saturday afternoons, when all the cleaning was done and there was nothing to do but curl up on the sofa and read a good book, Nancy would sometimes forget to feed Hamster. On those rare occasions when his internal clock beat her to his food bowl, he'd come up to the sofa and wrap gentle teeth around her arm and give her a little tug. Now, thousands of miles and a hundred eternities from those wonderfully languid afternoons, Nancy felt those same gentle teeth on her wrist. This time, however, the tug was more insistent. Hamster's meaning was unmistakable. He wanted her to follow him.

"You're kidding." Nancy groaned, astonished.

She remembered his doing this once before when it had nothing to do with food—he'd discovered a recently dead bird he wanted to share. What did he want to share this time?

"You can't be serious," she protested again. But he *was* serious—the pull on her wrist began to sting. *Well, why not?* she thought. *Staying in the light hasn't been all that safe, and being with Hamster's better than being without him.* "Okay, tiger," she said, twisting her wrist free, "where to?"

Chapter Twenty-Two

When Nancy's eyes adjusted to the night, the terrain underfoot turned from black mystery to ghost-gray manageable. Gripping Hamster's leash firmly, she skirted the pile of boulders and followed a rock-strewn route away from the dirt road. But even though the walk was easy, she knew that she could just as easily slip and twist her ankle or break a leg, or injure herself in some other way that would leave her lying out here stranded—just waiting helplessly for the coyote and his buddies.

In the distance loomed another, larger, pile of boulders, and Hamster headed for it. When they had circumvented it, a clearing sprawled dimly before them. In the center of it, maybe fifty yards away, stood a cluster of three buildings, a house and a couple of shacks—actually, they all looked like shacks. Yellow light spilled from an open door and glowed weakly from a window to reveal a low adobe fence surrounding the property. An unlatched gate clapped in an uncertain breeze.

"Fresh air nut," Nancy murmured, noticing the open door and feeling the cold she'd all but forgotten grate against her cheeks.

But fresh air nut or not, the shack was a place to spend the night. No one could possibly turn her away on a night like this.

When she was about ten yards away, her caution became curiosity. Something lay rumpled in the front yard, half in the door's light. After another few steps, Nancy saw the rumpled form take shape— a body clad only in a bathrobe.

She ran to it and as Hamster pushed a caring nose into the person's neck, Nancy knelt. The person lay face down, and from the sea of matted gray hair it appeared to be an old woman. Nancy carefully turned her over. In the dim, yellow light, Nancy made out an ancient sun-dried face. "She's still alive," Nancy told Hamster. Although she was unconscious, there was still evidence of shallow breathing. "But not for long if we don't get her inside."

Nancy pushed arms under the woman's back and knees, felt something metallic underneath, then tried to lift. But even though the woman's body was little more than a stick, it was a stick too heavy for Nancy. Tossing toiletries and purse inside the front door, Nancy grabbed the woman under her arms, lifted, then pulled her around and dragged her toward the shack. When she had done so, she saw that the woman had been lying on a Winchester rifle. Nancy decided to worry about the rifle later.

Naked heels bumped on worn, wooden steps, then cut two clear trails in the dust as Nancy dragged her to the sofa. After laying the woman as gently as she could, she closed the door. A brass lamp that hung from bare rafters gave enough light for Nancy to get a better look at her. A near skeleton, her skin was leathery and desert dry while her face, now with eyes closed and possessing a certain peace, had the angularity of a dried-apple doll. Her hands lay limply at her side, but Nancy could see the calluses. Although the specter of death now hung over this woman like the dust in the room, before it came visiting, this woman had worked.

An open door led to the bedroom and an unmade bed. Knowing the bed would be far better for her, Nancy grabbed the woman beneath the arms and prepared to drag her. But a thin, vaporous voice protested, "That hurts. I'll walk."

"Oh, praise the Lord. Here, let me help you. I was afraid—"

"No need to be afraid. I'm dying," the woman announced feebly. "Help me to my deathbed."

"Deathbed? Nonsense!" Nancy exclaimed, forcing a resolute smile. She wrapped the old woman's arm over her shoulder and eased her up. Lifting her this way was easier, but her steps were unsteady, like a rag doll's.

"You're a Christian," the old woman whispered.

"You too?" Nancy asked, dragging her along.

"Many years," the woman replied with a hint of sadness.

"Good. Let's get you to bed and then I'll get you a doctor. You'll be fine," Nancy reassured her as they reached the bed.

"No!" the woman said, lips trembling. "No doctors." She glared at Nancy for a moment then toppled into bed.

"That's silly—you need a doctor." Nancy lifted the woman's legs to the bed then stacked two pillows beneath her head. The prickly night chill had followed them into the house and now leaked through thin walls and up through cracks between the floorboards. To keep the woman from experiencing any more of it, Nancy covered her quickly with the blanket and bedspread. "Any more blankets?"

"I don't need a doctor. Look in the closet," the small voice said.

The bedroom, like the rest of the house, had walls of exposed studs, a plank floor with throw rugs here and there and a sparse population of ancient furniture. This woman lived with the economy of an ant. The linen closet stood next to the door back to the living room—stacks of linen were folded there, more than Nancy expected. She grabbed a couple of powder blue blankets and tossed them gently over her new friend.

Strong eyes peered up, "I'll sweat."

"There's not enough water in you to sweat. I want you warm." Nancy took another appraising look at her—so frail, so reluctantly frail. "What's your name?" Nancy asked.

"Sarah Redcloud," the woman answered feebly.

"Indian?"

"Native American," she corrected but not harshly. A bit of softness had seeped in.

"Native American," Nancy repeated.

"What's your name?" Sarah asked.

"Nancy Bernard, and this is Hamster."

Sarah chuckled feebly. "Welcome to my home, Nancy Bernard—Hamster."

"Thank you," Nancy said appreciatively. "Now, you need rest."

"On one condition—no doctors," the old woman repeated. "I'm happy I'm dying, and no doctor's going to change that."

Nancy brought her brows to a point. "Were you trying to kill yourself out there?"

"No." Shock spread over her eyes. "I heard a dog—musta been Hamster." Hamster now lay by the bedroom door on one of the braided throw rugs. "I thought the coyote was—did you get my gun? It's prob'ly still out there. Go get it. I don't want it to rust." Then the woman's expression softened. "A Christian—I've been praying for a Christian."

"I was too," Nancy replied, with a sudden sour look, "and he sent me a jerk."

"Huh?"

"Nothing. You get some rest now," Nancy said firmly. "I'll take care of things out here. And, whether you like it or not, I'm getting you a doctor."

Sarah grunted disapprovingly but her eyes closed obediently— she looked nearly dead, lying there stiffly beneath the thick meadow of sky-blue wool.

At the front of the house, Nancy grabbed the heavy Winchester and stood it against the wall near the door. She gathered up her purse and the toiletries and scanned the living room.

Like the bedroom, its walls were exposed studs and its floor, planks separated by cracks and pocked occasionally by knotholes. In one corner sat an old wooden desk. Dusty and stacked with books, papers, and an old, heavy black phone, the desk seemed promising. But after rifling through it for several minutes, Nancy found nothing to help her find Sarah Redcloud's doctor.

She looked carefully around the rest of the room, but she saw nothing resembling an address or phone book.

Heading back to the bedroom for another try at the old woman, she noticed a tattered cork bulletin board hanging near the bedroom door. A variety of scraps was stuck there, most noticeably family pictures—various people, various times, and in various poses. But in the corner, tacked at the bottom and hanging off the board was a church bulletin. Although faded with age, it had a phone number in the bottom corner—the woman's church?

Reciting the number repeatedly Nancy went to the phone. The receiver was lead heavy, the dial stiff, and after the fifth ring she decided to call again in the morning.

The old woman smiled triumphantly at Nancy's return. Although still on the beckoning edge of eternity, she seemed stronger. "I guess that tells you what side the Lord's on."

"He's on both our sides. He just wants you to rest tonight."

"Nonsense," the woman harrumphed. "He wants to bring me home unmolested. Within hours, minutes maybe, I'll be seeing him face to face."

"I suppose I could want worse things for you," Nancy said as she sat gently on the side of the bed.

"I told you I'd been praying for a Christian to come," the voice became tentative, indicating a request on the way. "Since I'll probably be going soon, could you read to me—from the Bible?"

"Sure, but shouldn't you be getting some rest?"

"I'll get plenty of rest soon—very soon."

Nancy's eyes darted around the room, and she found the large-print volume on an old dresser. "What would you like me to read?"

"Oh, this is wonderful. I so wanted to hear the Scriptures before I go."

"You're not going anywhere—what do you want to hear?"

"Well, now, how about Psalm 23, then 91, then anything you like."

Nancy nodded and found the Psalms. She'd finished 23 and was half through 91 when she heard Sarah's shallow but gentle breathing. She slept. Closing the volume quietly, Nancy flipped off the light, then stepped back to the living room.

Her adrenaline pumping, Nancy sat on the old, but comfortable, overstuffed sofa and allowed herself a moment to collect her thoughts. Things had changed so quickly. A half hour before she'd been cold, alone and vulnerable beneath a highway streetlight. Now she was reasonably warm and had a comfortable place to sleep. She even had company—morbid as it may be. As she pondered it all, she found her head shaking in disbelief. "Lord, you're incredible."

Nancy's eyes drifted idly around the room. Everything was gray and worn—the walls, the floors, the wooden furniture. The edges of some of the floor planks were split, causing great, secret gaps. One hole in particular was large enough for a very fat snake to easily ooze up into the house. Nancy felt uneasy about that hole until she remembered that snakes were hibernating. An insistent layer of dust encrusted everything—floors, shelves, lampshades, and the knickknacks.

Sarah didn't have as many knickknacks as Fletcher Harris, the mafia gun guy, had, but there were quite a few on bookshelves and end tables. But these weren't just knickknacks; they were works of art—wood carvings, bronze castings, and clay sculpture. Hanging on the walls were many examples of intricate bead work: some abstract designs, some representative, all splashed with brilliant colors, all beautiful. The small plaques and signatures all pointed to

Sarah as the artist. Nancy eyed each individually from a distance, but after a while she focused on one bronze casting in particular.

Standing beside it, she studied its haunting detail. Eight inches tall, twelve long, it told a sad story. A young brave, a single feather trailing down his shoulder, slumped upon his pony—the pony dragging himself forward, head down, both rider and mount defeated. Behind the pony dragged a sling—a wickiup. Upon it lay the brave's young wife. Covered by a frayed blanket, she clutched her swollen pregnant belly. So much promise—but so little future. Wonderfully and intricately done, it was sad yet symbolic. A young family with life ahead yet heading into the era of their own extinction. On the bronze base was a small plaque that read Inheritance—Sarah Redcloud.

Even though the pressures on the Native American were far different, their defeat not of their own making, the slumping stance of the brave brought her father to mind—his same drooping form perched on a bar stool. The image hung before her for a moment.

She moved about the room again. Sprinkled among the wall-art were plaques, testimonials, and degrees. The first to catch Nancy's eye was a Bachelor of Arts from Stanford University. Nancy's father had always wanted her to go to Stanford. "You'll *be* something if you graduate from there," he'd say about once a week, with greater emphasis right after she brought home a bad test score.

Catching her eye next was something very official-looking in French, and other honors, each eloquently singling out Sarah Redcloud. Most dates were in the '30s and '40s, some in the '20s, and a couple in the '50s.

There were also framed pictures. A husband and daughter and many with just the daughter. Nancy recognized the faces from the pictures on the bulletin board. There was another door in the far corner of the room, and she stepped outside into the chill. A narrow path led to two smaller buildings—Sarah's studio and a shed?

Nancy was too cold to find out. Back in the living room, she lay on the sofa. She'd been there for only a few minutes when she heard Sarah whispering hoarsely from the bedroom, "Are you still here?"

Nancy went to the bedroom door. "I won't leave you. I was just admiring your work—wonderful."

"Now they're the work of an old, worn-out redskin. When I die, they'll be art."

"They're art now."

"They are," the artist reaffirmed, coughing weakly. "They are, aren't they?" she said again, as if affirming it to herself.

"Do you have anything you're working on now?"

"I work at breathing—and it's getting more difficult. Arthritis. I haven't worked in five years—I love the Lord, but why has he kept me alive so long when I can't work? Why?"

"Maybe he had something else in mind," Nancy said. But Sarah seemed so frail and frustrated that Nancy found herself asking God the same question. She got no answer. "But they are beautiful."

Sarah grunted. "Let's talk."

Glancing at the luminous clock, Nancy frowned. "It's after ten. Shouldn't you—?"

"No. I'm rested. And the only things to talk to out here are coyotes."

"I met one," Nancy said with a small smile. "Out there by the highway."

"Come up and sniff you, did he?"

"You know him?"

"A devil. Diablo, I call him. He's been slinking around here for years. Wants this place. He'll not get it. But tell me, child, why are you here?"

"I'm on my way to California. I got left near here."

"Hitchhiking is dangerous."

"I was riding with a friend but we parted."

"A fight?"

"No. Not really. But that's not important now. Are you warm enough?"

"Was he the jerk you mentioned?"

"I really don't want to talk about it. If I do, I'll start missing him."

"A heathen?"

"The heathenest."

"They're trouble in a relationship. I know I was." Sarah's cloudy eyes looked off somewhere.

"You were?"

"My husband, Thomas, was the son of a missionary to the Native Americans. We fell in love and married against his father's wishes. I didn't know the Lord then. I was trouble to him every day of our married life. I only came to know Jesus after Thomas had died.

Thirty years ago." Her eyes again sojourned away but returned quickly. "Is the jerk receptive?"

"His name's Mark. No, but he's also gone. I just have to control my heart a little now."

"Pray for Mark. If you care for him, maybe the Lord will bring him in."

Nancy sighed. No, she couldn't hope for that. She'd just have to let him go.

"I'm hungry," the old woman announced abruptly. "I thought I'd die tonight, and I didn't want to waste the food."

"I'll work something up. Don't die until I get back—of course, my cooking might kill you anyway." Nancy laughed, but it was a weak laugh. Talk of Mark brought some of the feelings back, and as she laughed, most of her energy was spent in a vain effort to bury them again.

The kitchen was a messy little alcove in the back of the living room, strewn with pots, pans, dishes, and silverware—some clean, some dirty. After a few minutes of washing and straightening, Nancy grabbed a can of chicken noodle soup and heated it on the gas stove.

Returning to the bedroom, Nancy found Sarah's eyes closed. "Are you awake?" she whispered as she stood over the bed.

Eyes opened sluggishly. "Smells good."

"Can you skooch up a little?" Nancy asked, sitting on the edge of the bed.

Sarah managed an inch or two and when she was set, Nancy spooned the soup gently between weak and trembling lips. As she did, she remembered that only a few days before she'd done the same for Mark. The feelings broke free again, and she mentally kicked herself for missing him, but there was no denying it—she wished he was there with her—just to talk.

"Are you all right, child?"

"Huh? Oh, yes."

A few more spoonfuls and the soup was gone. Sarah still looked weak—she probably was going to die.

"Are you warm enough?" Nancy asked.

"It takes a lot to warm these old bones—but you've managed," Sarah whispered. "Read me to sleep again."

Nancy took the Bible in hand and rested it on her lap. "What this time?"

"John. I love John. I came to know Jesus reading John."

Nancy quickly found the book and began to read. But after she'd read only a few words, Sarah interrupted. "Nancy, how does it feel to be an answered prayer?"

Nancy smiled. "I might ask you the same question." And she continued reading.

▼ ▼

Nancy didn't know how long she'd been asleep on the sofa, but sometime through the cavernous darkness, she heard a loud, searching whimper, then crying, then choking. Not sure what to expect, she scrambled across the cold floor to Sarah's side.

The woman's eyes were frozen open and her hand stood erect, reaching for something, palm up, fingers extended and beckoning. "Oh, Thomas," she whispered hoarsely. Was she asleep? *She must be*, Nancy thought. Nancy laid a gentle palm on her forehead. As with those terrible nights with Mark, the old woman was burning up.

Nancy ran to the bathroom and wet a washcloth with cool water, pressed it to Sarah's forehead, left it there for a moment, then caressed her cheeks with it. Sarah remained asleep. Her dream must have ended, for her eyes shut and her arm dropped. But her breathing became more labored—another dream? Or was breathing becoming even more difficult for her?

After refreshing the washcloth, Nancy gingerly washed Sarah's arms, neck and cheeks. Refreshing it a second time, Nancy washed her face and arms. After tossing the cloth in the sink, Nancy sat on the edge of the bed and rested for a moment. Sarah's chest rose and fell more peacefully now, and her expression seemed less tense.

Maybe aspirin would help.

Aspirin and a glass of water in hand, Nancy jostled Sarah awake.

"What?" the thin voice said.

"You need to take these."

"What? Take what?"

"Aspirin—you have a fever."

"Aspirin? But I'm dying! Aspirin?"

"Aspirin's good for fever—so they tell me."

"Anything you give me keeps me from my Lord."

"Now, I may be a whole lot younger than you are and I'm certainly no artist, but the Lord gave us life. He doesn't want us to throw it away. He'll come and get you when he's ready—not just when you're ready."

The woman lay glaring up at Nancy for a moment, but soon her crust began to crack and she gave Nancy a faint nod. "You're right, I guess." Sarah sounded disappointed. Then she smiled. "If he's sovereign I won't die before he's ready anyway."

Nancy glanced at the clock by Sarah's bed. "It's almost three in the morning—not the time for theological discussions. Shouldn't you be getting some sleep?" she suggested with as warm a smile as she could manage.

But Sarah was awake now. "Have you had to sleep in your clothes? That's horrible. What kind of hostess am I? Get a robe and slippers from my drawer—old women get lots of stuff like that and I'm no exception. You'll be warmer and more comfortable."

Without much hesitation, Nancy did as she was told and found a thick blue robe as well as some slippers. She got undressed in the bathroom and was lusciously comfortable the moment she put on the robe and slippers. "They're wonderful," Nancy said.

"They're yours—a thank you."

"Are you sure?"

"Sure, I'm sure."

"Well, okay, but you really have to get some sleep. It's late."

"Time means nothing to people who are dying." Sarah grinned. "Read me Ruth. Thomas always reminded me of Boaz." The contented smile on the wrinkled face told Nancy she had no choice. Grabbing the Bible, she read from the book of Ruth, and Sarah didn't fall asleep until the very last word.

▼ ▼

The moment Nancy snuggled up on the couch beneath a warm wool blanket, the thick blue terry cloth wrapped tightly around her, she remembered sleeping in Fletcher's cabin a few nights before. Mark had been the one in the next room then. For a moment she wished he was again. But Nancy had hit the couch exhausted, and even though it was an old piece of furniture, the couch was incredibly comfortable. Before long, even though she tried to spend a moment or two with Mark's memory, she slept.

Morning came just a little after six. With the autumn sun only an amber hint on the horizon, Nancy heard Sarah's beckoning voice, "You awake yet?"

"I'm awake, sort of," she replied and swung from beneath the covers to the frigid floor. "I'll be right there."

Lack of sleep made everything burn and ache as she flip-flopped to the bedroom.

Sarah looked amazingly rested. Not strong or ready to spring from her bed, but rested. Her large radiant eyes were made more so by the shaft of dawn's light that came from the window opposite her bed, and a wonderful toothless grin greeted Nancy.

"Did you sleep well, child?"

"Not long enough to form an opinion." She fluffed Sarah's pillow. "Can I get you some breakfast before I call a doctor out here?"

"I thought you gave that up."

"No. Unless I get some sleep I'll need him more for me than for you."

Although the battered refrigerator had its handle hanging uselessly, it worked and inside Nancy found eggs, bacon, bread, and orange juice. The old lady must have had friends, because all seemed fresh. After they ate, Nancy washed the dishes then called the church. No one answered; it was too early. She'd call later.

She returned to the bedroom.

"Who are you calling?"

"Your church. I found a bulletin."

"Humbug! They don't care about me," she said bitterly.

"Somebody must. Who brings your food?"

"A delivery boy." She harrumphed again.

"Well, we'll give the church a chance. Would you like me to read to you again?"

The old woman's eyes lit, and Nancy grabbed the Bible and read from Romans.

Thirty minutes passed quickly, and Nancy set the book down. "My eyes are tired."

"We can wait a while."

"Good, then I'm going to take a shower." The fiberglass shower was small and, like the rest of the bathroom, seemed added on. But that didn't matter; the warm water refreshed her.

After dressing, Nancy got on the phone to the church.

Pastor Hopper answered and said he didn't know who Sarah's

doctor was but he'd find out, and both he and the doctor would be out before noon.

"You're being unfair. Pastor Hopper sounded very concerned."

Sarah grunted. "Concerned for what? An old useless woman. I loved the feel of clay, so cool, so pliable. Why did God take that away from me?"

"Well," said Nancy, searching for a reply, "I'm just glad I know you."

Sarah smiled warmly. "How are your eyes?"

"Tired. Can I take a break?"

Sarah nodded reluctantly. "I'll probably last a while."

"Well, praise God." Nancy chuckled.

There was a silent moment when Nancy thought about taking a nap, but that wasn't to be.

"You did the right thing when you dumped Mark," the old woman suddenly said.

"I guess. I do feel empty without him."

"You're being molded, child. Into a Christian woman—and God knows we need more of them these days—fashioned like that clay I miss so much."

"I'm already a woman," Nancy said with a touch of defensiveness.

"I have a feeling things will look different after this trip."

"Things look different now."

"There's a time when we change—when Christian childhood is over and Christian adulthood begins. I was only a Christian a year or so when the Lord matured me. When I realized what I'd done to my husband all those years—poor Thomas. Kept him from church, balked at his faith, laughed—yes, laughed when he told me to do anything that had a spiritual foundation. Made him miserable. Mark would do that to you. Christian adulthood begins when we see Christianity as more than slogans and rallies and exuberance and we see our place before God for what it is—beloved creature to Creator, sinner in need of sanctification—and that he's working in and on our lives all the time. You'll see him everywhere; then you'll stop worrying about getting and begin to give."

Nancy had no reply. She wanted to say that her moment of maturity had come last night when she gave up Mark. But now, as the memories were rekindled and her longing kept rising from the grave, she wasn't so sure.

Chapter Twenty-Three

Pastor Hopper had a tall, Lincoln-like sparseness about him and a long sun-worn face. After a few minutes of praying with Sarah, he took Nancy out to the front yard. "She looks like she's going to have her wish this time."

"What about the doctor?"

"Doctor Hornsby says he's seen her a couple of times. He'll try to stop by on his way home."

"But she needs him now. She has moments of clarity but sometimes—"

"I know, but he's as crusty as she is. Maybe more so."

"Well, if that's the way it is around here . . ."

Hopper glanced off toward the house. "She's so old, so very, very old. Can you stay until Hornsby comes? I should be able to round some people up to stay with her after that so you can get on your way."

Nancy shook her head, "I'll stay with her for at least a couple of days. We sort of hit it off."

The pastor nodded. "She's got an infectious way about her. I haven't seen her in a while. She came to church off and on for a couple of years. Seemed real distant. Sometimes Indians have trouble fitting in; sometimes they don't. She must have had trouble and just stopped coming. It's not to my credit that I let that happen, but old people come and go around here. They retire from somewhere else, then go live with family, and leave. I should have checked. Anyway, if you're staying, I'll stop back tomorrow. If you need me, call. I'll help in any way I can."

A few minutes later, billowing dust followed his Jeep all the way to the highway.

Nancy read to Sarah most of the afternoon. When she was not

reading, they talked—about Mark, Nancy's dad, Sarah's growing up on a reservation when there were still warriors around who remembered the relentless advance of the white man. They were warm conversations—at times friend to friend, at times mother to daughter. Toward late afternoon, when Sarah spoke of her early days as an artist, she became pale and her eyes went off to that distant place.

"Sometimes I'd wonder what I'd done wrong to be punished with age," she began. "Real age. I'm ninety-three now—I think. I'd see friends—and Thomas; when age would start to creep up on them, the Lord took them home. They never got to the point when they were incontinent or so arthritic they couldn't do what they longed to do. If the Lord loved me, I'd say—maybe I still say it—he would have taken me home years ago. I hate age. It's a jail. I hate walls and I hate age."

"But you live a full life. You're so creative. I saw all the plaques and citations."

"Worthless paper."

"No. Not worthless. Maybe they are, but they say you're not worthless. I played the flute, when I had a flute, but I just played what other people write. But, you—you shape things. Beautiful, haunting things. That one with the Ind—Native American dragging his pregnant wife on the sling . . ."

"*Inheritance*—you've a sensitive eye. But I *used* to shape things. Things like *Inheritance* used to pour out of my mind into my fingers and into the clay or the wood or onto the colored beads. Just poured out—gushing. I'd work all night on some things—all night and never tire. But at seventy-two my fingers began to bind; they'd ache like needles were in the joints, and then five years ago—I cried for a week when they stopped working—became too painful to be sensitive. He might as well have cut my arms and legs off and just stood me in a corner someplace. I prayed and prayed and cried and prayed and cried some more, but the hands just got worse. Maybe the art was coming before him, but why, then, did he give me such a longing for it?"

"I kind of know the feeling," Nancy said.

"It doesn't matter. I'll have relief soon and I can ask him face-to-face."

A renewed chill intruded on the growing darkness and brought a weariness that seeped into the bedroom like ground fog.

Nancy spoke, "I don't know why I cared so much for Mark. No, that's not true. I know why."

"I've only been in love once in ninety-three years, and I didn't know why I loved Thomas either. But I did. The Lord plants love inside, plants it like he plants a tree in the desert."

"I can tell you when I first loved Mark. When he came down and helped me after I hit the tree. Remember when I told you about that? He cared, Sarah. He really cared. I could see that. I can't remember anyone else ever really caring for me. My dad would have stood on the top of that cliff and shouted down to me—my mom too. I would have climbed up on my own. I guess I was ready, and suddenly there was this obnoxious guy who cared."

"We're always ready to be cared for," Sarah said gently. "But you did the right thing. You loved the Lord more." Her eyes became distant again. "I know the Lord cares for me, and yet in the past five years I've repented of hating him so many times. I'd curse my pain and my shaking. But the Lord allowed it and each time I cursed it I cursed the Lord too." Her voice rattled to a halt. Twilight invaded the room. "To die is gain," she whispered.

"But if you had died, I never would have met you."

"Now there's a treat to miss."

"No," Nancy protested, "I'm glad I met you. Maybe the Lord's telling you to give up death like I gave up Mark." She liked sounding so wise.

But the old woman said nothing in reply. Perhaps she hadn't heard. "Read to me. Read Luke and read Jesus' birth slowly—read it twice."

By the time Nancy closed the Bible, darkness had taken over. She turned the lamp on, and it bathed the room in its stagnant yellow light. Just as she was about to get dinner, a car pulled up.

Doctor Hornsby was a brusque little man with a black medical bag. He swept into the house before Nancy could open the door all the way and after only a few quick words swept into the bedroom. He closed Nancy on the other side of the door but left her there for only a few minutes. Soon the door opened, and he swept into the living room again. "I told her she had to go to the hospital," he announced. "She doesn't want to go to the hospital."

"She thinks she's dying."

"She's right. Even if she goes to the hospital, she's going to die. She's ninety-something."

"Ninety-three."

"Whatever. She's falling apart. I saw her about a month ago and gave her a year. I was optimistic. All you can do is make her comfortable. She wants to stay here, and there's no reason for her not to. Here's my card. Call if I'm needed."

He was gone.

Nancy was shocked at his indifference, and it took a long moment to calm her anger and gather enough cheer to rejoin Sarah. When she did, Sarah motioned her to sit. "He didn't even warm that stethoscope of his. Cruel man."

"Do you want some soup or anything?"

"Chicken noodle. I have a lot of it."

After puttering in the kitchen for a moment or two, Nancy turned to see Hamster standing rigidly in the bedroom doorway—half in and half out—his sense keenly focused on something beyond the closed front door. The coyote? Nancy became still, a little frightened, watching Hamster. Then he growled, that deep threatening growl of his, his eyes steady, his snout thrust forward.

"What is it?" she whispered as if expecting an answer.

Her heart gasped when suddenly there came a rapid, persistent scratching at the door very near the floor. It sounded very familiar.

"It can't be!" Nancy's fear dissolved to excited anticipation.

"Who is it?" Sarah called weakly.

Hamster knew. He leaped at the front door, shoved his nose in the crack by the floor, sniffed anxiously, then sat back on his haunches, waiting for Nancy to open it.

She did and immediately Naomi darted in. The little fur ball yipped and danced excitedly, while Hamster lost his characteristic reserve and woofed and whimpered joyfully.

But Nancy only glanced at the dogs. Her heart stopped as she stared into the night. First she heard his shoes scuffling as he ran, then a grunt or gasp of exertion. The light from the open door caught him. Mark was far more frightened than she had been a moment before. "Keep the door open," he shouted from a few feet beyond the adobe fence.

Nancy did and seconds later, lungs grabbing noisily for air, Mark fell through the door. "He's after me," he gasped.

"Who? And what are you—?"

"A coyote. Mangiest thing I ever saw. Hideous. Yuk!" He stopped to catch his breath and fell onto the sofa, his hand clutching his throbbing chest. "Naomi jumped out of the car window—never did that before. Went after her—coyote nipped at my heels—I thought he'd chew off my leg." Panting like a freight on a steep grade, Mark leaned forward then back in an effort to fill his lungs.

"What are you doing here?"

"What am I doing here? White Fang's out there, that's why."

"But why are you back here?"

"Just let me catch my breath. I was nearly killed out there—"

"Who's there?" came the ancient voice.

"Mark," Nancy called back to her.

"No kidding!" The voice, for reasons lost to Nancy, sounded excited.

"Now, why are you here?"

"I didn't plan on it, believe me," he said, starting to calm a bit. "I've driven through a whole gaggle of cats, and Naomi's never jumped out the window before. She must have sniffed the big guy—nothing stops love."

"But what are you *doing* here? You passed me going sixty yesterday on the highway. Me under a streetlight and you didn't stop."

Beginning to calm, he said offhandedly, "I followed you," as if there were an "of course" in there somewhere.

"Followed me?" Her brows scrunched up. "But I saw you go by."

"I turned off my light and doubled back. By the time I reached where you'd been you were gone. It took a while, but I found this place and I've been out there most of last night and all today. Caring about people can be very boring sometimes. It reduces you to doing stupid things—like juggling cacti." He pushed a hand toward her. "Which hurt."

"In your case being reduced to stupidity was just a minor reduction."

"Good one." His breathing was normal now, but he sat with an arrogance she didn't like—his arms stretched across the back of the sofa. "Why'd you stay? I figured I'd see you heading for the highway long before this. I had it all figured out how I was going to intercept you—or maybe be the one to pick you up when the old thumb went out. Who's in the bedroom?"

"Is that Mark?" Sarah's voice rattled out. "Show him to me."

"Come on, I want you to meet someone." Nancy grabbed Mark by the hand and over a shallow protest dragged him into the bedroom. When he saw Sarah, his expression grew apprehensive.

"This is Sarah Redcloud. She's an artist."

"Was," Sarah quickly corrected. "So you're Mark. Another answered prayer."

"What do you mean? What does she mean? Another answered—?"

"I love to hear a man read. And he has such a lovely voice. I've been listening."

"He does, doesn't he?"

"You'll read the Bible to me, won't you, young man?" Sarah smiled and although her eyes revealed that she wanted it to be a loving smile, she looked sadly comical with no teeth and all her wrinkles.

"Uh, I don't read very well," Mark said. "Nancy's the Bible person. Not me."

"Nonsense," the old woman frowned deeply. "I'm dying, and you can't deny a dying woman her wishes. Nancy's tired. I've driven her to her wits' end—isn't that right, child?"

"Well . . ."

"She needs a rest. You wouldn't deny Nancy rest, would you? I never sleep. Old people don't need much sleep, and you aren't going to find anyone older than me. Not around here, anyway." She laughed and in that toothless rattle of a laugh Nancy found something even more to admire.

Sarah must have been dynamite when younger—with her devastating charms and wonderfully disarming ways. With the remnants something to behold, the original package must have been incredible.

But there was no time for such speculation; Mark was being cornered, and like any other dumb animal in the same situation, he was getting ready to do something he might regret. He'd already tried to interrupt Sarah a couple times and, having failed, was now growing flushed.

Nancy touched him lightly on the arm. "Come on and help me. I'm making some soup for dinner."

"Great idea," Mark said, and Nancy could never remember him sounding more relieved.

"Well, come back soon, Mark," Sarah cooed.

Hamster and Naomi had no intention of following them. They'd already resumed their former positions as if they'd never been separated. Hamster lay curled up on his favorite rug and Naomi was snuggled within the curl.

In the kitchen Mark spoke in a forced whisper. "I didn't think you wanted to see me again. The fact you didn't use that rifle on me is encouraging." He indicated the Winchester leaning by the door.

"The night's young. But I have been thinking about you."

"You have?" He made a slight move toward her.

"Ease off. Maybe you should go feed the dogs."

"The car's a ways off."

"Drive it up and get the dogs fed," she ordered. He needed something to keep his hands busy, and that was as good a thing as any.

"You did see that I was chased in here by a coyote."

"I know the fella—I was standing out by the highway when he and I met."

"Both your legs are still intact, so it couldn't have been too traumatic. How'd you find this place anyway?"

"I didn't. Hamster took off on me and found it. He dragged me here. Or rather the Lord did. Isn't Sarah something?" Nancy glanced off toward the bedroom. "I'll miss her—she's right when she says she's dying. The doctor confirmed it today. Sometimes she's clear, like a minute ago. Other times she's not—and her dreams are real vivid. Sometimes she talks in her sleep. I'll miss her." Nancy grabbed a can of soup. "There's some hamburger in the fridge—looks a little old, but I think it'll be all right. We'll have soup and hamburgers—how's that sound?"

Mark had picked up one of the sculptures and eyed it critically. "She do this?"

"I like that one over there—the Indian with his pregnant wife."

Mark grunted appreciatively.

"She's quite an artist. But she hasn't been able to work in five years. It's made her a little bitter."

"Being forced to go out after the dog food's going to make me a little bitter too."

"Take the rifle," Nancy suggested, opening the soup can. "Sauce pans are under there, get me one."

Mark did and set it on the ancient white stove.

"I'm glad I met her. She's told me some motherly sort of things—you know?"

"I don't like old people," Mark said flatly.

"How can you not like old people?"

"It's easy. I don't want to read to her—especially the Bible. In fact, if she asked me to read *Playboy* to her, I wouldn't. Well, that's not entirely true—but I don't like being around old people. Especially when they're getting ready to croak. You're going to have to tell her that."

Nancy added a can of water and stirred the soup over the flame. "Come on, 'ye of little faith,' you have to admit that God brought you here to help me."

"I don't have to admit any such thing."

"She wants to be read to all the time, and I'm tired. She had me up most of last night and all of today, and she's going to be up most of tonight. I nearly fell asleep reading to her today."

"That's not my problem. I came back here to be near you. I'd still be in the car just being near you if it hadn't been for that dog of mine. I didn't come here to nurse old ladies."

"Well," Nancy began, her head cocked in thought, a spoon pointing his way, "I guess you have a choice to make. Help me help her, or get back in that rattletrap of yours—after you feed the dogs—and go on to California alone."

Mark's brows knit. "You mean if I help her you'll go the rest of the way with me?"

Nancy hesitated but only for a moment. Yes, that was what her heart had said.

"Okay," Mark jumped at it. "You win. But I don't have to like it."

"No, you don't have to like it."

Mark's smile grew broad, and he leaned forward and kissed her lightly on the lips. She pulled away at first, but then she couldn't help herself. She kissed him back. His lips were warm and yielding, and what frightened a good part of her was that the kiss felt like she'd come home.

He appeared weak in the knees as he pulled away. After a moment to collect himself, he looked toward the door. "Well, I used to shoot birds with a twenty-two; I guess a Winchester's about the same. See you in a minute."

Chapter Twenty-Four

Dinner over, dishes washed, Mark pulled two creaky, wooden kitchen chairs into the bedroom, and he and Nancy sat side by side while Nancy read to Sarah. But after only a few minutes, Nancy's eyes burned unmercifully, and she handed the heavy volume to Mark. "I'm going to lie down for a while, Sarah. Mark will read."

"Oh good. I've been looking forward to this since you came, young man."

"Couldn't I just find a nearby town where I can rent you a TV or something?"

"You need cable out here. I looked into it once. No, I just love a man's voice reading the Word. Thomas would read every night after dinner. Oh, such a deep, mellow voice he had. But I hated it. Until he died, and then I would hear his voice in my mind and I'd miss it. Such a bad wife I was to him. Soon I'll be able to tell him how sorry I am."

"I don't read very well," Mark said.

"It doesn't matter. It's the Lord's word. No matter how poorly it's read it will accomplish what it's sent to accomplish," Sarah said, winking at Nancy. Nancy leaned over and kissed the old woman's wrinkled cheek—it was cold, like a winter glove. Life was already ebbing.

From the couch Nancy could hear Mark reading. He didn't read well. Each word was an enemy to be struggled with, and the King James Version made it doubly difficult. But Nancy had to admit he was keeping his part of the bargain, for he persisted. Only a couple of times did he have to turn to Sarah for help, and Sarah got great pleasure out of giving it. After a half hour or so, Mark was given permission to take a deserved rest.

He excused himself and went to be with Nancy. She made room for him on the couch, and he sat down beside her.

"You understand that stuff?"

"Most of it," she said.

"I didn't understand a word of it. I might as well have been reading Greek or something."

Nancy said nothing for a minute. "She appreciates it though. I don't think it will be much longer."

"She better not die on my watch—I don't think I'd like that very much."

"Go on, read to her some more."

Mark groaned, but he got to his feet and went back into the bedroom. He felt like he was stepping into a mausoleum and the woman, though still breathing, already lay in her coffin. He hated old people and felt terribly uncomfortable around them. But a deal was a deal, and his reward would be worth the discomfort.

"Read Lamentations."

"I don't know—" Mark hesitated. "I'm not into funerals—that sounds like something you read at a funeral."

"In a way it was—Jerusalem's funeral. I feel like it now though. Find Psalms in the middle and page forward. It's right after Jeremiah—he wrote it."

"Got it," Mark said and began reading. When Lamentations ended, he leaned back in the creaking chair and yawned.

"Tired, Mark?" Sarah asked.

"Beat. I didn't sleep well last night."

"What do you think about Jesus, Mark?"

"I don't. You want something to drink?"

"No," Sarah said, "I don't need more trips to the bathroom."

"Well, I need a drink. I'll see you in a second."

But he didn't go to the kitchen. Nancy lay sleeping peacefully on the couch, and Mark had no intention of letting her enjoy that any longer. Without hesitation, he sat next to her and jostled her awake.

"You awake?"

"Huh?"

"I can't take this anymore," Mark whispered. "You've had a rest. It's your turn."

Nancy grabbed his arm and eyed his watch. "It's only nine. Take her 'til eleven, and if she's still awake, I'll take her after that."

"Eleven? Come on, have a heart!" But Nancy lay back and closed her eyes. "Okay, but not a second longer," he conceded.

Reluctantly, Mark returned to Sarah.

Eleven o'clock came and Mark stretched and put the Bible down. Eyes stinging, he was about to get Nancy when the old woman told him she was tired and wanted to sleep. Almost instantly she drifted off.

Alone, Mark wondered where *he* was to sleep. *Fine hosts these are,* he thought sarcastically.

He woke Nancy. "She's asleep. Where's my bed?"

But Nancy didn't answer him. Though her eyes opened, she wasn't awake, and after only a moment of staring up at him, they closed again and she curled up beneath the blankets. Dejected and feeling as if he'd made a mistake coming back, Mark returned to the bedroom and rummaged through the closet. He quickly found a couple of pillows and a worn sleeping bag. He unrolled it next to the couch, but just as he was about to stretch out, he heard Nancy groan, then say, "Not here—in the bedroom."

"Where?"

"On the floor or something. But not in here."

She turned her back to him.

Feeling lost, a vise of indifference closing in, Mark slumped over and grabbed the pillows. He jammed them under his arm, grabbed the sleeping bag, and shuffled back into the bedroom. The dogs were near the door, and he suppressed an urge to kick the big one as he passed. Seeing that the large braided rug at the foot of Sarah's bed would offer some protection from splinters, he laid the pillows and sleeping bag on it, unzipped the sleeping bag all the way and, after opening it, fell on top. He then pulled the other side of the bag over him. The fact that he was comfortable further irritated him. After a few minutes of fuming, he found himself really getting into and enjoying his anger.

He counted the things that angered him: Nancy for blackmailing him into this deal, Nancy again for making him sleep with the old lady and the dogs, the old lady for taking advantage of him, the old lady for being an old lady, himself for caring so much for Nancy that he'd let himself get imprisoned like this.

After all, this was a prison. Caring had always been a prison—it always meant giving himself away, subjugating himself to what others wanted.

He hated that feeling. He was a man—men were supposed to be in control. Yet whenever he got around an old lady she'd twist everything around so that he had to be something he wasn't, do something he didn't want to do, be somewhere he didn't want to be—so that he became nothing more than a slave.

And yet . . .

In his mind's eye he saw Nancy's face and the love for him there, her eyes searching over him, her lips pressing against his. He felt her lips and her arms pulling him tightly to her.

The vise began to loosen, and his anger began to wane, but only a bit, and as he lay there in the night, he decided that his anger was inappropriate and would bring nothing but more trouble. He pushed it away, buried it in the black grave that was all around him.

He knew he was exhausted, and as such it was easy to be angry and resentful. The morning would be something new—he'd be rested. He longed to be rested again—or just *to* rest again, to be somewhere that revived him rather than wore him out.

The bikers—the one with the Indian head shield on his roll bar—they were another reason he had stopped to keep tabs on Nancy. If he was off the road—their road—they'd never find him.

Their road. Another place he didn't belong. Mark longed for a place where he did belong—wherever that was. Such a place would know him, and he'd be safe there—safe to be himself, safe to be with friends, whoever they were. Safe to be with Nancy. He couldn't remember ever being with someone who loved him, who stayed with him through arguments and breakups. Who kissed him like she wanted to be kissed and held him like she wanted to be held.

He wanted to be with her too. He chuckled about the cows—the farmer with the gun was no picnic, but the cows were funny. And the snow fight. That was a kick. He hadn't laughed like that in—who knew how long. She brought out the kid in him—the all right kid, the kid who didn't hurt people or do stupid things, the kid who just had fun and enjoyed life. He loved her for that—whatever that meant.

Even though those thoughts wrapped him in a certain contentment, Mark still couldn't sleep. After listening to the dogs snore and whine in their dreams for a while, he turned on his back, rested his head on his hands and lay looking up at the ceiling. Although it was dark, a wash of gray stole through the window. There must have been a moon, for its light cast the room in a gossamer gray. Eyes wandering aimlessly, he came to focus on something standing in the corner of the room between Sarah's old dresser and the wall.

A sculpture of a person—no, two—about eighteen inches tall. The more it came into focus as his concentration separated the shadows, the more intrigued he became. Not normally drawn to art, Mark found the magnetism of the piece undeniable. Slipping from the sleeping bag, he crawled silently to it. It was an Indian woman, face stern, eyes defiantly forward, her shoulders sagging, but only slightly, with a world weariness—but so young for such weariness. At her side stood a boy, his chin coming to her waist, her hand pressing him protectively to her side. In the faint light Mark could see that the boy was crying, his face drooped, his eyes twisted, his lip extended in a pout. *Indian boys don't cry*, he thought. In the mother's eyes, though created with only a few quick strokes, was compassion—maybe she, too, was close to tears. She understood her son's hurt. This mother was protecting her son, consoling him against injustice. Her boy could cry—it was all right.

Mark lifted the heavy piece, felt the cold, lifeless clay yet knew there was much life in it, so much that touched him. He could imagine himself dropping and breaking it, so he gingerly set it down. But he didn't stop looking at it, drinking it in. The old woman had talent—she knew him—or people like him.

Mark suddenly hated her all the more for knowing him. She'd peeked into private places and he resented her for that—but then he realized how irrational that feeling was, and he tucked it away before he crawled back to the sleeping bag.

The moment his head hit the pillow he heard, "That you, Mark? I need help to the bathroom."

After the bathroom was more reading, more talking, some napping and finally, when she slept and he returned to his sleeping bag, she dreamed.

They must have been dreams because the old woman lay beneath the blankets, eyes shut tightly, her toothless mouth reciting strange noises that only resembled words. They drifted up with the rhythm of sentences—of one person speaking to another. Then they died away and a few minutes later, just as he was settling back in, Sarah woke. More reading and finally some more sleeping. When the gray dawn came, Mark was sure he hadn't slept more than an hour all night.

Nancy, on the other hand, woke refreshed. Standing at the bedroom door, seeing Mark struggle to wake, she said, "I thought you were going to wake me. But I'm glad you didn't. How are you feeling this morning?"

Sarah answered her, "Oh, Mark's been wonderful company."

"I need coffee," Mark croaked, hair askew, eyes red. He got to his feet and rubbed the stubble on his chin, then worked his knees to chase the aches away and left the two women.

Nancy followed him to the kitchen. "Thank you for letting me sleep."

"I couldn't wake you."

"You could have if you wanted to. Thank you."

He found the coffee, the pot and put them together to start the perking. "She got sugar?"

Nancy pulled a tin cup from the cupboard and found him a spoon.

He leaned against the wooden counter as the coffee growled and popped. "Did you ever hear one of her dreams?"

"Once."

"Weird, huh? I guess they're dreams. I woke up to this talking in her sleep. I couldn't make out words, but whatever they were seemed like sentences. Gibberish. I did make out a name—who's Thomas?"

"Her late husband."

Mark grunted. "Old people are weird."

"I'll miss her."

"I won't. When this is over I'm going to need a vacation."

"Sounds to me like you're always on vacation—but keep her company for a little while longer while I get breakfast, then you can get some sleep. You want a shower?"

"A shave too."

"I'll get breakfast—you listen for her."

The doctor called at about ten and the pastor at about eleven. They both expected the worst. Only the pastor sounded pleased when Nancy told him that Sarah was not only still alive but cheerful. By lunch, though, Nancy saw that Sarah was weakening; again her voice became strained, her eyes distant, and occasionally she'd lapse into a curious state between sleep and wakefulness that came on suddenly. Her eyes would become large and glazed, and she'd stare off somewhere above her, her breathing cavernous; her lips would move silently, almost imperceptibly, as if she were muttering to someone in a different world. It would only last for a minute or two, and when she returned. she remembered nothing.

Sarah would die soon. Nancy knew that and began to prepare herself. She told herself that this was only a woman she'd known for two days, that the only connection between them was this special event—Sarah's passing. She preached to herself about the better place Sarah was going and how much better off she'd be and how her hands would work there and that she'd be able to produce heavenly works of art again—works showing joy instead of sadness. But, for all that, Nancy couldn't shake the feeling of loss—yet another loss knocking on her heart's door.

As if to give credence to Nancy's mourning, a fever ignited toward evening but a couple of aspirin snuffed it out.

Mark had slept off and on most of the day, and by dinner he was fully awake and far more cheerful than he had been in the morning. Nancy prepared omelettes for dinner—omelettes were really the only thing her father had ever taught her how to make—and they ate together in the bedroom. They were a trio again.

After dinner, Mark read to Sarah—John again—while Nancy took a few moments and went out into the front yard. The dry, crisp air, not quite as cold as the previous night, revived her. But in spite of her earlier resolve to face Sarah's death calmly and maturely, to see it as a spiritual event in Sarah's eternal life instead of as an emotional attack, it still overwhelmed her. "Take her peacefully, Lord," she said finally. "And thank you for letting me meet her."

She shook the sadness away so that she could drink in the scenery that Sarah had relished for so many years—the rugged, purple foothills, the arid sea of shapes and shadows. Except for Mark stumbling over the words inside, there was complete stillness.

But beyond the stillness, Nancy suddenly perceived a presence—a movement in the gloom just beyond the light, then sounds of panting and nearly imperceptible footsteps. Clipped by the bedroom window's light, the coyote emerged then disappeared again. But that fleeting glance was enough to bring life to the shadow. Tail and head down, eyes riveted on Nancy, legs four naked sticks, the animal paced back and forth like an earthbound vulture. Nancy caught only fleeting glimpses of him as he moved in and out of the shadows, but he was out there stalking her—and stalking Sarah.

Inside, her resolve waning, the burden of Sarah's death growing, Nancy felt oppressively weary. Her mother's death had been a terrible ordeal. Sarah's passing was forcing her to relive it, and that was going to take more strength than she thought she had. Working her locket for the first time since she'd come to this old shack in the desert, Nancy stepped into the bedroom.

"How are you two doing?"

"I haven't read this much since the third grade. I hated the third grade."

"He reads very well," Sarah said.

"Not bad for having no idea what I'm reading. Words pass from ear to ear without sticking to anything."

"The Gospels are the most wonderful things to read. Jesus is our only hope, Mark," Sarah said firmly.

"And your only hope is a new body," Mark tossed back.

"Mark!" Nancy couldn't believe he'd said that.

"You're right, Mark. Actually my hope is in where I go to get it." Then Sarah added, her voice growing immensely weary, "I've prayed for you, Mark."

"Well, thanks," Mark replied dryly. "I'm going to get something to drink." He got to his feet and trudged from the room.

When they were alone, Sarah's hand went up and beckoned Nancy to take hold. The old woman pulled her down. "It won't be long now. But I'm sure it won't happen tonight. I want you to sleep. I'll keep him reading the Word. Perhaps the Lord will work."

"You've been doing this for him?"

"Who else?" she said. "He reads terribly. Third grade was not good to him. But faith comes through hearing and hearing from the Word of God. Even when it's read like that. And his stumbling around gives me time to pray for him."

Nancy laughed and wanted to weep at the same time. Even so close to death Sarah was thinking of someone else. "I'll pray too," she said.

"You mean you haven't been? Shame on you!"

Mark returned, a glass of water in hand. "It's after nine. I want a break. You take over for a while."

Mark went out in front as Nancy had, but he quickly returned. "White Fang's out there. I'll rest in here."

▼ ▼

At 2:00 A.M. Mark lay curled up in his sleeping bag unable to sleep. Nancy and the dogs snored away, the old woman had been sleeping for almost twenty minutes—a record—and all his efforts to sleep had failed.

He didn't like death. He didn't like to be around it. He didn't like its permanence, its stench, what it represented, and the memories it revived. Saying he didn't like it was an understatement—he detested it and whenever he could, he avoided it.

He glanced at the sculpture of the Indian woman and her son standing in the corner. "Why couldn't you have been my mother?" he muttered. "Maybe you were—she was cold and rock hard too."

But his sarcasm couldn't soften the knot that was forming in his chest.

He wasn't sure where it came from. There were so many possible reasons for it.

He decided to leave—he had to—death, the memories, what he was. Whether Nancy came with him or not, he had to get out of there.

A sound whispered up like rising vapor from the bed.

Oh, no—not another dream, he said to himself.

But the whispering persisted, and this time Mark heard Thomas's name quite clearly. It seemed eerie to hear it coming from the wings of darkness, a breathy whisper, a calling to the dead. Was *he* dreaming? No. He listened and heard the name again. Frightened, Mark rose and peered over the top of the bed.

Shocked by what he saw, he sat transfixed.

The old woman, who had been too weak to raise an arm earlier, now sat upright in bed, her eyes wide, staring through him as if *he* were the ghost. Then she whispered her dead husband's name over and over again as if she were in a trance.

Mark's heart thundered—had Sarah become a zombie? She certainly looked like the living dead. "Sarah?" He moved closer, but her eyes remained fixed on the darkness.

"Thomas?" She'd connected with his voice. "The money. Take it to the church. Dorothy mustn't get it. It's for them."

"What money?" He felt foolish asking.

"Under the green board," she whispered, a leathery hand on his cheek. The moment she touched him a peace settled on her face. "Oh, Thomas—soon, Thomas. Take it to the church, Thomas. It's for them."

"I will," Mark whispered, and the instant he said it, she collapsed on the pillows, relaxed, breathing heavily again—her dream over.

Mark didn't move for a while. Confused and still a little frightened, he had never been a part of a dying mind's ramblings before. Not sure what to do next, he stood over the old woman for several minutes. But he finally decided to put it all in its proper place. "Weird," he muttered and returned to the sleeping bag. But the experience had been too emotional to be quickly tucked away, so he lay awake for a while before finally succumbing to exhaustion.

The rest of the night passed with only one more interruption—a brief reading. But Sarah was failing fast, and before long she slept again as did Mark.

He woke remarkably rested at about seven to the aroma of bacon. Stepping into the living room, he saw Nancy in the kitchen still in a thick, blue robe. "That smells real good."

"Your coffee's on too," she announced.

"Maybe I'm the one who died and went to heaven."

Nancy laughed softly. "It's not all roses, Speedbump," she said.

"What do you mean, Chickenlips?"

"I think, after breakfast and after you finish your second cup of coffee—maybe even after your shower—we're going to clean Sarah's house."

"What? Why?" Mark's brows dipped.

"Because she's going to die, and I want her house to be clean when she does. A woman likes a clean house, and it's the least I can do for her."

"Like you cleaned my car?"

"At least she's not going to run away in a pout and leave me to freeze."

"All that aside, I've done enough for the old bird. I've been up half the night and I was up the night before. I have *officially* done enough."

"Mark." Nancy waved a spatula his way. "We're cleaning the house."

Mark cursed softly, but after his second cup of coffee—he was going to have to teach Nancy how to make good coffee—and after his shower, he got to work. Nancy worked harder, but he kept up and before long the living room looked less dusty, the windows less streaked, and the whole room less haphazard.

"Now for her room," Nancy announced, sweeping the last of the dirt into the front yard.

"The dust'll kill her," Mark said, whining just a little.

"Not if we're careful," Nancy told him, opening the bedroom door they'd closed to keep the dust localized.

The moment it opened, a toothless grin greeted them. "You two are so precious," Sarah said, a tear forming in her eye. "I'm so fortunate to have a God who sent me you two." She eyed them both in turn. "Even my daughter, Dorothy, won't find fault."

Dorothy—the name in the dream. Mark's ears perked, but he didn't have time to think about it, for Nancy shoved a dust cloth in his hand. "Be careful to wipe the dust, don't stir it up."

Mark nodded absently. Preoccupied with thoughts of the dream, he carefully worked the top of the dresser, pushing the dust that gathered onto the floor.

"Shake the rugs," Nancy ordered, and she lightly slapped the dogs with her broom. When they indignantly rose and left, Nancy waited for Mark to act.

He grabbed the rug the dogs were on and the one he'd been sleeping on. Outside he gave them an energetic shaking. When a century worth of dust died away, he took them back inside. He put the dogs' rug down and was about to spread the other out when he saw the green board. Faded with age, it was about eighteen inches long and eight inches wide and lay like a green patch with the rest of the planks.

Mark stiffened, both excited and disbelieving. Afraid Nancy might get suspicious, he quickly spread the rug with a flourish. He then excused himself for a second and went out into the living room. There he allowed himself to ask the questions. Was Sarah's dream all a dream? Was there really money under there? And if there was, how much?

Chapter Twenty-Five

From the moment Mark saw the green board, finding out what lay beneath it was all that mattered to him. Only two problems stood in his way. The first was to keep the old lady from telling Nancy what she'd told him; the other was to extract the money, if there, undetected.

Mark accomplished the first by staying awake with the old lady all day. Smiling cheerfully, he took complete charge of Sarah under the guise of giving Nancy a well-deserved rest. While Nancy lay on the sofa and read or sat with them or walked in the crisp, clear day with the dogs, he read to Sarah, fed her, talked to her, and stayed glued to her while she slept. Only twice did he leave her side, but after slyly questioning Nancy when he returned, he decided all was still on track.

"You're being so good to me, Mark." The old woman said several times during the day.

Mark responded to each comment with a forced smile and, "Well, I'm growing quite fond of you."

When Nancy first mentioned how helpful he was being, he said, "Well, I've turned over a new leaf. I want to help where I can. I care for you, Nancy, and I haven't been showing it lately."

Nancy instantly showed signs of an emotional meltdown, so he repeated himself and enjoyed the happy shock the words brought. Toward the end of the day, after he'd uttered his magic words for the fourth time, Nancy reacted more strongly. Wordlessly setting down the chicken noodle soup can she'd just opened for dinner, she wrapped her arms around his neck and kissed him, first on the cheek then on the lips. Any other time his heart would have turned to mush, but today he had something else on his mind. What lay beneath the green board was far too distracting.

His chance came after midnight. The old woman was weakening. The time between naps was growing shorter. At 1:00 A.M., when she dozed off, she'd only been awake for twenty minutes. On the other hand, the time she slept was growing—up to an hour. Although her sleep had become more restless, filled with dreams and talking that had become more agitated and less understandable, when she finally closed her eyes Mark knew she'd be out for a while.

He stood quietly and waited a moment to make sure she was sound asleep, then he checked on Nancy. Finding her asleep, he went quietly to the kitchen and got a knife, his heart racing. He pulled the sleeping bag away, and using the kitchen knife, he pried the board up. With no nails holding it down, it came up easily.

He looked down and saw a coffee can sealed by a thin plastic cover.

He lifted the can out and popped the lid. Wound tightly in every direction were bills—money.

Heart pounding, afraid to breathe, Mark reached into the can and immediately felt the very real, very cool, very special feel of cash. Painstakingly, he dislodged the bills, and when he unrolled them his heart thundered. There were mostly twenties and fifties—and an occasional hundred. When he'd finished the wonderful task of counting, he leaned back against the bed and surveyed the stacks— $14,860.

But his euphoria lasted only a moment. He heard the bed rustle, a prelude to the old woman's waking. He put everything back carefully: the money, the can, the lid, the board, and lifted his head above the bed. By the dim light, he saw that she was half-conscious and stirring restlessly. She'd be fully awake soon. Certain that she hadn't heard him, his plan was simple now: he'd read to her, wait until she fell asleep, grab the can, and leave.

He read faster in an effort to speed up time and tire her sooner. But neither occurred. An hour and a half crawled by before the old woman finally drifted off. Anxiously, Mark sat for several minutes watching her fall into deep unconsciousness before he moved. When he was sure she was really asleep, he rose to his feet, with fatalistic determination threw back the rug, pried up the board and grabbed the can; putting board and rug back, he stepped quickly past the sofa on his way to the front door to the car. Then he stopped, his heart suddenly in a vise, his shoes glued to the floor.

In the dim light, a thought spun a dizzy course in his head. It disturbed him and caused his head to ache with the pulse. It wasn't being a thief that disturbed him—it was that he was seriously considering *not* being a thief. He held nearly $15,000 that no one knew existed—money a dying woman would never miss. He not only could, but would, get away with this. There was no doubt; no one would ever know.

Yet he couldn't take it.

This sudden morality frightened him. Not that Mark thought himself particularly immoral but to change so dramatically so quickly thrust him suddenly onto shaky ground.

Something was changing that he didn't understand. It was this lack of understanding that he feared. If he stayed, he would change even further. Familiar anchors that moored him in safe harbors—the harbors that made up who and what he was—wouldn't moor him anymore. Set adrift, he would have to find other harbors, most unknown, and the unknown brought other fears—dark and foreboding fears. Nancy had entangled him and he was being changed. These changes might unlock doors that needed to remain closed.

Returning to the bedroom, he stood in the doorway for several minutes, frightened and confused.

Drifting meant finding new harbors and dropping new anchors. Emotional anchors must be attached deeply, on the solid bedrock of his identity. This situation required looking deeply into those things. But for Mark, looking deeply had long been forbidden—his core was off limits. The Do Not Enter sign posted on it was very real and to reopen and reenter that place were the greatest terrors of all. For Mark, this was all but impossible.

Although Mark didn't understand everything he felt, he understood enough about the dark clouds boiling up inside him to know that something had to be done to stop them and done quickly. He had to leave. Though he clothed his decision to leave in an illusion—he was eluding a trap set by two women intent on making him what he didn't want to be—there was still a small, very frightened part of him who knew the real reason: leaving would dam the current and allow the child within him a triumphant return to his hideout.

Now a man with a single thought, Mark quickly replaced the money, the board, and the rug and grabbed Naomi. After taking a deep, resolute breath, he headed silently for the dark front yard, coyote or not. He made only one detour. He grabbed the chicken noodle soup can from the trash—the one that Nancy had held just before she'd kissed him—and stuffed it in his jacket pocket.

Naomi in one arm, he walked to his car, grabbed a bag of clothes, found his screenplay, rolled it and stuffed it in the bag. Nancy would need the car—it was the least he could do for her. He closed the door as gently as he could and continued to the highway. He waited beneath the streetlight only twenty minutes before a Kenworth squealed to a stop, picked him up, and took him away.

▼ ▼

Nancy woke to Sarah's groaning and restless stirring. She called Mark's name through the yellow dawn. No reply. She crawled from beneath the blanket and set her feet on the cold floor. She ran into Sarah's room and found her gasping, her eyes closed, mouth open, laboriously sucking in all the air she could. There was drooling, too, and trembling hands reached for and clung to her heart. Sarah was dying, and Nancy stood by anxiously and helplessly.

Nancy gasped one prayer and then another, her hands reaching for Sarah then pulling back, her feet turning for the phone, then turning back to Sarah again, not wanting to leave her side. Much movement, all useless.

Sarah became stiffly silent, then a weak protest came from convulsing lips, then a rush of air as life escaped. In the dawn's dim light, her body lay still.

Nancy's heart went numb. "Oh, Lord, she's yours now." To save her eyes from burning tears, Nancy turned away from the frail old body that had been her new friend.

"Mark?" she cried. "Where are you?"

She grabbed her locket, and her thumb worked it feverishly. She saw that Naomi was gone, and when she went outside, she saw that he was nowhere in sight. The Pacer was there and that puzzled her, but there was little doubt he'd left. She was very much alone. She longed to talk to him and share her loss with him. She needed his support, and she longed for him more than ever before. Why had he left? It didn't matter; what mattered was that he was gone. Her friend had died, and she was alone.

Now there were tears. Rivers of them.

The doctor came some time later; more understanding now, he didn't seem to mind being awakened. He knew the pastor's number, so he saved Nancy the trouble and called him. "I hope she went quietly."

"It was terrible. I've never seen anyone die before—she was my friend." More tears.

When her tears had dried, the doctor said softly, "You never get used to it. The house looks nice. You cleaned the place up." He gave the house an appreciative nod.

Pastor Hopper came and soon thereafter the funeral home's old hearse arrived. While the pastor stayed with Nancy in the living room, the doctor went in with the attendants to supervise the handling of Sarah's body. When they'd disappeared into the bedroom Nancy noticed that she'd been rubbing the locket again—maybe for a long while, she didn't know, but her thumb and her hand muscles were sore.

"Pastor Hopper, I'll be right back," she said and stepped into the bedroom. The attendants were in the process of covering Sarah in a sheet. They stopped when Nancy entered. "She was my friend— could I be alone with her for just a second?"

The attendants looked to the doctor for direction, and he nodded quietly. When they'd left, Nancy stood over the lifeless form. She actually didn't look much different—with her dried-apple face, her high cheekbones. Nancy slipped the locket from around her neck and placed it around Sarah's and clasped it. Then she positioned the heart on her thin chest. "I guess it's time to give up childish things—from one mother to someone I wish was my mother."

Nancy bent down and kissed Sarah's cheek and found it not much colder than when she was alive. A few minutes later the hearse took Sarah away. The doctor left right after that, leaving Nancy with the pastor.

"I found a file on her this morning at the church. I must have just missed it before. There were a few notes I made after talking to her the first time. She had a daughter, Dorothy Guiterrez. I called her. She's not the most pleasant person in the world. A little angry she hadn't been contacted in time to come today. Called me incompetent. I feel that way sometimes. I'm sure she'll take charge of whatever happens next."

"Sarah was quite a woman."

"Oh, yes. I wish I'd known her better."

"I was wondering. Do you think I would be wrong to take one of the statues as a remembrance?"

"I think she'd want you to have it. She'd probably call it payment or something. They are beautiful, aren't they? Maybe she'll be famous now that—well, maybe she'll become famous. I remember a few years back that she gave a couple of small statues to a church rummage sale. She didn't like us much and maybe with good reason. We weren't as attentive to her needs as we should have been."

Nancy took the bronze Native American dragging his pregnant wife and cradled it lovingly. Her hands savored its detail. This was part of Sarah, and Nancy's hands were now touching secret places that Sarah's hands once touched, that her mind had once envisioned and obedient fingers had formed. For an instant she felt very close to Sarah and knew she'd always have a part of her.

"I guess there's nothing to keep me here," she said to Pastor Hopper. "I'll be going now."

She found the keys in the Pacer and pushed Hamster into the backseat. With the pastor in the front yard waving, Nancy fired up the engine, pulled out to the highway, waited for a couple of pickup trucks to whine by, and scanned the horizon for bikers. When all was clear, she eased onto the blacktop. Her heart still too numb to ask why everything had happened, she headed toward California.

Chapter Twenty-Six

Pacifica was cramped between ocean and coastal mountains. A little south of San Francisco, it waited for Nancy as she rounded the mountain to the north and headed down the irregular coast highway. Restless, foam-crested waves beat at the rust-rock shore while the sun struggled through gray morning fog. It was 10:30. Although she could have made it the night before, she'd spent the night at a rest stop, wanting to confront her father in the morning when she'd be refreshed and he'd be sober. After chasing away aching muscles, she washed in the rest room, did the best she could with her hair and dreamed of her next shower. No matter how her talk with her father went, there would be a shower soon.

When she rummaged in her purse for her lipstick, she found the small box, the one with Mark's heart in it. For an instant she thought about buying a chain so she could put it on. But she didn't. She pushed the box deep into the folds of her purse and left it there.

As the Pacer rattled along the coast road beside familiar sea-battered crags, Nancy longed to be somewhere else. With the Holy Grail of her trip within reach, the reason the Lord had given her for living through the events of the past days soon to be a reality—all she wanted to do was escape.

Her father still intimidated her. Fleeting angry looks, sighs of disgust, easy explosions, and a million other strategies had always kept her from really communicating with him. And over the years, alcohol had devoured most of his brain and his body, making it even more difficult.

And there was more—religious subjects were taboo. He'd boasted about never having set foot in a church, a boast Nancy had seen confirmed at a cousin's wedding. Rather than going inside, he'd paced impatiently out front and had finally ended his misery by finding a nearby bar.

The question everyone had asked before she left came rushing back at her. Why was she doing this?

He'd laugh in her face and probably throw her out of the house.

Only one thought kept her going: *With God, all things are possible*. The story of the rich young ruler who was too proud to give up his possessions. It is the Lord who saves. She'd read it to Sarah just the other day in Matthew. She'd thought of her father then. If Sarah were alive and with her, she'd know what to say. But then another thought came—the one who had made Sarah strong, the same one who had made her able to face death cheerfully, was with Nancy now. "With man this is impossible, but with God all things are possible," Jesus had said.

At least for the moment her spirits buoyed.

Her father had been a home contractor and the last she knew, earned a living putting together lumber lists from blueprints for other contractors. It was an exact science that forced him to measure every nook and cranny through a complex blueprint. From the measurements he'd build a list of the materials necessary to construct the house or the condominium or the office building. Errors were costly, but her father did his job well—when sober.

His office was in a small complex near the beach. Not because of the beach but because it was near the "best bar south of San Francisco."

The complex's gray wooden exterior seemed charmingly rustic and pretty much the way Nancy remembered it. At its entrance was a glass directory which had always proclaimed, among other enterprises, John Bernard Building Company. Her father liked the name because it meant nothing. He was neither a company nor did he build.

She parked in the adjacent lot, said a short, anxious prayer and stepped gingerly from the car. When she reached his office in the back of the courtyard she stopped, confused. John Bernard Building Company wasn't there. The name on the door was a mortgage company.

She backtracked to the directory. His company wasn't on it.

Had he moved?

She went back to her father's office and asked the woman inside if she knew anything about her father's business. No, they'd been there only a month.

On the other side of the parking lot was the bar. Nancy didn't want to confront her father in there, but there was no other choice.

But after a thorough look around, she determined that her father wasn't there either. She was about to to leave when she heard the growl of a motorcycle out front. Although she knew it unlikely that she'd been followed here, she opened the door just a crack and looked outside. It was a chopper, but not one of the two on her trail. It didn't stop. Rather, the guy in the saddle, his long, black hair streaming down from a red bandana, circled the Pacer twice, then gunned his engine and squealed onto the road and disappeared toward San Francisco.

Nancy stood there confused for a moment. Was he just interested in the car as a relic, which it certainly was, or did he mean her harm?

"Can I help you, miss?" the bartender, a man in his late fifties asked, wiping the mahogany bar.

"Huh?" she looked to the source of the voice. "Oh . . . uh . . . no." Then she remembered what she was there for. "Yes," she began, taking a step toward him. "There is something. My father works, or at least used to work, across the way there and probably comes here a lot—John Bernard. Do you know where he might be?"

"Who might you be?"

"His daughter. I need to talk with him."

"My, my, he talked about you a lot."

"Talked? Has he moved or something?"

"You're kidding. Are you sure you're his daughter?"

"I've been in Washington, D.C." Nancy's brows furled with questions.

"John Bernard was the best, and you didn't even know he died? What kind of a daughter are you?"

The news kicked her in the chest. "Died? When?"

"Six months. I think. This is October, and it was a heart attack in the middle of summer. In that booth over there. Just fell into the munchies. Didn't you ever call him? He talked about you all the time. There wasn't a day that went by that he'd not be sitting here for hours talking about you."

But Nancy didn't acknowledge the words the man said. She was confused, and mixed in with the confusion swirled guilt and a great sadness.

Without another word she made it outside into the sunlight.

Why hadn't she known? A better daughter would have known—somehow. She'd been the very worst of daughters.

There'd been too much death . . .

Why did the Lord send her out here when the mission was a failure from the beginning?

With a heart like a clenched fist, she wandered back to the car—Mark's car. When her hand reached for the door handle, she began to cry. At that moment, all she wanted to do was reach out to Mark. She wanted to lean on him, talk to him, be consoled by him. But she'd left him and then he'd left her. He'd been so nice that last day.

"Why Lord? I mean it's not like it's none of my business or anything! Maybe just a hint?"

Chapter Twenty-Seven

Naomi sat obediently at Mark's side while he juggled on Sunset Boulevard. Although there didn't seem to be other jugglers around, people were quick to point out that if there had been, they would have been better than Mark. Part of the problem was he couldn't get the finale to work. Things would just bounce off his nose, leaving it bruised and painful. Since things bouncing off his nose was funny anyway, he began to tell jokes—and money started to show up in his hat. He discovered that the dirtier the joke, the more money he got. After that, Mark spent a lot of time reading dirty joke books.

But jokes or not, no one wanted to read his screenplay.

After he had been there three days, he knew something had to be done. He decided to advertise.

The next morning passersby were greeted by a large, hastily painted sign leaning against the wall next to him. It boldly demanded, "While I'm juggling, read my screenplay. It's good." The screenplay stood in a pouch on the sign, a red arrow pointing dramatically to it.

The first day was discouraging. Not only did no one read it, most people laughed. Those who didn't laugh shook their heads in elaborate disbelief—he swore one of them was Steven Spielberg.

But on the second day a fellow in jeans and a blue and pink sweatshirt that proclaimed something ecological about rain forests walked by, eyed the sign, slipped the manuscript from the pouch and began reading. After reading three pages he returned it to the pouch and walked away. Hurt and depressed, Mark told only one more joke before gathering up Naomi, his juggling things, ten bucks in change, and leaving.

He lived in a cheap hotel with no name—only a broken neon sign that flickered eternally and said Rooms. The juggling business was good enough to make ends meet. All seemed well, and he was confident that before long he'd be writing movies all over this miserable town.

And then he'd think about Nancy.

Actually, there weren't many times when he wasn't thinking about her: at breakfast with a bagel, at lunch with a hot dog, at dinner with a hamburger, at bedtime when the sounds of L.A. were their harshest. His act of liberation had left him empty. But over the years there had been other things he'd learned to live without and Nancy was just going to have to be one of them.

Of course, the chicken noodle soup can sitting on his dresser wasn't helping matters much. He'd gone so far as to wash it out and set it on an empty tuna can he'd picked up somewhere, knowing it would make a good pedestal. Of course, he hadn't stopped there. Soon after he'd taken the room, he'd found an old black marker lying in the corner, and once, during a particularly bad spell of missing Nancy, he'd taken the marker, and while shakily holding the can, slashed out "noodle" and above it, boldly printed "LIPS."

Tonight, with Naomi cradled in his lap, the open wound of the screenplay rejection still festering, Mark stared at his trophy and missed Nancy all the more—it was a reason to get drunk. So he did. The last beer having a decidedly chicken-noodle taste, he drank it from the can just before his eyes finally drooped shut.

The next day he hit the street at about eleven, just in time to catch the lunch crowd. Having talked himself into it, he put his sign up again, and although business was good, no one paid attention to the screenplay. When he was about to break, however, the fellow who'd read the script the previous day returned. And he brought someone with him. The guy still wore the same jeans and sweatshirt, but the fellow with him, who had a long, horse face, was in a business suit.

When they stepped up, Mark stopped putting things away and straightened.

"Go ahead—finish up, but when you're done I want to talk with you," said the fellow who had been there the day before.

"Right," Mark replied and quickly gathered everything up into a pile and shoved it out of sight behind the sign. He scooped up Naomi and said, "Done."

"How about a drink?" the fellow said. "I'm Terry Short, and this is my associate, Don Brinker. We want to talk to you about your script."

"Mark Brewster," Mark introduced, thrusting a firm hand out and shaking both of theirs. "You want to talk—to me?"

Short laughed good-naturedly. "I know the old Hollywood success story is thought to be a thing of the past, but your little ad here worked. I liked what I read. Don, here, is an independent producer—low budget—sometimes only video. I've convinced him to read it."

"Really?"

"Why don't we go next door and talk?"

Brinker said nothing—it almost looked as if he thought nothing. His expression remained granite as he grabbed the script from its pouch and thumbed idly through it. They stepped into a dimly lit bar and found a booth. Mark set Naomi beside him and they all ordered drinks.

"What do you think?" Short asked Brinker.

"He read it in that time?"

"Needs work," Brinker said flatly. "Listen, I don't like dealing with amateurs. I told you that."

"I can rewrite. What do you want done?"

"Amateurs have the most dedication," Short told Brinker. "You know that. They dance better on the end of a shoestring."

"Shoestring?" Mark muttered.

"As independents we don't have the vast resources of the studios. But we get things done," Short explained.

"I'll admit that this one looks good," Brinker said to Short. "But there are a number of other good properties out there."

"Not like this one," Short fired back. "We can shoot it on a song—cheap."

"Real cheap," Mark echoed.

"And it's got all of it," Short sold hard.

"All of it—I know. I wrote all of it into it—and a lot of each too."

"And the other scripts need location. This is mostly interiors. More cheap."

"That part I like." Brinker's expression never changed. Their drinks came, and they nursed them slowly.

"How much do you want for your script?" Short asked Mark.

"How much? I don't know. A million, two million, ten bucks. I don't know."

"Writer's pay goes up and down the line. The budget for this gig is 50K," Short said.

"50K?"

"Fifty thousand dollars."

Mark's throat closed. "Fifty thousand dollars?"

"When the budget's put together that's what you'll get." Short turned to Brinker. "Do you want to do this or not?"

Brinker shrugged and took a long drink. "I have investors to consider. It'll take a couple days."

"But they do what you tell them to. Do you want to do it or not?"

"Come on, Short. You're an agent, not God. I'll make a decision when I want to make a decision. I'll see you later." Brinker stood, cast a stony eye down at Mark, then took a few steps toward the door. Just as quickly, Short rose and caught Brinker by the arm. Pushing machine gun lips close to the taller man's ear, Short started a rapid fire barrage of words that Mark couldn't make out as both walked toward the front door.

It was all happening a little fast for Mark. Yesterday he'd been brooding because he didn't have money enough to buy an old car he'd seen. Now there was the possibility he'd soon be holding $50,000. Was this the way of stardom? No wonder so many fell off the roller coaster. But no matter how many dips and long drops the ride took, he decided right then and there that he was in for the whole ride.

After a few moments of heated conversation, Short and Brinker parted. Short returned to Mark. Without sitting, Short grabbed his drink. "He's hooked," he announced, downing the glass in a single gulp.

"It's that easy? I get 50K."

"There's a catch." Short slid into the booth and got very near him. "But not a big one. He wants you in the deal. It means you'll get more than 50K because you'll be a stockholder, like an owner. It's his way of making sure you don't skip out. He wants a lot of rewriting done."

"I won't skip."

"He doesn't know that. He's gotten stung before. Independents have to worry about things like that where studios don't."

"So I'm a stockholder. That means I get my share later, right?"

"No. You get some of your fee for writing the script up-front, but now you need to come up with some money. About 10K." Short nursed the ice that remained in his glass.

"You're kidding. I don't have any money. I'm a street juggler, not a street owner." Mark tried to sound indignant, but the disappointment got in the way.

"If you want it bad enough you'll get it. Anyway, it could be worth millions to you—you know how much the writer of *Terminator 2* walked away with?"

"No, not really—you're crooks, right?"

"No, we're movie makers." Then Short chuckled. "I guess that's saying the same thing. Anyway, I can place this script of yours, but you need ten thousand. Let me tell you what that means. Your ten thousand-dollar script will become a five million-dollar deal and will probably gross over thirty million. Your 10K will get you nearly a million. Sound good? It'll buy a lot of bones for your friend here," he said, pointing to Naomi. He reached into his back pocket. "Here's my card. Call me." Short moved crisply. He tossed a card on the table, stood, and before Mark could read the card was gone.

For a second Mark wondered if any of it had really happened. The card was proof that it had. But that didn't end his confusion; it started it. He peered at the card in the dim light, eyed the door, then the card again. Then he just sat numbly. "Is anything easy in this world?" he finally said to Naomi. Only then did he begin to feel some emotion—but which emotions were legitimate? Should he be excited because someone liked his stuff? Should he be devastated because it didn't matter anyway? Should he be angry because he was probably being duped? After a distressing few minutes he returned to just being numb. It didn't hurt quite so much.

Back in the hotel room, Naomi planted her chin on his ankle while Mark lay on the bed. He stared blankly at the dirty-brown ceiling. He was so close, yet he might as well have been at the other end of the world—in another galaxy. Maybe they were crooks. Maybe all he needed was ten thousand to become legend—a legend with millions. After all, why would crooks hit on a street juggler in obvious poverty?

He could protect himself. Rather than giving them the money, he could put it in—watchamacallit—escrow or something.

I don't know why I'm worrying about any of this anyway. I don't have ten dollars, let alone . . .

That's when he remembered the old lady's green board and what lay beneath it. $15,000. Had anyone found it? Why would they? They wouldn't level the house. Who'd want the land? Would anyone go hunting for it? She looked excruciatingly poor.

And the beauty of it all was—things had surely changed. He couldn't take the money before for some misbegotten moral reasons. But those reasons didn't matter anymore. The woman was probably dead, and the money was just sitting there unclaimed and waiting for him.

He called Short and told his answering service that he'd figured out a way to get the money and he'd see Short in a couple of days.

Chapter Twenty-Eight

It took three full days for Mark and Naomi to get back to the old house. He'd spent much of the time between rides—waiting at truck stops and diners—but finally after several hours in snow-crowned Flagstaff, Arizona, the driver of a Kenworth, similar to the one that had taken Mark away, brought him back. It was mid-afternoon when the brakes squealed to a stop at the streetlamp. After dismounting from the cab, Mark found the landscape moon-dead and the chill predicting snow.

He set Naomi down, and she scrambled beside him as he shuffled down the dirt road, past the tall pile of boulders to where he could see the house.

It was still there, but now it stood lifeless, a growing wind whipping the dust in sporadic swirls, its door and window boarded up forlornly. A red For Sale sign hung crookedly on the gate, and another had been nailed to the few ragged boards tacked across the door.

The old gal died, Mark mused. *I hope it wasn't too hard on Nancy.*

When he'd advanced to a few feet from the gate, the wind blew it open. The rusty hinges whined, and Mark, a little tense, stepped back with a start. But it wasn't the rusty gate that caused him to stop short—it was what the opened gate revealed sprawling across the front step.

Naomi saw the coyote first and stiffened immediately and began to dance and bark at Mark's feet. Then Mark saw him; when he did, the coyote, his yellow eyes peering up from a slinking head, rose on skinny legs. The coyote bared his teeth and growled.

Naomi stopped yipping and took her post behind Mark's leg.

Mark quickly gathered her up. "Where's Hamster when we need him?" he said, glancing around for a weapon—a stick or large rock, anything.

He saw nothing.

Mark eyed the beast again. "I'm not particularly brave, ol' girl," Mark said to Naomi. "But he's standing between us and something we want. So hang on."

Mark dropped quickly and scooped up a handful of small rocks and with one motion threw them in the coyote's direction. By the time they clattered against the side of the house, Mark had grabbed another handful and thrown it. They struck the coyote's head and neck. The next handful did the same. The coyote had had enough. Lithely, the mangy critter ran to the side fence and leaped over it and disappeared quickly into the boulders beyond.

It was Mark's house now.

He set Naomi down and stepped through the gate to the door. Grabbing the rotting planks that boarded it up, he pulled them off easily. When the door was liberated, he tried the knob—locked. Without hesitation he threw himself against it. The door gave way as easily as the boards had come off, and seconds later he stood in the living room.

It hadn't changed much. The same dead chill, the same spears of light coming from the windows and the cracks in the walls, the same dust—the smell of it heavy in the air, a blanket of it covering everything. The ancient furniture and kitchen things obviously hadn't been worth taking, and cobwebs hung liberally from the naked light fixtures and the room's corners. Most of the old woman's art was gone. But some of it had been shattered; large jagged pieces were strewn along the floor, some just below scars on the walls where they'd been thrown. One of her beadwork pictures lay twisted and torn, some of the beads mixed among the chards.

"Dorothy," Mark muttered to Naomi. "The old woman didn't like her. She must have done this before she boarded the place up."

But none of that mattered—the only thing that did lay beneath a green board in the bedroom. As he had on that night of discovery, Mark stepped quickly to the kitchen, found a battered knife that had been left behind and, with his heart beating wildly, crossed quickly to the bedroom. Throwing the braided rug aside, he jammed the knife between the boards and pried the green one up.

The can was still there!

He grabbed it, tore the plastic lid off, and stared down at the rolled and folded crush of green. After staring excitedly at it for a long moment, he pulled a handful out. Then another. With each his excitement grew—with each came a freedom and exhilaration. Suddenly, as if the charge coursing through him needed release, he leaped to his feet, grabbed a thick handful of bills, wadded them into three balls, and while laughing uncontrollably, he juggled the wads. One of them actually held together through the second go around and almost stayed together through the finale. It started coming apart on the way down and completely disintegrated when it hit his nose. In one final carefree statement, Mark scooped up a handful of bills, tossed them in the air, then threw his arms out and spun. Batting bills everywhere, he cried to Naomi, "They may not see it too often in this God-forsaken desert, but our ship's docked— right here—in this room."

He was about to spin again and dance a little jig when he saw the eighteen-inch sculpture.

The mother and child was just where it had been that night he'd first seen it in gray shadows. Now it stood, bathed in a shaft of dusty light from a window behind him. And it haunted him just as it had that night. The mother's protective eyes, the child's dependence. He stared at it, unable to move—why?

Sure, this mother of clay forced him to focus on his own mother. And sure, he wished his had been as attentive as this mythical mother seemed to be. Sure he wished he had just once felt his own mother's protective arm on his shoulder or heard her express love for him, that she'd been a truer mother. But she hadn't been, and there was nothing he could do about it now. He knew that from long ago—then why were there suddenly tears?

Why were they searing his cheek, and even though they blurred his vision, why couldn't he turn away?

Deep inside his own graveyard of memories, where in moments of terror he'd buried and forgotten them, memories and feelings were beginning to stir. Ghosts were beginning to rise, their ugly faces becoming more than just decaying shadows. They took form and, like unwelcome vapors, seeped into and fouled his heart. Helplessness . . . unworthiness . . . inevitable defeat . . .

They visited like old, decrepit relatives, weighing him down with their abundance of baggage.

And rage. It boiled up like sulfur from a contaminated well. The instant Mark felt it coming he tried to cap it, tried to slam the lid down before it reached the light and spewed out all over everything—ruining all it would touch, even the things he loved.

Why was this happening now? Now, when the doors were beginning to open and the threshold was beckoning him—now when the light of promise had been launched like a flare in the night sky and he knew just which direction to aim the lifeboat? Why now? What was so different now?

Almost without thinking he began to gather up the wadded bills—one at his feet, then one next to it, then one next to that one, a trail that he suddenly realized led directly to the sculpture of the mother and child. With his hand poised to grab the next bill, he froze, eyes riveted on the mother's face.

"Oh, my God, it's happening again," he murmured.

He tore his eyes free. Then he spun his back to the mother. But his eyes fell on something else. Beneath a thick veneer of dust lay Sarah's Bible.

The words he'd read in it—they seemed like thin echoes in deep canyons, indiscernible. He liked them that way. But before he knew it, he found his mind dwelling on them—trying to remember.

He didn't want to remember.

He turned away, but his eyes fell on the sculpture again. His knees buckled and he sat down on the bed, a cloud of dust billowing up around him.

When do random impressions become thought? When does awareness begin? he wondered.

For Mark it began as a point far in the back of his head. As a child he'd burned himself with a magnifying glass by holding it just far enough away from his skin and focusing the light. The point of light was small, but there was no ignoring it. This point in the recesses of his brain seemed smaller still, but there was no ignoring it either.

He turned back to the Bible, then to the sculpture, and he thought of those endless hours of reading to Sarah—the mother, the Bible, and Sarah—all were in that point of light—all were one. They'd mingled and fused there—Sarah, the Bible, his mother.

Suddenly something pulled him back. Panting, the clicking of animal nails on wood floor—a form at the door. Naomi erupted—she danced on stiff legs and yipped at Mark's feet. Yanked back to the reality of the walls, the floors, the dust, the smell of dirty animal fur, Mark turned to see the coyote at the bedroom door. The coyote had already seen him, and each yellow eye seemed like the glowing end of a poker. Lips snarled and revealed angry teeth.

Mark grabbed Naomi and tossed her to the top of the dresser. Then as if he'd rehearsed it a hundred times, he rose, stepped over the hole in the floor to the sculpture, lifted it above his head, and hurled it at the intruder. The moment the coyote saw what was happening, it darted toward the front door. The sculpture hit the doorjamb and split. The head and shoulders shattered against the wall while the rest of it smashed against the living room floor and broke into several large, jagged pieces that skidded across the floor, chasing the ragged animal out the door.

The instant Mark heard the pop of exploding clay against the wall he never thought about the coyote again. He knew what he'd done. His awareness was now complete—the point that burned through the back of his skull now blazed before his eyes.

Almost in a trance, he bent over and picked up a small remnant of the mother's head—the eye? the ear? It didn't matter. "My God," Mark murmured, "I've done it again."

▼ ▼

Mark's footsteps rang hollow against the hardwood floor and echoed in the dark church. Even here the smell of dust was as thick as in Sarah's house. Sapped of energy, Mark walked stiffly, the can in one hand, Naomi cradled in the other. He held them both tightly as a child might hold a teddy bear. When he'd walked more than halfway down the aisle between the cushioned pews, a door on the far end of the sanctuary opened.

"Mark?"

"Yeah." His voice strangled with tension.

"You took a while—I was beginning to think you weren't coming."

"I had to walk. I couldn't get a ride."

"Walk? You should have said something. I would have picked

you up." Hopper stood in the doorway, his long, bony frame just touching the lintel. "Cute pup," he added.

"Right," Mark said as he reached the door. Hopper stepped aside and let the two pass into his study. It was a small room, books on all walls, a plaque here and there, only a few bits of memorabilia. His clean desk appeared richly brown in the twilight. A single lamp in the ceiling above Mark spilled light onto them.

"Have a seat." Hopper gestured to the two vinyl chairs in front of his desk.

"No. I only got a minute."

"Sit—let's talk," Hopper insisted, and Mark did while Hopper perched himself on the edge of the desk. Naomi lay at Mark's feet.

Mark leaned forward and pushed the coffee can at Hopper. "This is yours."

"Mine? What's this?"

"Fifteen thousand dollars—about."

The pastor's brows rose.

"It belonged to the old lady. Before she died she told me about it. It was hidden under the floor. She told me to give it to the church. I'm doing that now."

"She's dead now. That money probably belongs to her daughter—Sarah's heir."

"She said she didn't want her daughter, Dorothy, to get it."

"Well, I don't know much about wills, but I'll check with our attorney and see what he has to say."

"Whatever," Mark said. "You can take care of it now." He got to his feet.

"You okay?"

"Yeah, I guess. I gotta go."

"You came here for more than just this. You look troubled. What's going on with you?"

"Nothing. I'm fine. I came back here to take that for myself, but I couldn't. Now you can take care of it."

"Sit down, Mark. Talk to me."

"Listen, I came to bring that back, that's all. I don't want to talk."

"Sure you do. If you weren't going to take it, you could have left it in the house and told me to pick it up. You want to talk, and you walked all this way to do it. In fact you probably fought yourself the whole way. That's why you didn't have me pick you up. You probably wanted every minute to talk yourself out of talking. It must not have worked—you're here."

Mark looked down at the chair. It had happened just as Hopper said. He had fought himself the whole way. Even up to the front door. He thought of just leaving the can on the front steps and calling him with the news. But he hadn't.

"Go on, Mark. Have a seat."

Mark heaved a huge sigh, and as the vinyl creaked beneath him, he slammed his fist into his hand, then slammed it again. His chest constricted as if trying to hold in what was about to break out.

Hopper's firm hand was on Mark's. "Easy now—just let what you want to say come out."

Were there words to describe what churned there? There didn't seem to be—none came to mind. Mark heard himself stammer, then felt his head droop in defeat. But Hopper's calm whisper came to him, "It's okay—say anything—it's okay."

Anything?

"I'm no better than a grave robber," Mark said, eyes coming up to Hopper's.

"None of us is much better than that. At least you stopped yourself in time."

"This time. Not the last."

"The last?"

Mark suddenly realized that his hands were raw. Although he'd not slammed them together again, he'd been rubbing one into the other, knuckles to palm, and both were sore. "I can't believe what I did. I've been burying it, hiding it, pretending it didn't happen, and if it did happen that it was all right that it happened. But I can't bury it anymore. It won't stay buried—it's like the living dead or something. It keeps popping up."

"What does?"

More rubbing of his hands, so much so that Hopper again placed a calming hand on Mark's, Hopper's eyes searching Mark's. Because Mark could feel his eyes begin to burn with tears, he turned away.

"We're all sinners, Mark," Hopper said soothingly. "All of us. You don't have to tell me what you did. But if you did tell me, it wouldn't change the fact that we're in this life together."

Mark's eyes, tears and all, met Hopper's and in the tears was a touch of anger, "I killed my mother."

The words ricocheted off the walls of the study, but Hopper's expression didn't change. Finally he said, "Did you get the effect you wanted?"

Mark shook his head, then realized his childishness and sank back into the chair.

"Do you want to explain?" Hopper asked.

Mark took a long, disturbed breath. "I was sixteen and it was winter. My mom was sick—she was always sick—colds, the flu, fevers, sometimes her throat, anything and everything. The only time she got well was when she went out with her army friends. We were in Baltimore near Fort Meade. That particular illness lasted a long time. She got fired from her waitressing job and couldn't find another—but she didn't really look. After all, she had me. I'm a juggler."

"I bet that job has its ups and downs."

Mark just gave him a strange look and Hopper shrank back.

"I'm sorry. Please go on. I guess your father wasn't around."

"I never had a father—one that was around. My uncle tried to be nice to me, but he wasn't around much and he died when I was young. He liked me. Gave me money sometimes. But most of the time I earned it. I went out every day to juggle. Because it was winter and the pickins were slim, I had to go out every day. I'd catch a ride into Baltimore and stand on a street corner and juggle—snow, sleet, freeze—it didn't matter. I'd be there with my hat. Anyway, who's got time to watch some stupid kid juggle in the middle of winter? I'd get a few pity nickels but little else. But my mom needed medicine along with her food, and because I wasn't earning much, we relied on a little she had saved up."

"How long did that last?"

"February." Mark sniffled and brushed away an attack of tears. "We were down to my making some choices. She got both medicine and food and I didn't eat, or I ate and she just got food or medicine. I didn't eat for a couple days. Then there was just enough money to escape." He felt incredibly hard for a moment, as he relived that moment of decision—but only for a moment. Suddenly his chest began to heave spasmodically, and it took all his energy to beat the tears back. But they were being propelled by a heart yearning for release, and that heart wouldn't be denied. The tears burst out and Mark wept, tears running down his cheeks and his neck, staining his shirt and pants. Hopper grabbed a box of tissues and thrust a handful at Mark. Mark took them and worked his eyes and nose.

"You left her?"

Mark nodded, unable to speak; and then control began to return. "I took what was left of her savings—just a few bucks—and ran. A few days later she was found dead. There's no other way to put it. I killed my mother. Ever meet one of us before?"

Hopper said nothing for a while; he just kept the tissues coming.

"I guess you have these here for the women," Mark said.

"No, for me—allergies, and I'm not above a few tears now and then. Cry at movies all the time."

Mark felt some normalcy return, felt the wrenching of his chest go quiet. He started talking again. "But I had to live with myself. I couldn't fool myself into thinking what I'd done was okay so I just tried to forget. I buried it. I didn't think about it." He blew his nose and wiped his eyes and took a very deep breath. "But these past days—on the trip—I was constantly reminded. Old slums, coffee shops, even Sarah's sculpture. It was weird. Each time was like a shovelful of dirt was being taken from the grave, and each shovelful made it that much easier for the body to break free.

"When I went back to take that money from the old lady, it was like I was taking it from my mom again."

Hopper got to his feet and stepped over to the large window in the far wall. Night had come and the stars were out. "Why do you think all these things happened to you? Why do you think you feel this way right now?"

"It's God. I know it is. I don't believe in God, but when I was at Sarah's house tonight I knew God was there with me—he's slamming me. He's after me—he's going to punish me for what I've done."

"You became aware of God?"

"It has to be him. Ever since my mother died I've been afraid to feel anything—afraid to look inside at anything except what was on the surface. But in the past few days it's been one thing after another forcing me to look under there—making it so I couldn't avoid it. The main thing was I fell in love with Nancy. And she believes in God. There was Sarah who forced me to read the Bible to her—she believed in God. And that crazy waitress—oh, you don't know—it doesn't matter. God was suddenly everywhere."

"He certainly tends to be."

"And then today—he was telling me he was there."

"What do you think God is doing?" Hopper asked, eyes still searching the darkness outside.

"Getting even—punishing me. Or getting ready to."

Hopper turned, his expression wrapped in deep thought. "Mark, I'm not going to let you off the hook. What you did back there was bad. She was your mother and no matter what kind of mother she was, your first duty was to honor her and love her and see her through whatever lay ahead of you both. But there's something else to consider. We've all killed our mothers."

"What?"

"Not physically. But we've all said bad things to them, shouted at them, maybe even cursed them as we were growing—Lord knows I even deal with a lot of this today. The Lord tells us that all of that is just the same as murder."

"But everyone does that."

"That's the point. The Lord says that everyone sins seventy times seven times a day, and some of those sins are murder." Hopper sat on the edge of the desk again and looked down into Mark's uplifted eyes. "You should have stuck it out with your mother, but the Lord tells us that if we repent of our sins and ask for his forgiveness, he'll be faithful and just to forgive us and cleanse us from all unrighteousness. We're sinners, Mark. And before we come to know the Lord, before we commit ourselves to him, we're in rebellion against God. Your rebellion saw the death of your mother. He's not punishing you, Mark. He's bringing you in—he's showing you something."

Mark's eyes were still rimmed in crimson, his breathing was still erratic, but his attention was riveted on Hopper. "Showing me what?"

"That you need a Savior, Mark."

"Jesus . . ." The name slipped from trembling lips. " 'And Jesus came to save his people from their sins.' " Mark's eyes dropped away and just as quickly returned. "I remembered that from something Sarah had me read."

"The most remarkable thing about Jesus is that while we were yet sinners—while we were rebelling against him, while we were leaving our mothers, while I was stealing from my mother's wallet—and neglecting my flock—while we were doing all these things, Christ died for us."

Hopper paused a moment, and Mark saw him look off toward the window as if the meaning of the words was kneading and shaping him. Then he turned back. "He was the sacrificial Lamb of God. God is a just God. If you sin you pay. For him to forgive, the sins must still be paid for. Jesus paid for our sins, Mark. They nailed him to a cross, lanced his heart; then he spent the equivalent of an eternity in hell for us in those three days in that tomb. All God's wrath was poured on him—wrath that should have come to me." Now Hopper's eyes bored through Mark's. "Do you know that you're a sinner, a real sinner, in rebellion against God and deserving hell?"

Mark looked up, his expression grave. He nodded.

"Do you feel regret in your heart for your sins against God?"

"My heart's strangling with them."

"Do you know you need to be forgiven by God the Father?"

"Yes," Mark said without hesitation.

"Jesus Christ is the Son of God. He was sent by the Father to pay the debts of his people. The Lord promises that all who confess Jesus Christ as their personal Lord and Savior will be saved and forgiven and will inherit eternal life with God. Mark, consider the next question very carefully. Do you take Jesus Christ to be your personal Lord and Savior? Are you here seeking him?"

Mark had never experienced anything like this before—something within him compelled his eyes to search the pastor's, and he immediately saw a safe harbor there. "Yes." His voice was little more than a hoarse whisper.

"We need to pray to God the Father now—our petition is with him."

Whatever reservations Mark might have had dissolved when he felt Hopper's encouragingly firm hand on his shoulder. He picked up Naomi and bowed his head. Then, after they both prayed for a moment, Mark leaned back in the chair. His eyes still burned and his chest still hurt from the internal beating it had taken, but a satisfied smile spread across his face, and the single tear that now fell was a tear of joy.

Chapter Twenty-Nine

Nancy discovered the name of the executor of her father's will through the county recorder and quickly found that her father had left her a small legacy. There wasn't much; he'd borrowed heavily on his life insurance and put a second mortgage on the house—both in a concerted effort to make the San Francisco Bay area bar owners rich. But the house had appreciated a bit, he owned his car free and clear, and the insurance wasn't completely tapped out so when all had been converted to cash a month after his death, as his will had instructed, there was a little left: $23,047.

Nancy almost felt guilty taking the check, but she did have to pay Donna back for the lost trailer, and she did have a car to replace—her Champ only had liability insurance. So when the lawyer handed her the check she took it.

She decided to drive Mark's car back to Washington and figure out what to do with it then. If she took the northern route, Interstate 80, she thought she'd be safe from the bikers. Of course, they might not even be looking anymore. After all, she'd driven all the way to Pacifica without seeing them. Anyway, the trip and Mark and all they'd done together seemed far away, part of a dream that she found hard to remember, without hurting. Thinking of the bikers caused her to remember and she didn't want to do that anymore.

With all her father's affairs in order and with a few new clothes, Nancy and Hamster rose early, packed, and prepared to leave. She'd visited her father's grave soon after arriving. It was a place she knew well—it lay beside her mother's. The cemetery sprawled high on a bluff overlooking the ocean. She'd walked beside it a hundred times while growing up. The view reached forever in all directions, and in those frequent times of emotional difficulty she'd found a certain calm among the tombstones. It never occurred to her that one day she'd be visiting her parents there—especially her father. Visiting his grave had been difficult. Peering down at the headstone, she didn't know what she should feel. Quakes of guilt still persisted—she'd been so estranged that she hadn't even known he'd died, and yet she couldn't help feeling relieved that she didn't have to face him and be rejected again.

Was it all right to just be confused standing before the remorseless granite slab?

Now it was time to leave, perhaps for good, and she wanted to say good-bye to both parents once more.

The morning fog hung thick and cast the world in eerie shadows of light and gray. Ethereal, ghostly, it was perfect cemetery weather. Nancy drove carefully and after making the main gate, she wound slowly around the circular drive to the hill where her parents lay. Workmen were building a new, ornate mausoleum landscaped by a large pond and waterfall. She heard the loud grind of heavy equipment and the ragged clatter of a generator and jackhammer. She saw the busy construction scene through the gray haze, and it became clearer as she approached and parked nearby.

Hamster trotted next to her as she trudged up the winding path toward the graves. About halfway up the hill Nancy heard the rake of concrete against steel, an eruption of shouts, a few huge laughs, shattering glass, and the angry scream of twisting metal.

"Lady—hey lady," someone called to her.

She spun around and ran back down the hill. When she approached the car, the shadows clarified, and she gasped as she saw what had happened. An oversized dump truck loaded with huge boulders destined for the waterfall had gotten lost or something and had dumped its incredibly heavy load directly onto the Pacer. There wasn't much to see of the car now. Each boulder was gigantic, and there had to be fifty of them stacked helter-skelter in a pile, the Pacer somewhere beneath. When Nancy got close, while Hamster sniffed at the base of the pile, she scanned the bottom edges for some sign of the car. She finally spotted what was probably the front bumper, just a twisted bit of it, crushed against the street.

"Sorry aboutcher car, lady," a thick-armed fellow in a Giants baseball cap said, a fistful of gum keeping his jaws moving.

"It belongs to someone else," Nancy exclaimed, astonished that it had disappeared so quickly. "I can only make out the bumper."

"Kinda surprised you found that much. It's prob'ly about a foot high now—that's twenty tons of boulders there. But don't worry. We're insured." The guy searched through his pockets and came out with a soiled piece of paper. It started out about the size of a quarter but when he unfolded it became a legal-sized form. He handed it to her. "Fill this here out and mail it in. No sweat. I hope you didn't have no sentimental attachment to that car—if you did you could bury it in yer backyard or something."

Still in shock, Nancy stepped back, the enormity of what had happened slowly sinking in. When it had, she managed only a shrug and a couple of words, "Sorry, Mark."

The moment she mentioned his name, Nancy heard the guttural growl of motorcycles. Nancy's heart fluttered and leaped at the sound. When she turned, it stopped mid-beat. Off to her left, darkly silhouetted in the fog, two choppers slowly eased through the cemetery gates. Ghost riders—looking for someone, they growled slowly along the circular drive.

Nancy quickly grabbed Hamster's collar, sat him down beside her and turned toward the construction—as if she were an onlooker. When the choppers growled by, the ghost riders eyed her indifferently, then spoke to one another. Were they the ones following her? She got her answer immediately. When they'd passed she saw the Indian war shield. No doubt now. Had they recognized her? They'd come alongside the car that day the mountain cabin exploded just before the trooper chased them off. Had they seen her then? If they had, running now wouldn't do any good, so she just stood and waited. Thundering to the far end of the circular drive they stopped for a moment, looked around, then continued on around. A few minutes later they disappeared outside the cemetery gates.

"How'd they know?" she muttered to Hamster. Then she remembered the chopper that had inspected the Pacer the other day. She wondered if they had cellular phones and fax machines—the Hell's Angels in the age of communications.

She eyed the pile of boulders and the Pacer beneath it. "I guess we don't have to worry about them anymore."

"What should we do with the car, lady?" the guy in the Giants cap called to her as she started walking toward the cemetery exit.

"You have to ask that question here? Bury it."

She delayed her trip another day and bought a used Jeep; something wild in her needed satisfying and it seemed like the only vehicle with a pulse.

▼ ▼

When Nancy returned to her apartment in Washington, she quickly settled back in her routine. After arriving late on a Friday night, she rose early Saturday, eager for things at home to begin. She unpacked her few new clothes, she cleaned for a while, then went out and replaced most of the things that had been stolen—even her flute. Then she stopped by Donna's and wrote her a check. Although they hugged and talked for a while, Nancy found herself leaving out the intimate details and even some of the less intimate—she felt distant from Donna. Their friendship had faded.

After the Sunday service Pastor Bevel was excited to see her back and gave her an uncharacteristic hug and urged her to call him.

When she arrived at work on Monday morning, she felt surprisingly relaxed. Most of the way home she had dreaded going into the office, but now that she was home that had changed. Her boss, too, seemed more relaxed, and the two of them spent at least an hour before lunch just talking about things. As a result, Nancy was given some new responsibilities, and she took them over in the afternoon, feeling quite comfortable in her new role.

But then there was Mark. As a Christian with a renewed commitment to her Savior, Nancy couldn't give the feelings she had for Mark air to breathe. Out there somewhere was a good Christian fellow for her, and God would bring him in God's own time. So there were long, passionate prayers about Mark, endless hours spent rationalizing him away and trying to fool her feelings. But nothing worked. She loved him, and she would just have to pretend that he was dead—like Sarah and her father and her mother. If she did, then in time the feelings would fade. At first she cried herself to sleep pretending she was a widow in mourning. But soon she found that the sound of her flute brought some relief from the pain. Since she was playing it so much, she began to get good at it again—the purer the sound, the more soothing to the emotional burn.

A week passed and then another. Playing the flute each night became nearly ritualistic, and Nancy found that, instead of the memories fading, the sound of the flute made them brighten. But instead of the memories being edged in tears, they were laced with smiles. Instead of taps for the memories, the flute had become a wake-up call.

But life was for the living, and there were things to do. She did call Pastor Bevel that first week, and before the conversation was over she'd asked him where in the church she could help.

Without hesitation he said, "Junior high kids—we need some help there."

And she did help. She found that she related well to twelve- and thirteen-year-old girls. One Friday during a game night in the church rec room, she looked up from refereeing a volleyball game and saw two girls slumping in the doorway. One was thirteen, the other was ten. Suddenly transfixed, Nancy felt déjà vu when she looked into their eyes—the little girl at Harbor View where her car had been stolen. Vacant, frightened, they looked as if all feeling had been wrung out of them. Margie Whitcomb was the older, Millie the younger, and they were sisters. Their mother had abandoned them to an abusive father—a man in whom Nancy saw all the characteristics of an alcoholic.

Of course it took Nancy a few nights to find all that out, and in those nights, she committed herself to helping the children. But there was little she could do. Although emotionally abusive, the father wasn't physically abusive, so her only recourse was to befriend Margie and Millie, expose them to love and caring, and hope to share the Lord with them.

As days melted into weeks, they came to cherish their friendship with Nancy, and after a few weeks their reliance upon her convinced her to take a bold action. She visited their father, Howard Whitcomb. Although the hour with him was frightening, Nancy left him with two things: his respect and his okay to place the two girls in a Christian grade school that Pastor Bevel recommended. Nancy went on to secure a deacon scholarship for both girls and helped them buy books and school supplies. Of course, shopping with the kids was a kick. If Margie and Millie had been her whole life, all would have been well with Nancy. But they were only part of it.

Mark's memory was alive and well. Although it had started to fade, it came to visit now and then and when it did it was still warm and wonderfully real—which it was one Sunday when Margie and Millie were with her in the church rec room.

"Are you okay, Nancy?" Margie asked. Both sat on the floor, Margie doing a Christian crossword puzzle book that Nancy had bought her and Millie thumbing through a picture book about King David.

"Sure," Nancy said, her mind reentering the room. "I was just thinking about someone."

"Who?" Millie asked.

"Someone who's dead—I guess," she replied, smiling but feeling her eyes drift back to a more distant place.

Pastor Bevel's voice came from behind. "Nancy, you got a minute?"

"Sure."

Bevel took her gently by the arm and led her away from the kids. "A call came to the office this morning. Someone is looking for you."

"Who?"

"We told him we didn't know anything about you—we're hoping what Rahab did in the Old Testament justifies what we did. Anyway we thought it best. But I wanted to tell you."

"Mark?"

"Betty said he was very brief."

Nancy's brows knit. Not all of her wanted Mark to fade.

"Do you want him to find you?" Bevel asked pointedly.

Nancy could feel a sudden battle erupt, but she squelched it and shook her head, "No, it's best that he doesn't."

Bevel put a reassuring hand on her shoulder.

That night the flute came out early, and with Hamster sprawled across the foot of her bed, she played it late into the night. Before her eyes finally closed, she prayed that the ache in her heart would go away, along with Mark's memory. It was one of the hardest prayers she'd ever prayed. In the morning she found that the Lord had said no to both requests.

She had not thought much about Christmas. There was no one she really wanted to buy for. Or rather, the one she wanted to buy for she shouldn't. But Christmas was coming, and the stores had been decorated for months. And Millie was in the Christmas pageant at school.

"She's doing something special," Margie said to Nancy. "And she wants you there."

"Just try to keep me away," Nancy assured her.

Margie's eyes became big and doubtful. "Between you and me, she wants Dad there too."

Nancy nodded, her heart knowing all the feelings. "I always wanted my dad at these things too. And then, again, I didn't."

Margie nodded as if she understood. To see Dad there said he cared, but to see him there drunk said something quite different and destructive.

"I'll talk to him."

She did—that night when she took the kids home. She remained until he came home. Apprehensive, trembling at her core, she told Howard Whitcomb exactly what the kids wanted and then told him she'd be praying they get it. He said very little in reply.

Sitting next to Margie in the packed school auditorium, Nancy noticed how tense she was. How often had Nancy felt the same: longing for her father to take a step toward her, but afraid when he did he'd bring more pain than warmth.

"What part does Millie play?"

"It's kind of a variation on the little drummer boy."

"What does that mean?"

"She wouldn't say. She's got this crush on her drama teacher. I think she has some matchmaking with you in mind."

"I don't think I'm interested."

"I told her you were tied up in your own misery."

"Where'd you come up with that? Are you sure you're only thirteen?"

"I read Danielle Steele."

"Well, stop it!" Nancy laughed. But then she sobered. Standing in the back doorway was Howard Whitcomb—and *he* was sober.

The instant Margie saw him, she grinned from ear to ear. "Millie'll croak," she confided to Nancy and leaped to her feet, ran to her dad, and grabbed him by the hand. Nancy's heart turned to mush, and her smile stretched farther than it ever had as she watched father and daughter walk to the seats beside her.

"Good evening, Mr. Whitcomb," Nancy greeted.

Howard Whitcomb nodded and sat, Margie's arm entwined with his. Nancy smiled at them. There would be more hurts ahead for them both, but at least they'd have tonight and maybe there would be more nights like this in the future. A first step had been taken.

Nancy had a difficult time concentrating on the play. About every third line she found herself glancing at Margie and then at her father. Margie was losing herself in the moment and kept a tight arm in her father's and a loving eye on his face. The picture grew more heartwarming each time it was refreshed. So, when Millie stepped onstage and stood before the manger and the eleven-year-old Joseph, the ten-year-old Mary, and the cardboard cows and donkeys, Nancy viewed her entrance and performance as anticlimactic.

"And what did you bring our baby Jesus?" Joseph said, his voice as deep as he could make it.

"I have no gold," Millie said, each word an effort. There would be no acting awards tonight. "I have no silver. I only have what I can do."

"And what is that, my child?" Mary asked, stumbling a little on "child."

"I'll show you," said Millie. Then she reached down and gathered up three rubber balls.

She started to juggle.

Nancy's heart plunged. In the past few days she'd felt a certain freedom from Mark's memory. She'd thought of him the other night and realized it was the first time in two days. But now the memories flooded back, and her heart leadened.

"She's pretty good, huh?" Margie whispered. "She's been practicing for almost a month. When you see her, gush over her," Margie instructed.

But Nancy didn't want to gush. She wanted to crawl outside and have a good cry. Would the agony ever end?

Millie's performance was flawless. She didn't do anything complicated, but she did it well. Then she glanced offstage. Something special was in the wind. Millie slowed her juggling just slightly in preparation, then she tossed one of the balls higher than the others and after those two bounced away, she caught the third one on her nose—and balanced it there.

Nancy's brows instantly popped up, her heavy heart fluttered weightlessly, and she straightened in her chair.

"You okay?" Margie asked.

"Where'd she learn that?"

"That teacher I told you about."

"What's his name?" Nancy insisted.

Margie shrugged. "I said she had a crush on him. I didn't say she told me his name."

Nancy sat for another moment while the audience applauded enthusiastically. But she didn't hear any of it. If only she could see through those walls. "I'll be back in a second," she finally said as the applause was beginning to wane.

A moment later Nancy had made it out of the auditorium to the hallway and backstage. Among the kids there was only one adult, and he stood in the stage wings, his back to her. Nancy stood just inside the doorway and watched as Millie stepped offstage and her teacher stooped to give her a hug. "Praise God," the teacher said. "Great job!"

"Mark?" Nancy said, but his name caught in an anxious wad at the base of her throat.

But there was no need for her to speak. At that moment, Millie saw her, and her eyes grew even brighter. "Nancy, did you see it? I did it. I can't believe I did it."

Hearing the name he'd yearned to hear again, the teacher spun.

Now it was Mark who stood frozen. In the dim light it took him only a moment to steady himself, his heart beating like wings. "Chickenlips!" he cried. And then realized how loud he'd been.

"Chickenlips?" Millie said. "You already know Nancy?"

But Mark didn't wait to respond. His arms spread, and he crossed quickly to her.

"Oh, it *is* you," she exclaimed, both belief and disbelief in every word, her tears welling up. She sniffled them away, and, with an excitement that burst from the very heart of her, she said, "And you're a Christian." Now the tears broke joyfully from her eyes. "Oh, praise God."

"Oh, Nance. It's a long story but the Lord brought me in."

"Mr. Brewster's the one who taught me how to juggle," Millie said proudly, not fully grasping what was happening between the two people she loved.

Exhilaration and joy all over his face, Mark pulled back. "Would you believe it? I'm a teacher. Well, not exactly. But an aide. They actually pay me for doing this."

"No more dreams of Hollywood?" she asked coyly.

"I burned the screenplay. You were right. It was trash. I prefer Christian love stories now." He moved closer. "Know any good plots?"

"Just one," she said, her eyes filled with emotion. "I love you, Mark."

He threw his arms around Nancy and kissed her. And as he did, she wrapped longing arms around his neck and kissed him back.

"I've been looking everywhere for you," he finally said. "I called every Bernard and every church in the phone book."

"No wonder the Lord kept me loving you. Oh, Mark, promise to never leave me again."

"Is that a proposal?"

"As close as a speedbump could expect."

"Well, Chickenlips, my love, as a producer of this little stage thing, I've got a production to finish. After that what say we spend the rest of our lives together?"

Nancy kissed him again. But then she drew back guiltily. "Don't be too hasty. Something's happened to your car."

"What?" Mark asked, brows furled.

"It died in a rock slide in a graveyard."

"Ah," Mark said, not all that surprised.

About the Author

Bill Kritlow was born in Gary, Indiana, and moved to northern California when he was nine. He now resides in southern California with his wife, Patricia. They have three daughters and five grandchildren. Bill is also a deacon in his church.

After spending twenty years in large-scale computing, Bill recently changed occupations so that he could spend most of the day writing—his first love. His hobbies include writing, golf, writing, traveling, and taking long walks to think about writing.